ALL IS FAIR IN LOVE

A Regency Historical Romance

THE DUKE OF STRATHMORE
BOOK X

SASHA COTTMAN

This book is dedicated to all those who sail the oceans.

"may you have fair winds and following seas".

Chapter One

L*ondon Docks*

Just before dawn, late 1817

Poppy Basden slipped her hat from her head and leaned over the side of the ship. The wind whipped her fair hair in all directions, but instead of being annoyed, she simply smiled. The intensity of the breeze this far up the River Thames was much tamer than the gales out at sea, and she was prepared to risk getting a few tangles. Nothing was going to ruin this day.

Bliss. I can almost imagine that the air tastes sweet.

From her previous journeys to the English capital, she held no illusions about London. It was a dirty city with grey skies. The atmosphere around the docks was heavy with the almost heady stench of oils, animal skins, and rum.

But it was dry land, solid. And it held the promise of something which Poppy had long craved—the chance of a real home.

For much of her five and twenty years, coming into port

had been her favorite delight. Leaving port, her second. The lure of the salty sea had long held her heart.

But the footsteps of time had slowly changed her perspective—altered her view on life and what she wanted for herself. The woman Poppy had grown into had different needs to those of a windswept, adventurous child. The one thing which did, however, remain constant was the deep-seated longing to belong somewhere—and to someone.

Poppy was determined to build a life here in England. To create a future that was truly hers. The moment she set foot ashore this morning, her sailing days would officially be over.

With a keen captain's eye, she tracked the ship's progress into the docks. It glided gracefully through the water, weaving its way past the other boats which sat moored either side of the east and western quays. As the *Empress Catherine* slowed, Poppy raised her arm.

"Ready to let go the anchor!" she cried.

The ship slid silently into its allotted space at the dockside, giving the nearest vessel a respectable wide berth. Poppy dropped her arm and called. "Let go!"

"Aye, aye, captain!" came the reply from the deckhands.

Poppy glanced at her hands as she rested them on the ship's side railing. Her fingers shook as the chain cable rattled through the hawsehole. The moment the anchor hit the bottom; the chain pulled taut. A low groan reverberated through the ship's deck, and everything came to an abrupt halt.

She lifted her hand, her fingers seeking the silver medallion which hung from a chain around her neck. Poppy whispered, "Thank you, Saint Brendan. I shall take it from here."

After eight tiring months at sea and five ports of call, she had finally made it to her destination. London. Her new home.

"How do you feel?"

She turned as Jonathan, the ship's chief mate, came to stand alongside her. The note of weariness in his voice was unmistakable—whether it was from the long sea voyage or the fact that he, too, was about to give up the life of a sailor, she couldn't quite discern.

He must give it time. As will I. Only then will the lure of the sea release its hold.

"I must be honest—my heart is a mixture of sadness and excitement. It will take some getting used to, living permanently on land, but I am so looking forward to having a home. A place that is mine. I mean, ours," she replied.

"I wouldn't go so far as to call living in a shipping warehouse a home." Jonathan snorted.

Her gaze focused on the face of the man her father had chosen as her future husband, searching yet again for any sign of welcome regard. Anything that might spark some affection for him.

Nothing. I feel absolutely nothing for this man.

Why her father had settled on Jonathan was a mystery Poppy was yet to solve. The more time she spent with him, the greater her concern grew.

Relocating the headquarters of the Basden Line Shipping Company to England was a carrot her father had dangled in front of her for several years. But his last-minute declaration—that in order for the move to go ahead, Poppy must agree to marry one of her senior crewmembers—had come as a complete surprise to Poppy.

And while Jonathan hadn't exactly appeared all that enamored with the plan either, he had still agreed to it and sailed with her from Ceylon. Poppy didn't dare to imagine how much money her father must have paid to be rid of her. She had always been made to feel unwelcome in his life. Having his daughter married off and living on the other side of the world would no doubt be most convenient for George Basden.

Get through the next few days. Things will sort themselves out. Everyone is just tired.

She was nothing if not an optimist—a positive trait which at times had cost her dearly. But Poppy still clung to the hope that she and Jonathan would find a way to be partners and possibly more.

The gods of happiness surely had to smile on her at least once in her life, because the prospect of being wed to a man who cared little for Poppy, or her dreams was beyond even her wide boundaries of acceptance.

Turning away, she settled her gaze on the North Quay warehouses, a long, elegant row of sandstone buildings that were a part of the impressively constructed London Docks. Each warehouse was four stories high—plenty of storage space for the precious cargo of cinnamon bales which currently sat below the *Empress Catherine*'s deck.

Once the various contracts for the sale of the cinnamon had been filled, Poppy would have the money to properly set up the family company in England.

After I am able to grow the business and show him, I am a success, Papa will have to say he is proud of me. Surely, he will, especially when he sees that I did as he asked and married Jonathan.

She glanced at Jonathan, but he was still sneering at the dock. Poppy had long ago realized that changing the subject was the wisest thing to do when Jonathan was in one of his dour moods.

She pointed to the long row of warehouses which ran along the back of the recently constructed London Docks. "Just think how easy operating out of the more modern dock will be for us, Jonathan. No more lengthy delays while we wait to offload our cargo."

A sigh of disgust came from the man standing beside her.

"Urgh! Don't remind me. I almost went mad the last time we were in London. What was it, a month we had to wait for an available berth further down the river?" replied Jonathan.

"Something like that." Poppy had done her best to forget that last trip. As captain, she had endured not only a long delay, but a ship full of grumpy sailors.

Time was money for everyone. In the years since it had opened, the expansive London Docks on the River Thames at Wapping had become a godsend to shipping merchants and crews alike. The fact that the Basden Line Shipping Company owned a piece of the docks made things even sweeter. The berth at which the *Empress Catherine* now sat was also theirs.

Poppy pointed to the building which loomed in front of them. "That's our warehouse—the one on the corner. Number fourteen."

Our new home. I can't wait to move in.

And while Jonathan might yet again be in one of his dark moods, nothing was going to dampen her enthusiasm. She had a million things to do over the next few days. Her list of jobs was long and detailed. The thought of successfully working her way through them all had Poppy clasping her hands together in delight.

They both stepped deftly out of the way as the crew lifted and set the gangplank into place. A grim-faced Jonathan offered Poppy his hand. "Are you ready to go ashore, Captain Basden?" has asked.

Grateful that he was making any sort of attempt at ceremony, she took his hand and stepped up onto the walkway. A lifetime spent at sea meant Poppy had no problem moving on or off a ship unaided, but they both knew this was a special day. Such an occasion was worthy of all due pomp and ceremony.

It's a pity we don't have someone to pipe us ashore.

As soon as she reached the far end of the gangplank, Poppy jumped down. Her boots made a pleasing slap as they connected with the stone embankment which ran alongside the wharf. Her heart leapt at the sound. Long years of planning were finally coming to fruition.

Today is the day!

Jonathan, who had trailed behind in a more sedate manner, stood slowly shaking his head while Poppy performed an impromptu dance of joy. When her feet finally came to a halt, he nodded at the warehouse.

"What's first?" he asked.

She rummaged in her coat pocket and produced a large folded up piece of paper. Grinning, Poppy grandly unfurled it. "Top of the list. We need a key," she announced.

She pointed in the direction of a building situated at the western end of the quay, some fifty yards or so away. During her last visit to London, Poppy had paid a special visit to the docks and drawn up a plan of their layout. She had a captain's mind for organization. Knowing where everything was located would make the task of settling in that much easier.

Her first piece of business was to visit the superintendent's office and present her papers, after which she would receive the key to the front door of warehouse number fourteen. As soon as they had access, Jonathan would take charge of managing the crew. The cargo of cinnamon bales was to be carefully offloaded from the *Empress Catherine* and brought upstairs into the warehouse for secure storage.

Only after that task was successfully completed would she dismiss her chief mate and the rest of the crew. The faster they got the job done, the sooner they could find their way to the nearest dockside tavern and drink themselves into oblivion.

It's been a long sea voyage; the lads deserve a good drink and to have some fun.

Reaching into her coat pocket once more, Poppy pulled out a small leather pouch and handed it to Jonathan. "There should be enough coin in there to get all the crew fed and watered many times over. Of course, it goes without saying that the offer of drinking money should be held back until after the cargo has been offloaded."

A knowing grin crept to Jonathan's lips. "Aye, aye, captain. You go and fetch the key, and I shall make sure that the lads have the boat emptied in quick time."

As he headed back onboard the *Empress Catherine,* the first real doubt of the morning settled uncomfortably in Poppy's mind. Would there ever come a day when Jonathan stopped calling her captain and actually used her first name?

Give him time. Once you are both fully onshore, he will have no reason to continue addressing you that way.

She had been the one determined to draw a line under that life, but it would take time for her to get used to no longer being Captain Basden. After today, she would simply be Miss Poppy Basden. The concept was a strange one, and it left her emotions in an odd jumble.

Even stranger was the idea that at some point she would become Mrs. Jonathan Measy. She would still be notionally in charge of the shipping business, but as her husband, Jonathan would be able to wield some power over her—something he couldn't currently do.

Will we be a partnership in life and business, or will I have to fight for every inch of ground? I don't want a marriage where I am lost as me.

Poppy pushed that thought firmly back to the dark recesses of her mind, to the place where it usually lurked.

Checking one last time to make sure that the company papers were in her possession, Poppy straightened her spine and with head held high, went in search of the superintendent's office.

Today was a day for taking a great leap forward.

Chapter Two

Francis Saunders had woken in a foul temper, and not even a full plate of breakfast could remedy the situation. He was seeking solace in his third cup of tea when his father, Charles, arrived in the family breakfast room.

"*Bonjour*, Francis. *Comment vas-tu par ce beau jour?*" said Charles, in his typical cheerful manner.

"*Bonjour*, Papa," grumbled Francis.

He wasn't in the right frame of mind to tell his French-born father that there was nothing beautiful about the morning. He couldn't even manage a polite smile. Fortunately, the look on Charles's face was enough to inform Francis that his grim mood was apparent.

"What has you in a fit this morning?" asked Charles.

Money. Contracts. Missing cargo. All of the above.

Francis set his cup of tea on the saucer and sighed. He had never thought that taking over the family shipping business would be this hard. That his worries about all manner of things would consume his every waking moment. And an uncomfortable portion of his sleep.

There had to be a secret to it all. His father was even-tempered. Francis had never heard Charles raise his voice with the staff, and it was rare for him to work late at the office.

There has to be a trick. Something he has kept from me until now. What can it be?

He leaned forward over the table and met his father's keen eye. "How do you do it? I mean, manage the business as well as everything else?" asked Francis.

In the years that Francis had worked alongside his father, he had never questioned any of this, but now, as responsibility began to fall on his youthful shoulders, he found himself at times almost paralyzed with self-doubt.

Charles leisurely poured himself a small cup of coffee. In typical French style, he eschewed the use of milk or sugar. Francis shuddered at the sight. How anyone could drink such a strong brew first thing in the morning was beyond him.

His own plate, which had been filled to the edges with a full English breakfast, sat in stark contrast to Charles's which had a small, sweet bun sitting all alone in the middle.

Charles took a sip of his coffee and sighed. "The first coffee of the morning is always the best. And the most necessary."

Francis raised an eyebrow at the remark. The coffee in his father's hand would be the first of many. A long procession of cups of coffee would follow in Charles's wake throughout the long day ahead.

"As I have told you before, Francis, this next year is going to be a tough one for you. But if you want to successfully manage the Saunders Shipping Company, you are going to have to find a happy medium between business and your private life. I can't begin to tell you the countless hours I worked when I first started the company. Of the many meals and family occasions I missed. And if your mother hadn't finally read me the riot act, I expect I would have continued in that same vein 'till the day I died."

As a young boy Francis had always thought it unfair that his father put business ahead of family, but lately, he had begun to understand the reasons why. Work was never-ending.

Of course, he and his siblings had all been present that night when Lady Adelaide had brought her protest down to the old docks. Francis still remembered being rugged up in the family carriage watching as his mother berated her husband in the middle of the street. She had threatened to burn the Saunders Shipping warehouse to the ground if Charles didn't immediately pack up and come home.

To her credit, Adelaide had actually managed to find a copy of the *Riot Act* and quoted Charles the section where it commanded him to peaceably depart to his habitations. Her husband had sensibly taken heed. It was the last time Charles had ever worked late at the shipping office.

In the intervening years, the Saunders Shipping Company had grown steadily. Charles must have found a solution to the problem of never-ending work, but as things currently stood, Francis couldn't see it. At the moment, he was not only stuck in the trees, but he was also trying to find a way to climb to the top of them so he could map his way in the world.

There was, however, one spark of hope in his life. A highly lucrative tender for handling spices from Ceylon and India had recently been announced. A contract which was only open to those who had warehouses at the London Docks.

If Francis could win the contract, many of his problems would be solved. He had worked hard on the proposal. It was well costed and sensibly priced. He would be able to make a solid profit on every shipment from the far east. Nothing would stand in his way of becoming one of the biggest shipping merchants in London.

Then I won't just be 'young Francis Saunders.'

"I've done the numbers, Papa. If I can win that new spice tender, then I think I can make things work. You will be able to retire confident that I have things under control. That contract would give me enough money to be able to expand into the warehouse next door as well as employ more clerks. I could then step away from the books of account and focus on growing the business. I have grand plans."

Charles raised his small cup of coffee to his lips and took a sip. As he set the cup back down, he fixed his gaze firmly on Francis. "Speaking of plans, your mother asked if you are still intending to travel up to Scotland with us? I promised I would seek an answer from you this morning. Adelaide has her own plans to finalize."

Deft and sly change of subject, Papa.

Francis reached for his cup, taking the time to drink his cold tea slowly. He had been hoping to avoid having this conversation until closer to Christmas. But no time was ever going to be a good one. He would simply have to bite the bullet and deal with it.

"I'm thinking perhaps I might stay in London for the festive season. I can have Christmas Eve supper with Will and Hattie," replied Francis.

With the rest of his siblings having all taken spouses this year, Francis was the only Saunders offspring left unwed. And while the thought of spending Christmas at Strathmore Castle with the rest of the extended Radley family held much appeal, being around his mother and her not-so-subtle hints about the need for him to find a wife made it less so.

In the months following his sister Caroline's marriage to Earl Newhall, and her subsequent departure for Derbyshire, Francis had become Adelaide's pet project.

"Your mother will be disappointed," said Charles.

I know, but I can't spend four weeks in Scotland with her while she is on this matchmaking crusade. I shall go mad. Besides I have far too much work to do.

He shot his father a pleading look and was nearly overwhelmed with gratitude when Charles slowly nodded in response. *Thank God someone else in this house understands my predicament.*

"I shall speak to your mother and let her know that you have pressing obligations at the shipping office, which will give you a few days in which to prepare to give her the bad news. When you do speak her, you had better make it clear that you are saddened not to be able to undertake the journey to Scotland this year."

Thank you, Papa. Thank you. Thank you.

Charles paused, and Francis instantly ceased his silent gratitude.

"But in return for me helping you to delay your announcement, you have to do something."

Francis gritted his teeth, fearing what might come next. His father had been the one to build the family company up from nothing. Charles Saunders's skills at being able to secure contracts and form strong alliances with business associates was the stuff of legends. He was a first-rate negotiator, one whom Francis hoped he would one day be able to emulate. Charles drove a hard bargain with everyone—including his children.

"What is it that you demand of me?" replied Francis.

He stifled a grin when Charles, mimicking his own action of a moment or two ago, picked up his coffee cup and took a slow, considered sip. Like father, like son—he was taking his time. Making his opponent wait.

Francis's heart sank. Charles always won the cup game.

If I could just be half the businessman that you are—no. I want to be better. I have to be better. No one will take me seriously unless I am a success.

"Not demanding—just asking. In return for helping to smooth things over with your mother, I would like you to attend some parties and balls in the early part of the new year. Son, you need to have more in your life than just the company. The shipping business might eventually fill your coffers with gold, but it will not keep you warm at night. And it most certainly will never bring you the sort of joy that finding love will," said Charles.

Francis was cornered, with little room to maneuver. If he wanted his father to help him navigate this next phase of his life, he was going to have to agree to some concessions. But he was determined that they would be on his terms.

I can attend the odd ball or two. Papa hasn't stipulated that I have to remain long at any of them.

He knew plenty of other bachelors in London high society who were masters of the art of making an appearance at a social function and then quietly disappearing out a side door. It wouldn't take too much effort for him to join their ranks. Love wasn't something Francis considered important right now.

"Alright, you win. I shall do as you ask. I promise. Commencing in January, I shall attend at least one ball a week," replied Francis.

"And a dinner party or a supper. Come now, Francis, you need to try. If not, then how else do you expect to ever find yourself a wife?"

Oh, not you as well, Papa. I am not on the hunt for a wife. Marriage isn't in my plans.

Not for the foreseeable future at least. He was only two and twenty; he had time. A wife and family would no doubt eventually happen, but not until after he had made his mark amongst London's business elite.

The sound of servants moving about in the hall signaled the impending arrival of Lady Adelaide Saunders. Francis quickly downed the last of his tea and got to his feet. He had won, while also making some concessions this morning. It was enough. But if his mother got wind of him cancelling the annual trip to Scotland for Christmas, he wouldn't ever get out of the house.

"We have an accord. Please give Mama my apologies; I have to leave for the office. I shall see you a little later this morning."

Francis was out of the breakfast room and headed for the stairs at breakneck speed, his father's hearty laugh in his wake. After swiftly collecting his hat and coat from a waiting footman, he was out the door to the rear mews in less than a minute. He hastened toward the waiting carriage at a fast trot. He would do anything to avoid his mother.

Adelaide would no doubt be disappointed to have missed her youngest son this morning, but Francis knew full well that if she did get hold of him, she would make him sit and chat while she ate her breakfast. And no matter how clever a negotiator his father was, even Charles wouldn't have been able to save him.

As soon as he was on board the carriage and the door was closed, Francis rapped hard on the roof. "Coutts Bank, The Strand, and please make haste. I have a busy day ahead."

He had a meeting with his banker. Time was money. And he didn't have either to spare.

Chapter Three

The superintendent's office at London Docks was a hive of activity. As soon as she arrived, Poppy was directed to the end of a long queue of people all waiting to speak to a clerk. The docks might well have been a modern construction, but the bureaucratic wheels of customs and excise still turned slowly.

Poppy's private dreams of marching straight up to the front desk, presenting her papers, and being graciously handed the key to warehouse number fourteen evaporated in a puff of disappointment.

By the time she finally made it to the head of the line one frustrating hour later, Poppy was hot and tired. Her heavy coat and woolen scarf had both been removed and were draped over her left arm.

"Next," announced the clerk.

Poppy stepped forward to the wooden counter. She met the clerk's gaze with all the authority that years of being a sea captain had instilled in her. "I am Poppy Basden, captain of the *Empress Catherine,* and legal representative of the Basden Line Shipping Company. I have come for the keys for warehouse number fourteen, building two, North Quay. These are my papers."

She handed the company identification papers over, waiting impatiently while the clerk slowly examined them. This was not how she had planned her day.

I have things to do apart from standing in a queue.

Peering over the rim of his spectacles, the clerk looked her up and down, then quietly snorted. "Do you have the title of ownership papers with you, miss?"

Poppy had dealt with enough port officials during her life to have everything well organized in advance. Delays in getting ships processed through customs and excise could well mean the difference between making a profit on a shipment and losing money.

She cleared her throat. "I am Captain Basden. And I am of the clear understanding that our company solicitor delivered the title papers to this office some months ago. All fees should have been paid. My ship has just arrived, so I am keen to get this matter settled and my cargo offloaded. Would you please go and check with the head clerk? I am, however, quite willing to deal with the superintendent himself if required."

The clerk's gaze shifted from her face, and Poppy endured his slow eyeing of her body. His eyes tracked down over her jacket and past her just-below-the-knee skirt. A frown followed. When he got to her trousers, the frown deepened.

Yes, I am wearing trousers. One can hardly stand at the wheel of a ship in a roaring gale whilst clad in a full-length gown.

It wasn't the first time, that a man had taken the time to conduct a slow study of the female captain standing in front of him. It was rare for a woman to be in charge of a ship, especially in this part of the world. Men seemed to find it odd that a young woman could actually have the brains to command a crew. And also dare to wear men's trousers.

She bit on her bottom lip as the man's gaze drifted back

up, then settled on the swell of her breasts. There were times when being well endowed was a blessing, but not when she was trying to get a male of the species to take her seriously.

Stop staring at my titties.

Poppy cleared her throat more loudly this time. "When you are quite ready, sir."

The clerk startled at her words and muttered an apology before hurriedly scurrying off.

While she waited, Poppy let her own gaze roam over the numerous notices which were pinned to the back wall of the office. Ships for sale. Cargos requiring transportation to various places. Missing crewmen.

She snorted at that last one. Sailors had a happy knack of disappearing when they decided they didn't want to leave port. More often than not, a pretty little lady was the cause.

Another notice caught her attention. She leaned forward, silently mouthing the words as she read the details.

Public Tender number 145. London Docks.
Superintendent's Office.
The procurement, shipping, and safe storage of spices from India and Ceylon is required.
Reliable and experienced vendors only.
Contract duration is three years commencing February 1st, 1818.
Tenders, in writing, to be submitted by end of day December 12th, 1817

This was exactly the sort of contract Poppy was looking to secure. The *Empress Catherine* had arrived in port with a size-able cargo of cinnamon bales from Ceylon on board. They were going to be stored in the warehouse before being delivered to the local merchants with whom her father had already secured contracts.

If she could find another ready-made customer, it would make things that much easier for her to get the company established in England.

That contract could set me up quite nicely. I have to win it. I know I can.

The clerk soon returned with a small pile of papers in his hand. He spread them out on the counter. Some nodding and humming followed before he finally let out an approving sigh. "Well, everything seems to be in order, Miss Basden."

Poppy ignored his lack of manners. The man clearly had no intention of acknowledging the fact that she was a sea captain. And while that might be true for only a few hours more, it still meant something to her. That *something* was respect.

She wriggled her fingers as the clerk dropped a ring of keys onto the desk. They landed with a clang. All worries about her status disappeared in an instant.

This is real. Those keys are mine.

"This is the front door key. That one is the rear door key; it opens up onto Pennington Street, but the London Docks requires that all business be conducted wharf-side," said the man, pointing to various keys. He shuffled up the papers then pushed them, along with the keys, across the counter toward Poppy. "You will find the relevant title documents and letters approving you to use the facilities at the dock. There is also a formal letter from the superintendent explaining your responsibilities for use of the warehouse, including but not ending with the exclusion of storing any tobacco and explosives."

Poppy nodded. It was nothing she hadn't dealt with

before. She pointed to the spice tender notice pinned to the wall. "Would you have a copy I could take with me, please?"

The clerk glanced over his shoulder, then turned back to face her. "I don't think we have any left. But since the tender is due at the end of today, I don't see why you can't have that one."

"Today? Oh, no," said Poppy.

Dates and deadlines often lost their meaning at sea. A ship arrived when it arrived. She had thought it was earlier in the month, but the weather off the coast of Portugal had seen the *Empress Catherine* delayed.

It would take most of the morning to shift the cargo and get things in the warehouse properly set up. Her day was already spoken for several times over. And completing a tender document required time and a good deal of attention. She had just lost a valuable opportunity to get established in England.

If only we had arrived yesterday. Damn. There must be a way I can put in a bid.

"When it says end of day, I assume that means office hours?" asked Poppy.

The man shook his head. "This is the London Docks. We never close."

Hope sparked anew. "So, I have until the end of today—I mean, midnight—to get a submission in?"

"Yes." The expression on the clerk's face was one of thinly veiled scorn. Poppy could just imagine what he was thinking. *Foolish female attempting to take on a man's job. She should be at home with children gathered around her skirts, not sailing the seven seas, and playing at captain.*

Eager to get on with the day and her ever-growing list of tasks, Poppy pointed to the tender sign. "Could I please, have it?"

"Oh, alright," he huffed.

While the clerk trudged over to the wall and tugged the notice down, Poppy wrapped her scarf around her neck and put on her coat. The superintendent's office might be warm, but the breeze outside was chilly. The last thing she needed was to catch a cold.

Accepting the rolled-up tender paper, Poppy tucked it under her arm. She quickly gathered the rest of her things before dropping the keys into her coat pocket.

"Thank you," she said.

Once outside, Poppy stopped and unfurled the notice. Three years. That was a princely contract. If she could win the tender, her future in England would be secure.

And with the money which such a business arrangement would bring she could finally have what she had always wanted.

A home to call her own.

Her gaze took in the busy western part of the docks. There were carts and people milling about the wharf. Tall sailing ships lay at anchor in every berth. The shifting cables and chains in the rigging around the mast of each boat provided a never-ending symphony of clatter and jangle.

It was music to Poppy's ears.

If she was going to give up her days of sailing on the ocean, living in the London Docks wasn't a bad place to start her new life. Every morning, she would be able to step out of the warehouse and take in the sight of newly arrived ships. And with them they would bring the scent of the sea.

Who said she couldn't have her cake and eat it too?

Chapter Four

Poppy spent the better part of the morning inside the ground floor of the warehouse, sweeping cobwebs from the ceiling with a long-handled broom and brushing away the inch or so of thick black filth which she was certain covered every surface.

The windows were coated in a pale grey sticky ooze which filtered out the daylight and kept the space in a state of semi darkness. The sooner she had scrubbed and wiped the glass clean, the better.

Warehouse number fourteen had apparently been vacant for nearly two years, but Poppy had assumed someone would keep it clean in the meantime. That had been somewhat of a foolish assumption on her part. From the look of things, the previous owner had locked the front door and simply walked away, not caring about the condition of the place.

"I swear all I can taste is dust," she muttered.

The front door opened and Jonathan marched in. "Everything is off the ship, and the last of the crates will be brought up shortly," he announced.

Inside the warehouse, the heady aroma of cinnamon now

replaced the stench of neglect. The cargo had been carried upstairs to the third floor and was safely stored. This left the second- and ground-floor main rooms empty. There was ample space in which Poppy and Jonathan could work. And, for the foreseeable future, live.

Jonathan wiped the sweat away from his brow. "Oh, and we cleared all those barrels and things away from around the front door and our side of the wharf pavilion. It looks like the neighbors had taken over the extra space for their unwanted stuff."

Poppy had first noticed the odds and ends dumped outside her warehouse when she returned from the superintendent's office. She hated clutter. Messy decks were dangerous. A good captain always kept a weather eye on the safety of the crew.

"Thank you; we need to keep our part of the wharf clear. I suppose our neighbor has encroached on our property because the warehouse has been empty for such a long time. But I expect that whoever they are, they will soon realize we have taken possession, and will no doubt make suitable accommodations," she replied. Poppy couldn't blame the neighbors for having used the extra space while it was available. If she had been in their position, she would likely have done the same.

The front of the warehouse was earmarked for some potted plants and perhaps even a small garden bench. Poppy planned to sit outside each morning and enjoy the sunshine while sipping at her coffee and observing the latest arrivals into port. Little touches and special moments would go a long way to making the warehouse feel more like a home.

I wonder if curtains would be going too far. Floral curtains, with a matching tea set. That would be nice.

She stirred from her thoughts of decorating. There was

still plenty of other work left on her current to-do list—work she would love a hand in getting finished.

"What are your plans for the rest of the day?" she asked.

Jonathan had the money to shout the crew drinks, but Poppy was quietly hoping that he could see there was still plenty of work to be done.

His gaze roamed lazily over the dust piles that Poppy had swept up and for just the briefest of moments, she thought he might offer to stay and help. If he did, then she would be able to get to work on the all-important spice tender submission.

"I'll be off to the Prospect of Whitby, and an ale or three," he replied, patting his jacket pocket. The clink of coins echoed in the empty space.

Of course, you are off to the nearest tavern. Why would I expect any different?

Her future husband wasn't one for doing anything more than the minimum which was asked of him. For a moment, Poppy simply stared at Jonathan. If they did marry, she was going to be left to do the lion's share of the work both with the business and any family they might have.

For the second time that morning, she questioned her father's choice of Jonathan as her intended spouse. Poppy was blind to whatever George Basden might have seen in him.

Perhaps that is the truth. There is nothing. Jonathan was simply a means to an end.

It was a sobering thought.

There was no point in arguing with him. "Could I ask you to try and not be all sheets to the wind when you get back? There is still a lot of work to do. I was hoping to be able to get this place cleaned up and ready for us to move in," she replied.

She hated the pleading in her voice. On land, she wasn't Captain Basden, she was merely Poppy, and her authority could be easily challenged.

Jonathan gave a pained sigh. "You can't let me have a day with the lads? We are in London and the cargo is all upstairs. Just leave the rest of it until tomorrow. The dirt and mess will still be here."

And there was his answer. As far as Jonathan was concerned, he was already halfway to the waterside tavern and ready for a long afternoon of heavy imbibing. If things went as they usually did when the crew was in port, Poppy would be fortunate to see him again before sometime late tomorrow. And even then, he wouldn't be in any condition to help her.

Reliability was not Jonathan's strong suit. The pattern in their relationship was already well set. She could just picture a future where constant disappointment would eventually breed bitterness and resentment between them.

The little voice in the back of her mind whispered the warning it had long been offering—a warning she could no longer ignore.

You need to do something, and that doesn't include marrying this man.

But worrying over what she was going to do about Jonathan would have to wait. Poppy had an important business proposal to prepare and cost. Winning the contract was her topmost priority.

"Have a good afternoon with the lads. Give them my thanks for all the hard work," she said.

She followed him out of the warehouse. While Jonathan headed toward the entrance to the docks, Poppy made a beeline for the gangplank and the captain's cabin of the *Empress Catherine.*

I need that contract.

If she could secure her financial future, then she might well be able to address the issue of Jonathan Measy—and how she was going to get him out of her life.

Chapter Five

As the carriage drew up outside warehouse number twelve, building number two, North Quay of the London Docks, Francis leaned forward in his seat and pressed his face to the window.

"What the devil is that?"

The usually empty berth out the front of the warehouse which adjoined his own was occupied. A strange ship was moored at the wharf. And it was of such an unusual construction that it immediately captured his interest.

Francis was still staring at the vessel long after he had climbed out of the carriage. Rather than his usual polite 'thank you', he gave a halfhearted farewell wave to the Saunders's family driver.

Walking closer, he was greeted with the sight of an ornate crowned lion which sat proudly at the ship's bow. Under the masthead was a red and white plaque with the year *1703* emblazoned on it. He hadn't ever seen a ship that old which was still in service.

Francis narrowed his eyes. He knew enough about boats to know that something wasn't quite right. The ship was old, and yet, it clearly had some modern features. It was a three-masted topsail schooner, which correctly matched its age, but the sails were of a later design. It appeared that someone had taken a one-hundred-year-old ship and given it a major refit. A costly exercise in anyone's language.

Why would you do that? Why not simply have a new ship built?

Intrigued, he wandered past the row of low-roofed pavilions which were located between the warehouse buildings and the waterfront. When he got to the fourth of these, he stopped. Just as the berth was no longer empty, neither was the pavilion. In the spot where he normally sat and enjoyed a quiet midafternoon coffee, numerous crates and barrels had been stacked.

"Where is all this coming from?" he asked, throwing up his hands.

He didn't like surprises. Spontaneity made him uncomfortable. Francis liked the surety that came with well-ordered plans, especially the ones which he personally created and commanded. Other people making unexpected changes set his nerves on edge.

"Coming through," came the cry from a group of sailors who were lugging a large wooden chest. They were bearing down on him at a fast rate, and Francis barely had time to step out of the way as they passed him by.

More dockworkers followed. A small procession made its way from the lion ship, through the pavilion, and across the service road right up to the warehouse next door to the one occupied by the Saunders Shipping Company.

If the sight of the odd ship and its cargo hadn't already knocked Francis for six, bearing witness to the front door being opened, and the chest being carried inside would have done the trick. His mouth snapped shut.

Someone had moved into warehouse number fourteen.

This couldn't be happening. In his mind, he had already

claimed it as his, along with the dockside berth, and the cargo-sorting pavilion. The space along the wharf embankment from number twelve to number fourteen and the short gap beyond was meant to be his. A small kingdom over which he intended to rule.

That's mine.

His plans for managing the new spice contract rested on him being able to take over the lease of the long-empty premises next door. Without them, he would struggle to meet the terms of the tender.

"Damn," he muttered.

Leaving home this morning, he had gone to an important appointment with his banker. A meeting during which it had been made plain to Francis that he would need to find a great deal more money if he planned to grow the Saunders Shipping Company. The bank had offered to lend him money but at an eye-wateringly high interest rate. He had politely refused the loan.

He didn't want to be in debt to the bank; nor did he wish to ask any of the extended Radley family for a private loan. When he took over from his father, Francis wanted it to be on his terms. Saunders Shipping would grow in the years to come, but he was determined that it could only be funded by the money he made. Francis Saunders was going to be known throughout London society as a self-made man.

Securing the lucrative spice contract was crucial to his plans for expansion. As was the empty warehouse next door where he had intended to store the spices. The warehouse which had, until today, been vacate for almost two years. Francis's day was fast turning into a disaster.

He needed money. And now it looked like he had lost the warehouse.

Who are these people? And how did they get a hold of the keys to the warehouse? I've been trying to get the owner to lease it to me for months.

Watching the activity on the dockside, his mood slowly darkened. From the way the sailors from the lion ship, worked, it was obvious they knew what they were doing. This was a professional outfit. He would look foolish if he marched up to them and demanded that they stop unloading the cargo.

Turning from the dockside, Francis headed toward the entrance to the Saunders Shipping Company. The heat of his temper soared as he caught sight of the barrels and piles of rope sitting either side of the door.

Who had dumped all that rubbish in front of his offices?

He stopped to check out the markings on the side of one of the barrels, ready to go and have firm words with its owner. The name had him swearing under his breath.

Saunders Shipping Company. Warehouse 12, Building 2, North Quay, London Docks.

It was one of his own barrels. A quick glance at the rest of them revealed the same result.

Lifting his head, he took in the tidy, clear walkway out the front of number fourteen. It wasn't normally in that sort of neat condition. Mostly because it was where he dumped his extra barrels and odd bits of rope.

And then it hit him. Someone, he assumed the new tenant, had kindly moved his property back to his side of the wharf.

For a moment Francis was tempted to simply leave his property where it was or instruct some of his shipping staff to move the barrels inside and out of the way, but his stubborn mindset whispered another solution.

Start as you mean to go on. Don't make them feel the least bit welcome.

Whoever these people were, Francis had to get them out

of the way and quick smart. His heart raced as nervous adrenalin pumped furiously through his body. Mouth dry and on the edge of losing his composure, he hastily considered his options. Conclusion? This called for drastic action.

If he could make life difficult for the new tenants, then perhaps they might come to realize that London Docks wasn't for them. There were plenty of other places where they could berth their lion-headed ship. *They can take their peculiar little boat and find a new home for it.*

Without another thought, Francis bent and picked up a pile of ropes, and carried them back to outside the front of number fourteen. He threw them on the ground. The rest of the barrels and ropes quickly followed.

When he was finished, Francis silently congratulated himself as he stood wiping the dust from his hands. If anyone had an issue with what he had done, they could come to his front door and take it up with him.

But you had better come prepared for a fight.

As far as he was concerned, it wasn't anything personal; it was just business. And when it came to business, Francis Saunders approached everything like it was a war.

There could only be one winner.

Chapter Six

Poppy sat back in her favorite chair and rubbed her eyes. She was exhausted. The proposal had taken her all afternoon and most of the evening to prepare, but it was finally done.

She had double-checked her calculations, making certain that they not only reflected a fair price, but one which allowed her to make a solid profit. Her father had taught her that commercial contracts which were based on mutual benefit always lasted the longest. Trust was something Poppy valued highly.

"Now just to add in the final details of the Basden Line Shipping Company and put father's stamp on the signature."

Her stomach gave an unwelcome growl of protest. She hadn't eaten anything since scoffing down a stale bread roll just after the *Empress Catherine* had berthed earlier that day. The only sustenance she had managed over the subsequent hours were the countless cups of strong, black coffee which she had brewed on the ship's galley stove.

Poppy was tired, but she was also wide awake. The

tremble in her fingers confirmed that she was more than a little edgy after all that caffeine.

From the desk drawer of the tiny captain's cabin, she retrieved a small ebony wooden box and opened it. Inside were several pieces of paper, including the official notices of her legal capacity to sign on behalf of her father, George Basden. There were also three stamps and accompanying wax seals.

After selecting the one which had her father's name and address on it, she inked the stamp and carefully placed it at the bottom of the contract proposal. She then added her own signature to the document. She wondered how much longer she would be able to manage the company affairs in such a manner. As an unwed woman she could sign these papers, but the moment she married Jonathan, her legal standing ended.

Poppy stared at the paper, waiting for the ink to dry. This wasn't the first contract she had pitched for, but it was, to all intents and purposes, the most important. Her father wouldn't arrive in England for another year. He had made it clear that in the meantime, he was trusting Poppy to get things up and running. To have a firm base established by the time he finally did make it to London.

As soon as the paper had dried, she neatly folded it, then sealed the document with wax. "It's done. Now just to deliver it and have the lodgment time stamped. Then I might actually get some sleep."

She pushed back the chair and slowly, stiffly, rose to her feet. Her tired muscles joined her stomach in making their protest.

With both hands placed carefully in the small of her back, Poppy leaned backwards and stretched. Head turning from side to side, she sought to loosen the kinks and knots that long hours at the desk had created. "Oh, that's so tight. I would love a hot bath to ease my aches and pains."

Now that's an idea. I could put a bath in the warehouse. There is plenty of room for one.

It didn't need to be anything fancy—just a copper tub, which could be carried outside and emptied after its use. The mere notion of actually being able to soak and relax in hot suds sent a smile to her lips.

A bath would be pure heaven. It would also be a major step up from what Poppy was used to making do with for her daily ablutions while onboard the ship. Long sea voyages required the steadfast use of a wet cloth and a small amount of precious fresh water to keep oneself clean.

Poppy sighed. "All that hot water would be so lovely."

She made a mental note to locate a suitable bathing spot at the back of the ground floor of the warehouse. A place which she could claim for herself.

That idea got her to thinking about how best to utilize the space. "There should be plenty of room for some walls to be erected so I can have a spot of privacy. The front of the warehouse can still be a functioning office."

If she was going to spend the next year living in the warehouse, she may as well be comfortable.

But before she could start thinking about where rugs and a comfortable sofa would fit, Poppy had a tender bid to deliver. She checked her pocket watch. It was a little after ten, which still gave her plenty of time to line up at the superintendent's office and submit her proposal before the deadline.

Hopefully they can also recommend a respectable place where I can get food at this hour. I am utterly famished.

Buttoning up her coat, she grabbed the papers and headed for the weather deck of the *Empress Catherine*. Up on the deck, she stopped and took in the sight.

London Docks was set out in a large square grid formation. On either side of it was a series of long, low-roofed pavilions, all stacked high with cargo. The end in which her warehouse was situated, faced out toward the River Thames and the entrance to the docks.

It was a busy place, with ships moored up to three abreast in some places. Poppy counted another fifty ships at anchor alongside one another in the middle section of the main dock. All these ships were waiting for an available berth so their cargos could be unloaded.

She glanced up at the smoky haze which sat low in the sky over the city, a grey cloud created by the thousands of fires burning in London's chimneys. Fortunately, when the smoke reached the river, the wind whipped it away leaving most of the air above the docks clear.

Poppy took in a deep breath. The air was clean enough, but it lacked something. She nodded to herself. She knew exactly what it was; it was the fresh, salty tang of the ocean. The River Thames was in fact an estuary, a saltwater extension of the North Sea, but it had an unpleasant brackishness about it that the tide couldn't ever wash away.

Living at the London Docks would mean an existence somewhere between the land and the sea. It wasn't perfect, but she had made her choice. If she wanted a home, she had to make sacrifices.

"It's the start of a new life. It makes sense that you are a little afraid," she whispered.

The deck of the *Empress Catherine* was devoid of any crew, the men having gone to drink with Jonathan. Some of them would likely return later this evening while others would find themselves a local brothel in which to spend the night. The sailors had the same routine with every call into port. Drink, get drunk, then seek out the comfort of a warm and willing woman. As long as the seafarers had a coin or two in their pocket, they were happy.

She didn't give much thought to where Jonathan might

end up tonight. Where he went and with whom, when they were in port, wasn't something they had ever discussed.

For a moment, Poppy pondered the fact that it didn't bother her, but like many things about Jonathan Measy, she found it impossible to have a care. Giving a disinterested shrug, she headed for the gangplank.

On the way to the superintendent's office, she passed by the warehouse. It was late and the area was not well lit, but even at a distance she could immediately spot the problem.

The barrels and ropes which Jonathan and the crew had shifted earlier in the day were back in front of number fourteen. The next-door neighbors must have moved them.

Why would anyone do such a thing? It's obvious our warehouse is occupied.

She was tempted to go and knock on the door of number twelve and have a polite word, but the front door was closed, and she couldn't see any lights shining through the windows. At this late hour, it was more than likely that everyone had gone home for the day.

"I shall take it up with them in the morning," she promised.

Making herself known to the neighbors was on her list of things to do but banging on their door and demanding that they move their barrels and ropes wasn't quite the way Poppy planned on making their acquaintance.

Who knows? They may not have realized that number fourteen is no longer vacant.

Giving the neighbors the benefit of the doubt, she headed toward the nearby superintendent's office. As she stepped through the door, Poppy gave a sigh of relief. There was only one other person in front of her in the queue.

At the end of a long, hard day, all she wanted was to go back to the ship, have a quick wash, and then crawl into her tiny bed.

Sleep. Oh, yes, that would be bliss.

"Next."

Poppy stirred from her standing snooze and approached the counter. She handed over her documents. "I am submitting a bid for the spice tender, which closes at end-of-day today. I trust the bids are sealed and kept secret."

The clerk, who was not the same one Poppy had dealt with earlier, considered her for a moment, then he frowned. "Yes madam, the bids are kept secret. But I'm not really sure if women are actually allowed to put bids in for contracts. You might need to go and find your husband."

She may have been having a touch of a nap only moments before, but the man's words, coupled with his condescending tone, immediately brought Poppy fully awake. Her shoulders snapped back, and her spine straightened. She held his gaze.

"I am the captain and owner of the *Empress Catherine*. I have sailed the seven seas since the day I was born. I have been at the helm of ships as they rounded Cape Horn six times, and I have successfully navigated the Cape of Good Hope twice. Men eagerly sign up to work on the ships I command."

Her blood was getting up, and with it her temper. When it came to customs officials, being polite had never gotten Poppy anywhere. No matter the port or the country, males seemed to only listen when she raised her voice. *I hate having to be this way with people. Why can't we just be polite and respectful?*

The clerk shuffled the papers about on the counter, clearly looking to be rid of the feisty woman as fast as possible.

Poppy pointed to the document. "It has been signed and noted. The Basden Line Shipping Company, owner of warehouse number fourteen, North Quay, is officially placing a bid. I request that you complete and stamp a notification of receipt for me. Please."

She placed a hard emphasis on the please, ensuring that the clerk understood she was not only here to conduct business but that she wasn't in the mood to argue with him.

The man collected and inked a stamp, then affixed it to the front of Poppy's paperwork. He signed and dated it.

I know how these things work.

While he completed a separate receipt, Poppy dipped her hand into her coat pocket. As the clerk handed over the completed record of lodgment, she slid some coins across the counter to him. "For your trouble, my good man."

He quietly took the coins.

Transaction complete, Poppy gave a nod, and headed for the door. She was almost outside when a sudden thought sent her racing back to the counter. "One last thing. Could you please tell me when the winning bidder will be informed?"

The clerk glanced up from counting his coins and nodded. The money clearly had softened his attitude. "Officially it will be when the notice is printed in the Port Gazette mid-January. But the custom here at London Docks is to let the winner of a tender bid know privately a week or so before that. Which in your case, Captain Basden, would mean that the successful bidder should expect to hear something just after the start of the new year."

"Oh, that is good news. Thank you."

At least she wouldn't have to wait long to know if she had secured the spice contract. Win or lose, she would have her answer soon. The prospect of securing the contract put Poppy in a much happier mood.

"I owe you a freshly baked apple pie for all your assistance," she said.

"Thank you, Captain Basden, that would be very generous of you."

A hopeful Poppy made her way back to the quayside. As she drew close to the row of warehouses, she noticed an elegant carriage standing out the front of number twelve. When the door of the warehouse opened, Poppy hurried her steps.

A tall, white-haired gentleman appeared and made his way toward the carriage. For a moment, Poppy thought he might be an elderly man. His shock of white hair caught her eye. But his stride, which was sure and confident, was that of a young man.

She held up her hand and waved to him. "Hello!"

He, gave one brief look in her direction, shook his head, and climbed aboard. Poppy caught a glimpse of a haughty glare through the window as the carriage passed her on its way out of the docks. Hands on hips, she stood and watched as it travelled through the front gate and turned right.

"How rude. I was just trying to be friendly."

If that was the owner of number twelve, it certainly went a long way to explaining the situation with the barrels and ropes. The arrogant man clearly thought he owned the dockside. Perhaps he even viewed her arrival as that of an unwelcome interloper.

Poppy softly chuckled. She couldn't wait to see what the pompous ass would make of things when come tomorrow morning, he found his discarded junk once more tossed back in front of his warehouse.

When she reached the front of number fourteen, Poppy slipped off her coat and set to work. Ropes went first, then the barrels.

By the time she finally headed back to the *Empress Catherine,* having given up on the idea of seeking a hot supper, the area in front of her warehouse was clear. Her back ached, but the job was done.

The gentleman next door might well be full of himself, but he hadn't dealt with Captain Poppy Basden before. She had spent much of her life waiting for her father to arrive into port and show her the slightest amount of attention.

While those long years had been painful, and at times lonely, the lessons they had taught her still ran deep. If it meant her moving the barrels and ropes every morning for the rest of her days, she would do it.

And a smile would be on her face as she worked.

My snow-haired friend, if you seek to take me on in a game of wills, you will find that I have endless patience.

Chapter Seven

Francis sat back in the seat of his carriage and fumed. It had been a long trying day. First with the bank, then the new neighbors, and finally with a cancelled shipment. He couldn't decide which of the three vexed him the most.

Actually, I can. It's the bloody neighbors. How on earth did they take over the warehouse?

To top it all off, a lady of the night had tried to hail him outside the front door of his warehouse. He would be having firm words with the port authority people in the morning. The last thing he needed was for the local street walkers to start touting their business along the North Quay.

Cheeky minx.

There were plenty of unofficial brothels in the area, all discreetly situated in nearby houses where the needs of passing sailors could be met. The girls who worked the streets had the area around Spitalfields market well staked out. No one had any call to be crowding the docks. It wasn't good for business.

As far as Francis was concerned, everyone had a right to make a living—just as long as it didn't interfere with his plans.

But with the arrival of the new tenants next door, and the loss of the dockside berth, his scheme to make money was now in serious jeopardy.

What did I miss? I was polite in the letter I sent the owner. He knows who I am. So why didn't he offer me the lease?

None of it made sense. The only thing that did was that these new neighbors had to go.

If he couldn't get hold of the warehouse through the owner, then surely there had to be a way to make the tenants want to leave.

"Ah, now that's a thought. There has to be some legal technicality to the lease. I did make an offer to take over the premises at least two months ago. I should have had first right of refusal."

The bones of a cunning plan began to form in his mind. Tomorrow morning, he would speak to the superintendent of London Docks and demand to see the lease agreement. Seek to challenge its validity. There had to be a loophole. An *i* missing a dot; a *t* not crossed. He would put the contract in the hands of his lawyers and demand that they find a fault. Something that would allow him to challenge the lease.

As far as Francis was concerned, strange lion-headed ships had no place in the London Docks, nor did their owners warrant a place at the North Quay warehouses. No matter what it took, he was going to make certain that warehouse number fourteen was his for the taking.

Without the warehouse, he couldn't fulfil the spice contract. And without the contract, he...no, he wouldn't even consider that option.

"Tenants of number fourteen, I suggest you stop unpacking this very minute. Tomorrow, you leave."

Chapter Eight

Some of the crew had made it back on board in the wee hours of the morning. Poppy had stuffed her pillow over her head in order to drown out the loud drunken singing that had taken place on deck. There were going to be plenty of sore heads and queasy stomachs in the morning.

After coming up from her cabin, Poppy had stopped and tossed a blanket over one of the men. She'd noted that Jonathan was not among the snoring bodies scattered around the deck. There was too much work to do today for her to waste time in wandering the streets in search of him. Jonathan being Jonathan, he would return to the ship when it suited him.

Outside her own door, she glanced over at warehouse number twelve. It was early; the neighbors likely hadn't arrived yet and seen her handiwork. The battle over the fate of the barrels may yet have to be fought.

If that was the case, then there was every chance that an unpleasant altercation was brewing. The memory of the foul looks the white-haired gentleman had given her as he departed late last night fanned the flames of determination burning in Poppy's belly.

He was rude, and she knew only too well that people like him only responded properly when treated in the same haughty manner. If he wanted to take issue with her, he could come and knock on her door.

Poppy took the key from out of her pocket and slipped it into the lock. The click of the latch bolt sliding back had her smiling. *My own front door. I can come and go as I please.*

Once inside the warehouse, Poppy set to work sweeping the rest of the ground floor. She cleared away the dirty holland covers which had been thrown over the odd pieces of furniture the previous owner had left behind.

There was a broken chair. "That can be repaired with a nail and glue." And a small step, which she decided might come in handy for reaching high places.

"Oh, this is wonderful," she exclaimed, as she pulled the next cover away. Underneath lay a proper table. A good half-dozen people could be seated around it quite comfortably.

The sight of a real table, one which didn't hang from the wall, set tears brimming in her eyes.

Poppy rested her hand on the smooth oak. She could just imagine sunny mornings sitting here while enjoying a hot coffee and a plate of eggs. *The Times* would be spread out before her, along with the *Port Gazette*. And every morning she would take the time to read them both from cover to cover.

Her mind happily filled in the rest of the blanks. Small cakes on a plate. Freshly baked bread. And seated across the table from her would be her husband.

A scowling Jonathan.

That image yanked her violently out of her sweet dream. All pleasant thoughts disappeared; in their place sat a cold, sense of dread.

Poppy found herself resenting Jonathan. He hadn't spared a thought for her, nor the heavy workload she had been burdened with last night. Within a day of them arriving in port, he had already been unsupportive of her efforts.

He wouldn't have dared to do that while they had been on board her ship. The power dynamic between them was now changing. Poppy didn't like the way the wind was shifting the sails. A storm was brewing. And at sea or on land that was never a good thing.

Her hands slapped against the table as she slumped over it. Was the price of finally having a home going to be that she was doomed to spend the rest of her life bound to such a sour man? A man who clearly didn't give a damn about her.

Because if Jonathan Measy did care, he would be here right this very minute helping her to get things set up. Instead, he was more than likely lying in a drunken stupor. Heavens knew where.

Her father had chosen Jonathan. Made his decision clear. If she wanted to base herself in London, she had to have a husband. At the time, her agreement to his terms had been heavy with desperation. But eight months after departing Ceylon, the more she thought about it the less appealing it became.

This is a city of over a million people. There must be plenty of men in need of a wife. I might not be the prettiest girl in town, but I still have much to offer the right man.

If only she could find someone who would be willing to create a true partnership with her—a meeting of minds. A bonding of equals. Respect. Affection. Unity. The things she had always craved.

Pushing away from the table, Poppy angrily scooped up the holland cover, not caring about the dust which now covered her clothes.

During the long voyage from Ceylon, Jonathan hadn't

once raised the subject of marriage. Nor had he ever attempted to share Poppy's bed. She had been too busy running the *Empress Catherine* to pay it much mind, but it was quickly becoming a matter of importance.

George Basden had left the matter of his daughter's betrothal somewhat vaguely incomplete. And while she had always assumed that there was an understanding of sorts between Jonathan and her father, nothing had ever been set in writing.

What seemed at the time as an oversight on her father's part now presented itself as an opportunity. If Jonathan was in no hurry to wed, then neither was she.

Perhaps Jonathan had also viewed the opportunity to move to London as a means for him to escape George's sphere of influence. The Ceylon spice trade was a fiercely competitive one, and Jonathan had made little headway in it over the years. If that was the case, did his plans actually include her?

It would go a long way to explaining how cold and distant he is with me.

With the covers wrapped up in her arms, Poppy headed toward the door and back to the ship. The covers would be hung over the rope lines on board the *Empress Catherine* and the wind would do much of the work of blowing away the dust.

As a captain, she had always been fair with her crew and that included Jonathan. She would give him one last chance to show he was serious about their partnership. And if he didn't take it, then as far as she was concerned, they were done.

With a year before her father was due to arrive, she would have plenty of time to find herself a suitable husband. One who would pull his weight. One who valued her.

And when George Basden finally did make it to London,

he would have to accept that his daughter had not only decided her own future, but with whom she would share it.

~

Francis set his coffee cup down with a sigh and pushed back from the breakfast table. Charles glanced up from his newspaper and slowly shook his head.

"Pouting is something reserved for children, not a businessman such as yourself, Francis. You are going to have to accept that the warehouse next door to the shipping office has been let. Being petulant about it won't get you anywhere."

He might have been in his early twenties, but Francis was not above a scolding from either of his parents—the price of being the last of the offspring left at home.

"You know I need that storage space and the dockside berth," replied Francis.

"Want, not need. Saunders Shipping lasted all those years at the old docks before we moved to London Docks. Granted, there were times when it was difficult to manage cargos and ships but manage I did. You will do the same, extra warehouse notwithstanding," said Charles, continuing to shake his head in obvious parental disapproval.

Hand resting on his knee, Francis clenched his fist. He hated it when Charles offered him these words of wisdom. They grated on his nerves.

The dark side of ambition was an inability to accept criticism. He was thin-skinned and easily offended. Francis knew it was fault in his character. It hadn't always been a problem, and he had kept it mostly under control. But over recent months, as the time for his father to retire drew closer, Francis had loosened his hold on the reins.

He wanted to be a success, to be able to stand alongside his titled relatives and know they viewed him as an equal. For his father to not only see him but be proud of his achievements.

I don't have the mental capacity this morning to endure another lecture.

Rising to his feet, he stretched his six-foot, six-inch frame to its full height and bowed to his father. The shipping office beckoned.

"While I appreciate the history lesson, Papa, I must respectfully disagree with you. I need that warehouse. When the spice contract begins, the space we have will not be sufficient. Renting storage away from the docks will cost both time and money."

"So, what are you going to do?" challenged his father.

Francis held Charles's worried gaze. His father was on the verge of retiring, but he was still very much involved in the shipping business. Saunders Shipping had been built up over the years by Charles, and its reputation as a reliable, honest company was well known. If Charles thought Francis was about to do something rash, he might well reconsider his plans to leave the business. That would put Francis in an untenable position.

He might well be a hot head, but a fool he was not. Francis understood the precious and fragile nature of a company's good name. Once damaged, it was nigh on impossible to repair. The London business community had a long memory.

"I am going to go and speak to the superintendent of London Docks. I want to know who this new tenant is and how they managed to get the lease," he replied.

Charles frowned. "You are going to look for a loophole—is that what you really mean? A way to void the contract. If so, I caution you to tread carefully. May I remind you that you do not take over full management of the company until the first day of January. I won't have the Saunders name dragged through the mud."

Yes, I am well aware of the fact that it is still your company. When will you learn to trust me?

He had no intention of doing anything rash, but he wasn't going to simply let someone else, some unknown interloper, steal his future out from under him. There had to be a way to overcome this unexpected and unwelcome turn of events.

"I never said I was going to cause trouble. I am just going to have a quiet word with the superintendent. Make sure everything is above board. We can't have the wrong people taking up valuable warehouse space in the docks."

His father held his gaze for a little while longer. The warning was clear in his eyes. Francis had better not do anything reckless.

With a resigned sigh, Charles went back to his paper. "I shall see you at the office in a little while. When I arrive, you can inform me as to how things went with the port authorities."

The message, while clearly heard and understood, was entirely unwelcome.

Teeth gritted firmly together; Francis headed for the door. Charles Saunders knew everyone at the London Docks, so there little to no chance of Francis getting away with anything. He would have to tread carefully with his inquiries.

Whatever I say will get back to you.

He loved his father and had learned a great deal from him, but there were times when Francis feared Charles would never understand his burning drive to succeed. That in his father's eyes, he would always be that little snow-haired boy desperate for his papa's approval.

As he made his way from the house and out to the rear mews where his carriage was waiting, Francis stopped briefly to glance up at the window of the breakfast room. Charles had his back to him, no doubt still deeply engrossed in his newspaper.

His father was fascinated by the constant comings and goings in London society. When he arrived at Saunders Shipping later in the morning, he would as usual give Francis a well-considered précis of the most interesting snippets of information and gossip. And his firm opinion of them.

But with each one would also come some carefully crafted words of advice. A lesson which Charles would no doubt expect Francis to not only ponder, but to put to good use.

After six years of being an understudy, Francis was chomping at the bit. He couldn't wait until the day his father retired.

An apprentice could only learn at the side of his master for so long. Eventually, he had to be given the freedom to make his own decisions. To endure the pain of his mistakes and learn from them.

"I can't do that while you are constantly looking over my shoulder."

Stubborn and single-minded, Francis was more than ready to make his own mistakes. It was the learning part where he found himself failing.

Chapter Nine

Travelling east across London was a painful endeavor at the best of times. Carts, carriages, and wagons jostled with one another in the crowded streets. Some mornings, Francis was sorely tempted to get out and walk the four miles from his home in Dover Street to the shipping offices at London Docks. This morning was one of them.

After pulling his pocket watch out from his waistcoat, he checked the time. His carriage hadn't moved for the past twenty minutes.

What on earth is going on? I have work to do.

He rapped on the roof of the carriage. "Why aren't we moving?"

"Some sort of accident by the look of it, Mister Saunders. Everything has come to a complete stop," came the reply from the driver.

"Bloody hell," he muttered.

After gathering up his papers, Francis stuffed them into his leather satchel, then set it on the seat. From here to London Docks was another two miles. He could comfortably cover that distance in less than an hour.

Gripping the handle, Francis swung the carriage door open. Not bothering with the step, he jumped out and landed on his feet in the middle of the road.

The sight which met his eyes had him cursing under his breath.

His carriage was stuck in the middle of a long line of other vehicles, which were all banked up through the Poultry thoroughfare and across Threadneedle Street. He moved in front of his horses, glancing across to the right. More vehicles were stuck in Cornhill. The entire intersection of the three streets was a convoluted mess of horses, carriages, and irate people.

He waved up at his driver. "Let me go and see what's happening. If things are too bad, it might be easier for you to turn around and go home. I can always walk or try and catch a hack on the other side of this mess. I will be back shortly."

There had to be a clear spot somewhere up ahead.

Making his way forward, he eventually reached the crossing point of the streets and came upon the cause of the traffic chaos. A large wagon laden with sacks sat in the middle of the road. The horses which had been hauling the load were tangled in broken reins. The backband on one of the harnesses had twisted and was causing obvious distress to one of the animals.

As the driver of the wagon worked to free the stricken horse, another of the wagon team broke free of its reins and bolted away. It headed straight toward Francis.

He had but a moment to decide what to do. Either step out of the way and let someone else deal with the problem, or help.

Francis chose the latter.

He held his arms out wide and stood his ground. The horse slowed. Fortunately for Francis, the skittish beast hadn't had time to lift its pace to more than a slow canter.

"Shh. Shh. Good lad," said Francis, in a calm voice. He was keen to reassure the spooked horse that he posed it no threat.

Making sure he avoided meeting the horse's eyes, he moved forward, his right hand lifting slowly as he did. As his fingers touched the leather of the loose reins, Francis took a firm hold. "It's alright. No one is going to hurt you."

To his relief, his words and calm manner had the desired effect. The horse didn't struggle against Francis's hold.

The liveried tiger from the Saunders's carriage appeared at his side.

"Mister Saunders, shall I take the reins?"

He nodded. "Yes, thank you. Just keep him calm." The young man took the horse.

Francis pondered what else he should do. He could go back to his carriage, retrieve his satchel, and then be on his way. This situation wasn't his problem.

The air was blue with the foul curses of various drivers and passengers, but no one was making any effort to help clear the obstruction.

Abusing the poor man and his animals won't do any of us an ounce of good.

It would cause disruption to his plans for the day, but he couldn't just walk away when he could do something to help.

Arriving back at the middle of the crossroads, Francis made his way over to the wagon. The red-faced driver was doing his best to untangle the other horse, while at the same time stopping it from running away. From what Francis could tell, the poor man was making little progress.

Adding to the bedlam were the other vehicles which were trying to get around the scene. Horses and carriages squeezed through a gap that left little room for error.

"Here, let me hold the reins and keep the horse still. You

see what you can do to clear the tangle. One of my servants has your other horse," said Francis.

The wagon driver appeared close to tears. "Thank you, kind sir. You are the first person who has offered to assist. Everyone else is too busy abusing me or shoving their way through."

"You look like you need help, and it wouldn't sit right with my conscience not to do what I can."

It took some time, but finally, with Francis's assistance, the driver was able to set the harness to right. Francis then handed him the reins and went back to his own carriage. He returned a few minutes later with the other horse and a spare length of leather.

He fashioned the leather into a makeshift rein and secured it. With both animals back under control, the wagon driver was able to move the wagon out of the way. Movement across the intersection immediately gathered pace. The life and blood of the city began to flow once more.

"Thank you, sir. I don't know what I would have done if you hadn't come along. I expect I would have been stuck there for a long while yet," said the driver.

Francis offered the man his hand. "It was my pleasure. I am just glad that your horses are safe, and you can get on your way."

The wagon driver glanced at Francis's hand. He took it, then bowed. The expression on his face said it all. He wasn't used to well-dressed, upper-class men offering to help, let alone shake his hand.

"God bless you, sir."

As Francis made his way back to his own carriage, he checked his pocket watch again. He would have to hurry if he was going to be able to see the head of London Docks this morning.

It would have been so easy to have done the same as everyone else and simply left the wagon driver to deal with his problems on his own. But situations like this called for good men to step up and do what was right. And while he had his faults, Francis Saunders was a good man at heart.

Chapter Ten

Poppy was having the time of her life. She had gone in search of food earlier in the morning and had been delighted to discover that the dock area was well serviced by roaming pie men, selling all manner of hot and delicious baked pastries.

With her belly full, she had set to finishing the task of cleaning the warehouse. Hours later, she was covered from head to toe in dust, and her hands were blackened from scrubbing around the window frames.

And she was loving it.

Slowly but surely, the ground floor of her new home was taking shape. Another day of this and she would be able to move some of her personal possessions off the *Empress Catherine* and into number fourteen. She couldn't wait for the moment when her soft, feather mattress made its way down the gangplank, across the wharf embankment, and through the front door.

Tomorrow night, I am going to sleep in here. Claim this place as my home.

She had just set her hands back into the bucket of soapy

water and was wringing out a cleaning rag when the front door opened. A pale-faced Jonathan closed the door quietly behind him.

"Good morning," said Poppy.

He winced. "Could you not yell? My head is ready to split wide open."

"I wasn't speaking loudly," she replied, lowering her voice.

Jonathan waved her words away with the barest movement of his hand. "A whisper would be good."

Oh dear, that bad?

"I was wondering when you would make an appearance. Some of the crew arrived back at the ship earlier this morning. What's left of them is dotted about the deck," she said.

She had press-ganged a couple of the less inebriated crew members into helping her hang the holland covers over the ropes, then let them go back to sleep. There wouldn't be a great deal of work getting done on board the *Empress Catherine* this morning.

Jonathan's gaze settled on the freshly cleaned and polished table, but he said nothing. "We gave it a good nudge. Your extra coins lasted a couple of hours, after which we pooled the rest of our money into a kitty. I don't remember much of what happened after that. I woke somewhere out near the burying grounds in Bluegate Fields."

He couldn't have picked a stranger place in London to end his night of celebrations. From the taverns of the waterside to waking up beside the dead. Then again, by the state of him, Poppy decided she should be pleased that Jonathan had at least made it back to the dock in one piece.

He doesn't smell like he visited one of the brothels. No aroma of cheap perfume. His miasma was a fog of whisky, ale, and something damp.

For a moment, Poppy was tempted to ask Jonathan what he had planned for the day but recalling their disagreement of the previous morning and his hungover state, she left it unsaid. The last thing she wanted was to start another fight.

"You look like you have been busy," he said, and there was a familiar defensive edge to his tone. One which challenged her to say something about his lack of help. Of her near constant disappointment with his efforts.

Don't give him an excuse to play the victim. He will latch onto it as soon as he can.

If she did give him the opportunity, there was every chance that Jonathan would be out the door and headed back to the ship. There, he would find himself a sympathetic ear which he could bend with his tale of self-pitying woe. Of how Poppy was forever expecting him to be at her beck and call.

After that, he would be back, demanding more coins from her so he could retire once more to the nearest tavern and resume drinking.

No. We are not playing that game.

An awkward silence descended, during which Poppy was sure she could hear Jonathan taunting her under his breath. Whispering, "Go on. Say it."

But when it became clear that she wasn't going to take the bait, he let out a tired sigh. "I am going to go back on board the ship and get some sleep. I shall see you later."

His gaze drifted and settled on the far wall. His brows knitted as his eyes focused on it. Poppy turned, interested to see what had caught Jonathan's hungover attention.

"I'm surprised you haven't tried to move that," he said.

He was pointing at the large black partition, which had been erected against the brickwork. Poppy had noticed it when they first arrived, but she had been so preoccupied with cleaning that she hadn't given it a second thought.

"Why? What's so important about it?" she replied.

She caught sight of the rare smile on his lips as Jonathan

stepped past her and headed over to the wall. An intrigued Poppy followed.

"It's not often that you surprise me, Poppy. I would have thought this was the first thing you would want."

As her gaze drifted up, past the partition and toward the ceiling, Poppy let out a gasp. "It's a chimney, which means . . ."

"Exactly. There must be a fireplace behind that wood panel. And if they have just put a screen in front of it, I would bet five shillings it's still in working order."

A fireplace. Tears pricked at Poppy's eyes. She had longed for a home, but her secret desire had really been for a place where she could bake. A proper cooking area instead of the tiny oven she'd had on board the boat.

Hearth and home.

"Oh, Jonathan," she whispered.

To her surprise, he took a deep breath and made what appeared to be an effort to shake off the effects of his hangover. "Let me get some tools from the ship."

He disappeared out the door, returning a few minutes later with a crowbar. Two crewmen trailed slowly into the office in his wake.

Poppy kept out of the way while the men set to the partition with tools and hands. They might well be suffering from the night before, but these men were well versed in being dragged from their hammocks in the middle of a stormy night at sea. Compared to having to go up on deck and haul rope, the job of clearing away a wooden wall inside a dry warehouse presented little challenge.

The panel broke free from the wall with a satisfying crack. As Jonathan and the crewmen lifted it free, a cobweb-covered fireplace was revealed. Poppy clapped her hands with glee. Images of a piece of roast beef turning slowing in front of a well-stoked fire immediately sprang to her mind. This was more than she had hoped for. Why anyone would cover up a fireplace was beyond her.

"We will take this panel upstairs and put it somewhere out of the way. It looks a useful piece of wood, so we should keep it," said Jonathan.

He might have been a source of continued frustration for Poppy, but she had to hand it to him. Jonathan did have the occasional moment when he could be useful. Her resentment toward him thawed just a touch.

While the partition was carried upstairs, Poppy grabbed a broom and set to the maze of cobwebs with unrestrained enthusiasm. Quickly sweeping to and fro, she had years of intricate spider weaving cleared away in a matter of minutes. By the time the men returned downstairs, she had worked up quite a sweat.

"You didn't waste any time," observed Jonathan.

Poppy had waited long years for this day. For when she had her own front door. Her own table. And now . . . She blinked back tears. "I have somewhere I can really cook. To create."

The two crewmen exchanged an odd look. They clearly didn't understand why this was such a momentous occasion. Or why the captain of the *Empress Catherine* was in tears. Poppy rarely showed emotion while on the high seas. Keeping her boat and crew safe meant having their respect. Weeping women didn't command ships.

They will never understand.

How could they? Only Poppy had experienced her life. No one else had suffered the exact same empty, motherless childhood. Been left at strange ports by a father who headed out to sea for months at a time.

She forced back her tears, afraid of what would happen if she let them have free rein.

"Could I ask one more favor of you before you all head back to the boat?" she asked in a tremulous voice

"Does it come with a coin or two?" replied Jonathan.

"Yes."

He had done his good deed for the day. Anything else that she required was going to cost Poppy a spot of drinking money. But for this request, she was prepared to pay.

"I would like to bring my mattress off the *Empress Catherine*. I am going to sleep here in the warehouse from tonight."

She had thought to wait, but with the sudden discovery of the fireplace, Poppy wanted nothing more than to be able to rest in front of the light from a fire's golden flame.

Jonathan nodded at the men. "You heard the captain. Let's go and get the mattress. After that, we can go and get a bacon roll and a tankard of ale for our breakfast."

He held out his hand, and Poppy dropped several coins into his palm.

As Jonathan and the men disappeared out the front door, she turned and faced the fireplace. Not even his demand for money could dampen her mood this morning. She had somewhere she could bake.

Thoughts of hosting lady guests for tea and cake filled her mind. Lace tablecloths and polite conversation would be the order of the day. It didn't matter that Poppy hadn't any female friends in London, nor that her temporary home was a dockside warehouse. All that was important was the hope that one day she would be accepted as a member of English society.

"Now, what shall I make first?"

Chapter Eleven

"I'm sorry, Mister Saunders, but the contracts are all legally binding. The transfer of occupancy is valid. There is nothing I can do to change it."

Francis did his best to steadily hold the gaze of the grey-haired superintendent of London Docks. Sitting in the man's office always reminded him of being sent to the head of house when he was at school. It hadn't been a pleasant experience when he was younger, and this wasn't much better.

But at least he knew his knuckles were not going to be rapped with a heavy cane at the end of the conversation. That was a small blessing.

Francis took a slow deep breath, doing his best not to shift about in his seat. He would have shaken his head, but Charles was a personal friend of the superintendent of the London Docks. Any outward signs of disappointment on his part would surely get back to his father.

The contract was valid; he was stuck with his new neighbor. But it still didn't answer the question of why he hadn't been offered the lease. His overtures to the owner had been rejected without reply. He'd made a misstep somewhere but for the life of him, Francis couldn't comprehend when or where.

"Does the lease have yearly options?" he pressed, leaning forward. If it did, he might be able to make the owner a better offer this time next year. A year's delay in getting his hands on the warehouse would be a major inconvenience, but he could bide his time if it meant securing a long-term lease. The spice contract was hopefully just the first in a long line of many.

And who knows? If I work at it, I might be able to convince them to give up the tenancy a little earlier. Grease their palms with some coin.

Or make things so difficult for them that the new tenants came to him and asked that he take over the lease.

Now there's a tasty thought.

Once Charles handed over the reins of the shipping company in the new year, Francis would be free to conduct business on his terms. Without his father's interference.

But the second that the superintendent fixed him with a steely glare, a shiver of dread slid down Francis's back. He knew that look only too well.

Did he and Papa go to the same school of parental disapproval?

"There isn't a lease on the warehouse, Mister Saunders. The Basden Line Shipping Company owns the building."

He lifted a piece of paper from the bottom of the file and slid it across his desk. Francis glanced at it and immediately recognized it as a deed of title. His heart sank to the bottom of his boots.

Oh, no.

"I am of the understanding that they purchased the warehouse some time ago but only took physical possession in the past day. I am led to believe that the owner currently lives in Ceylon. His representatives are getting the place ready for his arrival, which I expect will be soon."

Little wonder the previous owner hadn't bothered to return his correspondence. The building wasn't his any longer.

Defeat settled heavily on Francis's shoulders. The warehouse was lost. He fought the temptation to snatch up his hat and make a hasty departure. He was impetuous at times, but even he knew better than that. The earliest of Charles's lessons had stuck. Just because one door closed didn't mean that there weren't others about to open.

"Are there any other warehouses in the North Quay possibly becoming vacant in the next year?" asked Francis.

It was a long shot. Competition for storage space at the London Docks was fierce. But as far as Francis was concerned, if you didn't ask, you didn't get.

The superintendent closed up the contract file and set it aside on his desk. With hands clasped gently together, he settled back in his chair and considered his visitor.

And here commences the lesson.

"Not that I am aware of, young man. If I may offer you a suggestion, it would be that you might want to make friends with the Basden family. I hear one of them arrived this week. Since they are just getting operations set up, they may offer to lease you some of their warehouse space."

That's all well and good for you, but a portion of the warehouse won't be enough to generate the money I need to grow the business. I intend to fill every inch of that warehouse.

Francis's interest stirred at hearing the news that one of the owner's family was here in London. *Interesting.* If they were fresh off the boat from Ceylon, they wouldn't likely know how the port worked. How the rules could be twisted and applied to his favor.

Whereas I do.

He might have lost out on the warehouse, but he had an edge over the neighbors. If he turned the screws just tight enough, they might come to see that London wasn't the place for them. That doing business here was harder than they could ever have imagined.

And then they might leave.

Making friends with the Basden family was one option. Becoming their nemesis while operating within the boundaries of English law was a far more attractive proposition. He didn't want to negotiate for a spare spot somewhere next door; he wanted it all.

By the time he was finished with the Basden Line Shipping Company, they would be begging to sell him the warehouse.

Francis got to his feet. "Thank you for your advice. I shall call on the new owners of number fourteen at my earliest convenience. Who knows? We might have similar business goals and find a way in which we can work together."

Not bloody likely.

The superintendent rose from his chair and offered Francis his hand. "I am pleased that you have come around to this way of thinking. Your father said he was worried that you might be taking a hardline approach, but I can see that is not the case."

A smiling Francis shook hands. "One should always look for options when it comes to business."

And for a way to get an edge over the competition.

"This is coming together quite nicely," said Poppy. She had made good progress in cleaning the ground floor. Her initial idea had been to clear out the first level and convert that into living quarters, but the discovery of the fireplace had seen a quick change to her plans.

The warehouse had a large enough footprint for her to be

able to set up a small office for conducting business and handling company accounts just inside the front door.

Her amended plans included erecting a temporary wall a few feet to the left of the office space. On the other side of that, she would set up her private quarters, utilizing the fireplace to both cook and keep warm.

A knock at the door disturbed her from her happy musings.

That had better not be one of the crew coming to ask for yet more coin.

She would have firm words with Jonathan if that was the case. Him demanding money from her was one thing; sending the men to beg on his behalf was another. Her patience had some limits.

A second knock came, and with a resigned huff, she set the broom down and headed for the door. To her surprise, the clerk who had handed her the keys at the superintendent's office the previous morning was waiting on the threshold. He wore a worried expression on his face.

This doesn't look good.

"May I help you?" she asked. It was always a good idea to be accommodating with port officials—even ones that had been on the end of your tired temper.

The clerk glanced over his shoulder in the direction of the warehouse next door. Poppy poked her head out and was relieved to see that the barrels were still in front of the Saunders Shipping Company, right where she had left them the previous night.

"Could I please have a moment of your time, Captain Basden?" asked the clerk.

Those words rarely meant good news. A pensive Poppy stepped back and ushered the man inside. He closed the door behind him.

Just listen and get the problem straight in your head. Whatever the matter is, you can deal with it. But it must be bad if he is addressing me as Captain Basden.

"We have had a complaint," he said.

Oh, no. What has the crew done?

It wouldn't be the first time the men from the *Empress Catherine* had caused trouble while on shore leave. Sailors arriving into port always gave the booze a hard nudge, and what followed was often a bloody disaster. Yet Jonathan hadn't made mention of there having been any trouble. While he wasn't the most reliable person in her life, Jonathan usually kept an eye on the crew.

"What has happened?" she asked. The sooner she knew the situation, the quicker she could deal with it.

The clerk scowled. Whatever news he had come to impart, he was clearly uncomfortable with telling her. "When I say complaint, I mean more of an enquiry. Have you met your next-door neighbors yet? The people in number twelve?"

"No, I haven't. But we do appear to be having a silent tussle over some barrels and ropes. They are clearly marked as belonging to the Saunders Shipping Company. So, if that is the problem, let me tell you that I am well within my rights to move them out of the way of my property," she replied. That had better not be what this was about. If it was, the Saunders didn't have a leg to stand on.

"I don't know anything about the barrels, Captain Basden. But I thought you should know that one of the gentlemen from next door, Mister Francis Saunders, paid a visit to the superintendent's office this morning. He was looking to see if your ownership papers were in order," he whispered.

Considering they were in her warehouse, and the door was closed, the man's behavior struck Poppy as rather odd. Who were these Saunders people? And how much power did they wield around the London Docks?

"I trust that your employer explained that all the titles

were clear of any encumbrances and the Basden Line Shipping Company are the rightful owners," she replied.

He nodded. "Yes. Mister Francis Saunders was none too pleased. I just thought that you should know. Rumor has it that he has been wanting to lease this building for some time. Your arrival has not gone down at all well."

This wasn't the first time Poppy Basden had had to deal with a male trying to muscle her out of the way. She didn't respond well to threats, but she most certainly didn't take them lying down. If this Francis Saunders person wanted a fight, she would gladly give him one.

But who was he? If she had a bright and shiny new nemesis, it made good business sense to understand as much as she could about him.

"These Saunders people. Who are they?" she asked.

"They are well connected. The older gentleman, Mister Charles Saunders, is married to the sister of the Duke of Strathmore. That family, the Radleys, are one of the richest and most powerful families in all of England."

Poppy could understand why the clerk felt it necessary to warn her, but it didn't explain his motivation. Had his employer sent him, or was this a personal matter?

"Why are you telling me this?"

No one trusted a tattler, and the hairs on the back of her neck shifted as her sense of unease grew. The next words out of his mouth had better not be asking for money.

Poppy, you fool. You shouldn't have given the other clerk those coins last night. They must now see you as an easy touch for cash.

She was going to have to stamp down hard on that and quick smart.

A red blush rushed to the clerk's cheeks. "Please don't get the wrong idea, miss. I mean, Captain. I am only here to warn you. I have nothing against the Saunders family, but if I was being honest, I would suggest that young

Mister Francis could do with being taken down a peg or two."

Now the story gets interesting. Do tell me more.

Poppy could confess to being just as intrigued by dockside gossip as the next sailor. "Why? What has he done?" *Apart from dumping his stuff in front of my building.*

"Mister Charles Saunders, who is an honorable man, is due to retire shortly. Francis will be taking over the family business. To say that he has been strutting about like a peacock of late would be an understatement. He is not a bad chap, but he is a little too eager to show everyone that he is as good, if not better, than his father. If you get my meaning."

Now things made sense. The young pup was trying to mark out his territory, but rather than lift his leg and pee on her doorstep, Francis Saunders was using the barrels.

I know exactly how that feels.

Poppy nodded. She wasn't angry—rather, she felt a sense of understanding. Trying to stake her claim as a woman in a man's world was a constant battle. There were many men who simply refused to take orders from a female, ship owner or not.

"Have you come to warn me or is there something else?" she replied. Information rarely came without a price.

The clerk dropped his gaze to the floor. It was clear he was having second thoughts about this visit. Perhaps he had set out from the superintendent's office with the intention of asking her for money, but now, having spoken to her, he seemed more than a little uncertain of himself.

The man shrugged but wouldn't meet Poppy's eye. She took that as a good sign. If he had come seeking a coin, this would have been the perfect opportunity to put out his hand.

"Thank you for coming to talk to me today. I appreciate your candor. And I will respect that this conversation goes no further," she said.

Her words were crafted with care. She would no doubt have to deal with this man in the future. And the spice contract was yet to be announced.

"Could I perhaps bring you some cinnamon biscuits? I will be hoping to bake some in the next day, and you look the sort of chap who likes to have something sweet with his tea."

He gave a quick nod. "Thank you, Miss Basden. I mean, Captain. Well, I had better be going. I have work to do."

As the clerk headed for the door, a question dropped into Poppy's mind. "This Mister Francis Saunders. Could you possibly describe him to me? I mean, if we encounter one another along the wharf embankment, I would like to be prepared."

The man nodded. "He is easy to spot. Very tall, with a shock of white hair. Mister Charles is French, and rumor has it that Mister Francis was gifted the Norman side of the family. The original Viking bit."

"Thank you."

The rude man from last night had indeed been the self-important Francis Saunders.

I'll give him filthy looks.

Poppy opened the door and stepped out into the sunshine. She checked that no one was in the vicinity, then beckoned for the clerk to follow. "Before you leave, do you know where I could buy some supplies? If I am to bake you those cinnamon biscuits, I shall need some flour and butter."

"Spitalfields market is a half hour walk from here, but there are a few grocers along the way who sell goods. If you head out the front of the docks and turn right on the Ratcliffe Highway, there is a grocer just past the draper's shop."

Excellent. The fireplace inside the warehouse might not yet be ready for use, but the small stove onboard the *Empress Catherine* could be fired up to bake biscuits. "Thank you for your warning about the neighbors. I shall pop by your office in the morning with your reward."

With a tip of his hat, the man beat a hasty retreat toward the entrance to the Superintendent's Office.

Poppy, meanwhile, pondered his words. "Francis Saunders wanted this building. Well, he is too late. The Basden Line Shipping Company owns it. And I am going nowhere."

Poppy could only hope that the well-connected and wealthy Radley family members would respect her rights to live peacefully at the docks. The warehouse was now her home, and she would defend it to the bitter end.

No one, not even a self-important son of nobility, was going to take it away from her.

Chapter Twelve

An hour later, Poppy was returning from the local grocer with ingredients for her cinnamon biscuits. The grocer in question sold all manner of produce, which to her relief meant she would be spared the long walk to the market each day. She immediately asked to have an account arranged with them.

The prospect of being able to drop into the shop whenever she needed something was a far cry from her life on the ship. A life on land brought with it conveniences that she would never take for granted.

She called into the drapery next door and was delighted with their selection of fabrics. A pretty blue and cream floral pattern caught her eye and she decided it would be perfect for curtains.

All those little feminine touches that go to creating a home.

After making a quick perusal of the display garments, including a ready-to-wear collection, Poppy resolved to come back another day and try on one or two of the simple but functional gowns. Her woolen trousers and knee-length skirts were going to be relegated to the past—only brought out on the rare occasions when she might need to work on board one of the company ships.

While most other women were skilled with a needle and therefore able to make their own clothes, sewing garments and fancy stitches were not Poppy Basden's forte. She could, however, repair a sail in the middle of a storm.

Catching a glimpse of herself in the shop window, she sighed.

I don't think I own a single article of clothing which isn't salt-stained.

On her way back to the docks, baking ingredients in hand, Poppy crossed the road and stopped at a display outside a general trade shop. Four large ceramic pots had caught her eye.

"Good morning," said the shopkeeper, coming out to greet her.

He looked exactly the same as every other store owner Poppy had encountered in her world travels—short, rounded, and with ruddy cheeks. The only difference she could discern was the language they spoke. It was as if God had decided that this was the perfect template for a man who worked in a shop.

"A good morning to you too." Poppy pointed at the nearest of the pots. "Are these for sale?"

The portly man smiled. "Of course. Everything in my shop is available for purchase. I also have a range of plants and herbs for sale if you are interested."

And a cheery smile for a customer. How could I have forgotten that?

Herbs would be the most practical use for the large pots, but Poppy had something else in mind.

"What about flowers? I am thinking daisies or something with a little color. I have spent a long time at sea and want to see yellow, or even purple buds when I step out my front door. But they must be hardy."

It was a small indulgence. But as far as she was concerned, she had well and truly earned it.

As she stared at the empty pots, Poppy could just picture them full of blooms. They would look a treat standing either side of the warehouse entrance, creating a pretty welcome to her new home.

Hopefully they will also help to solve the problem of Mister Pompous Saunders and his stupid barrels.

Even he wouldn't be so petty as to block her plants from the sunshine. Could he?

"I can arrange for whatever sort of plants you would like, miss. We also deliver if you live close by," replied the shopkeeper.

Poppy nodded. "Yes, I live in one of the warehouses at the London Docks, so it's very close. Would tomorrow be too soon to have them brought over?"

The man motioned toward the door of his shop. "If you would like to come inside, we can easily make all the arrangements right now. If we do, then this time tomorrow your home will be gaily decorated with flowers. I also have some planter boxes which I think you might find of interest."

A delighted Poppy followed the man through the door. True to his word, within a matter of minutes, he had written up her order for the four large pots and two planter boxes. They were to be delivered along with some pansies early the day after tomorrow.

Her heart was light as she stepped out into the street and resumed her journey home. *Very soon, I shall have a garden. Or at least the beginning of one.*

She would have to wait until her father arrived in England for them to buy a proper house and for her to have a real garden. But Poppy was well versed when it came to waiting for what she wanted. She had infinite patience in being able to hold her heart's desire at bay.

Glancing down at the bag of flour, fresh eggs, and pat of wrapped up butter in her hands, Poppy's thoughts turned back to her plans for the morning. She wouldn't have to wait long to savor the taste of freshly baked biscuits.

A contented smile found its way to her lips. It was still there when she turned off Nightingale Lane and headed through the gateway which led into the London Docks. Poppy's happy mood disappeared the moment she passed by the superintendent's office.

Oh, no. Not him.

Coming toward her, striding with great purpose and clear self-importance, was Mister Francis Saunders. His shock of white hair was mostly hidden by his top hat, but Poppy recognized him in an instant. The insolent look he had gifted her the previous night had burned itself deep into her psyche. She would recognize that face anywhere.

She hesitated, unsure as to what to do. The temptation to confront him over his behavior was tempered by the fear of what he might decide to do in retaliation. If he had already been to the port authorities about her, who was to say what else he might do if she crossed him? Experience had taught her the prudency of keeping her powder dry—of waiting for the right moment to confront someone like Francis.

It took a great deal of willpower not to glare at her nemesis as the distance between them quickly narrowed. Poppy repeatedly tore her gaze away, doing her utmost to focus on the brickwork of the first row of warehouses.

Don't stare. Don't look at him. Just keep walking.

Much as she fought against herself, the lure of the approaching gentleman was too much. Her eyes kept darting back and forth from the wall to Francis Saunders and then away again.

Stop it. Just don't.

When her gaze drifted back to him once more, it lingered, taking in his tall, elegant form. His broad shoulders. Expertly tailored jacket. His gruff chin.

She didn't notice the small bag slip from her fingers until it was too late. Poppy let out a gasp as the eggs landed with a terrible splat on the stone roadway. "Oh, deuce," she muttered.

The angry Viking hastened his steps, bearing down on her at a rapid rate. Poppy staggered back.

To her surprise, he didn't glare at her. She had fully expected him to shoo her away, the same as he had done the previous night. Instead, he bent and picked up the bag of broken eggs. He took one look at the package and its now dripping contents and winced. "I don't think any of your eggs survived the fall."

"No, it doesn't appear so," replied Poppy. She held out her hand. "Here, let me take the bag. You don't want to get egg on your fine clothes."

He hesitated for a moment as their gazes met. A quizzical look crossed his face as he narrowed his eyes at her. Francis Saunders was clearly trying to recall where he had seen her before.

They were alone in the road. A prick of fear reached out and touched Poppy. She wasn't quite ready to take him on, just yet. Not until she was certain of his motives.

Please don't let him remember.

She could only hope he hadn't got that good a look at her face in the dark. Sucking up her courage, Poppy stepped forward and gently took the bag of broken eggs from out of Francis's hand. "Thank you."

All she wanted to do was keep walking, reach the safety of her home, and lock the front door behind her. "Good day to you, sir," she said.

Her heart raced at a furious pace, beating hard in her chest as she continued on her way. She didn't dare look back.

This is ridiculous. You have torn strips off the crew of your ship when they didn't lash the sails down properly, and yet you can't face the spoilt brat from next door.

"Miss!" came a cry from behind.

Poppy kept walking. There were still a good eighty yards or so between her and sanctuary. The crunch of boots on the road behind her had her gritting her teeth and hastening her steps.

Poppy pressed on. As the footsteps grew louder, her demise appeared certain. He must have remembered where he had seen her.

There was a whoosh of air and Poppy's world turned to black as a body crossed in front of her and came to a sudden stop. She staggered to a halt, but not fast enough to avoid hitting the mass which now blocked her way. "Oof!" she cried.

A pair of large hands settled on her shoulders, steadying her. "Don't be in such in a hurry, young lady. You forgot this."

Francis Saunders drew back, and a blinking Poppy caught sight of the bag of butter in his hand. In her haste to get away, she had dropped yet another item of her shopping.

She took a short, shallow breath, and reached for the bag. "Once again, sir, thank you."

Her gaze remained glued to her old cloth bag. To the fibers which laced together to make the fabric. To the faded markings on the side which had once read *Cal Corderet*.

The bag had come from the wax chandler's shop in Tarragona, Spain, where she had spent time in a nunnery while her father was at sea. Unsure of what to do with the strange English girl, the head nun had regularly sent Poppy into town to buy the prayer candles.

As much as those memories were filled with pain and

bitterness, she still preferred them to the task of meeting the gaze of the large man who now stood before her. A man who didn't appear in any hurry to move away.

She had the bag of butter. Francis Saunders had returned her things. There was no need for him to linger.

Poppy cleared her throat. "Once again, thank you, sir. I won't delay you any further."

"Where do I know you from?" he asked.

She shook her head. "Nowhere. I am just delivering some supplies to one of the ships. I work in the grocers' shop on Pennington Street. There is a chance that we might have passed one another by at some other time."

If you know what is good for you, you will leave me alone.

An uncomfortable moment of silence ensued, followed by a resigned huff.

"Right. Well, I had best not delay you any longer. I am sure you will have to make another trip to the docks once your customer discovers you didn't bring any eggs."

Poppy kept her eyes cast downward. Despite the strange warmth of his crisp voice, she wanted nothing more than to give this upstart a piece of her mind.

But not yet. And not here. Not in public.

To her relief, he suddenly stepped away. Light filled her vision once more.

"Thank you. Good day, sir."

"You can look at me. I don't bite," he replied.

Considering his behavior toward her thus far, Poppy would beg to differ on his self-appraisal. Mister Saunders certainly had a bark that would give most people enough reason to have second thoughts about engaging with him.

Slowly, reluctantly, she lifted her head. When her gaze settled on the sapphire and silver of his cravat pin, she let it linger. Inanimate objects were always a safe bet. The elegant pin was in the shape of a silver ship.

That is a beautiful piece. I expect it cost a lot of money.

"Do you think perchance that you are Lot's wife? That if you actually look at me you might be turned into a pillar of salt?"

He was mocking her. And from the lilt of mirth in his voice, the scoundrel was enjoying himself. Poppy was determined not to play his game. "No. I just don't make a habit of staring at strangers. The London Docks is not a safe place for women, so my employer has always pressed upon me the need to make my deliveries and then return to the shop forthwith," she replied.

"Look at me, please," he said.

Poppy dragged her gaze from the pin over his expertly tied cravat, all the way up to his face. She took in his firm, square jaw. Then his pale pink lips. His strong, well-formed nose. And finally, his eyes.

And that was a mistake.

She couldn't decide whether they were the hue of a cloudless blue sky or indeed the deep blue of the Mediterranean Sea. The morning light had them shifting from a dark sapphire to the brightest of blue.

"Your eyes," she whispered.

His slow, languid blink sent a jolt of lust-filled heat racing down her spine.

Talk about being tempted by the devil.

"My mother says my eyes are Bleu de France, the royal color," he said.

Poppy licked her lips and nodded. He could have said that his eyes were the color of mud; she really wasn't taking much of anything in. She was imagining Francis without his fancy clothes.

"Then again, my mother says she enjoys boiled cabbage and peas, yet I have never seen them served at our dinner table," he added.

Peas and cabbage? What?

The mundane topic of food snapped Poppy out of her sexual fantasy and back to the real world. To the reality of where she was and with whom.

Mister Francis Saunders. The barrel-and-rope bully from next door. The man who had lodged a complaint about her to the London Docks authority. And who had glared disdainfully at her as he rode past in his shiny carriage.

"I have to go. I have deliveries to make," she said. She gave a quick nod in farewell and scurried away.

The encounter had been peculiar and most unsettling. It was rare for a male of the species to leave her in such a state of flummox. It had only happened to her once before, and she had sworn never to let it happen again.

Handsome, alluring men held too much power. A woman was sure to make life-altering mistakes if she allowed herself to come under such a man's sway.

To her relief, he didn't follow. If she dropped anything else, she certainly wasn't going back for it. Nor would she wait for him to catch up.

Poppy's footsteps remained at their fast pace. She walked straight past her own warehouse and all the way to the end of the North Quay. Only then did she dare to stop and turn around. Her gaze searched the waterfront, seeking him, but Francis Saunders was nowhere to be seen.

She let out a huge sigh of relief, then quietly swore. If she wanted eggs to make her cinnamon biscuits, she was going to have to take the long way back around to Pennington Street.

But if it meant avoiding Francis Saunders, and the wicked things that he made her feel, it would be well worth the effort.

Chapter Thirteen

"I'm pleased to see you have shifted our ropes and barrels from out the front of number fourteen. Are you going to move them upstairs?" asked Charles.

Francis stirred from his musings of buxom delivery maids and glanced at his father.

"Pardon?"

"I said I am glad you moved our barrels and things from out the front of next door," replied Charles.

Oh, that. Damn.

Francis gritted his teeth, annoyed with himself. After his meeting with the superintendent of the London Docks, and then the strange encounter with the girl who had dropped the eggs and butter on the roadway, he had made his way back to the Saunders Shipping offices. Passing the barrels, he had made a mental note to move them back in front of the other warehouse, but several other matters had arisen during the morning that required his attention, and he hadn't got around to it.

Now I will have to wait until Papa has gone to move them again.

He was being petulant, but he wasn't ready to give up on

making the new warehouse occupants feel thoroughly unwelcome.

By the time Charles had arrived, Francis was up to his elbows in paperwork. All thoughts of petty games had been set temporarily to one side.

His cousin James Radley had worked for the Saunders Shipping Company for a time, handling many clerical tasks, and it wasn't until after he had left to go and live in Cornwall with his new wife that Francis finally realized just how much work James had been able to get done in a day. He had lost his most efficient employee and now had to take up the slack himself.

I must get another clerk as soon as possible. This bookwork is not my destiny.

He was quickly learning that it was nigh on impossible to create new business strategies when your head was stuck in the books of account.

A cup of steaming coffee was placed in front of him on the desk as an all too chirpy Charles pulled up a chair and took a seat. His father wanted to have a little chat.

I do not have the time nor patience for this.

The last thing he needed was yet another session of fatherly advice. He couldn't wait until his parents left for Scotland. He was counting down the days.

"Are you sure you don't want me to help carry those bits and pieces out of the way? It was good of you to move them, but now they are making the front of our warehouse look untidy," said Charles.

They won't be there for much longer.

He would have to wait until after Charles had left for the day before once more resuming his mean game of dumping barrels and ropes. Not that Francis viewed it as being cruel. This was serious business. They could keep the barrels and rope if they wished. Who was he to quibble if the soft folk at number fourteen didn't view it as a kindness?

"I shall attend to them later," replied Francis.

And by that, he meant he'd drag some extra barrels from the second floor and add them to the collection he intended to dump in front of next door.

Charles leaned back in his chair and sipped at his own coffee. "Are you looking forward to tomorrow? It's been such an age since the Radley family gathered together. I think your mama still feels somewhat cheated over the fact that both your sisters didn't have proper London society weddings. You know how important these things are to the mother of the bride."

Francis frowned. Tomorrow. Something was happening tomorrow. He racked his brain, trying to remember what it was. And why was his father going on about weddings?

"Did you have a chance to select a wedding gift?" added Charles.

Oh.

It was his cousin Maggie Radley's wedding tomorrow. How could he have forgotten?

He'd been so busy dealing with shipping business that it had completely slipped his mind. And no, of course he hadn't bought a gift. His mind had been on business and business alone.

The impending marriage of his favorite cousin Maggie wasn't even penned into his diary. But he certainly wasn't going to tell anyone else that.

I don't have time for anything other than the company at the moment.

Business had always been important to him, but Francis was fast losing perspective on the other things in his life. Taking over the running of the company had become somewhat of an obsession.

Charles looked at him expectantly. The expression on his face clearly one of doubt over whether his son had picked out a present after all.

"I have chosen a nice silver travel clock from Rundell, Bridge, and Rundell. I'm due to pick it up this afternoon," replied Francis. That was a barefaced lie. One he could only hope his father didn't seek to challenge.

Charles raised an eyebrow. "That's a generous gift. I thought you were minding your pennies."

I was, but if it gets you off my back it's worth it.

He gave his father a confident smile. "Yes, well it's not every day that one of your cousins get married. I am so looking forward to the ceremony and the wedding breakfast."

If he was going to be false, he may as well lean into the lie. A silver clock would set him back a princely sum, but the cost to his pride of confessing the truth to his father would be far greater.

Charles finished the rest of his coffee, then got to his feet. "Well, I had better let you get on with things. I expect you have a lot to get done before you leave at three o'clock."

He bent and gave Francis a friendly pat on the shoulder. "Because that is the time the silversmiths close, just in case you forgot."

Francis gave a nod. "Of course."

Three o'clock. Who closes at that hour? I won't have scratched the surface of all this work by the time I have to leave. But if I don't arrive with clock in hand tomorrow, I will never hear the end of it.

He silently gave his father his dues. Charles had him, and they both knew it.

Checkmate, Papa. Well, played.

~

There was still a mountain of untouched paperwork on his desk when Francis rose to leave midafternoon. Placing his hands in the small of his back, he stretched his tired muscles. They gave an unfamiliar twinge. *That will teach me to drag barrels around when I am in a temper.*

Charles had left the warehouse a little while earlier. His days of staying late at the office were long gone. In the lead up to his impending retirement, Charles usually managed no more than a few hours, much of which was spent sipping coffee and offering his son sage words of wisdom.

And while Francis appreciated his father's advice and privately enjoyed his company, he was eager to take over the reins for himself. The shipping clerks still referred too many things to Charles for his liking. The sooner they deferred to him, the better.

He would have preferred to remain at work, but the wedding gift for Maggie and Piers couldn't wait. Knowing Charles, he would already have made mention of the clock to his wife. Expectations had been set in place.

After gathering up his papers, Francis collected his hat and coat, making ready to depart. At the door, one of the senior clerks caught up with him. "Mister Saunders, I wanted to ask you about the barrels and the ropes which are cluttered about the front door. Would you like them brought inside and carried upstairs? I did ask Mister Charles, but he said to ask you."

Deuce, I had forgotten all about them.

The wedding service and festivities scheduled for tomorrow would take up much of the day, so neither he nor Charles would be making an appearance at the office, which meant that now was the perfect time to move the barrels back in front of number fourteen. The neighbors would have a whole day to deal with the problem while he was out celebrating.

He was being more than a little childish. A rational adult wouldn't stoop to doing such a thing. But simmering frustration clouded his vision. The burning desire to make his mark, to teach these people that they couldn't just move in next door and expect him to welcome them with open arms, had Francis, contemplating actions that he knew were shameful. He couldn't help himself.

This behavior wasn't typical of a gentleman, but politeness didn't always get you what you wanted. A strong businessman had to have a sharp edge—one which made people think twice about crossing him. He might well have family connections, but he wasn't in possession of a title, nor about to inherit vast wealth.

He had to make his own mark on the world. And if it meant not being friends with the neighbors, so be it.

"No, I don't want the barrels and ropes brought inside. What I want is for you to arrange to move them back to where they were in front of number fourteen."

The clerk scowled, but wisely held his tongue. In a matter of weeks, Francis, not Charles, would be the man's employer.

After pulling a handful of coins out of his coat pocket, Francis pressed them into the clerk's palm. "Go and find a couple of dockside workers and get them to do the job." Francis leaned in close. "But maybe leave it until a little bit later in the day. When the sun has gone down. We don't want to start any trouble. Of course, it needs not saying that you won't mention any of this to Mister Charles."

"Yes, of course, Mister Saunders."

The battle over the barrels would only have a finite lifespan, but at least he now had another day to come up with another plan. To find a more decisive way to be rid of the people in number fourteen once and for all.

To show them who was the boss.

Chapter Fourteen

The scent of freshly baked cinnamon biscuits filled the cramped galley kitchen in the *Empress Catherine*. Poppy worked on the ledgers while the cookies cooled on the tray next to the oven. She was the queen of doing more than one thing at a time.

Her original intention had been to take the books of account back to the warehouse, but by the time she had returned from the grocers, replacement eggs in hand, it was getting late in the afternoon. She had promised to deliver the biscuits to the clerk at the superintendent's office, and Poppy Basden was a woman who never went back on her word.

By warning her about Francis, the man had done her a great service. One should never underestimate the value of having people looking out for them. Especially in a city where she barely knew a soul.

If she had to work late into the night, so be it—she would get all her tasks completed. Poppy rarely went to bed without having everything done.

She set her pen back into the holder and rose from her chair. "Those biscuits should be cool enough by now."

After collecting two small clean dishcloths, she wrapped half the biscuits in each, then set them on top of her closed ledger. The delicious cinnamon goodies would be coming back to the warehouse with her. She wasn't going to risk leaving any food onboard for the crew of the *Empress Catherine* to gorge themselves on when they returned to the boat later in the evening. They could fend for themselves. Tomorrow she would officially retire from being the captain and the men would be paid out for their articled services, after which they would be free to sign up with any other ships who were looking for crew.

With ledgers and biscuits in hand, Poppy made her way up to the deck. She stopped for a moment, taking in the view. The sails were tightly lashed away. It was still hard to imagine that the *Empress Catherine* had sailed her last great ocean voyage under Poppy's command.

Perhaps I will take her up the coast for one final time. Give the girl a proper farewell.

Poppy's gaze landed on the Holland covers she had brought over from the warehouse, and she made a mental note to come back and gather them up before it got dark.

"I wonder where Jonathan is," she mused.

With the first consignment of cinnamon bales scheduled to start leaving the warehouse over the next few days, Poppy had to make sure she got all the paperwork ready. Invoices needed to be prepared and left waiting for the merchants who were purchasing the spices. That was her job. Managing the cargo was meant to be Jonathan's role.

I might have to hire some other hands to do the work if he decides to stay away.

The familiar sound of a heavy object being dragged over stone had her looking from the ship to the shore.

"Oh, no. Not again."

On the roadway across from the wharf, several dock

workers were busy hauling the barrels from next door and dumping them in front of her warehouse. Her hopes for Francis Saunders to have set his childish games aside were dashed.

This is ridiculous. Who does he think he is?

Putting a finger either side of her mouth, Poppy let out a shrill whistle. The men all stopped at once. Their heads turned back and forth as they searched for the source of the noise. As she climbed up on the gangplank, she let out another warning signal.

Closing in on where the men stood, Poppy pointed at the barrels. "I don't care who you are or who you work for, but if those barrels are not removed from my property in the next two minutes, I shall summon the port authority and they will deal with you."

The men exchanged a worried look, then approached her. "We were given instructions to move the barrels and ropes to your door," one of them said.

"Who gave you those instructions?" she demanded.

She knew full well who was behind it, but it always paid to have such pertinent facts confirmed.

"The Saunders Shipping Company. They said this spot is their property," replied the nearest man. Putting his hand into his jacket pocket, he produced a folded-up note. Taking a tentative step toward her, he gingerly offered Poppy the paper.

The Saunders Shipping Company has made a claim of adverse possession over the front of warehouse number fourteen, North Quay, London Docks. As such, the area marked from the boundary of warehouse number twelve to the end of building two is under its control.

F. Saunders, Esq

Saunders Shipping Company.

Poppy's blood shot to boiling point as she took in the contents of the letter. This was beyond the pale. How dare he attempt to stake a claim over her property.

She took a deep breath, doing her best to calm her temper. Francis Saunders might think he had the right do as he pleased, but he hadn't dealt with her before. Long years of dealing with port officials and stubborn sailors had left Poppy well equipped to handle one overindulged son of society. She had handled every situation ranging from a minor argument to a near riot on board a ship in the middle of a perilous storm. This wet-behind-the-ears boy had no idea who he was going up against.

Poppy Basden knew how to deal with intractable people, and for those occasions when she failed, she always had her pistol close at hand.

She didn't have any wish to point a weapon at these men. They were clearly just doing what they had been told. But she wasn't going to stand quietly by while some pompous ass attempted to bully her into submission.

And to think he was the perfect gentleman this morning when he handed me over the butter.

Pushing her disappointment away, Poppy pressed on. "Gentlemen, this warehouse is the property of the Basden Line Shipping Company. Rest assured that if I am forced to summon the London Docks authorities to deal with this matter, you will be leaving here in irons."

It was enough to have the men quickly moving the barrels back to the front of number twelve after which they beat a hasty retreat.

"Bloody cheek," Poppy muttered.

Thank heavens she had caught the men before they'd finished the job. If not, she would have had to move everything back tonight to make room for her large pots and planter boxes. No one, least of all Francis Saunders, was going to stop her from starting her garden.

"Maybe I will have to draw my pistol on someone if this nonsense continues."

This was London, and the law tended to take a dim view of duels. But if worst came to worst, then the pompous Francis Saunders might find himself in need of a new hat.

Crushing the letter in her hand, Poppy turned and shook her fist at the empty warehouse next door.

"You may well be a blue-eyed devil, but you are no match for me."

She was more than prepared to take him on. And while some might view it as an unfair match, Poppy was quietly confident of being able to best Francis. His money and connections were nothing to the wealth of experience she could call upon.

Bring your top game, young Saunders. You are going to need it.

After depositing the ledgers and the baked cinnamon biscuits on the table inside the warehouse, Poppy went back to the *Empress Catherine*. When she returned, it was with a small keg of gunpowder tucked firmly under her arm. In her left hand she held her trusty pistol. Her coat pockets were stuffed with lead shot. A smile sat on her lips.

If Mister Francis Saunders wanted a war, she was going to give him one.

Chapter Fifteen

The third time Adelaide Saunders turned around in her pew and smiled sweetly at him, Francis decided he would much rather spend the whole day moving barrels and ropes than be at a wedding. The look of expectation on his mother's face made his skin crawl.

She's imagining me standing up there in front of Uncle Hugh while he marries me off to some sweet little thing.

If Francis had his way, he would have positioned himself at the rear of St. Paul's cathedral alongside his brother, Will, and made his escape as soon as the wedding service was over. But family expectations were set in stone. He was doomed to sit just behind his parents, close to the front of the congregation. The long day was just beginning.

And where the devil is Gideon?

The day might not be so boringly arduous if he could team up with his cousin Gideon, but the Marquis of Holwell was nowhere to be seen.

After dropping his prayer book accidently on purpose, Francis rose from his seat and bent to pick it up. As he righted himself, he took the opportunity to make a quick examination of the rest of the wedding guests seated in the rows behind. His gaze flitted from one relative to another, searching.

As he dropped down into his seat, his mind was filled with concern. Not one of the Duke of Mowbray's family were in attendance. And while Gideon and his father were not partial to weddings, the young women of the Mowbray title, Lady Victoria, and Lady Coco Kembal, were avid attendees of marriage celebrations.

They wouldn't miss Maggie's wedding. Not on purpose. What has happened?

It did occur to him that they might have decided to miss the nuptial service and only attend the wedding breakfast, but he doubted that was the case. Hugh Radley wouldn't take kindly to his brother-in-law skipping the wedding of his eldest daughter.

I'm sure there is a perfectly reasonable explanation. Someone might have taken ill. Perhaps several of them, and they decided to stay home and not pass their malady on to the wedding guests.

Making the bride and groom ill on their wedding day wouldn't be the nicest of gifts.

Yes, that's probably what has happened. That's one way of getting out of the drudgery of a wedding breakfast. All those dull speeches.

He loved his cousin Maggie dearly. Seeing her so happy with her new husband, Piers Denford, had Francis blinking back a tear.

But celebrations and joy aside, being at the nuptials still meant a full day away from the office for him. Work would be piling up.

Then there was the matter of the ongoing argument with the neighbors. *Those barrels had better be out the front of number fourteen when I arrive tomorrow morning.*

His lips formed a tight, forced smile. It was the best Francis could muster in his current state of mind. He trusted that the Saunders Shipping head clerk had found someone to move the barrels late last night. And for Francis's threatening legal letter to now be in the right hands. *Good old adverse possession. That will give them something to think about.*

The spot out the front of number fourteen had been left vacant long enough for him to consider it his. Now was the time to press his claim.

"You look like someone who has swallowed a frog," said a voice to his right.

Francis snorted at his sister's unkind observation. Eve, who was seated between him and her husband Lord Freddie Rosemount, gave him a nudge. "What is the matter with you this morning? I thought you would be thrilled to see our cousin Maggie get married. You look such a grump."

He sighed. Of course, he was happy for Maggie. She was getting on with her life. Everything she had ever wanted was coming to fruition.

His plans, meanwhile, were mired in the ongoing battle with his next-door neighbor, and the warehouse he coveted.

"I am happy for Maggie. Piers is a good man. They are well suited. I just don't have time for all this," he replied.

"You mean family, love, and all the good things," muttered Eve, with a sarcastic huff.

Francis kept his gaze trained on the wedding service, praying it would all be over soon. He didn't want to admit it, but Eve's words stung. It wasn't nice having family members brand you as being cold and lacking emotion.

She doesn't understand what it is like for me.

His unfeeling heart did a little dance of joy as Piers Denford leaned in and kissed Maggie, his new bride. Francis joined in the applause.

See? I am not made of stone. Why, even yesterday I stopped to help a poor delivery girl who needed my gallant assistance. She appreciated that I was a warm-hearted man.

He turned to Eve. "I value lots of things. It's just that I have other priorities at present. Family and the rest of it is, of course, important. Just not right at this minute."

Tears brimmed in his sister's eyes. Francis flinched. He hadn't expected his words to give rise to that much emotion.

Eve gave his hand a gentle squeeze. "Please don't make the same mistake that Freddie almost did. Don't lose your soul in an effort to prove yourself to the world. No one says you can't have it all. You have as much right as any man to be loved. But you have to understand that love is as abstract a concept as time. Neither can be planned. They simply happen."

When had his sister become such a font of wisdom?

Can I have it all? A woman who loves me and also understands my drive to succeed. Does she even exist? I have never met anyone remotely like that.

Lost for words, Francis remained long in his seat while Eve took her husband's hand and they rose. A smiling Freddie Rosemount gently brushed his thumb over his wife's face and whispered, "My sweet, you are just like my mother. She always cries at weddings."

At the sight of such open, unrestrained affection, Francis tore his gaze away. He had a horrible suspicion that Eve had it wrong. He wasn't cold or unfeeling.

Of one thing he was certain, as he attempted to swallow down a lump of emotion. He had two frogs in his throat.

Francis's faint hopes for his day to improve were dashed not long after he arrived at Denford House for the wedding breakfast. His cousin Alex Radley, the Marquis of Brooke, cornered him. "Who died? Or is that supposed to be your happy face?" asked Alex.

Francis downed the last of his glass of wine, pausing for a moment to compose a suitable response. No matter how hard he tried, his smile simply wouldn't work. "I have a large number of worries on my plate at the moment. None of which are being resolved by me having to spend an entire day away from the shipping offices."

Alex slowly shook his head. "Is this about the new tenant next door? The one who has taken over the warehouse you wanted? Uncle Charles was telling my father all about it earlier and how angry you were."

Wonderful. Just what I need. Papa is getting around telling everyone that I am being a petulant child. And letting them know all about my business plans.

"What did my father say?" replied Francis.

Alex slipped an arm around him and gave Francis a friendly squeeze. He suffered the indignity with little grace. There were few people tall enough to be able to actually put their hand on his shoulder without it looking awkward, so being hugged wasn't something he was particularly used to or comfortable with.

"He says you and some chap that represents the Basden Line are conducting your own private war over some bits and bobs. I didn't believe it at first, but from the look on your face, I can see that you have indeed sunk to that level of pettiness."

There was no doubt that his cousin was supremely amused at hearing this tale. But if Alex dared chuckle, there was every chance Francis was going to punch him.

"It's not pettiness; it's principle. The man can't just arrive in port and take over the wharf," he snapped.

"You mean the part of the wharf embankment that the Basden Line owns? The bit along the front of his warehouse? I'm afraid I am going to have to side with your father on this one, Francis."

Please not another lecture.

"I don't know you anymore, Alex. I swear you have become a stranger, since taking a wife," said Francis. It was going to be a long afternoon if this was how his family was going to take the news of his problems. More wine and brandy would be required.

I wish cousin Gideon was here. He, at least, has some understanding of my point of view.

Alex handed his half empty glass of wine to a passing footman. Francis blinked twice, unsure of what he had seen. The Marquis of Brooke, the one that he thought he knew, would never let a drink go unfinished.

"I am not a stranger, Francis; I will never be that to you. I just grew up. Set aside my childish ways and accepted that I now have responsibilities," replied Alex. He nodded in the direction of his wife, Millie, and Francis's gaze followed. The Marchioness of Brooke was deep in conversation with her sister-in-law, Lady Clarice Radley. From the way both women kept rubbing their pregnant bellies, it didn't take much to discern what their discussion was likely about.

"Why don't you go and talk to your wife?" suggested Francis. If people left him alone, he might just get through this family ordeal without committing murder. But if the expansive grin on his cousin's face was anything to go by, Alex was just getting started.

Alex shook his head. "I am keeping well away from her."

That doesn't sound good. "Trouble in paradise?"

"Never. My wife is utterly besotted with me. No, I am staying clear of Millie and Clarice as they are having another one of their nice little chats. I swear, if I have to listen to one more conversation that revolves around swollen feet and indigestion, I might just head down to London Docks and shift those barrels of yours myself," replied Alex.

Francis grinned. It was both amusing and surprisingly sweet to see the Marquis of Brooke so taken with his wife.

"Subtly is not one of your strengths, Alex. Best that you don't pay a visit to Wapping."

The docks had strict rules regarding behavior within its boundaries. Anyone who caused trouble suddenly found themselves waiting lengthy periods for customs and excise clearance.

"Besides, I don't want to have to face Millie if you go blundering around and get yourself arrested."

They both laughed at that remark.

"There has to be another way to get this Basden chap to move. Or if not, perhaps rent you part of his warehouse. One thing marriage has taught me is the value of compromise," said Alex.

Movement behind Millie and Clarice had Francis gritting his teeth. His father, along with the Duke of Strathmore, was heading his way. His cousin David Radley was bringing up the rear. From the expressions on their faces, they were getting ready to share more words of wisdom with him.

Turning, Francis summoned a nearby footman. "Could you please get me a strong brandy?"

If he was going to survive the quickly gathering posture of males, he was going to need to down more than just wine.

Chapter Sixteen

The brandy wasn't hitting him fast enough, or if it was, Francis didn't feel it. An hour of listening to his well-meaning male relatives, followed by the wedding speeches, and he was ready to throw himself out the nearest window and into the street. Death seemed a pleasant option compared to the long endless hours of the wedding breakfast. Every time a footman was in reach, Francis ordered another brandy.

"You have to work with people, negotiate," offered David.

"As the old proverb says, you get more flies with honey than vinegar," added Ewan Radley, the Duke of Strathmore.

"But you use honey to attract flies in order to be horrible to them," replied Francis.

"Yes, but do you really need to be horrible to the people of the Basden Line? You could always look to work with them. To collaborate," offered Charles.

Francis threw up his hands. He had heard more than enough. His male relatives might have thought they were helping him, but all they had succeeded in doing was to make him feel a lesser man than all of them.

Among his titled and rich family members, he was the only one who had nothing he could call his own. Even his brother Will, who had always been on his side, was more exalted than him. He was a much-lauded former spy, recently knighted by the Prince Regent. He had a home full of elegant antiques, and a wife who was carrying his child.

No one seems to understand things from my point of view. They don't appreciate just how hard it is to be the last one trying to make his mark in this family.

When he swayed unsteadily on his feet, Francis sent a silent prayer of thanks to heaven. The alcohol was mercifully kicking in. The welcome arms of inebriation were ready to take him lovingly into their embrace.

"Excuse me, gentlemen, your grace. I need to go and get a spot of fresh air. I shall return momentarily."

As he made his way toward the terrace doors, Francis sent a second note of gratitude to the gods on high. With the happy bride and groom having slipped quietly out a side door an hour earlier, he was now spared the torture of having to linger and make further small talk with other guests. The official part of the evening was over, and he was well within his rights to make his own escape.

On his way outside, he grabbed another drink and downed it quickly. The footman didn't have time to move away before he grabbed a second glass.

The brandy was finally starting to have the desired effect. He no longer cared what his father or family thought. They were wrong, and in due course, he would be proven right. In the meantime, he was going to avoid them for the rest of the evening.

There is not enough alcohol in me to go back and face that pride of lions. I am done.

A friendly face caught his eye. Clare Radley waved him

over. She rose from her chair as Francis approached, motioning to the terrace doors. He followed her outside.

The second he stepped through the doors, a chill breeze smacked him in the face, and he staggered back. He had never understood how one could be relatively sober inside a building, but suddenly be four parts to the wind the second you breathed a spot of fresh air. He was no longer just a little tipsy; he was drunk.

"You have been giving the brandy a bit of a nudge, cousin dearest," said Clare. She reached out and took a firm grip of his arm.

"Is it that obvious?" replied Francis.

"Well, it is considering that every time I have glanced in your direction over the past hour or so I have seen you lifting a full glass of brandy to your lips. Lady Denford went and had a word with the head butler the second you downed that last drink."

Oh, wonderful.

If Viscountess Denford had spoken to the servants about his imbibing, they would be avoiding Francis like the plague. He wouldn't be getting another glass of brandy anytime soon.

I had better nurse this one. Or leave.

"Why are you drinking so heavily this evening, Francis? You are not normally one for making a mess of yourself," said Clare.

She was right. Francis normally prided himself on restraint in public situations. He had learned the lessons of his father, who had secured a number of important business deals through people he had met at social functions. A sober mind gave a man control over his words and, most importantly, the impression he made on others.

Clare's words resonated as strongly with him as Eve's had.

How was it that the men with their lecturing hadn't been able to reach him, yet the women had?

Business might well be of great importance to him, but it still didn't give him the right to go getting drunk at a family celebration. To go shaming both himself and his parents. Clare had a valid point. He had to stop drinking.

"I'm sorry. I have a lot on my plate at the moment, and today has just not been the sort of day that I needed."

She touched a hand to his cheek. "And Aunt Adelaide is not making your life any easier by putting pressure on you to find a spouse. Believe me, I am getting the same from my parents."

Francis raised an eyebrow in response. He hadn't thought that the rest of the family knew about Adelaide's plans to marry off her youngest son.

"You and I are some of the few eligible offspring left in our families. With Maggie now married, it is only a matter of time before my parents start throwing every bachelor in London in my path." Clare shuddered. "I will be expected to choose one of them. God help me."

In silent accord, they moved away from the doorway and any prying eyes. Clare wrapped her arms about her. "I just don't understand why they feel that we have to rush into marriage."

Francis stared at the brandy glass in his hand and sighed. "I know we all want to find a life partner at some point. I don't want to be alone. A wife and family would be a wonderful thing to have. But not just now."

"At least you can use the shipping company as an excuse not to be on the hunt for a wife. According to my mother, finding a husband is the only thing I should be putting my efforts fully into. I am not looking forward to the trip to Strathmore Castle this year. Mama will be dropping hints the moment we leave town."

Francis pitied Clare. While the coming weeks of Christmas and Hogmanay would likely involve their usual fun and family games, it also meant the matchmaking mamas would have their unwed offspring captive within the castle. He had been planning to leave it to the last minute to tell anyone else in the family that he wasn't going to join the Radley family expedition up north but lying to Clare wouldn't be fair.

"I am not going to Scotland. I have too much to do here," replied Francis.

Clare let out a gasp. "You swine. I was counting on you to spirit me away whenever Mama wanted to have a private chat. Now what am I going to do?"

"I'm sorry, Clare. But please don't mention my not going to your parents. Not yet. I have already told my father and he agreed to wait a few days before telling Mama."

The brandy has loosened my lips.

"I thought you loved coming up to Strathmore Castle at Christmas."

"Oh, I do. I just cannot spare the time this year. A major shipping contract is due to be announced early in the new year and I fully expect that it will be awarded to Saunders Shipping. Besides, I am not the only one eschewing the trip this year."

"True. But those who are not coming are either recently wed or heavily pregnant. Or both."

Francis couldn't argue with that. "I will make the effort to come to the family gathering at Strathmore House in late January. But Scotland is out of the question," replied Francis.

He would do anything to avoid the long days of travel with his parents and the inevitable conversations with his mother. He was certain that somewhere in Lady Adelaide's writing desk was a list of potential brides for her youngest son. And that, when she did soon pack for Scotland, the list would be coming with her.

Even if he had been on the hunt for a wife, Francis

couldn't honestly name a single woman who had caught his eye. His special lady was out there, but unfortunately, she would have to wait.

After raising the brandy glass to his lips, he downed a mouthful, then offered it to Clare. She finished the rest of it in swift time, then handed it back. "Not my favorite tipple. I suppose that is one thing to look forward to during my stay at the castle. Good Scottish whisky."

Francis chuckled. The Duke of Strathmore always had a generous supply of whisky at the castle in readiness for the annual family gathering. Ewan Radley also had a tradition of making sure that no one was ever seen without a glass of it in their hand. Scotland could be bitterly cold in December, and a dram of fire in the belly was always welcome.

The evening had now reached a crossroad for Francis. It was nice talking to Clare, but he should get back to taking his leave. It was only a matter of time before another of his well-meaning male relatives found him again. Or worse, his mother.

A sense of impotence settled uncomfortably in his liquor-addled mind.

I can't stay here, and I don't want to go home.

Today had been a loss when it came to getting work done. He had accomplished nothing of value. It was late, and he was more than a little drunk. So of course, the notion of going to the office and attempting to get some work done made perfect sense.

I bet the representative of the Basden Line got plenty done today.

That thought sealed things. Decision made, he glanced around the night garden. There had to be a rear entrance to the grounds of Denford House. A way for him to make a stealthy escape. He was not going back inside under any circumstances.

His gaze settled on a small gate in the far wall. With luck, it would lead out into the mews and the rear laneway.

"I shall bid you a fond farewell, Clare, and if I don't get to see you before you head off to Scotland, have a wonderful Christmas."

Clare Radley offered him her cheek, and Francis gifted her a quick cousinly peck. "Where are you off to now? Please tell me it is home," she said.

"Just a few business things I need to attend to tonight. After that, I promise I shall seek the comfort of my bed."

He might have well been inebriated, but he wasn't about to confess to Clare that instead of going to London Docks to catch up on some paperwork, he had decided his time would be better served with checking on the barrels and rope situation.

The brandy was now talking loudly in his head, and it liked the idea of a trip across town to visit the neighbors in warehouse number fourteen.

To cause a spot of late-night mischief.

Chapter Seventeen

By the time the hack finally made it across London and through the entrance gate of the London Docks, Francis had sobered a little—but not enough. He had come up with an idea. In the morning, he would meet with his solicitor and begin the process of exploring any and all legal avenues which might still be open to him. There had to be a loophole or two which he could exploit in order to make his new neighbor think twice about setting up shop at the docks.

Who knew? Perhaps he did have a claim for adverse possession.

"It's not personal. It's just business."

If he said it enough times, he might truly come to believe it. Becoming a hard-nosed businessman would take time. But if he was going to succeed, he had to grow that tough outer shell—become impervious to emotion and focus on the task of making money.

People will then see Francis Saunders as more than just another member of the Duke of Strathmore's clan. I will be respected. Claim my place. Be an equal among my peers.

The moment the carriage slowed as it neared his warehouse, all thoughts of cold, detached behavior flew straight out the window.

His barrels and ropes were back, but this time they had been stacked hard against the front door of the Saunders Shipping Company offices.

Francis saw red. He flung open the carriage door and jumped from the hack, landing with a hard tumble on the roadway. Staggering to his feet, he rummaged in his pocket and tossed a coin up to the driver. He then walked away.

The coachman pulled up the horses. Francis caught some of the foul oaths the man muttered as he was forced to climb down and close the door of the hack. He was still swearing into the night as he drove out the front entrance.

"You think you have problems! I bet someone hasn't blocked your door, have they?" Francis bellowed.

Marching across to the pile of flotsam and jetsam which had been purposely dumped right in front of number twelve, he muttered, "I am going to commit bloody murder."

A note nailed to one of the barrels caught his attention. He angrily swiped at it, tearing it away. From the look of it, he and his nemesis could at least agree on one thing. Threatening missives was the best way for them to communicate.

Holding the letter up close to his face, Francis strained to read it in the dim light. The brandy coursing through his veins wasn't helping. With the door to his company offices blocked, he couldn't go inside and avail himself of a candle.

With paper tightly held in his fist, he marched back toward the entrance and the gas lights which blazed outside the superintendent's office. As he drew close, he slowed his steps. There were a few people about the place; the docks were never empty.

Whatever the contents of the note, he didn't need other people to bear witness to his drunken rage. Trying to calm the fury which boiled within, Francis took a deep breath, then held the letter up to the light.

It took a long moment for him to be able to focus properly.

Saunders,

This game has been amusing, but even children understand when it is time to put away their toys. Keep your cursed barrels away from out the front of my offices. The same with your confounded ropes. If your barrels cross the line between our buildings one more time, I shall be forced to punish you by throwing them off the dock and into the water.

Be a good boy and find someone else more your age to play with. Let the grown-ups handle the business side of things.

Yours

P. Basden

It was fortunate that Francis was a healthy young man as the contents of the note sent his blood pressure rocketing to a dangerous level. He swayed on his feet, utterly gob smacked that someone would think they could do this to him.

Who the devil does P. Basden think he is?

Francis screwed the paper up into a ball and stuffed it into his coat pocket. He wasn't about to throw it away—no, he was going to shove it down his neighbor's throat.

"I am the one being childish?" He snorted. "And it's three times that you have moved the barrels back over to my part of the wharf, not two. You should learn to count."

He returned to the front of the warehouse, picked up an empty tea chest, then carried it over to the edge of the wharf and threw it into the water.

"See? I can throw my own rubbish into the dock."

The tea chest landed with a splash. But being empty, it didn't sink. Instead, it gently bobbed up and down on the waves, taunting him.

"That's it. I am going to have it out with this bloody interloper, and right now."

Francis stopped outside warehouse number fourteen and glanced up. The top floors were all in darkness, but there was a faint light shining through one of the windows on the ground floor. Someone was in the building. And they were about to feel the lash of his tongue. Hand fisted, he pounded on the door.

"Open up, Basden!" he bellowed.

When he didn't get an immediate response, Francis attacked the door once more.

Bang. Bang. Bang. It hurt his hand, but at this juncture he was beyond reason.

"Open up, you blackguard!"

The clang of a key being turned in the lock had him ready to rush into the warehouse and confront his enemy. The door barely released, just a crack. Light shone through the opening, but he couldn't make out who stood on the other side.

"You might think you can send me threatening notes, but I am Francis Saunders, and you clearly have no idea of the sort of power I wield," he demanded.

The door opened a little more and Francis moved forward. The sight of a pistol had him skidding to an abrupt halt. It was pointed directly at him.

Francis was rendered speechless as a young woman stepped out of the warehouse. And she wasn't just any woman—it was the girl he had met along the wharf road. The grocer's assistant. She was clad in a low-cut nightgown.

What is she doing here?

Her long, fair hair tumbled down to kiss the top of her bare shoulders. A medallion on a gold chain sat between her breasts. As his gaze settled on her pale, cream flesh, all thoughts of violence fled his mind. She held him spellbound. Even the fear of the pistol couldn't stop Francis from sneaking a peek at the swell of her bust. It was generous, buxom. And perfect.

It was only when his brain finally registered the click of the gun being cocked that Francis finally tore his gaze from ogling the woman and shifted it back to the weapon.

Her skills with a pistol seemed far better than her ability to carry eggs and butter. There seemed little chance of her dropping it.

"You have until the count of three to move away before I put a bullet in your head," she announced in a calm voice.

"I . . . but . . ."

"One."

"I need to talk to P. Basden. Is he your employer?" he replied

"Two."

A now frantic Francis rummaged in his pocket, hurriedly searching for the letter. He held the screwed-up paper in his trembling hand. "I have a letter. This is London. Y-you can't just go shooting people."

"Three."

The loud echo of gunfire rang in his ears, and he dropped like a stone.

Chapter Eighteen

The instant Francis cracked open an eyelid, he was certain that his head was about to explode. Pain screamed down his back. Even his toes uttered their protest.

"Oh, bloody hell!" he cried.

"That's one way of putting it," said a female voice.

He squinted through the agony, trying to focus on where the sound was coming from. Something pale pink and yellow filled his vision. When his sight eventually cleared, he realized it was a woman's face.

The blonde beauty stared down at him. Her rosy cheeks were a perfect flush. Unfortunately, her similarly hued lips were set in a hard, disapproving line.

"I expect you are in a spot of discomfort," she added.

Woman. Pain. Gunshot.

It all came rushing back in a fury. He had knocked on the door of number fourteen and the woman from the grocery store had answered it. His last memory was of her pointing a loaded pistol at him. Not exactly the sort of welcome he would have expected to receive from a girl in service.

"You shot me."

A soft chortle echoed in his pain-addled brain. “No, I didn’t.”

A hand took hold of his and gripped tight. There was a tug of upward pressure, which took Francis a second or two to comprehend.

“Oh, come on, don’t be completely useless. You are more than capable of helping me to get you upright.”

While the woman pulled on his left hand, Francis scrambled to place his right hand on the stone floor. He flinched as he put pressure on it. Even his palms hurt.

Between the two of them, they worked to lift him to a seated position. As soon as he got upright, all the blood rushed to his head and Francis clutched at the woman’s arm. A wave of woozy nausea washed over him.

“Oh, my head,” he complained.

He tentatively reached for the back of his skull, searching for the part where he was certain it had been split wide open. His fingers, however, found only rumpled hair.

“If you didn’t shoot me, then why am I in such agony?”

The woman snorted. “Stop grumbling; this is all your own fault. You were the one who did the dramatic leap out of the way and clipped your head on the planter tub as you fell. Just be grateful that you didn’t damage any of my petunias. If you had, I would have put a bullet in you.”

Francis flinched at her harsh words. She was certainly angry with him. He wasn’t used to women speaking to him in such unfriendly tones.

But he had heard the sound of a gun being fired. He pointed at the weapon in question, which was poking out of the woman’s blue bridge-coat.

She wasn’t wearing a coat when she answered the door.

His head might have been spinning, but he still had a clear recollection of pale skin and bountiful breasts.

If she had time to change, how long was I unconscious?

"You aimed that weapon at me. I heard you cock it. And I am convinced that you fired it at me."

She gave a disinterested shrug. "Oh, yes, I did let off a round. But I shot wide. If I'd meant to kill you, I would have done so. Just be grateful that this is London and bodies aren't so easy to dispose of. You are a big chap, so the chances of me being able to drag you across the road and dump your body into the River Thames without being seen was always going to be a slight one. Besides, your family has money, and that means people might actually miss you."

Francis caught the obvious sneer in the word *miss.* Whoever she was, this woman didn't think too highly of him. He would think twice next time before stopping to help a damsel in distress. Or at least a girl who had dropped her eggs.

And why should she care about you? You came to the door in the middle of the night making demands to see her employer. If she had shot you, she could easily have claimed self-defense.

Behind her fair hair and sweet cheeks was a woman who knew how to handle herself in a dangerous situation. And that included taking down strange men who foolishly pounded on her front door in the wee hours.

She got to her feet, and a rather chastened Francis struggled to his. He swayed unsteadily, but this time she didn't offer him her assistance. Clearly, the limits of her hospitality had been reached.

Sucking in a deep breath, he caught the strong scent of cinnamon, which hung in the air. The cases he had seen being carried over from the ship must have been full of the expensive spice.

That thought had him scowling. The last thing Francis needed was a neighbor involved in the spice trade. It was bad enough that they had his warehouse.

Thank heavens the tender is closed. I don't need that sort of competition.

Hands on hips, she glared up at him. "What do you want, Mister Saunders? It's late and I am tired. And your breath reeks of brandy."

He had come here for a reason, not just to lay on the floor of the warehouse.

Wait. How did I get in here? I was outside.

"Who else is here?" he replied. Someone must have helped to carry him in.

Her hand moved slowly from her hip toward the pistol. Her fingers wrapped comfortably, familiarly around its handle. She shifted her stance, her feet slightly wider apart.

"No one. But if you think to try anything, I promise you will be dead before you get near me. After that, I will take my chances with the hangman," she replied.

While her voice and accent were different to that of the women he knew, the tone was exactly the same. Francis would bet a guinea that if she was given an elegant gown and dropped into a high society gathering, this intriguing female would be more than capable of holding her own with the sharp-tongued matrons of the *ton*.

"I was only asking because someone helped to drag me inside this warehouse. I am not a small man, so I assume you didn't manage the task on your own."

She chuckled softly. "Yes, you are a very large lump of male. But you are not the first unconscious man that I have had the displeasure of dragging around. Sailors might boast that they can drink, but many are hopeless after a few rums. Besides you came around for a moment earlier and crawled inside on your hands and knees. It wasn't an elegant endeavor."

That explains why my palms are so sore.

Francis let his gaze take in the woman standing before

him. She wasn't petite by any standard. And while the coat was large on her, he could still make out the generous pair of hips and pleasing bust which lay beneath it. She had some strength about her.

"And speaking of being a lightweight with his drink, why are you here? I am assuming you had a few brandies tonight and decided to take the fight over the barrels to the next level. If that is the case, then you are wasting your time. Adverse possession is invalid in this case. A handful of barrels does not give you squatter's rights."

A horrible thought crept into his mind as Francis continued to stare at the woman.

She is not a delivery girl. That was a lie.

Not only did she have some understanding of the law, but she was also not behaving like a mere employee. More like an owner.

Which makes me look nothing more than a foolish shit.

"You are P. Basden? I thought he was a man."

She leveled him with a look which said that he wasn't the first to have made that mistake. "Captain Poppy Basden. The ship which is berthed across the way is the *Empress Catherine.* She is my vessel. This warehouse belongs to my father's company, as does the shipment of cinnamon which I brought with me from Ceylon. And of course, let us not forget the clear space out the front of this building."

Francis scrubbed his hand over his face, wishing he was anywhere but there. His grand plans for becoming a well-respected businessman did not include threatening young women in the middle of the night. The fact that the female in question could clearly protect herself didn't figure into his self-disgust. He was rogue. A brute.

If my parents could see me now, they would disown me.

And he wouldn't blame them if they did.

All his brandy-fueled intentions of offering harsh words to

the owner of warehouse number fourteen fled like a thief in the night. Now, if only he could do the same.

"I don't know where to begin to make amends for my behavior," he said.

Captain Basden pointed at the door. "I would suggest that you start with a polite 'good evening' and follow it up with a hasty departure."

She was offering him an easy way out. Surprising. Most other people would have sent for a constable and had Francis arrested. He would have done that if a stranger had appeared at his door in the dead of night and made threats.

He was still considering his good fortune as he took his first step toward the exit. Then he stopped. Her actions didn't make sense.

"Why are you being so magnanimous toward me? I certainly don't deserve it," he said, turning to face her.

Her fingers dropped from the pistol, and her arm hung loosely at her side. "I don't know. I just hope it won't be something that I live to regret."

Francis managed a tentative nod. The notion of battling against a young woman didn't hold quite the same appeal as taking a man on. He wouldn't be praised by society, or his family for that matter, for having been the aggressor in this situation.

Rogue. Harasser of women. Bully.

The list of dishonorable names continued to grow as the sharp edge of the brandy began to wear off. Francis's mind slowly cleared. Shame filled the spaces where rage had once reigned. "I am sorry. I had no right to come to your door," he said.

Captain Basden met his gaze. Her hazel-colored eyes shone bright. "No, you didn't. But I suspect that when it comes to someone like you, Mister Saunders, there are many things which you think are yours simply by right of birth and status."

Under most other circumstances, Francis would have taken her to task for what he considered an unfair critique of his character, but tonight he stood like a little boy and took his punishment. His only response, a chastened, "You don't know me."

A flush of heat raced up his neck and settled to burn uncomfortably on his cheeks. Being of such a fair complexion there was no chance of Francis hiding his embarrassment.

An expression of pity appeared on the captain's face. She sighed. "Oh, for heaven's sake, why does everything in this city have to be so difficult? And why do you hate me?"

Hate was a strong word. Dislike, disapprove were closer to his emotions—not hate. Captain Basden was a problem he needed to solve—nothing more.

"I don't hate you. I just . . ."

She stepped closer. He knew that move; it was a challenge. To force him to speak his mind. "Just what?"

"It's not personal; it's just business."

A knowing grin sat on her lips as she slowly shook her head. "Mister Saunders. Tell yourself all the lies you wish, but we both know that business is personal. If it wasn't, then you wouldn't have taken up the battle over the barrels, nor tried to intimidate me with that pathetic letter using legal jargon you clearly don't understand."

She was mocking him. Showing Francis just who was the more worldly. And it certainly wasn't him.

"I should leave," he offered.

It sounded like he was being polite, but in truth he was close to begging. Anything to gather up the crumbs of his pride and flee.

Her shoulders slumped. "Stay. I baked an apple pie earlier.

You are welcome to a slice. Consider it a peace offering. That is, of course, if you are prepared to call an end to this war."

Always be gracious in defeat. She has bested you.

His father's words of advice echoed loudly in Francis's mind. He had lost the battle over the barrels and ropes. Made a fool of himself in the process. Captain Basden was being more than generous.

"Thank you. That would be nice. I take it you went back to get more eggs, Captain Basden," he replied.

He took comfort from the hint of a smile which sat at the corner of her mouth. For the first time since he had regained consciousness, Francis sensed the captain felt it safe to relax in his presence. "Yes, more eggs. And I was very careful with them as I carried them home. But if we are going to share a meal, I think we can dispense with the formalities."

A hand was extended, and Francis offered his own.

"Poppy Basden. You may call me Poppy," she said.

They shook. "Francis. Honored to make your acquaintance."

Chapter Nineteen

The following morning Poppy was lovingly tending to her new flowers; the bright colors gave her such joy. She hadn't slept all that well. While the visit from the odious Viking next door had ended in what she hoped was an ongoing peace agreement, its aftermath had resulted in her lying awake for hours pondering the possible repercussions.

Francis Saunders clearly had an issue with the Basden Line Shipping Company taking over the warehouse. With a belly full of booze, and the note clutched tightly in his hand, he had come seeking P. Basden. His haughty demeanor and puffed out chest displayed all the signs of a man spoiling for a fight.

But you encountered an opponent ready to take you on. Someone armed with more than just her pride.

Adrenaline had been pumping furiously through her veins as she'd fired the pistol. Even now, she still felt a little nauseous at the memory of having discharged her weapon.

Taking on the towering Viking should have frightened her, but Poppy had found it thrilling. She knew how to handle a pistol. But her intent had never been to hurt him.

Hopefully Francis had learned his lesson. He had seemed genuinely ashamed of himself as they sat and ate apple pie in the early hours of the morning. While Francis chewed his slice of pie, Poppy hadn't been able to stop herself from privately studying him.

Her thoughts had started with wondering about what sort of man he really was, but they quickly turned to slowly undressing him. To imagining if his manhood matched his large stature. She should have stopped herself, but the temptation was too strong.

Poppy wasn't naïve when it came to sex, nor to the ways of men. A man like Francis rarely took defeat well. For all she knew, he had gone home and after a good night's sleep was back to plotting her demise. If that was the case, she wouldn't be granting him any further mercies.

Or pie.

"You will have this place looking like a home in no time," said Jonathan.

She glanced up to see her future intended making his way toward her. Jonathan had been absent for several days, so if she held any sort of romantic thoughts of him, his reappearance should have evoked a sense of happy relief in her. Her heart felt no such thing. In fact, the sight of Jonathan sent a spark of unease racing to her brain. She tried to fight it, but the habit was well ingrained.

You are just tired. Don't start an argument with him. It won't serve any purpose.

Jonathan stopped at the end of the planter box. He rested his grubby, scab covered hands on the edge. The cracks on the knuckles were a tell-tale sign of him having been in a tavern brawl or two.

Poppy took a good look at him. Jonathan's clothes were rumpled, his hair a mess. She didn't want to even think about the last time he had attempted to bathe.

She didn't want to think about him at all.

"What's wrong?" he asked.

Poppy hesitated for a moment. Francis Saunders might well be a stuck-up hot head, but her ship's chief mate was a man used to a hard life of throwing punches. If the two of them ever came to blows, she would have all her money on Jonathan.

Yet all-out war with the neighbors wouldn't do her chances of winning the spice contract any good.

"Poppy?"

"Just getting things sorted out with the Saunders Shipping Company. I had an unpleasant encounter with one of their principals late last night," she replied.

A firm hand gripped her arm, and she was pulled away from the planter box. Taking a deep breath, Poppy met Jonathan's gaze.

"What happened?" he demanded.

As if you really care.

If he gave a damn about her, Jonathan wouldn't have left her sleeping alone in the warehouse. But that was what he had done every night since they had arrived. He was out drinking, and Lord knew what else, until the sun came up or he ran out of coin. Where Poppy was or with whom likely didn't even merit his time or consideration.

Poppy held back those words. This wasn't about protecting her; it was about his manly pride. "Mister Saunders paid me a visit. He had a note in his hand. I had a loaded pistol. We discussed the issue of the barrels and the ropes. I granted him a painful understanding of the situation. Whether he truly gets that, only time will tell," she replied.

She held his gaze, silently challenging him to finally step up and show that he cared about her welfare. Her hopes for him to take an interest in the shipping business had died many months ago. But she was the woman he was supposed to be marrying. The future mother of his children. *That has to count for something.*

"Well then, I expect you will deal with any problems in the same efficient way you normally do. Just let me know if you need anyone beaten up, though I am sure you could also handle that if you had to," he replied in a voice dripping with disdain.

Or not.

He gave a tired put-upon sigh and let go of Poppy's arm. "I'm going to go back to the boat and get some sleep. My head is pounding, so I'll grab some of the laudanum from your cabin."

And that was it. No offer to go and have chat with the neighbors. No suggestion that perhaps he might consider staying in the warehouse with her at night. Nothing.

Jonathan wandered off in the direction of the *Empress Catherine*, leaving Poppy to tend to her flowers.

She was considering where she could put some more pots, one for herbs, when Jonathan reappeared. "One last thing," he said.

He had better not be asking me for more money.

"Yes?"

"One of the chaps in the tavern last night happened to make mention of the tall white-haired gentleman from next door. Apparently, everyone knows that he has put in a bid for the spice contract. And he has made it clear that he fully expects to win it. Thought you might want to know."

The events of last night might have surprised her, but this particular piece of news left Poppy shaken to the core.

"Do you think that is why he has been so unwelcoming? But he couldn't know that we are also in the running for the tender, could he?" replied Poppy.

The bids were meant to be secret; that was why they had been sealed. The only way for anyone else to know about the

Basden Line bid would have been for either her or Jonathan to have let that information slip.

Please don't you have said anything to anyone.

Jonathan shook his head. "If he does, he didn't hear it from me. You and I might not agree on many things, but this contract is important. Word is the young Saunders is taking over from his father and is keen to build his reputation as a hard-nosed bastard. The old man is well-regarded around the docks, but Francis Saunders is yet to make his mark."

Her suspicions were confirmed. Other people in the docks saw Francis Saunders as just an eager pup trying to show everyone that he was better than his papa.

"I have been made aware of Francis Saunders and his ambitions. He has already been to see the superintendent of the London Docks, querying the Basden Line Shipping Company's ownership of the warehouse. Hopefully last night will have given him enough to think about so that when it comes to dealing with us in the future, he might be more circumspect," she replied. *He better be. Or next time I aim a pistol at him, I won't miss. Hulking Viking or not, a bullet will still stop Francis in his tracks.*

At least Jonathan seemed to be thinking along the same lines as her this morning. As her future husband, he had a vested interest in making sure that the Basden Line got a fair shot at winning the spice contract.

"Do you think you could continue to keep an ear to the ground for any other useful tidbits while you are out and about? After last night, I don't want any more nasty surprises." Poppy wanted to be ready just in case Francis did have a change of heart.

"Aye aye, captain," replied Jonathan, giving Poppy a half-hearted salute. He tipped his hat, then walked away, whistling as he went. His self-important swagger had her stomach tightening into a knot.

Jonathan would never love her or be her true partner in life. He cared about the contract and the money it would bring. But that was as far as it went.

He neither respects, nor cares about me.

Poppy stood, hands on hips, staring out over the wharf as Jonathan made his way onboard the *Empress Catherine*. Despite his reassurances that he valued the shipping business, she was certain he was more than happy to leave things up to her. That she was, in truth, on her own. And always would be.

Papa, he might have been a convenient solution for you, but Jonathan is fast becoming a real problem for me. And I have more than enough to deal with at the moment.

When it came to the man next door, she was going to have to tread carefully. It wouldn't be wise for her to give him the slightest excuse to escalate any future disagreements. Unwanted attention from the superintendent's office could reflect poorly on her and directly impact her chances of securing the tender.

Recalling the events of the previous night, Poppy winced. What if someone had heard the sound of a firearm being discharged? There weren't too many things that could be mistaken for a gunshot.

Perhaps firing a pistol might have been a little rash on my part.

And there must surely be a rule or two about the use of weapons around the dock area.

"Good morning."

Poppy turned. A few feet away stood a well-dressed gentleman. He slipped his hat from his head and gave her a bow. "Charles Saunders, at your service," he announced.

She swallowed a lump of dread. Was last night's little misadventure about to come back to haunt her? And if so, where was his son?

Don't tell me the Viking can't even fight his own battles? He has to send his papa.

Her hopeful opinion of Francis faltered. Anger stirred.

Mister Saunders righted himself. "Welcome to the North Quay warehouses. I have seen you around the area over the past few days, so I am assuming you work for the Basden Line. Would you know if Mister Basden is about this morning? I would like to make my introductions."

A cautious Poppy wiped her fingers on her apron, then offered him her hand. "I am Captain Poppy Basden, part owner of the Basden Line." She nodded in the direction of the *Empress Catherine.* "My crew and I arrived from Ceylon earlier in the week."

To his credit, Mister Saunders did a solid job of hiding his surprise. He accepted Poppy's hand and shook it firmly. "I haven't ever met a female captain before; this is quite an honor." He glanced at Poppy's boat. "That is a fine ship you have there, Captain Basden—very unique in its design. The lion figurehead is magnificent. Ceylon, you say. Which means you went around Cape Horn. How did the *Empress Catherine* handle the weather?"

"She did well, though the wind and seas on this trip were a lot calmer than usual. I am afraid I cannot take too much praise for our safe passage; I merely guided her."

Charles's eyebrows raised at her words. "How many times have you been 'round the Cape?"

There was a spark of genuine interest in his voice, unlike with most men who discovered she was a sailor; Mister Saunders wasn't just patronizing her.

Let's not rush to conclusions about the father or the son. Maybe there is hope.

Poppy couldn't hold back her grin. "Thirteen times all told, but only six as the captain. The trick to ensure you make it safely 'round is to stay away from the reefs near Cape Agulhas. That's the point where the Atlantic and the Indian

Oceans meet. Cold and warm currents crashing together make for turbulent and unpredictable waters."

"I would love to sit and hear your stories of life on the sea, Captain Basden. You must have had many interesting journeys. So, what brings you to the London Docks?"

Jonathan's words of caution rang quietly in her mind. Not everyone who wished to spy on their competition did so by banging on the door in the middle of the night. There were other more subtle ways to gain vital information. A polite question here or there asked under the guise of making friends.

Mark your words carefully.

"We have brought a shipment of cinnamon up from Ceylon on this trip. There are a number of buyers already lined up to take the bales."

"So, you won't be staying long?" he asked.

His smile was easy, alluring. She had to hand it to Mister Saunders; he was good. If she didn't already suspect he was fishing for information, Poppy could have let slip more than was wise.

It was time to turn the tables. Give him and his impetuous son something to think about.

"Oh, no, we are staying here permanently. The company owns the warehouse. And I am waiting for another ship to arrive. Once that comes into port, I will be working out of the docks."

Her gaze tracked his face, searching for any sign of annoyance but to her surprise, he simply kept smiling. "Well, it will be nice to have someone living next door. The warehouse was empty for too long," said Charles.

He pointed at the barrels and ropes which sat out the front of number twelve. Someone had moved them so that they no longer blocked the door.

"I must apologize for us leaving our bits and bobs cluttered about the place. We got so used to your warehouse being vacant that I think we came to see this area as ours. I know my son, Francis, certainly did."

It was Poppy's time to gather intelligence. To gauge just how in step father and son were when it came to opposing her occupancy of number fourteen.

"Yes, I spoke briefly to Francis yesterday, and we cleared up our little misunderstanding," she replied.

Charles frowned. "You mean the day before yesterday? Francis and I were at a family wedding and celebration all day yesterday. Neither of us made it to the shipping office."

Poppy let her gaze drift away from Charles and out over the water. For a moment, she let it linger on the morning light which danced over the bobbing waves.

Francis had come to see her without his father's knowledge. It was likely the older Mister Saunders had no idea as to what had transpired last night.

She had just been handed a golden opportunity. One she would be wise not to fritter away. It gave her real power over Francis. If he hadn't told his father about coming down to the docks late at night, she would bet a thousand guineas Charles had no idea what Francis had done. Nor why he might have a sore head this morning.

Her silence could be bought, but it wouldn't come cheaply.

"Ah, yes. I am mistaken. It was the day before yesterday, and it was only a few words that we exchanged. I must confess that I am still at sea when it comes to time and days. Apart from the phases of the moon, the calendar has little relevance until you arrive in port," she said.

She turned as the salt-and-pepper-haired Charles came to stand alongside her. Taking in the older man's features, she noted that he and Francis shared a similar-shaped nose. They also had pale eyebrows, though only Francis had ones which matched his snow-white hair.

I wonder where in your family history he gets such fair coloring from.

"You are not the first captain who has told me that time loses meaning on the sea, though from my side of the shipping business, time means everything. A day here or there and I stand to lose money," replied Charles.

Poppy nodded. She knew both sides of the shipping business only too well. Had spent her whole life involved in it.

"My Francis keeps a chart of when ships are due into the docks. The day they are scheduled to arrive, he starts scanning the horizon," Charles said.

Francis Saunders appeared to live his life at the mercy of his impatient nature. He had chosen the wrong line of business if he expected ships to come and go on his command.

Speak of the devil. His father is at the docks, but I haven't seen him.

"I don't see Francis here this morning. Did he arrive early?" she asked.

Keeping an eye on the comings and goings next door had become her topmost priority in the past day.

This morning, as with most days, Poppy had watched the sun come up over the masts of the ships on the far eastern side of the docks. She had seen Charles and various other members of the Saunders Shipping Company personnel arrive during the morning. But there had been no sign of Francis. So, unless he had slept overnight in the warehouse, she was convinced he wasn't here.

"My son is a little unwell this morning. Self-inflicted, if you get my meaning."

"Oh, that is not good news. Please send him my best wishes for a speedy recovery," replied Poppy.

Tsk, tsk, Mister Saunders. You lack the fortitude of a sailor.

Poppy was enjoying this conversation. Not only was she secretly relishing the fact that Francis did indeed have a sore head this morning, but she was gaining valuable information. Getting a clearer picture of the dynamics between the two Saunders men. And in particular, what each man was keeping from the other.

Secrets meant leverage.

"Do you like cinnamon, Mister Saunders?"

He nodded. "Please. Call me Charles. We are neighbors, so there shouldn't be any need to stand on ceremony. And I am French, so of course I like cinnamon. We do so love our *pain perdu*. Cinnamon toast is our national dish."

"Excellent. Would you like to join me for a spot of sweet toast? I have a fire going and can warm up a pan in no time," replied Poppy.

She found herself liking Charles Saunders. He had an easy-going nature, which gave her comfort. While she couldn't say the exact same thing for his son, Poppy could privately admit that Francis Saunders had his own unique appeal. He was frustrating, pig-headed, but there was something about him.

The memory of kneeling over him in the warehouse the previous night, of staring into those mesmerizing blues eyes as they fluttered open, smashed without warning into her mind.

You should have kissed him.

Her breath caught in her throat. And no matter how hard she tried to force the foolish notion away, to dismiss it right out of hand, she couldn't.

This is ridiculous. The man is a rude and self-important brute. He was ready to run roughshod over me. To force me from my home. He only apologized because I pointed a gun at him.

No. Thoughts of kissing Francis were a girlish infatuation. An interest merely brought to life by pent up sexual frustration. Of wishing for things that she hadn't experienced with a man for a very long time. For something that she could never have with a man like Francis Saunders.

Poppy was still trying to shake off the unwelcome and prickly thought of having discovered an unexpected attraction to Francis when she ushered Charles through the front door of her warehouse a few minutes later.

Ending the war over the barrels might well have been the gravest mistake she had ever made. She could dislike Francis if he was her enemy. Possibly even manage to work it up to outright hate.

But if they became friends?

I don't know what to do if he is nice to me.

Chapter Twenty

Francis stared at his reflection in the mirror. His jaw was set hard as he considered his next move. After leaving warehouse number fourteen in the early hours of the morning, the taste of freshly baked apple pie sitting sweetly on his lips, he had stopped by Saunders Shipping and shifted the barrels away from the front door. The note Poppy had left him, he quietly destroyed.

And while his head had been pounding from where he had smacked it against the planter box, the pain of that was nothing compared to feeling like he had his tail firmly wedged between his legs. As he slowly sobered up, his sense of disgust with himself had grown.

In all of his two and twenty years, he had never been so ashamed of himself. The brandy had played a part in his terrible behavior, but he had been wound up long before he got the first glass in his hand. His outrageous conduct was his and his alone.

Instead of rising early this morning, he had remained hidden under the bedclothes. When his valet knocked on his door and asked if he was ready to dress, Francis had sent him away. His aching head wasn't the issue; it was more the fear that if anyone took one look at him, they would know what he had done. Poppy's acceptance of his apology could only undo so much of the damage.

But as much as he wished he could remain hidden in his bedroom; he couldn't stay away from the docks. He had to man up and face the consequences of last night. Of his actions.

But what was he to do?

His brash side offered up several unpleasant suggestions, all of which involved him marching into the offices of the dock authorities and demanding something be done about the mad woman who had shot at him. She was a menace to all. A danger to public order.

That thought, however tempting, was quickly rejected. His bull-in-a-china-shop approach was what had got him into trouble in the first place.

Besides, such heavy-handed tactics would no doubt result in Francis having to answer some uncomfortable questions himself. The first one being, why was he rousing the neighbors at such an ungodly hour? Followed quickly by the suggestion that he had been drunk and was therefore the one who had posed a risk to public order.

With the spice contract still in the balance, only a fool would go stirring up trouble with the port authorities. He could just imagine how him being excluded from the tender over poor behavior would go down with his family.

He pushed away from the dresser and sighed. The painful truth was that he had behaved like an entitled bully. Had frightened a vulnerable young woman. And got exactly what he deserved.

"This isn't you," he muttered.

The drive to succeed was one thing, but of late, he had started to do and say things that were not part of his nature.

His father had warned him about losing himself in the business. Of the risk of corrupting his character.

He hadn't understood what Charles had meant. Nor the danger becoming too invested in one's work posed. Not until last night.

"And what I did last night was exactly that. I put everything we have worked for in peril."

What if she had fired the pistol at him? If his parents were right this minute sitting in the family drawing room, consumed with grief?

You had a lucky escape. Another adversary might not have shot their weapon wide.

That settled the matter. There was nothing else for it. As soon as he arrived at the warehouse this morning, he would pay Captain Poppy Basden a visit and offer up his full, unreserved apology.

What he was going to do about the spice contract, he had no idea.

This morning's attempt to speak to the occupant of the Basden Line warehouse was in stark contrast to that of the prior evening. Instead of Francis pounding his fists on the door and demanding that it be opened, he politely knocked. Then he waited.

He opened his mouth, ready to begin to apologize as the door creaked open, but the sight of his father, snapped his lips shut.

"Ah, Francis! We were just talking about you. Come in," said Charles.

Oh, no.

The faint hope that he might be able to make amends

with the neighbors while keeping the events of last night from his father disappeared in a puff of disappointment.

Charles ushered him inside. "I was just saying to Poppy that normally you are at the office much earlier in the morning." He gave Francis a cheeky wink. "I might have let slip that you gave the brandy at your cousin's wedding a little too much of a nudge, yesterday."

Oh wonderful. Now she knows that I was drunk as a lord.

Words failed him. This was awkward beyond even his worst imaginings. The idea of walking straight across the road and throwing himself into the water was becoming more appealing by the minute.

Trapped, he followed Charles farther into the warehouse. His gaze roamed left and right, taking in the space and all the things he hadn't noticed while his head had been woozy last night.

Rounding the end of a tall cupboard, he stepped into a wide-open area. There were various items of furniture, but he didn't pay them any heed. His gaze immediately settled on the young woman standing in the middle of the room. On her light gold hair.

And that smile.

Francis swallowed deep. There was nothing else for it but to press on.

"Poppy, may I formally introduce my youngest son, Francis. I know the two of you have spoken, and I am sure he regrets playing that silly game with the barrels and ropes," said Charles.

She met Francis's gaze. To his surprise, the smile on her face only grew wider as she stepped forward, her hand extended in greeting. "Francis, what a pleasure to finally meet you properly. We didn't get much of an opportunity to talk the other day when we met; you were leaving in a bit of a hurry if I recall."

Poppy nodded at Charles. "And yes, I have enjoyed the game of the barrels immensely. Though I think we can all agree that it's time we called a halt to it. We all have better things to do. I promise to be a gracious winner."

And while her tone brooked no argument, there was a definite lightness to it. A certain something which set Francis's pulse to a fast clip. He took her hand, and they shook.

"Touché, Captain Basden," he replied.

Her sparkling hazel eyes carried more than a hint of mischief. She was silently challenging him. Daring him to say otherwise.

Francis wasn't a dull man. He prided himself on being a quick learner. And this Captain Poppy Basden was full of clever lessons. He was more than happy to play along with the ruse she had constructed.

His gaze dropped instinctively to the swell of her breasts. They were bound beneath a burgundy leather vest, which was laced tightly at the front. The white linen of her undershirt did far too good a job of hiding the delights of her flesh from sight.

He missed the way her nightgown had hung off her shoulders something fierce. Her creamy skin. Without thinking, Francis licked his lips.

I wonder what else you could teach me. I would be willing to learn.

"Please, call me Poppy. All my friends do, and I am hoping that, as next-door neighbors we shall become more than just business acquaintances," she said.

Francis cleared his throat—anything to distract his mind from the direction it was heading. Which, at this very moment, was right to his manhood. It gave a twitch of interest.

Oh, no you don't. Not after all the rotten things I have done to this woman.

Indulging in sexual fantasies of having a strict, female pirate captain take him firmly in hand would be an act of utter stupidity.

Forcing his lustful thoughts aside, Francis squeezed Poppy's hand a little too tightly. She squeezed back. His gaze dropped to their joined hands, and he quickly released his grip.

Make small talk.

"Poppy. Is that short for something? Petunia, perhaps? Though you don't look like a Petunia."

For heaven's sake, shut up. What a stupid thing to say. Who knows what a Petunia looks like?

The smile on her face dimmed, along with Francis's hopes of getting out of the place without his father finding out just how much of a cad his son had been.

"No, just Poppy. My mother apparently chose it. And since she died giving birth to me, my father was loath to give me any other name. It might sound a little girlish, but I can assure you that my men only use it with the utmost of respect."

Francis could have hugged his father when Charles cleared his throat. "Poppy is not only an excellent seafarer, but she can also bake."

A dazed Francis turned to his father. "Pardon?"

Charles held up a flat golden piece of toast. "*Pain perdu*. Freshly baked and absolutely delicious."

Francis's buxom nemesis hurried away. He tracked her steps to where she stopped in front of the fireplace and bent to pick up something from a flat tray. She quickly returned to his side and offered him a piece which looked very much the same as the one his father was happily chewing on.

Poppy had made Charles's favorite food. The dish that so many times had brought Francis's father to the edge of tears. Francis and his siblings had spent many hours listening to their dear papa regale them with tales of his home as he sat and nibbled on his cinnamon toast.

She could have baked anything else in the world, but she had to choose this simple dish. Charles would be forever under her spell.

The waft of warm cinnamon and milky eggs filled his senses. His stomach growled its eager appreciation. It seemed that everything this woman did made his body react. If he didn't take care, he too would soon be at her mercy. Accepting the offered food, Francis took a hearty bite. "Hmmm."

He was powerless to stop the hum of appreciation. *Pain perdu* was nothing new to his experience, but this was hot, crispy, chewy heaven. Better than anything the Saunders family cook had ever made.

Charles laughed. "Now you can understand why I have eaten three of Poppy's cinnamon creations already. It's a good thing that I am retiring in the next month. I wouldn't fit any of my clothes if I remained working nearby."

"Could I possibly tempt you with a fourth piece, Mister Saunders?" asked Poppy.

His father waved her generous offer away. "No, thank you. I actually have an appointment with one of the traders over in the tobacco warehouse in a few minutes, so I must be going. But I am sure Francis will be happy to stay and sample some more of your delicious toast."

"Another time, perhaps. Now that I have managed to get the fireplace set up, I will bring some more baking trays over from the *Empress Catherine*. And once I get the time to purchase a good pot, I might attempt to roast a piece of beef as a practice run for Christmas. I hear that is what people in England serve on Christmas Eve," she replied.

Charles nodded. "The English do so love their roast meat."

Poppy escorted Charles to the door, leaving Francis alone for a moment. As soon as he had swallowed the last mouthful of food, his gaze went to the fireside, straight to the tray where the remaining cinnamon toast sat.

I am surprised Papa stopped at three.

Given half a chance, Francis would polish off a good half a loaf, then go back for the crumbs.

"Would you like another slice?"

He turned as Poppy reappeared. The welcoming smile on her face had his guilt quickly returning.

"I don't deserve your good grace. Not after the way I have behaved," he replied.

She had obviously kept silent over the incident of the previous evening. Charles Saunders was an even-tempered man, rarely to rage, but even he would have torn strips off Francis if he knew what his son had done.

Poppy shrugged. "From the way you slunk out of here, I guessed you had learned your lesson. I noticed that the barrels had been moved inside your warehouse, so I took that as you having decided to keep to your word. Besides, when you spend a long time at sea on a crowded boat, you learn to let bygones be bygones."

She paused for a moment, and Francis sensed she was waiting for his response. For him to confirm that the battle was indeed over.

"I am sorry. I truly am. When I arrived here this morning, it was with the express intention of apologizing to you. I wasn't looking for my father."

"I expect your heart was in your mouth when he answered the door," she replied.

He caught the hint of a teasing grin on her lips. It was similar to the one she had offered him last night.

I expect you have a very good idea as to how terrified I was when

I discovered my father was already here. And from the look on your face, you think it highly amusing.

"How is your head this morning? You gave it a decent whack when you fell," said Poppy.

Francis managed a tentative nod. "Sore, but nothing more than what I deserve. Brandy and bad tempers never go down well together. And thank you for not saying anything to my father."

She waved his words away. "What sort of a friend would I be if I didn't allow you to get away with lying to your parents?"

It was odd but hearing her claim their friendship had Francis breaking into a smile. Before last night, he had been determined that the people of Basden Line were going to be his enemies. Poppy had clearly decided otherwise. Her choice held sway. And he was more than content with that outcome.

The door of the warehouse opened with a bang, startling them both. Heavy footsteps and much swearing proceeded the arrival of a disheveled male. "Poppy. I've changed my mind about working on the ship this morning; I am going back to the tavern. I want more coins. Now."

The instant the stranger met Francis's gaze; the fuming man narrowed his eyes. "What do you want? Don't tell me it's about your bloody barrels."

What a pleasant chap. I must ask Mama to have him over for supper.

"Poppy and I were having a chat, and she was feeding me some of her delicious cinnamon toast," replied Francis.

Francis had spied the stranger lurking around the wharf side over the past few days, and from what he had seen, it was clear the man was part of the crew of the *Empress Catherine*. And if the way in which he spoke to Poppy was any indication, she and this man were somehow personally connected too.

He shuddered at the thought.

With the filthy state of the other man's clothes, coupled with the stale stench which hung about him, Francis decided that he wasn't about to offer to shake hands.

Poppy huffed. "Jonathan, I gave you coins when we arrived and more yesterday. And plenty of them. You can't just come into port and get drunk every day. I am not made of money."

Jonathan stepped past Francis, brushing firmly against him as he did. Francis decided this was a man he would be more than satisfied to make his enemy. They could never be friends. If polite introductions were going to be ignored, then the rules of good manners didn't apply.

He had a sudden compulsion to punch this man.

"If I want to drink every day, I will." Jonathan held out his grubby hand.

Francis knew there were times when a man had to hold his tongue and mind his own business. This was one of them.

Poppy threw up her hands. "Alright. But I am not the Bank of England. Everything I pay you from now on comes out of your share of the contract."

While Poppy made her way to a nearby table and unlocked a small cashbox, Francis quietly ground, his back teeth. He and Jonathan exchanged cold, hard glares.

"Here. This is all I have to spare." Poppy slapped some coins into Jonathan's hand.

He glanced down at them, then snorted in disgust. "You had better go to the bank and get more, because this pittance won't last me for long."

Jonathan drew closer to Poppy, and he towered over her. It was a move of pure intimidation. A ball of dark shame welled within Francis. This was exactly how he had been behaving lately. He might be better dressed and have actually washed, but in truth, he was no better than Jonathan.

To her credit, Poppy didn't flinch.

"We aren't at sea anymore, Captain Basden, and I think it's about time you started to learn who is going to be in charge from now on. When you are my wife, you will do as you are told," growled Jonathan.

Francis's hand instinctively tightened into a fist. The air was thick with tension. If this man was Poppy Basden's betrothed, it was little wonder she was handy with a pistol.

A snarling Jonathan turned toward the door, then stopped just as he reached the cupboard. He pointed a finger at Poppy "Make sure you go to the bank today. If I come back and there is no money, you will regret it. Your father isn't here to protect you."

The windows rattled as Jonathan slammed the door behind him.

What on earth would make Poppy even think of marrying such a man?

Francis knew little to nothing about Poppy Basden; they were barely even friends. But there was one thing of which he was certain. Hell would freeze over before he let her marry that drunken scoundrel.

Chapter Twenty-One

When the echo from Jonathan's slamming of the door finally dissipated, there followed a moment of awkward silence.

"Would you care for a cup of coffee to go with your cinnamon toast?" Poppy offered.

She couldn't think of anything else to say. Nothing could take the sharp edge off the humiliation that currently filled her. She was used to Jonathan speaking to other people in his rough-and-tumble manner, but this was the first time he had ever used that sort of intimidatory language with her.

I hope he is only speaking to me that way because he is hungover, not because he feels he can.

Jonathan was no longer under her command. His whole manner of behavior spoke of him looking to claim what he rightly saw as his entitlement, Poppy's obedience.

Francis nodded. "That would be nice. Thank you, Poppy."

She let out a small sigh of relief, grateful that Francis hadn't immediately fled the warehouse. The heat of embarrassment burned her cheeks, and she did her best not to raise her hand to her face. Her father had taught her that blushing was simply a physical response to an uncomfortable situation. Nothing more.

She poured them both a hot cup of the black, bitter brew, and handed Francis a mug.

"Thank you," he said.

"Do you take sugar or milk with your coffee? If you do, I'm afraid I don't have any, I used the last of the sugar to make the apple pie. The milk went into the toast mix. I can, however, give you a drop of honey."

She was clutching at social niceties. Small talk to help her navigate her way out of the swirl of shock and embarrassment. The threat of violence in Jonathan's voice had left her rattled. He was right; her father wasn't here to protect her. Then again, George Basden had rarely ever been present when his daughter needed him.

Do. Not. Marry. Jonathan.

She glanced at Francis and caught his comforting smile. Her heart gave an unexpected lurch.

"This is fine. My siblings and I were raised to drink coffee in the French fashion. That means bitterly strong and in very small cups," he replied.

"Your father speaks perfect English, but there is a definite lilt to his voice. I've spent time in Monaco and so I am used to hearing French accents, but I wasn't sure if I had picked it right. Then he happened to mention that he was originally from France," she replied.

Francis nodded. "My father is a French *émigré*. Our original family name was Alexandre. He moved to England after he married my mother. My grandfather, François, was a royalist who helped fight in the uprising in the Vendee. He was executed after the Battle of Savenay. When he discovered what had happened to his father, Papa renounced his country and changed his name to Charles Saunders."

She had heard of the thousands of French *émigrés* who had

fled to England during Robespierre's reign of terror but hadn't actually met one before. "And your father hasn't ever been back to France?"

"No. But one day perhaps he will, especially now that the war is over. I long to travel to France, to visit the town of my ancestors, and make the connection to the other half of my bloodline. My mother's family is Scottish, and I'm well acquainted with that side of the family, but at times, it feels like a part of who I am is missing," he replied.

Suddenly shy, Poppy glanced at the cup in her hand. She wasn't used to having people share such personal information with her. Her friends were few and all were on the other side of the world. She had never considered Jonathan as someone she could call her friend—more a commitment.

Yet this man, who only a matter of hours ago had been pounding his fists on her front door, was conversing with her in such a warm manner that Poppy genuinely hoped they might indeed become friends.

Don't get your hopes up. You don't know Francis. Tread carefully.

Jonathan might be an unpleasant man at times, but Poppy was sure she understood him. She also had strong suspicions as to the root of his current troubles. For the way he was behaving.

But when it came to Francis Saunders, she had little on which to base her opinion of him. He was being polite and friendly enough this morning, but how much of that was due to him discovering his father at the warehouse when he arrived?

I bet that came as a bit of a shock.

Then again, he clearly hadn't liked what he saw during the exchange between her and Jonathan.

The odd, inexplicable feeling she'd felt earlier returned as Poppy met Francis's gaze. That undeniable attraction.

They were alone in the warehouse. They had also been

alone here in the early hours of the morning, but that had been different. He had been injured, and she had been holding a pistol.

Damn. I left the pistol onboard the ship this morning. Foolish girl.

Now, all that stood between them were manners and pleasantries. Coffee and cinnamon toast were her only weapons.

As the morning light streamed through the upper windows at the front of the warehouse, Poppy studied Francis. His piercing blue eyes were more powerful than they had been when she'd looked at them in the dim light of the night. She hadn't imagined that possible. His white hair gleamed like a nimbus.

And he was tall. Exceptionally so, even for a man. His beautifully tailored coat displayed his broad shoulders to perfection. The white linen cravat with its silver ship pin had been expertly tied. This was a man who took great care with his appearance.

Everything about Francis Saunders spoke of a well-bred gentleman, yet it had been an ogre whom she had greeted at her door. An angry, drunken beast.

The most handsome ogre I have ever seen, but a beast, nonetheless.

Fine attire and a polished accent did not make a man. His actions did.

"About last night," he began. He stopped and nervously cleared his throat. For a moment, Poppy feared he might have been reading her mind.

"I am sorry. I behaved terribly toward you." He raised a hand to his head, raking his fingers through his snowy mane. "You might be surprised to know that it is not in my nature to be so horrible. People might say I look like a Viking, which isn't surprising considering I have Norman ancestors, but the whole 'sacking of villages and pillaging of loot' really isn't who I am. Or at least, I hope not."

Poppy nodded. "Yes, I did think you a Viking. You do have that hard glare about you when you are irate."

I seem to be dealing with a number of stubborn, angry men in my life at present.

"I'm taking over the shipping company from my father shortly and I think I might have let the pressure of it get to me. Of course, none of that excuses me in the slightest for the way I have treated you. I was a drunken brute last night, my behavior a shameful disgrace."

He does wear grumpy like an ill-fitted coat. It's almost like he feels he has to be that way in order to succeed, but it doesn't sit easy with him. I wonder what it would take to make him laugh.

Having to confess his sins was also a challenge to him, if the tight way Francis was gripping hold of his hair, was any indication.

Francis's confession, while clearly uncomfortable for him, did at least endorse Poppy's decision not to throw him to the wolves. If he was ashamed of how he had behaved toward her and was prepared to make amends, she, in turn, was willing to keep her mouth shut. He had made a mistake and regretted his actions.

But if you try anything else, I might not be so accommodating.

"If I may make a suggestion?" she offered.

There was an expression of uncertainty on his countenance as Francis met her gaze. "Yes?"

"Lay off the brandy for a bit. Give your thick skull time to heal."

His shoulders shook as he chuckled. "That's a capital suggestion."

See? You can laugh.

"I am grateful that you didn't mention last night to my father. He wouldn't have taken it well. My sore head would have been the least of my problems."

Her former nemesis had suffered enough for one day.

"How about we take our coffee out into the sunshine? I expect you could do with a spot of fresh air," she offered.

Francis nodded, and Poppy led the way outside and across the road to the edge of the wharf. She knelt and took a seat on the wooden beam, swinging her legs so that they dangled over the side of it. A bemused-looking Francis joined her. She grinned as his enormous boots almost touched the water.

How strange. I had forgotten that the tide was in. A couple of days in port and I am already losing my touch.

"I don't expect you come and sit here very often, do you, Mister Saunders? It's a pity; there is nothing better than taking the time to smell the sea air."

He glanced over at her. "No, I haven't the time. Whenever one of our ships is in, I am often down in the hold checking the cargo. The rest of my day is spent on paperwork and haggling over contracts."

This was encouraging news. Francis actually worked in the shipping company. He wasn't just here to indulge his father. Poppy could respect a man who made a real contribution to the shared workload. That sort of person was someone she could value.

"And please, call me Francis. You joked about us being friends earlier. I am hoping that we could soon come to share a common regard," he added.

His formal manner of speech spoke of him having received a quality education. His finely cut clothes marked him as someone who had never known anything other than a life of privilege.

It was a stark contrast to Poppy's own life of living in foreign ports and at times wondering where her next meal would come from. Or when her father would return. Her own schooling, attained in various places across the globe, had been haphazard at best. She was fluent in Spanish and French. Had a fair grasp of Italian. And her rough command of several other languages meant that Poppy was able to negotiate her way into ports from London to Singapore.

The main things George Basden had taught her were how to read the stars, maps, and strike a fair bargain. His greatest gift had been to make his daughter a first-rate mariner.

At the age of eighteen, she had taken full ownership of the *Empress Catherine* and for the past seven years, she had captained a crew of, at times, rough sailors. Poppy was her own woman.

With their dissimilar backgrounds, they should have little in common. Any relationship, a distant one. Yet, she found it hard not to like Francis.

There was a certain something about him. One which had her staring into those blue pools of his, long past the point when she should have looked away.

"Poppy?"

She blinked back to the now.

Oh god, I was staring at him.

There was no point in trying to pretend that she had been doing anything else. "Sorry. I just find your eyes to be such an interesting shade. They remind me of the clear blue waters of the Maldives."

"That's a new one. I shall add that to the list. People are always trying to come up with comparisons for the color of my eyes. It's the same with my hair," he replied.

Poppy tore her gaze away, determinedly focusing on the gold crown which sat on top of the lion masthead of her nearby ship. She had sailed the *Empress Catherine* for many years, knew every inch of its timbers, but in an effort to avoid having to actually look at Francis, she searched for something new.

A soft, knowing laugh reached her ears.

Don't look at him. Look at the lion.

"Did you know the tips of your ears have turned bright red?"

Poppy shook her head. No. She would not look at him. The boat was much more interesting. She kept her gaze steady.

Francis let out a sigh. "Alright, let's not discuss my eyes or your ears. And since you are so keen to study your own ship, how about you explain its provenance. I have honestly never set eyes on such a vessel before."

She risked a sideways glance in his direction, catching the grin on his face.

He isn't just being polite.

"She is modelled on the original ship the *Shtandart*, which was the flagship of the Imperial Russian Navy. Tsar Peter first commissioned it in seventeen hundred and three—hence the date on the masthead. They were raising it out of the water to do a refit twenty-odd years later but the cables they were using accidently cut the hull in two. The ship was so badly damaged that it was decided it was easier to break her up. They were supposed to have built a replacement, but that never happened."

"So how did you end up with a copy of the ship?" he replied.

There was an unmistakable glint of interest in his voice. Poppy loved it whenever someone asked her this question; she could talk about the *Empress Catherine* for hours. Wax lyrically about the ship's statistics, mention how much cargo it could carry, and how well it sat in the water.

"I found some of the original plans for her in a chandler's shop in the Port of Civitavecchia, Italy. I was fourteen and immediately captivated by its design. My father commissioned the *Empress Catherine,* and I became captain of her the day I turned eighteen."

She could continue to talk about her ship, but when it

came to Francis, Poppy decided she would much rather show him.

Drawing her legs back up to the wharf, Poppy scrambled to her feet. "Come, Mister Saunders. Let me show you around my boat."

It was an innocent enough offer, but the way the words came out made it sound more alluring than Poppy had intended. Dare she say, sexual?

Francis scowled. "Are you sure? I mean, what would Jonathan say to you inviting a man on board your ship? He clearly didn't like finding me with you in the warehouse. I don't want to get you into any sort of trouble."

Poppy didn't give a damn what Jonathan thought. The *Empress Catherine* was her vessel; she could do with it as she pleased.

But if you marry him, it will be his.

Her future intended had shown an ugly side of himself this morning, one which only added to her growing unease. Every encounter with him pushed her closer to what was fast becoming an easy decision.

"Jonathan has no say over me. No rights to claim. I am the captain of the *Empress Catherine,* and I decide who comes on board my boat." Even to her own ears, Poppy's voice held the weight of authority and defiance.

How dare Jonathan think he can demand money from me and that I will simply comply?

This morning was the first and the last time he would ever speak to her in such a disrespectful manner. He had shown his true colors. Now it was time to draw a line in the sand.

Poppy held out her hand. A grinning Francis waved her hand away. "I can manage."

With startling speed, he leapt to his feet, and Poppy took a hurried step back. For a tall man, Francis was surprisingly agile.

"Lead on, Captain Basden," he said.

Unlike Jonathan, there was clear respect in the way Francis said captain.

As Poppy headed toward the gangplank, with Francis close on her heels, a flicker of something lit within her. This could be the beginning of a friendship. One that might come to be important to them both in the future.

Don't be silly. You are clutching at straws yet again. People like Francis Saunders don't make real friendships with people like me.

Making peace with the neighbors made good business sense. And if Jonathan's information was correct, then of course it was in Francis's best interests to keep things sweet with her.

What he would say if he discovered that she had also put in a bid for the spice contract, Poppy didn't wish to consider.

Chapter Twenty-Two

Francis had to admit that following Poppy as she made her way up the gangplank was the highlight of his day. She hadn't bothered with a coat, which meant he was granted a pleasurable view of her swaying hips as she climbed onboard the *Empress Catherine*.

He licked his lips as he took in the sight, imagining the secret delights which were hidden by her dark grey skirt and trousers. The color of her garments might be dull, but they did little to dampen the wicked images which popped into his mind.

"Welcome aboard the *Empress Catherine,* Francis," announced Poppy.

Her words stirred him from his lustful thoughts.

What are you doing, ogling the poor girl? She is an intelligent and skilled sailor, and you are back to behaving like a cad.

He was a grown man, yet every time he got close to Poppy, Francis couldn't seem to stop himself from reverting to a callow youth. Back to a time when his manhood did the majority of his thinking.

As he stepped onto the deck, Poppy turned to face him.

His gaze followed the twirl of her skirts. Then it shifted higher, taking in the swell of her generous breasts. It continued on up all the way to her face, where it lingered on the smattering of freckles which kissed the bridge of her nose and upper cheeks.

You really are rather lovely. I can't believe I was horrid to you.

At that moment, the late morning sun peeked out from behind a cloud, and its light caught Poppy's hair. Her pale strands magically transformed into spun gold.

Francis halted, enchanted by the sight.

And then she smiled. Her obvious happiness and pride in showing him her ship lit up Poppy's face.

All those times when he had observed couples in love and mocked them for their open displays of affection came rushing back to haunt him. He had done his best to convince everyone that he viewed love and all its so-called grandeur as being only for fools.

And yet, as he took in the sheer loveliness of Poppy Basden, Francis's heart gave a little pitter-patter. A dance of joy.

What is happening to me?

"We are all fools in love," he muttered.

"What did you say?"

Blast.

Here he was, quoting a line from one of Eve's romance novels, and Poppy had heard him. A sensible man of business shouldn't even know about such books.

And he most certainly shouldn't have stolen the odd volume or two and hidden them away in his bedroom. Nor should he have repeatedly read them, cover to cover.

His private hunger should remain just that. His secret.

"I said, only a fool would sleep above," replied Francis, realizing Poppy was still waiting for some kind of explanation. He hastily pointed toward a nearby pile of blankets. The crew had obviously been sleeping on the deck.

"Oh. For a moment there I thought you were quoting *Pride and Prejudice* to me," said Poppy, with a soft chuckle.

Francis stifled a snort and quickly adopted his best business face, the one he used for haggling over contracts. He wasn't about to confess his dirty little romance novel secret to anyone. Least of all Poppy.

She had more than enough leverage over him as it was.

"Do I look the sort of gentleman who reads soppy love stories? Though, I am led to believe that my sister Eve has read *Pride and Prejudice* on more than one occasion. She even claims to have met the author."

Shut up. What are you doing? You are meant to be talking about boats.

Poppy's eyes grew wide with interest. "Really? Who is it? The cover of the book only says it is by the same author as *Sense and Sensibility*. I would love to know who wrote such wonderful stories."

It hadn't occurred to Francis that Poppy would know of the books. She was a ship's captain, busy sailing the seas. When had she ever had the opportunity to purchase such novels?

His lips were moving before he could stop himself. "Apparently the author was a Miss Jane Austen. Most people in London society knew of her. Her identity was an open secret, but she didn't move among the *haute ton*. Rather, her family was good country folk."

"The author was Jane Austen? You speak of her as if she has passed away," replied Poppy.

Francis sighed. "Yes. I'm saddened to inform you, but Miss Austen died earlier this year. But I am of the understanding that some more of her works are going to be published posthumously by her family."

You can't help yourself. She shows an interest in something that you love, and you become insufferable.

He dropped his gaze to the deck of the ship, hoping that Poppy wouldn't ask him the obvious question. Why would a young man, a future leader in commerce, have any reason to follow the work of a recently deceased female author?

She didn't need to know that he had quietly reserved a copy of both the soon-to-be-published novels with Hatchards book shop in town. The order had been placed under the name of Lady Adelaide Saunders, but his mother would never know anything about it. Nor would she ever see the books.

Poppy sighed. "That's a pity. I enjoyed her books. I bought *Pride and Prejudice* when I was in London three years ago. I cannot begin to tell you how many times I have read it during the long nights at sea."

Imagine being able to sit beside her and talk about the books. Of the stories and the wonderful characters. Having someone who understands the joy that they bring me.

How could he even suggest such a thing? He pushed the thought away. He'd obviously banged his head harder than he had realized.

"Would you like to come below deck and have a look at the rest of the ship?" said Poppy.

Francis nodded, grateful for the change in subject. As he followed Poppy along the deck and toward the steps which led from the weather deck to the lower decks, he silently berated himself. When it came to this young woman, his skills of conversation failed him. His silver tongue became a lump of wood in his mouth.

Talking to the female sex wasn't normally an issue for him. He was self-confident, if not outright cocky most of the time. But Poppy Basden had him stumbling around like a foolish schoolboy desperate to impress and appease the headmaster.

He wasn't certain which was worse. Him battling her over

the barrels and ropes or doing his utmost not to behave like a blathering buffoon.

Get your head together. It was just the sunlight on her hair and the gentle sway of her hips.

The sea air was playing tricks with his mind. A temporary madness had seized him, and he would shortly return to a state of sanity.

I hope so. If not, I am in serious trouble.

He followed Poppy as she climbed down the short, narrow set of steps which led to the lower deck. While her fingers barely brushed the handrails, Francis found himself having to hold on tight.

There were few portals or windows below deck, and it took a few moments for him to become accustomed to the dim light. He peered into the semi darkness, unsure of where to place his feet. Poppy, meanwhile, moved with the confidence of someone who knew exactly where everything was.

Using her pale hair as his guide, Francis tracked behind Poppy as she made her way along the lower deck. When she came to a sudden halt, he stumbled into her.

"Sorry. My eyes are not yet adjusted to the lack of light," he said.

She turned and took a hold of his arm. "It's a challenge all sailors face—being able to come out of the brightness of the ocean and safely move around below deck. Nuts are good for eyesight; so are oysters. I brought several large barrels of cashews with me for the voyage from Ceylon. I might have some left if the crew haven't already eaten them all."

She was practical as well as pretty.

Ruddy hell, this woman has me all at sea.

Her grip on his arm firmed. "We are about to pass through the galley kitchen. There is a stove on the starboard side. From the warm air, I would say some of the crew stoked the fire this morning in order to make themselves a hot meal.

Just be careful where you put your hands, Francis. You don't want to get yourself burned."

He had been down into the lower decks of enough ships to know that small vessels such as the *Empress Catherine* were equipped with sheet-iron stoves, which could be used to bake food in. They usually also had a cooktop for pots and pans.

"It must be nice to have use of a proper fireplace, now that you are settled in the warehouse," he said, as they continued into the kitchen.

Poppy bent and picked up a flat baking dish. "I might take this back to the warehouse. I would like to be able to cook a roast, so I could use this as a lid over the other pan I have. Things are slowly coming together. I must say, I am happy with the flower pots. Now that the area around the front door is clear, I would like to put some small, boxed garden beds in for herbs."

Francis took the subtle rebuke over the barrel war with good grace.

He could see clearly now that his eyes had become accustomed to the dull light. "Here, let me take that," he offered. Poppy handed him the heavy baking dish.

Mama would be proud of me, offering to carry kitchen dishes.

Actually, no, she wouldn't.

Adelaide would have taken him to task for his boorish behavior. Then she would have started in on him. Made clear her firm opinion that this sort of incident would never have happened if he was a happy married man. She would impress upon him her further thoughts that marriage would solve much of his frustrations. If he had a sweet wife waiting for him when he returned home at night, he would be calm and not feel the need to go off causing a rumpus.

Rumpus was Adelaide's favorite expression when she wished to give any of her children a lecture on their mood or poor conduct. If you weren't paying attention before, you certainly were as soon as that word reached your ears.

Poppy opened a small wooden cupboard and rummaged around in it. "Ah, another handy little item." A large metal pail appeared in her hand. "I need a bucket to cart water, and this might just do the job."

The main water station for this end of the docks was situated near the gate at the entrance to the docks, but there was a handpump in the laneway which ran between the end of their block of warehouses and the next one. Who was to say that Poppy hadn't been made aware of the other water pump much closer to home?

"You have discovered the pump beside your warehouse, haven't you?" asked Francis, taking his growing interest in her welfare to an even higher level.

"Oh yes, I found that on the plans our solicitor provided. Not that I am going to drink any of it, since water from the River Thames is not much better than seawater."

Francis cleared his throat, eager to share his knowledge. He was excited that he finally knew something which Poppy did not.

"The water from the pumps at the North Quay is fresh water. It doesn't come from the river. You still have to boil it, but you can drink and bathe in it," he said.

One of the major advantages of the new London Docks was the supply of fresh water piped in by the Shadwell Waterworks.

"Really? That's wonderful!" she exclaimed. "I was going to ask about the roof of the warehouse and whether we could collect rainwater. But this is even better. I have a copper tub arriving today. I plan to use it to indulge in many long, hot baths."

Francis's head was instantly filled with images of Poppy reclining naked in a copper tub. She was seated before a crackling fire, enjoying its warmth. In her hand was a glass of fine French champagne.

The fire may well have taken the chill from the air, but it didn't stop her nipples from becoming hardened pebbles. Soapy bubbles hid the rest of her form from his imaginary sight, which only served to heighten his lust.

His imaginary Poppy glanced over her shoulder and met his gaze. "Come and join me, Francis. You know you would love to share my bath."

Don't think about her like that.

The air in the cramped galley kitchen suddenly became uncomfortably warm. Francis's cravat grew tight around his neck. He desperately wished he could loosen the knot and take it off.

"I could . . ." He struggled with his breathing. "I could organize for some of my staff to help bring water over to your warehouse. We have several fit, strong lads who could assist. It wouldn't be any trouble."

Her face lit up, and his pounding heart skipped a beat. "That would be lovely. Thank you, Francis."

She motioned toward the rear of the ship, to a closed door. "Would you like to see the captain's cabin? It's not much—just a table and a bed. Though you do get a good view out of the rear portal."

Francis nodded. He wasn't all that interested in the view of London Docks. His mind was now concentrated on the prospect of actually seeing Poppy's bed. It wasn't just any old bed; it was *her* bed. The one she had slept in for countless nights. Where she had lain beneath the bedclothes.

Where you probably touched yourself when you were alone at night.

The soft cry of her completion as she reached orgasm echoed in his imagination. What he would give to hear it in reality.

I'm done. If I set foot into her bedroom, it will be the end of me.

It was a step, in self-control that seemed too far. If he didn't pull back now, heaven knew what aroused state he would be in by the time they left the boat. In the cramped, poorly lit space of the lower deck, he might be able to hide his growing condition, but up on the weather deck . . .

Francis swallowed deeply. It was time to concede defeat. And as much as he disliked the idea, Poppy was engaged to be married. He had no right to be fantasizing about her.

"Actually, I have to get back to the office. I lost a day with the wedding yesterday. And there is a mountain of paperwork I need to get through before the next ship arrives. Let me know when you want the water, Poppy, and I shall arrange it," he said.

"Of course. I'm sorry. Forgive me, I have already taken up far too much of your time this morning." The note of disappointment in her voice tugged at his conscience.

He reached out and took the bucket from her hands. "Let me take this. I insist."

With Francis carrying both the bucket and the baking tray, they climbed back up to the weather deck. Putting his foot on the gangplank, he gave a nod to the *Empress Catherine*. "She is a fine vessel. I promise to come back soon so that you can finish our tour."

"It would be my pleasure."

As soon as they reached the front door of warehouse number fourteen, Francis handed Poppy the pail and baking tray. He had to escape. "I have some tea chests which need urgent attention. I shall bid you a good day, Captain Basden."

Doing his best to ignore the expression of sadness which sat on Poppy's face, Francis scurried off toward a pile of crates on the Saunders Shipping side of the nearby wharf pavilion.

The tea chests had been happily sitting there for several months. Until this morning, their fate hadn't been much of a priority. Now, there wasn't anything more important in the entire world than making sure they were in the right place.

I am an utter lecherous coward.

When Poppy's words of farewell carried to him softly on the wind, Francis dared not look back over his shoulder. It was taking a herculean effort to walk away, all the while his heart was demanding that he turn around and go back to have another coffee with her. To stuff himself full of cinnamon toast until he couldn't breathe.

To spend the rest of his day in her delightful company.

Upon reaching the sanctuary of the pavilion, Francis mindlessly picked up a coil of rope. He then proceeded to make a thorough study of it. Anything to avoid Poppy's gaze. He could feel it burning into the back of his head.

When the click of a door being closed finally reached him, Francis dropped the rope with a tired sigh. He glanced over toward warehouse number fourteen and let out a breath of relief. Poppy was gone.

For a moment, he stood slowly shaking his head. Last night he had been more than ready to do battle with the occupant of the warehouse next door. Now, he had no idea what to do about her.

In the bright morning sunshine, Poppy's warm smile, and easygoing nature had battered his steel-encased heart. A heart which Francis had been resolute in his determination to keep under lock and key.

He had made a pact with himself. Sworn a solemn oath to keep it. Before he would even entertain the notion of looking for a wife, he had to have become an acknowledged success in the shipping business. The jewels and fine clothes he intended to give to the woman he eventually married had to come from the money which he had earned.

On the day of his wedding, he wanted his male relatives to be standing in awe of him. Of what he had achieved. And if they were a little envious, it would only serve to make the champagne which they toasted Francis and his new bride with, taste all that much sweeter.

His grand plans had not figured on him meeting Poppy Basden. Nor on his mind tempting him with a different stream of thoughts. Delicious, enticing thoughts.

A bath.

A naked Poppy.

And him.

All he could think of was Poppy's lush breasts, of how wonderful they would look as the soapy suds slid over them.

What color would those peaked pebbles be? A dusky rose. Or perhaps a light caramel brown. She was fair in her complexion.

"A delicate blush," he whispered.

His body hardened as lust crept through his veins. By the time Francis had finally got himself back under control, he had licked his lips raw.

He stared at rope which lay at his feet. He could do battle over barrels and ropes, but when it came to sunny-natured Poppy Basden, he hadn't a clue.

What the devil was he going to do about the temptress who had moved in next door?

Chapter Twenty-Three

Francis had made a rather hasty departure, but Poppy didn't have all day to sit and ponder as to the reasons why. She had barely got back inside the warehouse and set the bucket and baking tray on the table when there was a knock at the door.

"Oh, good. He has come back," she muttered.

She hurried to the door, but instead of finding the tall figure of Francis Saunders standing on her threshold, she was greeted with the sight of a large, round-bellied man who promptly announced, "I have a delivery for a P. Basden."

Poppy glanced past him to the wooden cart which was pulled up outside. All thoughts of Francis disappeared in a flash as her gaze settled on the large copper tub which was being lifted down from the cart. She clapped her hands together with unrestrained delight as it touched the ground. "My bath! Oh, how wonderful."

The delivery man raised an eyebrow and Poppy laughed. It was likely he didn't get that sort of response when he usually made his rounds. Her previous visits to London, had taught her that bathing wasn't as popular in England as it was in other parts of the world. The knowledge that the water from the nearby pump was clean and fit for her to bathe in had her giddy with glee.

Poppy promptly signed for the tub, then stepped out of the way as two burly men carried it inside.

"Where do want us to put the tub, miss?"

Darting over to the fireplace, she quickly moved a chair and some odds and ends out of the way.

"Right here if you would be so kind. Thank you."

She had chosen a spot to the left of the fireplace. Close enough that she would be warm while she bathed, but still far enough out of the way for her to be able to use the hearth to cook meals.

The tub was set gently on the stone floor, and Poppy checked its position. She nodded; it was exactly where it should be.

"Perfect. Thank you so much. I know it is only a bath, but you have delivered to me the promise of much joy." She pressed a coin into the hand of each of the bemused delivery men, then politely showed them out. As soon as she closed the door, Poppy raced back to the fireplace and her beloved copper tub.

"It's bigger than I imagined." She bit back a giggle. "And roomy."

If she and another sat close enough together, the tub could comfortably fit two people. "Now I just have to find the right person with whom to share my bathwater."

But they had to be someone who appreciated the fine art of bathing. Of soaking their cares away in front of a warm fire. Bathing wasn't just for the mundane task of getting one's skin clean. She had learned from her time in the far east that it was a way to soothe the soul.

All she had to do was to fill it with warm water and bath oil, strip off, and let her worries disappear.

"Bath oil. I need bath oil."

She was in London, and the best bath oil in all the world was sold at Floris, the perfumery in Jermyn Street. But what sort of perfume would she want for her bath oil?

Gardenia? Lavender? Or something less floral, spicier perhaps?

A scent that might entice the right man to make Poppy an offer to share her bath.

Things had been so busy since her arrival; Poppy hadn't had the time to venture much outside the docks. Two short walks to the local shops, and one longer sojourn to Spitalfields market in order to purchase meat and vegetables was the most she had managed thus far.

And while the ready-made garments at the drapers would do for her everyday wear, Poppy's heart's desire was for a gown tailored to her own personal tastes. Something elegant and feminine that she could wear on special occasions.

She glanced down at her gown and frowned at the numerous grubby marks and stains which covered her skirt, trousers, and bodice.

I look like I have been scrubbing the decks on my hands and knees. I can't possibly go into a respectable shop dressed like this; no one will wish to serve me.

Being the captain of a working ship meant she had had little use for fine clothes. Silk didn't respond well to being soaked in seawater. And fine lace had a horrible habit of catching on things.

She was now a resident of London, and while the warehouse wasn't an elegant abode, it was still her home. The money from the cinnamon contract would allow Poppy to indulge herself and purchase some brand-new clothes. "Perhaps I shall buy myself a fine feathered hat and take walks in Hyde Park like I hear the ladies of quality do each day."

Poppy shook her head. The mere thought of mixing with London's elite was preposterous. She was a stranger, an outsider, and the *haute ton* never permitted those sorts of people into its ranks. The closest she would likely ever get to rubbing shoulders with the upper class would be to have business dealings with people like Charles and Francis Saunders. And even then, the connection would be purely about contracts and money.

More's the pity. Though Francis strikes me as the sort who might attempt to break free of those social shackles. He is in an awful hurry to make his mark.

There was every chance that he would go to great lengths if there was a penny to be made. Anything to show the world that he was a successful man of business.

Her father had taught her that for a man to really stake his claim, he had to forge new paths. To be the first, and not just one of the others who came after.

Alone in the warehouse, Poppy took in the scene. There was a table. Her mattress was tucked away in the corner. And now she had a copper tub. Slowly but surely, she was transforming the once dirty space into somewhere she could live. Into a home.

She had even managed to make peace with the neighbors. That was a particularly worrying problem which had been solved. "If I can just win that spice contract, everything will be set."

The only other major problems left to overcome were that of her finding a suitable husband, and by way of that also solving the sticky situation with Jonathan. She also had to negotiate changes to the existing deal for the cinnamon bales, that they had brought with them from Ceylon, making sure, it was not placed in jeopardy.

It wasn't going to easy. Men like Jonathan Measy didn't tend to go quietly.

When Poppy woke the following morning, it was to the sight of Jonathan slumped fast asleep at the table. Sometime during the night, he had arrived back at the warehouse, picked the lock, and let himself in.

The two loaves of bread she had baked late yesterday on board the *Empress Catherine* were gone. All that remained were the crumbs scattered across the table. Jonathan lay face down in them, snoring loudly.

That was my breakfast and midday meal for the next few days. He's eaten it all.

She shook him firmly by the shoulder, but Jonathan didn't stir. He remained deep in what she surmised was an alcohol-induced slumber.

"What am I going to do with you?" she muttered.

With the food gone, a resigned Poppy got dressed and headed out in search of a pie man. She was too hungry to wait the time it would take to bake another loaf of bread.

When she got back to the warehouse, Jonathan, along with the small pile of coins Poppy had carefully hidden under her mattress, was gone.

She sighed. "You have gone too far, Jonathan." She was going to have to have a deadbolt installed. "I can't have you breaking in and stealing from me whenever the mood suits."

For the first time since she had arrived in London, Poppy's new home felt less secure. When she next saw Jonathan, she would give him the news. He was no longer welcome at the warehouse.

It would cost her a pretty penny to be free of him, but it would be well worth it.

Chapter Twenty-Four

Following his visit to the *Empress Catherine*, Francis did his utmost best to avoid Poppy. With Charles and Adelaide shortly heading off to Scotland for Christmas, he had more than enough to concentrate his mind on.

But try as he might, as soon as he stepped down from his carriage at the docks each morning, he found himself looking for her. His routine was thus—a quick glance toward the door of number fourteen. Then a slow search of the wharf embankment, and finally, a check of the deck of Poppy's ship, all in the secret hope of catching a glimpse of her.

He shouldn't look for Poppy. Shouldn't be the least interested in what she was doing. But every time his efforts didn't result in a Poppy sighting, the same dull pain of disappointment settled heavily in his gut.

The complicated ledgers and shipping records no longer held the same fascination as they usually did. Francis worked late into the night adding and tallying figures, all in the vain hope that they would somehow concentrate his mind.

"That's it. I am done for the day." With a sigh, he closed up the books of account and leaned back in his chair. He had caught three of his own errors in the past hour but suspected he had made more. Tomorrow, he would need to go back over the figures and correct his own work.

After wiping the ink from the end of his pen, he set the instrument back into its box. It took several attempts to put the lid back on the ink pot. These were simple tasks that Francis had done every day since coming to work with his father, yet now, they seemed to pose him a problem. His fingers wouldn't work in concert with his mind.

"I am hungry—that is the only cause of my muddled head. My stomach is too busy making demands for my brain to function properly."

It was well past nine o'clock, and he was the only person left in the company warehouse. The last of the clerks had packed up and gone home several hours ago.

If he'd had any sense, he would have done the same. Instead, he had wasted the best part of the evening trying to get sales figures to reconcile to his cash balance. They hadn't matched up.

Rising from his desk, Francis collected his coat and some papers. Hopefully his head would clear after having taken some supper at home, and then he could work on the balance again.

Time is money. You don't have enough of either.

Charles had taken the Saunders family carriage home earlier in the evening with the offer to send it back to collect Francis, but Francis had politely declined. The nearby Ratcliffe Highway was a busy thoroughfare, so flagging down a hack at this time of the night was never a problem.

Francis undertook his usual tour of the office, making sure that all the candles and lamps had been properly extinguished. He stopped by his desk on the way out and turned down his desk lamp. The flame slowly flickered, then went out.

Standing in the darkness, he was reminded of being below deck on the *Empress Catherine.* Of the warm touch of Poppy's hand on his arm.

The time they had spent alone together on board the boat was seared into his mind. She affected him like no other woman had ever done.

He wasn't an innocent when it came to sex. His last term at Eton had put paid to both his virginity and his youthful lack of knowledge about pleasuring women.

Back then, the women he'd met were professionals. They'd demanded payment for their services. Sex was merely a business transaction. Money exchanged for a short period of indulgence. Hearts were not risked, nor offered. It kept his world neat and his emotions on ice.

In the more recent years, he had restricted his occasional bedroom encounters to the bored, experienced matrons of the *ton*.

The arrival of Poppy Basden had thrown Francis. He couldn't stop thinking about her. The last two nights his sleep had been interrupted by vivid dreams of her in the copper tub. Those wicked imaginings made stronger by the knowledge that a bath had indeed been delivered to the warehouse next door. He wasn't sure what he would do if she took him up on the offer to cart water for her tub.

"Time to go home. You can't stand here in the dark indulging in sexual fantasies about the next-door neighbor," he muttered.

Stepping out onto the roadway, Francis closed the door, and turned the key in the lock.

"You can't keep doing this Jonathan, I need your help. We are meant to be partners in this venture."

That voice was a familiar one. Francis whirled around and caught sight of Poppy and Jonathan standing face-to-face in the middle of the road. Poppy stood with her hands on her hips, while Jonathan swayed gently in the breeze. The man was clearly drunk.

"I know. I know. But we were at sea for months. Can't a chap have a little time to enjoy himself? You won't be happy until you have my balls firmly in your grip and you can just squeeze them whenever you want to bring me into line," complained Jonathan.

This was a private disagreement and Francis should take his leave. He didn't. Instead, he stood stock-still in the doorway of his warehouse, watching as the argument continued.

Poppy threw up her arms. "I just want you to take some of the weight. We agreed with Papa that you would help. If you weren't going to do that then why did you sign up? As it is, you have started drinking your part of the proceeds of the cinnamon bale sales."

Jonathan shrugged. "Well, all your money will be mine soon enough anyway, so I don't see the problem."

Francis backed away from the door. He shouldn't linger. None of this was any of his business. Unfortunately, his movement had both Poppy and Jonathan turning in his direction.

"What the fuck are you staring at, pretty boy?" spat Jonathan.

Poppy didn't flinch at the foul language. Francis wasn't surprised. He expected she had heard much worse over the years.

"I am not staring at anything. I was leaving my warehouse to go home. It's your fault if you are the one causing a scene in public. Any louder and you will surely wake the dead," replied Francis, coolly.

His gaze went from Jonathan to Poppy. She looked downcast, defeated. How many times had the two of them had this conversation? From the expression on her face, Francis guessed that Poppy had long stopped counting.

I hate the way he makes her look small.

It wasn't just a physical thing. Francis worried that Jonathan was the kind of man who stole the light from a woman's soul. That in her efforts to placate him, she would be reduced to an insignificant version of herself.

"I am sorry, Francis. We shall take our personal business inside," replied Poppy.

She headed for the door of number fourteen. Jonathan lingered out in the roadway for a few moments after Poppy had gone inside. Francis clenched his fists, ready to do battle with the man he had decided was his sworn enemy.

Jonathan didn't move from his spot. He pulled a handkerchief out of his coat pocket and wiped it over his face. Francis dreaded to think what was on that square of fabric. Poppy's intended was still dressed in the same clothes Francis had spied wearing him on the first day he'd arrived in port.

I'd hate to see the color of the bathwater if he climbed in.

The mere thought of Jonathan being naked around Poppy had Francis clutching his fist so tight that his knuckles cracked. He really didn't like this man. And if the way Jonathan spoke to him was any indication, Francis was certain the feeling was mutual.

Jonathan took a step toward him, and Francis readied himself for a physical altercation. The sailor might well be a strongly built man, but Francis was tall and could move fast. He also had the advantage of being stone-cold sober.

"I'm not going to fight you," huffed Jonathan. "You are not worth my time."

He spun inelegantly on his heel and headed in the direction of the *Empress Catherine*.

Francis breathed a sigh of relief. He wasn't particularly fond of bare-knuckled boxing. His cousins Alex and David Radley had a penchant for it, but he had always found it too savage. His choice of battlefields were the floors of the shipping offices and the London Stock Exchange. To his way of thinking, money spoke louder than fists.

Something had to be done about Jonathan. He and Poppy were a disaster in the making. The drunken, lazy seaman would ruin her life. Francis feared for Poppy's safety.

But what could he do? He and Poppy had come to a détente of hostilities, but they were barely friends. He couldn't simply go telling her how to run her life.

But someone needs to protect her.

His thoughts drifted back to the wagon driver he had assisted. The poor man and his distressed horses had been abandoned, left to their fate in the middle of the road. If Francis hadn't stepped in, more than likely the horses would have been badly injured, and then been put down.

Poppy was all alone in London. And while she was a strong sea captain and more than capable of handling a pistol, she was still vulnerable. She didn't need him quietly ogling her or indulging in wicked thoughts of the two of them together. She needed a friend. A protector.

Francis Saunders, it is time to stop watching the drama unfold. You need to help Poppy change her fate.

Chapter Twenty-Five

The tradition of getting up early to watch the sunrise was one Poppy had established as a child. During the long absences of her father, she would look up at the pale morning light, knowing that he was one day closer to returning.

And while it had been many years since she had given up on racing down to the dockside of whichever port George had left her in just to see if his ship had dropped anchor, Poppy still rose early to greet the dawn.

Mug of coffee in hand, she was seated, legs dangling over the side of the wharf when Jonathan made his appearance. She glanced up at him as he dropped beside her. The stench of rum and lord knew what else hung around him like a foul miasma.

Don't ask him where he has been—you don't want to know. And truth be told, you don't care. You just want him gone.

She had no idea where he had ended up. Or with who. But their relationship was surely headed for dangerous reefs. Whatever their agreement had been before they left Ceylon, It was time to make a change.

Jonathan nodded at her coffee cup, and she handed it to him. He noisily slurped down the rest of its contents before handing it back. "Thank you. My head and queasy stomach appreciate it. I should have stuck to ale, not rum."

"There are the remains of a piece of pickled pork inside if you are looking for food. I do ask that you leave me the small loaf of bread. I am not in the mood to go shopping for more ingredients at this hour," she replied.

Jonathan sighed. "I don't deserve your hospitality or your good favor. I am sorry, Poppy. The lads got drinking and the next thing I knew, I was lying in a laneway just off Threadneedle Street."

He glanced down at his clothes. "I should get these washed. I stink like the Fleet Prison."

Poppy wasn't going to offer to do his washing. Nor was she about to give him first use of her beloved copper tub. If Jonathan wanted to be clean, he could avail himself of a washcloth and a dip in the river.

If she won the new spice contract, it would mean Poppy would be staying in London for the foreseeable future. Success would bring further complications to the already unsteady relationship between her and Jonathan. She was at breaking point.

When George Basden had bid them farewell from Trincomalee Harbor, it had been with the express understanding that Poppy would make things official with Jonathan once they reached England. When he arrived in the new year, he would fully expect to be greeted by his daughter *and* his son-in-law.

But her father hadn't been on board the boat; nor was he here in London to witness Jonathan's behavior.

Taking a deep breath, Poppy steeled her nerves for the conversation that had to be had. The one she had sat up late last night and rehearsed.

"I have been thinking about us," she said.

"I am leaving."

Her head whipped 'round so fast, it cricked her neck. "What?"

Jonathan slowly shook his head. "I can't stay here, Poppy. I hate London. The idea of living in this god-awful city for the rest of my days makes me feel ill."

Poppy fiddled with the pearl and sapphire ring on her right hand all the while doing her best to dampen the spark of hope which had suddenly flared in her heart. Jonathan was leaving. She couldn't believe her luck.

"I am not meant to live in one place, Poppy. You must know that already. I thought I could do it—follow through on the agreement I made with your father—but I can't. I would rather die than stay in this city. I am sorry. I cannot marry you."

Tears filled Poppy's eyes and she let out a loud sob. "Oh, thank heavens. You have no idea how much of a relief it is to hear you say that. I've been trying to find the right words to tell you that marriage between us would be an utter disaster. We would both be miserable."

For the first time since they had left Ceylon, Jonathan actually smiled. For a time, they sat staring at one another, sharing both tears and laughter. When Jonathan reached out and put an arm around her shoulder, Poppy rested her head against his chest. Her head was so light, she feared she might faint.

"You are a wonderful woman, Poppy Basden, and you deserve better than to be bound to a man who will drink himself drunk every day in order to hide his misery. The sea has always been my mistress. I can never love another."

To some, his words may have sounded cliched, but as a sailor, Poppy understood his sentiment only too well. Some men were not destined to remain on land. They found no joy in feeling solid ground underfoot. Jonathan was one of those men.

A few days in port was enough for him. He could stand it as long as he knew a ship was leaving soon and that he would be on board when it sailed. She could just imagine how he must have felt when the *Empress Catherine* drew up to the dock for the last time.

Poppy sat up, wiping away her tears. "When do you leave?"

Jonathan nodded. She knew he could understand the truth behind Poppy's question. Her words weren't meant to be cruel; she simply wanted confirmation.

"When I was at the pub last night, I signed up for a ship which is sailing for Cape Town later today. I came back this morning in order to collect my things from the *Empress Catherine* and to say goodbye to you."

"Where will you go after Africa?" she asked.

Cape Town was a good three months away by ship. Longer if they stopped on ports along the west coast of Africa.

"The contract is for a round trip. So, I will be back here in London by June. After that, who knows? I might even sign up to a ship sailing west to the Americas. I've never seen the Caribbean," he replied.

"It's a beautiful place. Hot, but not like the subcontinent. The heat in the West Indies is a dry one, so they don't get the blessed monsoon rains. They do, however, get huge storms. Hurricanes. I pray you never get caught up in one." Poppy had lived through one during a brief stopover in Port Royal, Jamaica, when she was young. The winds and howling rain had been terrifying. George Basden had been on a run to Belize at the time and Poppy had been left in the care of a madam in a local tavern. She had made her father swear to never leave her alone in such a place ever again.

And now I am to be alone once more.

She was older now. Capable of taking care of herself. The warehouse had locks and she had a pistol.

Jonathan got to his feet. "George will of course be disappointed; I have only fulfilled half the bargain we struck. But I am hoping that you and I can at least part as friends. Your father is not a man I wish to make my enemy."

Poppy caught the underlying message in his words. Jonathan had seen the cargo of cinnamon to London, and while he wasn't going to marry her, he would of course expect to receive payment for having completed some of the contract.

If it meant he went quietly, it would be worth every penny.

"Go and get your things from the ship, then come back to the warehouse and have some food. We can discuss a financial settlement over some cold cuts and another cup of coffee." She lifted her gaze and met his.

Jonathan nodded. "Thank you. If there is one thing, I have always known about you, Captain Poppy Basden, it's that you are fair and honest in everything you do, and that includes your business dealings. Someday, a fine man will come into your life, and he will learn that your word is your truth."

Jonathan tapped his forefinger to his head in salute, and Poppy offered a kind smile in reply. Them parting on civil terms was an unexpected victory—one she was not going to jeopardize.

Sitting watching as Jonathan made his way across the wharf and onto the gangplank of the *Empress Catherine*, Poppy considered his words. She had always made a point of being honest with her work, never seeking to undercut a business acquaintance or go against the spirit of a contract. Jonathan would get what was rightfully his from the cinnamon shipment. She would even handle the banker's order herself.

With her empty coffee cup in hand, Poppy headed back to the warehouse. The second she closed the door; the flood of tears came. When Jonathan departed later that day, she would be alone once more. No family. And few, if any, real friends.

Always by myself. I just wish I had someone to share my life with. To love me. Someone who wouldn't leave.

Knowing that she would be the only person living here for many months to come suddenly made the cavernous space seemed even more empty than usual. A shiver of fear gripped her. As a young woman sleeping alone at the London Docks, Poppy was in a vulnerable position. Perhaps even a dangerous one. She could only point her pistol at so many people before something bad happened to her.

Wiping her hands at the tears, Poppy wished desperately that they would go away. Weakness wouldn't do her any good. She had to be brave. It was the only way she could survive.

"You have done this before; you can do it again. Papa will be here soon. You just have to hold on," she comforted herself.

But the mantra by she had lived for so many of her younger years no longer held the same weight it once had. She was slowly losing faith in the promises her father had made.

George Basden hadn't always come good on them. And she knew not to question him when he failed her. He was his own man, and she was a lifelong inconvenience. One he had hoped that, through marriage, he would finally be rid of once and for all.

And what if he didn't make it to London? She had spent long years without her father, living on the prayer that wherever he was, he was safe. When she moved to London, he in turn had remained in Ceylon on the understanding that Poppy was with Jonathan. That he would protect her.

What would she do if her father never came? Ships were regularly lost at sea. The journey around the bottom of Africa was a perilous trip even in the best of weather.

The front door swung open. Poppy turned as Jonathan appeared. His woolen seabag was slung over his shoulder. She flinched as he dropped it to the floor. It was heavy and the sound of it hitting the hard stonework echoed around the room.

"That's everything. Oh, and I did take my spyglass from your cabin, just in case you went looking for it," he said.

Poppy sniffed back her tears of self-pity. "Of course. It is your spyglass; you have every right to take it with you. Will you stay and have some breakfast with me? Cold cuts? A final meal before you go?"

"Perhaps just a coffee, but I would prefer that we settle the financial arrangements as soon as possible. I want to be able to leave England with my share of the cinnamon money. Less, of course, the coins you gave me."

Having made the decision to leave, it was clear he wasn't even going to bother with more than the barest of niceties. In his mind, Jonathan was already on that ship, and she was but a distant memory.

"Let me get the banker's money order drawn up. You can cash it this morning and then be on your way," she replied.

"Thank you."

Poppy unlocked the top drawer of her desk and took out a pile of papers. In the middle of them was a letter she had written but not dated instructing her bank to pay Jonathan Measy the amount of two hundred pounds. It was a princely sum, more than what a first captain in the British navy would make during the same time it had taken them to sail from the far east. But the contract was clear, and notwithstanding his lack of effort since their arrival, Poppy was determined to abide by their agreement.

Laying the paper out on the desk, she dipped her pen in ink and wrote the date at the bottom of the letter. After affixing her father's stamp, she signed her own name.

"I think you will find the amount is correct," she said.

Jonathan took the letter and checked it. "Yes, thank you."

When he offered her his hand, Poppy stared at it for a moment. This was not how she had expected things between them to end, but as they shook hands, she knew it was for the best.

"I wish you all the luck in the world, Poppy Basden. And much happiness here in England. When I return, I shall call in and see how you are faring."

She nodded her thanks. "As for you, Jonathan Measy, may you have fair winds and following seas."

It was the only way for sailors to part and wish one another safe travels.

When the ink had dried, Jonathan carefully folded up the letter and stuffed it into his coat pocket. He retrieved his bag from the floor and headed toward the door. Poppy followed him out into the early morning sunshine.

"Before you go, could I ask one small favor?" she said.

A grinning Jonathan nodded. "Yes. I will keep my lips shut about the spice contract. It's no one else's business, and I would never do anything to harm your prospects of making it a success. I am sure you will be the winning bidder."

He pointed toward number twelve, the offices of Saunders Shipping Company. "If I can give you one piece of advice before I go, it would be to keep your lips sealed until after the official announcement. It's clear that you and Mister Francis Saunders are on good terms. If he knew you were competing against him, he might not be so friendly."

Poppy glanced at the warehouse next door. It was still

closed up, with no one about at this hour of the day. "I am sure Mister Saunders has plenty of other irons in the fire, but yes, I won't be saying anything until after the official announcement is published in the gazette."

Jonathan took one step away, then stopped. He turned and came back to Poppy, pulling her into a brief hug. "Good luck. Take care of you," he said.

He had drawn back and was most of the way down toward the end of the wharf before Poppy finally pulled her gaze from his retreating figure.

There went the man she was supposed to have married. The man her father had chosen to share her life. She should be feeling utterly bereft. Shattered at his leaving. At his abandonment of her all alone in London.

As he disappeared behind the bulk of a ship and was lost from sight, Poppy whispered, "Thank god, he is gone."

With Jonathan out of her life for good, she was finally free to make her own choices—to decide on her future.

Chapter Twenty-Six

Francis watched Poppy and Jonathan's parting with more than a little interest.

He had arrived early this morning, keen to get in a full day of working the books of account, but the sight which met his eyes as he made his way from the superintendent's office tore his thoughts from the long columns of numbers and dates.

From where he stood, it appeared that Jonathan Measy was leaving. The sailor was carrying a large duffel bag slung over his shoulder. He was going somewhere. And Poppy was staying behind.

Perhaps it was just a short voyage to a nearby port and he would soon return.

But what if it isn't?

What if his silent prayers had been answered and Poppy was now free?

Francis continued on toward the warehouse, torn as to what he should do. By rights, he should go into number twelve and get on with his work. Mind his own business. That was what the Francis of only a week ago would surely have done.

What if she is heartbroken over him? I know the man is a pig, but they must have a long history together. They were about to get married.

His mind was still not made up by the time he got to the front door of Saunders Shipping. *Do I go and see her? Or should I give her a little time to compose herself?*

He didn't know what he would do if he found Poppy in tears. Wrapping her up in his arms was the obvious solution. But that might only complicate matters.

The little voice of reason sitting in the back of his mind cautioned him against going next door. It might seem callous to leave Poppy to her own devices but sometimes you had to be cruel to be kind.

It would be better to wait for Poppy to come and see him. Let her decide when and what she was going to say. If Jonathan had indeed gone for good, then that most surely changed the dynamics of the friendship between him and Poppy.

She didn't need Francis and his growing attraction to further complicate things.

Poppy is a smart girl, and right now, I expect she is reconsidering a great number of things in her life. When she is ready, she will talk. Until then, you should give her time and space to think.

And for once, Francis actually showed some restraint.

Chapter Twenty-Seven

The following morning, the foyer of the Saunders family home was piled high with travel cases and boxes. There were only two people travelling to Scotland, Lady Adelaide, and Charles, but they had packed enough luggage that an expeditionary force would view it as overkill.

"How long did you say you were going to be away?" asked Francis.

His mother shot him a look of disapproval, which he calmly ignored. She had been throwing them his way since the day she had discovered her youngest son was not making the trip north.

"We will be back late January. If you were coming with us, you wouldn't have to ask," replied Adelaide.

Grin and bear it. They will be gone within the hour.

"I'm sorry, but as I explained to Papa, I have a great deal of work to do over the next few weeks and I cannot spare a festive jaunt." Francis took a deep breath, doing his best to continue with his carefully adopted air of disinterest. His mother was looking for an excuse to berate him, or worse, cry, and he wasn't going to give it to her.

I am a grown man. The days of me having to sit with my parents in the family carriage are over.

Charles appeared at the top of the stairs, and Francis turned his pleading eyes to him. "Your mother and I understand. Besides, with the spice contract about to be announced, you can't possibly be out of town. There will be much to do apart from just signing the papers," said Charles.

"Exactly," replied Francis.

Charles took Francis by the arm and led him away from where Adelaide and her lady's maid had begun to perform another check of the various leather hat boxes. Knowing his mother, it wouldn't be the last time she examined the cases before the footmen finally carried them out to the Saunders family travel coach. Adelaide wasn't anything if not meticulous. One year, she had made the coach turn round on the outskirts of London so they could return home and collect a pair of boots.

"What are your plans if you do secure the contract? I mean, about the storage space," asked Charles.

His father might well be leaving the company in Francis's hands, but that didn't mean he wasn't going to be checking things before he left.

He's not trying to undermine you. He is just asking.

Much as he tried to convince himself, Francis didn't believe that for one moment. Everything Charles said about the business in the lead up to his departure felt like he didn't trust him.

On January 1st, the company is mine. Humor him.

"I am considering. And grant that this is not final. But I am thinking of possibly moving the clerical office space out of the warehouse. If I rent a small shopfront in one of the nearby streets, that will free up most of the bottom floor," replied Francis.

It wasn't the best solution, but it was the most cost effective. In the meantime, he would keep an eye out for any other possible warehouse vacancies.

Charles nodded. "I suppose that could work. Your clerks don't need to be at the warehouse every day. You could maintain a small area with a desk or two for those who need to be on the spot when a ship arrives. Yes, smart thinking."

His father went to step away, then stopped. "Of course, you could always speak to Captain Basden and see if she will rent you some of her space."

Things were at a delicate stage between Poppy and himself, and Francis was loath to make matters more complicated. He was yet to understand the situation regarding Jonathan. Asking Poppy if he could sub-let some of her property might put her in an awkward position.

And if she is still going to go ahead and marry the brute, the last thing I want is to have to bear witness to their domestic disaster every time I visit the warehouse.

No. His solution was the best in the circumstances. Keeping business and personal relationships separate was the smart way to handle things. He liked Poppy, and as much as he would like to punch Jonathan, Francis had no time in his life to get mixed up with the people next door.

"I did consider that option, Papa, but I think it best that I look at finding a space for the clerks and our shipping records. Hopefully that will create enough room."

Francis was in a reflective mood when he arrived at Saunders Shipping later that morning. Adelaide and Charles were on their way to Scotland, and for the first time in his life, he was alone at both home and work. A mixture of excitement and trepidation bubbled away in his stomach. He had waited for this day for many years, but now that it had arrived, he found himself wondering how on earth he was going to get through the next month.

Much as Charles frustrated him at times, he at least was a solid sounding board. With both his sisters at the estates of their respective new families, the only family member left in London whom Francis could possibly turn to for advice was his brother Will.

And even then, that relationship was problematic. Will had only recently returned to England after many years abroad. In the time that he had been gone, Francis had grown from a gangly youth to a man. Will had also changed. They were taking slow steps toward rebuilding their brotherly connection. To setting it on a new, more equal footing. This would take time. But all good things did.

After having spent the afternoon working through the books and getting the ledgers up to date, Francis took a break in the early evening. With no one at home, he intended to spend as much time as he could at the docks over the next few weeks.

When he was announced as the winner of the spice contract, which he would be in a few days, he would have everything ready. The day the contract commenced would be the day he had truly arrived.

Perhaps I should treat myself to a new suit and a fine pair of boots.

As the Bard himself said, apparel oft proclaims the man. A fresh look would help stamp his authority. Let everyone in the London Docks know that Francis Saunders was a man not to be trifled with; he was to be respected.

Pushing back from his desk, Francis rose stiffly to his feet. He had spent too many hours hunched over the books of account.

"There are knots on the knots of my shoulder muscles. I need a long soak in a hot bath," he announced.

The last clerk had packed up and left a short while ago, leaving Francis once more alone in the warehouse. It was fast becoming a habit of his to work well past normal business hours. Skipping supper meant he often returned home late at night and then had to throw himself on the mercy of the Saunders family cook for a plate of cold leftovers.

He could go home. He should go home. But the paperwork mountain never seemed to get any lower. The work which he didn't get to tonight would have more work added on top of it come morning.

I might go and see if I can scavenge up some food from one of the nearby taverns. They surely must have a pie or two to spare.

With ships arriving at all hours into the docks, the local taverns never closed. Hungry and thirsty sailors were always on the hunt for sustenance.

He grabbed his coat and wrapped his scarf around his neck. December could be surprisingly cold in London. Not as chilly as Scotland, but even at this time of the year it wasn't unheard of for snow to fall in the capital.

Stepping out of the warehouse, Francis slipped the key in the lock and secured the door.

"Francis?" came a familiar voice—one he hadn't heard for several days.

He steadied himself and turned to face Poppy.

She was standing on the other side of the wharf road, and after checking right and left, she quickly crossed to his side.

"Working late again?" she asked.

"Yes. I have a lot of paperwork to get through before Christmas," he replied.

He avoided her gaze, instead choosing to stare down at her boots. When he had talked himself into avoiding Poppy, he'd thought it was the sensible thing to do. Now, seeing her, it seemed all wrong.

For heaven's sake, speak to her. Don't be a cold fish. Ask her how she has been.

"Where is Jonathan? I saw him lugging a sailor's bag yesterday. The two of you were saying your farewells, and he looked to be going somewhere," he said.

He hadn't meant to ask that, and especially not right at the outset of their conversation, but the thought of what had happened to Jonathan Measy was inconveniently at the forefront of Francis's mind. "Sorry. That was rude of me. He is none of my business. Forgive me."

When Poppy moved closer, Francis had no option but to shift his gaze upward to meet her face.

She greeted him with a soft smile. "Jonathan is gone. Signed a ship's articles to join a complement crewing a vessel to South Africa. He sailed on the evening tide last night."

This was the best news Francis had heard in a long while. He searched her face, looking for signs of distress. There were none to be found. If she was heartbroken over the departure of her intended, Poppy certainly hid it well.

"And will he be back?" he asked.

The disinterested shrug he got in response flooded Francis's heart with warmth. Jonathan was gone, and Poppy didn't seem to mind.

This might be the way of the sailor life. He goes off to sea, then comes home when it suits him. She remains here, waiting.

"The contract is for six months, after which he says he might seek a new contract on a boat to the West Indies. Not that it matters to me. He is gone."

Even as hope flared, Francis was determined to tread carefully. The last thing he wanted was to get the wrong idea about Poppy and Jonathan's personal arrangements.

"Are you alright? I mean, did you ask him to stay?" *Please tell me you threw him out.*

She let out a sigh. "He went of his own volition, and I

must say, when he told me he was going, I could have wept with relief. Actually, I did."

"But what about your betrothal?"

"There never was a betrothal—just a gentleman's agreement between Jonathan and my father. Papa expected that Jonathan and I would marry, but the truth was this trip to England was merely a means to an end. Jonathan got some money from the cinnamon bales we brought with us while I was given the opportunity to set up the shipping business. We both went along with the idea of marrying because it made sense at the time when we left Ceylon. But the sea is Jonathan's home. He was miserable here. We agreed to part as friends."

Jonathan was long gone. Poppy hadn't ever loved him. This was good news.

Francis quickly lowered his head and rummaged around in his pocket for something. Anything. He needed a moment to absorb the news. *This is excellent. But why is it so wonderful?*

The voice in the back of his mind softly whispered, *"Because you like her, you great big fool."*

He caught a glimpse of her boots as Poppy shifted away from him. Francis glanced up.

"I haven't seen you around the place for the past day. You are normally everywhere," she said.

There was a note of sad accusation in her tone, and it went straight to Francis's heart. While he had been keeping his distance, thinking he was doing the right thing, she had been left wondering why.

You have hurt her.

Ashamed of himself and his thoughtless ways, Francis raked his fingers through his hair. "What . . . what will you do now that he has gone?" he stammered.

"Do what I always planned to do. Stay here. Work. Wait for my father," she replied.

So, George Basden was coming to England—that was encouraging. Poppy wouldn't be alone once he arrived. But in the meantime, who would look after her?

"And when is your father due?"

"Soon. He always comes, eventually." Her simple answer was delivered in such a cheerful but clearly rehearsed manner that it set a frown to Francis's lips. How much of Poppy's life had been spent waiting for her father?

Deuce. How many years has she been on her own?

Francis had a horrible inkling that Jonathan Measy hadn't been the villain of Poppy's life story. Her father had.

Anger and curiosity got the better of him.

"When you say soon, what does that mean?" he pressed.

"He is due to have the house packed up by May. After that, he'll be on board his ship by June, which puts him into London early to mid-December."

"Next year?"

Poppy nodded. "Yes."

It was going to be a whole year before her father arrived.

If Francis could have reached across the wide seas and found Poppy's father, he would have punched the man in the face. He had sent his daughter to England and pressured her into making a loveless union, yet the man didn't have the good grace to even bother setting sail for another six months.

When George Basden did finally set foot ashore in London, he was going to have to deal with Francis Saunders. It was not going to be a pleasant encounter.

Chapter Twenty-Eight

After breakfast the following morning, Francis made his way downstairs to the kitchen and sought out the family cook. The moment he entered the room, the servants stood stiffly to attention. All except the cook. She gave him a look that spoke of her disapproval of his violation of her sacred place.

"Good morning. Cook, I was wondering if I could have a word?" he said.

He was certain Cook had a real name, but he had never been privy to it. She was Cook, and that was that. This was her domain and if she chose to use that moniker, he had no authority to ask for anything more.

Cook cleared her throat, after which all the other household servants immediately made themselves scarce. It was only after everyone else had gone that she turned back to Francis. "I know Lady Adelaide and Mister Saunders are gone, but that doesn't mean we should permit anarchy to reign," she announced.

Translation: Don't think you can come wandering into the kitchen when it suits you.

Francis bit back a grin. In his younger days, the Saunders family cook had been given a free hand when it came to disciplining the children as and when they crossed a line with her. More than once, he had felt the hard wood of her oval-headed spoon as it was firmly applied to his backside.

"I actually came to ask your considered professional advice. But if you are too busy, I fully understand," he replied.

She narrowed her eyes at him. His feeble attempt at flattery wasn't going to get him anywhere, and they both knew it.

"What do you wish to know, Master Francis?" she replied.

Two and twenty he might well be, but he would always be Master Francis in this kitchen. Age would not weary the memory of the snow-haired boy who had spent many an afternoon seated on a high chair eagerly waiting for the next batch of hot buttered bread to appear.

Charles Saunders had insisted that a proper brick oven be installed in the kitchen. He flatly refused to have his family be served the locally make bread, as he considered it to be of poor quality. As a Frenchman, he took the whole business of bread and pastries seriously.

"I was wondering what you would recommend as the best sort of kitchen implement that I should purchase for my friend who has recently moved into a new home. They have lived much of their life on board a ship and cooked their meals using a small galley stove."

The idea of finding something that Poppy would find useful had only occurred to Francis late last night, and he found it most appealing. While he could simply buy her more flowers and pots for her rapidly growing garden, Francis was keen to ensure that his gift was one which was not only practical but added to Poppy's comfort.

He could also privately confess that he wanted her to think of him every time she used his gift. At some point, he had stopped viewing the next-door neighbor as a nuisance. Poppy had become something else. A friend.

One who found her way into his thoughts at odd times of the day and night.

"A large fireplace?" replied Cook.

"Yes. Oh, and my friend likes to bake. She is good with biscuits and cinnamon toast," he added.

As a soft smile appeared on the woman's face, Francis silently chastised himself for having mentioned that his friend was, in fact, a she.

The servants will have a lovely time gossiping over that gem as soon as I am gone.

To his relief, Cook simply turned and made her way over to the nearby fireplace. A selection of pots and pans sat to one side of the main grate. She picked up a three-legged round pot and brought it back to where Francis stood.

"This is what they call a Dutch oven. One of the most useful inventions ever made for the kitchen," she said.

He took hold of the pot. It was heavy. "What is it made of?"

"Iron. They cast it in sand molds, and that gives them the nice smooth surface inside. Stops things sticking to the bottom. The three little legs are so you can stand the pot either in the hot coals of the fire or near them."

It looked sturdy, reliable. Something that would last a lifetime. He was certain Poppy would appreciate the practicality of it.

"It's not the most romantic of gifts," said Cook.

Francis set the oven on the floor. She was, of course, completely right; a cast-iron pot didn't quite send one's pulse racing. He hadn't meant it to, but now that he thought about it, perhaps that was a misstep.

No. No, it's not. Remember, you like Poppy. You want to be on friendly terms with her. Anything else is an unnecessary obstacle.

"The lady in question is just a friend. Well, more of an acquaintance," replied Francis. He kept his gaze from meeting Cook's, fearing what he would see in her eyes. The lack of conviction in his voice was bad enough.

Cook picked up the Dutch oven and replaced it back beside the fire. "If you are still set on buying one of these for a gift, I can give you the address of the ironmonger Mister Saunders has an account with in Thames Street."

Francis was caught in a bind of his own making. If he said no that he would find another more suitable present, Cook would have won. And if he kept on with his original plan, he ran the risk of appearing stubborn and thoughtless.

I lose either way.

It was the thought of Poppy and her delicious baked goods that finally settled things. He was being a good friend by gifting her an oven which would enable her to make more sweet treats and tasty bread.

And if the cast-iron pot means that she is inclined to bake every day, then it goes without saying that she will need a friend with whom she can share her food. Perhaps even a gentleman who happens to have a shipping office close to hers.

Poppy was living alone. It would be impolite of him not to call in each day and spend a little time with her. And he could hardly refuse if she asked him to stay and give her a spot of his attention while she served up elevenses and a cup of tea.

Francis swallowed down a lump of imaginary cake. "I would be most grateful if you could write the address down on a card, thank you, Cook."

Cook opened the drawer at the end of the large kitchen work table and sorted through a small stack of cards. "Ah," she muttered, before handing one of them to Francis.

"Just let him know who you are before you begin to conduct business; that way, you will get the best quality Dutch oven. It might cost your father a pretty penny, but I am sure that if it has the desired result with the young lady in question, he will think it money well spent."

"Thank you, Cook. But just so as we are clear regarding this cooking pot, it is a gift to a friend, nothing more."

"Of course, Master Saunders."

Francis took both the card and his leave. As he climbed aboard the carriage in the mews at the rear of his family home a short while later, he swore he could hear the buzz of the rumors which his visit to the kitchen had already started.

Just a pot. Not a proposal.

Chapter Twenty-Nine

Poppy had burned the cakes in true King Alfred style. She had gotten busy with some paperwork and forgotten that they were cooking on the small iron tray on top of the grate. The smell of burnt butter and sugar alerted her to the impending disaster.

"The cakes!" she cried, pushing her chair back from the desk and leaping to her feet. She scurried over to the fire and took a hold of the tray with the edge of a folded-up dishcloth. Her grip wasn't sure, and the hot platter slipped out of her hand.

The six little sugar cakes fell to the floor, scattering in all directions.

"Oh, no. Now look what I have done."

Dropping to her knees, she gathered four of the cakes up, tucking them into her apron. One had rolled under a nearby chair. She bent, stretching to collect it.

Knock. Knock.

"Oh," she muttered. Talk about terrible timing.

With a huff, Poppy got to her feet. She dropped the cakes onto the table and headed for the door.

Francis Saunders was standing on the threshold; he held a wooden box in his hands. "Good afternoon," he said, offering up a cheery smile.

Thank heavens we are no longer enemies. His smile lights up the whole of his face.

"Not such a good one for me unfortunately. I have just burned and then dropped a whole batch of sugar cakes," replied Poppy. She beckoned for him to come inside, and Francis followed her. "I am still in the process of locating the last one of them." She glanced back over her shoulder. "Feel free to put your box down next to the table. It looks heavy."

Francis set the box on the floor. "It is rather. But it's not my box; it's yours."

Poppy stopped mid-way to the fireplace. She was sure she hadn't ordered anything. Turning, she considered the plain wooden box. "I wasn't expecting a delivery. Was it outside when you arrived?"

He shook his head and the grin on his face grew even wider. Francis might well fancy himself a hard-nosed businessman, but if he had any idea as to the power of his smile, he would know that it was all he would ever need to secure a deal. Charles might be the one blessed with a friendly, disarming nature, but Francis could also hold his own.

You just need to decide that being pleasant with people can get you a long way.

It was a lesson she had learned at an early age. It served as a means to an end. Making sure she survived on her own in a foreign port when her father had yet again gone off on one of his journeys and left Poppy behind.

"I brought the box with me. I have been to Thames Street to the ironmonger," he announced, proudly.

Poppy's brows lifted. She didn't think someone like Francis would even know what an ironmonger did, let alone know where to find one.

Her mind was still tackling that thought as Francis bent and removed the lid from the box. His hands then disappeared inside the wooden frame. When they reappeared, they were holding a cast-iron pot. He lifted it free, then stepped forward and placed it on the floor in front of Poppy.

"It's a Dutch oven, for you."

Poppy's hands went to her heated cheeks in an instant. Francis had brought her a present. A rather grand one, from the look of it.

"Note the matching lid and the three little legs on the bottom. I have been assured that this pot should last you a lifetime. In fact, your grandchildren will very likely be cooking with it long after you are gone," he said.

Her eyes darted from Francis to the pot, and then back to him. Poppy couldn't believe what was happening. No one had ever given her such a thoughtful gift. While many might think it odd to buy a new friend a Dutch oven, Francis, of all people, seemed to genuinely understand her.

A Dutch oven. Oh, my.

Flowers of course would have been nice. A fancy handkerchief welcome. But a pot which would enable her to bake bread and full-sized cakes was like being handed the keys to El Dorado.

Her vision grew misty, clouded with tears.

"I . . . I don't know what to say," she stammered.

Francis drew close. "Tell me that it is something you can use. I wasn't sure what to get you, but I remembered you bringing some small baking trays off the *Empress Catherine.* I spoke to our cook at home, and she said this would be something she would want for cooking in a fireplace."

Poppy nodded. "I have seen smaller iron pots in various places, but these cast iron designs are considered to be the best. You even managed to get a tripod one. Thank you. I really don't know what else to say, other than that."

She couldn't imagine what it must have cost Francis. Good quality Dutch ovens were an investment piece, something she had always promised herself that she would one day own.

And that day is today.

It was an expensive gift. It bordered on extravagant. And in her world, such gifts rarely came without ties.

"I don't wish to appear ungrateful, but why?" she asked.

It was a question which she felt had to be asked. She needed to understand him, and this moment in particular.

In the short time since she had known Francis, Poppy had developed a sense of being able to read his moods. He wasn't one who could easily hide his emotions. At times, he barely seemed able to keep them under control.

This morning, however, he appeared hesitant, almost unsure of himself. This was not a version of Francis she had encountered before now. The closest he had been to this was when he'd arrived at the warehouse the morning after the pistol incident and discovered his father happily sitting with her, sharing French toast.

Poppy's senses clicked into self-preservation mode. They were heightened but not alarmed. She searched his face, trying to get a clearer understanding of him.

Another step brought Francis to within a short arm's reach. "I was unkind to you when you first arrived. And while we have been able to establish a peace, I thought it only right that I offer you this gift. Please accept it with my best wishes for your future happiness here."

Disappointment dropped like a heavy stone into Poppy's stomach.

His gift was a peace offering. A token of his ongoing guilt over the barrels and ropes. Of course, it was.

"You didn't have to do that, Francis. The fact that we are on speaking terms and good neighbors is more than anything

I could honestly have asked for," she replied, pushing down her unexpected sadness.

A perplexed look appeared on his face, then it suddenly cleared, and he took hold of Poppy's hand. "I've made a mess of things again, haven't I? I don't mean this gift was something I felt obliged to do. I wanted to give it to you. It wasn't just to say how sorry I am, but rather— to say welcome."

Francis was an extremely tall and solidly built man. He towered over other people. But there was also a kindness about him, a surprising amount of tenderness which he now displayed to her.

As she stared up into his sky-blue eyes, Poppy remembered that morning on the wharf road when she had dropped the eggs, when Francis had hurried after her and offered his assistance. The more she got to know this man, the more convinced she was that his conduct toward her over the barrels hadn't been true to his nature.

Something else had driven him to behave that way. She would love to know what it had been.

Her gaze dropped to where Francis still held her hand. "Thank you. This is a generous gift, and I shall treasure it always."

"But will you use it?" he asked.

Poppy rewarded his question with a beaming smile. "Oh, yes. I have a dozen recipes already planned in my head. Not just bread, but stews and roasts. And when I can source the right spices, a good strong Ceylonese Kari."

"Kari?"

"Or what the English call curry. It's from the Tamil language. We ate it all the time in Ceylon. Cinnamon, black pepper, and coconut milk. I might see if I can find a good fishmonger at the market, or if not, then somewhere that sells cured tuna."

Francis's stomach rumbled and they both laughed.

"Have you eaten this morning? I have some bread left over. I promise I won't press my burnt cakes upon you," she said, taking a step back. "And I have freshly brewed coffee if you would like some."

"Thank you. That would be nice. Where do you keep your cups?" he replied, letting go of her hand.

"On the second shelf," she said, pointing to the nearby cupboard.

By the time Poppy had returned from the fireplace with the pot of hot coffee, Francis had collected two cups and arranged them on the table.

"Oh, and I found this. I accidently trod on it, so I would suggest it is beyond repair," he said, holding a squashed object in his left hand.

It took a moment for Poppy to realize what the item was, then she shook her head. It was the missing sixth cake. By the look of it, Francis was right. There was nothing to be done about the poor burnt creation.

"Shall I throw it and the others into the bin? Or feed them to one of the dockside cats?" he asked reaching for the other cakes.

Poppy playfully batted Francis's hand away. "Don't you dare! I will cut the burnt pieces off these remaining cakes, and then eat them myself. Food onboard a ship always finds its way to the floor. There is no standing on ceremony when it comes to food. You simply scoop it up, dust off any dirt, and stuff it in your mouth."

The chastened expression on Francis's face told her all she needed to know. It hadn't occurred to him that the food might be salvaged. That she would actually eat it.

This is a man who has servants to make sure his food never hits the floor.

It would be all too easy for her to judge Francis for his privileged upbringing, to view him as being pampered and soft. But Poppy was quickly learning that when it came to her next-door neighbor, there were different layers to him. His weaknesses were more than offset by his strengths. A one-dimensional dandy he was not. Francis was complex. It made Poppy want to get to know him better.

She poured them both a cup of coffee and handed one to him. While he took a seat, Poppy found a knife and proceeded to cut away the burnt bottoms of the cakes.

Francis picked up one of the sugar cakes, examined it briefly, then bit into it. Poppy's gaze shifted from the half-eaten food to Francis's face. Their eyes met. There was a distinct glint of mischief in his, an open challenge for her to say something.

Poppy picked up another of the cakes and took a bite. After finishing her mouthful, she washed it down with a sip of hot coffee.

For a few minutes they sat in contented silence, eating and drinking. She couldn't remember the last time she had indulged in such a simple pleasure. The sense of easy calm which settled in her mind was most welcome.

Brushing the last of the cake crumbs from his fingers, Francis sat back in his chair. "That was delicious. Even the burnt bits were tasty," he said.

She shot him a disapproving but mischievous glance. "Don't be cheeky. The sugar caramelizes when it is hot. That is what you tasted; there were no blackened edges."

Rising from her chair, Poppy collected her cup. Francis followed suit. They narrowly avoided colliding with one another as they both stepped away from the table.

"Sorry," she said.

Francis shook his head. "I should be the one apologizing. I do tend to take up a lot of room."

His gaze dropped to her lips, and Poppy's breath caught.

The silence in the room was so heavy it was as if time had suddenly stopped. It took all her energy just to blink.

He bent forward, and her vision was filled with his smiling face. A hand reached out and touched her cheek. Strong, but gentle fingers brushed over her skin. "You have a crumb or two of cake on your face," he said.

The warmth in his voice sent a frisson of heat racing down Poppy's spine.

Touch me. Please.

His fingers wiped another crumb away from the corner of her lips, and it took every ounce of her self-control not to open her mouth. Poppy was certain that if she did, Francis would slip his thumb inside and let her play. She was desperate for the salty taste of his skin.

"Poppy," he murmured.

Francis lowered his head. She didn't pull away, silently begging the heavens to allow what she hoped was about to happen to take place.

This man, the one who had tormented her when she had first arrived in London, was about to kiss her. Claim her lips with his. Take and plunder. She wanted nothing more than for this Viking to do as his ancestors had done. Seize everything. Her lands were ready to cede all power to him.

Yes. Oh, please yes.

His fingers continued to brush over her cheek. She didn't care that her face was hot and flushed. He was doing this to her. He had to know the effect he was having on every nerve in her body. When she drew in a shaky breath, she could have sworn he growled in response.

"Francis," she gushed.

Bang. Bang. Bang.

What the devil?

The crash of someone pounding on the front door tore Poppy out of the moment. Francis immediately stepped back.

No. This can't be happening.

The knock came again. Whoever it was outside, they were most insistent.

"You had better get that," he said.

Dropping her cup carelessly onto the table, Poppy marched around the dividing wall and opened the door.

"This had better be bloody important," she muttered angrily.

On the doorstep stood a young lad, no older than ten. In his arms was a large leather satchel.

Contracts. Damn, I had forgotten about those.

"Delivery for Captain Basden. Is he about or can someone else sign for this?" asked the boy.

Poppy snapped out of her lust haze and sighed. "I am Captain Basden. I can sign for the delivery." She held out her hand and the delivery boy passed her his notebook and a pencil. She scribbled her name in the required space, then handed them back, taking the satchel in exchange.

The boy lingered on the threshold for a moment before an embarrassed Poppy, reached for her jacket pockets. They came up empty.

"Just a minute," she said, turning to go back inside. Francis met her; he was on his way out. "I have to go; I have a ship at dock which needs my inspection. Thank you for the tea cake and coffee, Poppy."

"Thank you for the Dutch oven," she replied.

Disappointment stabbed at her heart. By the time she returned to the front door, payment for the delivery boy in hand, Francis was gone.

After closing the door of the warehouse, Poppy went back to the table. She pushed the freshly arrived satchel out of the way, resumed her seat, and reached for another of the tea cakes. Within minutes, there were none left.

Her stomach was full, but her heart was sad and empty.

Chapter Thirty

What was bright, shiny, and utterly under his skin? Answer: Poppy Basden.

A matter of a week ago, Francis had been ready to go to war with his neighbor. Now he was sharing coffee and burnt cakes with her. He had also bought her a gift.

Those facts would rightly have been enough to concentrate a man's thoughts, but he had gone one step further. He had touched her. And while his fingers had brushed over her skin, his mind had been filled with all manner of heated longing.

When had a stray cake crumb on a woman's mouth been so sexually provocative? Even now, a full day later, it was all Francis could think of, and it clearly muddled his mind.

He had spent yesterday afternoon in the hot and stinking hull of a ship sorting through barrels of black molasses. The task would normally have had him in a foul mood by the time he'd finished. Instead, he'd barely noticed the acrid air and heat. His thoughts had been concentrated on Poppy and how close he had come to kissing her.

If the courier hadn't knocked at the door, he would have

claimed her mouth with his. Taken those soft pale pink lips of hers and kissed her senseless. It would have been heavenly.

The morning saw him in a more sober mood.

He had touched Poppy. Crossed clear boundaries that society put up for very good reasons—to protect vulnerable females from predatory males. He had taken advantage of the situation, and lord knew what would have happened if they had remained alone.

It was fused into his brain. You never touched a woman without asking first. And if she agreed to let you put your hands on her person, you only proceeded in the full understanding that you might well have to offer for the lady's hand in marriage.

After a breakfast where he barely touched his food, Francis aimlessly wandered the upper floors of his family home. When he made no sign of heading to the office, the Saunders family butler sent word to the mews that the town carriage could be unhitched from the horses.

After dragging a book down from one of the shelves in the library, Francis slumped into a chair and attempted to read. The words on the page didn't register in his brain; his eyes merely danced across them. Finally, he snapped the book shut and set it on a nearby side table.

He leaned forward, hands clasped together, head hung while he stared at the carpet.

What am I going to do?

The problem with Poppy Basden wasn't so much that he had taken advantage of their friendship. It was that he couldn't find it in himself to regret any of it. She was a warm summer's day in his winter of discontent. He craved the sunshine she had brought into his life.

He should have been ashamed of himself. Especially after having lured her with that gift. She'd probably felt obliged to let him touch her face. To have his fingers linger on her skin.

"Damn. That is not how I want things to be between us, or the grounds on which our relationship could be based," he muttered.

His own words pulled Francis up sharp.

He had been trying to frame his connection with Poppy as being purely a business one. At a stretch, a convivial friendship between neighbors. Nothing more.

Who was he trying to fool? Himself? Not likely. So, what was he to do?

Poppy Basden hadn't ever been in his well-ordered and set-in-stone plans. But it was becoming apparent even to him, that everything she did caused a major ripple in his life.

She had moved into the warehouse he had wanted. Her odd but rather cleverly designed boat was berthed at the wharf, right where he had planned to offload the new shipments of spices.

And now, every time he saw her, his thoughts turned to muddled mush.

If his mother could see him right this very minute, she would be grinning from ear to ear. Adelaide would know exactly what ailed her youngest son.

The toe of his boot tapped a quick but steady rhythm on the floor. It matched that of his heart. The tune which they beat out in time with one another was one which many a man had danced to down the ages.

It was sure, and it was sweet. The addictive music of love held Francis in its sway.

Chapter Thirty-One

The late afternoon breeze blowing in from over the River Thames brought a chill with it. Poppy, who was seated up on the weather deck of the *Empress Catherine,* sewing curtains for the warehouse, didn't pay the wind much mind. Others might think London cold in December, but those that did likely hadn't ever sailed around the bottom of South America in the middle of a storm sent straight up from the Southern Ocean.

"Now that is a freezing wind," she said.

She paused her stitching and took in the sight of the docks. Her gaze shifted from the river across to the rows of warehouses which ran along the North Quay. There were five main blocks of buildings, each comprising eight sets of warehouses. From where she sat, opposite building number two, Poppy could just make out the last building. Farther past that was the Tobacco Warehouse, at Tobacco Dock, which was one of the busiest places in all of London Docks.

She had pictured this place in her mind, imagined she was seated right where she was this very minute. But her visions hadn't ever been able to convey the emotion that finally being in London and living her lifelong dream would bring.

Her heart swelled at the knowledge she wouldn't ever have to leave this place. That she was home.

A carriage drew up outside the Saunders Shipping Company offices, and Poppy's attention immediately focused on the passenger door. She hadn't seen Francis this morning.

Not that I was looking for him.

But after yesterday, when she had been convinced that he was going to kiss her, Poppy was keen to speak to Francis. To clear the air. He shouldn't feel a sense of awkwardness over a moment of temptation. They had both been on the verge of changing their relationship. She had hoped it had been a mutual decision to do so, but she had her doubts.

He had dashed out of the warehouse before the delivery boy had even got his gratuity from Poppy. Francis's farewell had been yet another hurried goodbye.

After that, she had made several trips across the wharf road back and forth to the *Empress Catherine,* hoping to catch a glimpse of him. To have a quick word and make sure things were alright. But, typical of Francis, he had disappeared from sight.

The tall sailing ship, which was berthed astern of her boat, had arrived early in the morning and from the small army of dock workers marching up and down the gangplanks, lugging barrels, it soon became clear that the captain had no plans to linger in port.

This morning, as she sat sipping her coffee, the ship had weighed anchor and headed back out into the Thames. The only evidence that the ship had been at the dockside was the cargo, a hundred or so barrels stacked under the Saunders Shipping side of the wharf pavilion.

Poppy narrowed her eyes and peered at the carriage, which had come to a complete stop. One footman climbed down from the back and moved around to the side. Meanwhile, another footman, in matching livery, climbed to the top of the coach. He unstrapped a large trunk, then lowered it to the waiting footman.

Between them, they carried the trunk to the front door of number twelve, and after a short interval, the door was opened, and the luggage taken inside.

"I wonder who that is. It looks like someone is moving into the warehouse."

The door of the carriage now opened, and a familiar figure stepped out. It was Francis. There couldn't be too many other men in London who matched his description. Tall, broad-shouldered, and with a shock of white hair.

Intriguing. I wonder what he is up to.

She set her sewing aside and continued to watch the goings on at the dockside. Francis was far more interesting than stitching curtain hems. He went inside the warehouse but was back out in the roadway in less than a minute.

Poppy's heart gave a little skip as Francis made his way next door to her warehouse and knocked. No one answered the door.

"Oh. I am here," she muttered.

How foolish was she, sitting there waiting for someone to open her own door?

She rose to her feet, sighing with relief when Francis, who had turned away from the front of number fourteen, trained his gaze toward the *Empress Catherine*.

He waved. She waved.

His long legs ate up the distance from the road, across the pavilion space, and up the gangplank of Poppy's ship in no time.

"I saw you knocking on my door, and for a moment I couldn't understand why I didn't answer it," confessed a blushing Poppy. She giggled nervously at her own words.

He muddles my mind at times.

Francis laughed. "I have confidence that you are blessed with many skills but being in two places at the one time is beyond even you. Good morning, Captain Basden. May I come aboard?"

"Of course, you may, Mister Saunders."

Their banter was light, but it held an uncomfortable edge. Had he also been thinking of her and that almost kiss?

Shifting the swath of fabric, she had been sewing out of the way, Poppy pointed to the space on the wooden bench. "Have a seat."

Francis glanced at it, then shook his head. "I don't know if I should. Not after yesterday."

Poppy forced a smile to her lips. The lightness in her heart dimmed.

He regrets the almost kiss. I knew it.

There was nothing she could do about it. You couldn't make a person feel something that they didn't. Her non-existent romance with Jonathan had driven that message home. But unlike Jonathan, Poppy wanted Francis to be a part of her life. Even if they were just friends.

Friends wasn't a bad thing. It was good to have them. She didn't have anyone in London. Friendships weren't something she had managed to maintain. With moving countries and continents every few years, she was well versed in starting all over again.

"About yesterday. I don't know what it was, but nothing happened. Could we just leave it at that? Pretend we ate cake and drank coffee, and then said our goodbyes?" she said.

Francis pinched his lips together, and for a second, Poppy feared he was going to leave. His shoulders rose and fell as he sucked in a deep breath. "Let's do that. Well, at least for now. At some juncture, you are going to have to accept another one of my apologies."

Were they ever going to be able to move on from his constant sense of guilt over her? The seeds of worry were already planted in her brain. Francis wanted to be friends, but he didn't know how to be friends—or at least not with her.

Poppy nodded toward the gaily patterned fabric she had been hemming. "Do you like my new curtains?" Anything to change the subject.

"They are lovely. Are you going to put them up in the warehouse?" replied Francis.

"Yes. I want some more color inside. They will afford me a bit of privacy, especially around my sleeping quarters."

Perhaps mentioning that I sleep in the warehouse wasn't such a good idea.

While Francis didn't say anything about the slip-up, he did settle into a spot at the other end of the long, narrow bench. He was perched on the edge of the seat, his posture stiff.

"My sisters are both skilled with a needle and thread. For all her hot-headed temper and her tendency to be flighty, Eve has an eye for detail. The embroidery work she has done on the edge of my shirt cuffs is outstanding," he said.

He pulled the sleeve of his coat and jacket up, giving Poppy a glimpse of his white linen shirt. Her mouth opened as she took in the sight of a pale blue sailing ship sewn into the cuff next to the sleeve button. On the button itself was a clever representation of a whale.

I wish I could sew that beautifully.

"Your sister is very clever. I'm afraid my skills begin and end with large pieces of fabric. Usually sails. I can't embroider or make nice clothes, but my sails do last," she said.

"You don't make your own clothes?"

"No. Wherever Papa and I have travelled over the years, he has always found a local tailor or seamstress to make our clothes. I didn't learn to sew as a child."

Without a mother to teach her such domestic skills, Poppy had instead learned how to tie knots, trim sails, and navigate.

~

Poppy had grown up without a mother—that much was obvious—but with things between them still unsettled after yesterday, Francis didn't wish to impose by asking personal questions. He wanted to know more of her past, of where she had been before she stepped ashore and into his life.

She had seen places and people he would never know. If he trod carefully, behaved less like a heavy-footed clod, then she might come to trust him with the stories of her life. The ones that really mattered. The events and people which had come to shape and define the woman.

"I would love to hear some of your tales of the great wide world. I expect you have experienced things beyond those which have been written in the traditional travel guides," he said.

He could also admit to a peculiar degree of envy over the things she had done. His privileged upbringing afforded him comfort and security that few others had. Yet it also brought with it a life of expectation. Of adhering to social norms.

And until he had met Poppy, Francis had never questioned any of it. His sole aim had been to become a captain of business. To rise up and be celebrated by his family and peers.

So much of what he had always taken for granted, the path which had been clearly set for him, now chafed. The things that he considered bright opportunities, were nothing compared to the interesting life Poppy Basden had led.

Even his decision to temporarily move his things from home into the Saunders Shipping offices was something that a mere week or two ago he would never have considered as anything other than preposterous.

And yet he had done it. Packed up his travel trunk and left his perfectly good home in Dover Street in order to go and sleep in a warehouse. His major concession to comfort, the purchase of a bed and mattress. He knew that testing the chains that bound would take time, and a good night's sleep should never be treated with anything less than sacred regard.

I surely must be going mad. I am on the verge of getting everything I have ever wanted, and yet here I am . . .

Poppy folded up the curtain fabric and placed it in her lap. Francis avoided her gaze for a short time, sensing that she was going to ask him about the trunk. She must have seen it being taken down from the carriage. Her vantage spot on the deck of the *Empress Catherine* gave her a commanding view of the dockside.

"Who is moving into the warehouse?" she asked.

I knew it. She doesn't miss anything.

Francis sat up tall in his seat, his answer at the ready. "I am. My parents have gone to Scotland for Christmas and most of January, which means I am the only member of my family in residence at Dover Street. Considering the long days, I am working and the unsociable hour at which I return home, it makes sense for me to decamp here for a time."

He wasn't going to make mention of the mountain of work he would need to undertake on the new spice contract, or that he had several particular and delicate issues which would require immediate resolution as soon as the tender was announced—securing another ship being paramount among them.

Where I am going to find the money is another question.

"I thought it might be nice to let some more of the servants take time off over the festive season. Cooking meals and lighting the house fires for just one person does not make sense."

A footman would come every few days and collect Francis's dirty clothes, and they would be returned to him the following morning, freshly laundered and pressed. There were limits as to how far he was prepared to take this new warehouse living experience. Dirty garments were one step beyond his comfort.

Poppy rose from her seat and collected the curtains. She glanced up at the sky.

"It's getting late, and the wind will soon have its evening teeth. I am going to head back to my warehouse."

Francis got to his feet. He held out his arms. "Please let me carry those for you." When she shook her head, he stepped forward and took them from her. "I insist."

"Alright, but only if you agree to come and share supper with me later this evening. I've been cooking a stew in the Dutch oven since midday, so it should be ready soon."

"Are you pleased with the oven?" he asked.

"Oh yes, it is wonderful." Poppy beamed.

She was actually using his gift. A spark of joy lit Francis's heart.

I am falling for this woman.

He had never thought it would happen to him. Yet every moment he spent with Poppy; his feelings grew deeper. She was becoming his everything.

As he followed her down the gangplank, Francis prayed no one of his acquaintance could see him. The white-haired Viking, a hard man of business, carrying a set of pretty floral curtains. On his face was a happy grin.

How the mighty have fallen.

Chapter Thirty-Two

Poppy lit some lamps and candles as dusk settled and the warehouse grew dark. She set the table for two. Excitement danced in her belly. The precious cotton cloth she had purchased on a voyage to India the previous year was going to get its first public viewing. A hot iron carefully applied to the creases had resulted in a flawless surface.

I am finally going to have a guest for supper in my home.

Her attempts to convince herself that it was only the next-door neighbor coming to share a meal failed dismally. After Francis had carried the curtains back to the warehouse and given his promise that he would come to dine at eight, Poppy had spent the rest of the late afternoon dusting, sweeping, and cleaning every surface she could find.

It's a pity the curtains are not finished. They would have looked lovely.

She made a mental note to hurry up with her work tomorrow and have the window coverings hung before the end of the week.

If only her clothing situation could be so easily rectified. With Christmas fast approaching, no dressmaker of any worthwhile reputation was taking on new customers. They and their staff were far too busy completing existing orders.

The ready-made garments in the local drapery store were functional but plain. For her new life in London, Poppy wanted to wear the sort of gowns a lady of quality would consider acceptable. She would of course keep her old dresses for days when she had to check the lower decks of ships or do some spring cleaning.

In the new year, she would treat herself to a trip into the city. To finally purchase the bath oils, she hadn't had time to get. Buy some new books. And hopefully find a lady's seamstress who would welcome her as an ongoing client. But before then, she still had to win the spice contract.

Poppy smoothed the folds of her best skirt. To cover her light stays, she had chosen a short red silk jacket which finished at her hip. Her attire was not the latest of London fashion, but it was all she had.

I want to look like I belong here. Like London has always been my home.

After all those years of being denied the little things, like a pair of fine gloves or a lace shawl, she was eager to step into the world of fashion. Or at least have a taste of it.

I shall have some nice gowns, and a hat for Sunday best and trips into the city.

And a collection of fancy reticules. Poppy had promised herself that indulgence. She couldn't wait to be able to slip her gloved hand into her beaded purse to pay for her purchases when she was playing the grand lady on Jermyn Street.

None of it could make up for her lonely childhood. Nor for the no-nonsense and at times hard demeanor she had been forced to adopt in order to maintain control of her crew and ship. But this was her new life, one where she could finally discover the truth of herself. Where happiness might find her.

A gentle knock at the door roused her from her musings.

"He's here."

After one final check of her hair, Poppy took a deep breath, and opened the door. As Francis stepped into the light, he snatched her breath away.

"Good evening, Captain Basden," he said.

Francis was dressed in a fresh shirt and an elegant black jacket. Poppy's eyes took it all in, but her brain had turned to porridge at hearing his voice. It seemed lower than usual, and it sent heat to her most private of places.

It was a moment or two before her mind managed to scoop itself back into some semblance of rational thought. "Good evening, Mister Saunders. Please, do come in."

He crossed the threshold, and as he did, Francis produced a small box and handed it to Poppy. "This is for you."

The scent of lavender and lily of the valley filled her senses. A flustered Poppy stared at the package. "What is this?" she asked.

He leaned forward and whispered in her ear, "Something to go with your copper bath."

With trembling fingers, she opened the box. Inside were two jars of bath oil. The labels on the front read *Floris London*.

"Oh, my. How lovely. Francis. Thank you. This is such a wonderful gift."

Francis took the jars out of her hands while a stunned Poppy did her best to comprehend that he had once again brought her the perfect present. She followed him past the dividing wall and into the private space of the warehouse. He set the oils down on the occasional table next to the copper bath; his manner was so comfortable and easy; it was as if he did such a thing every day.

"And my offer to have the lads bring you water still stands. You only have to ask," he said.

Poppy's gaze lingered on the bath for a moment longer than it should. She had managed to use the tub for small strip washes so far but hadn't ventured to the point of trying it out as a full bath.

Her heart whispered, *"It's big enough for two."*

Indeed, it is.

From the folds of his coat, Francis magically produced a bottle of wine and Poppy laughed.

"You are the most excellent man I have ever met. When it comes to gifts, none can compare."

Francis held up the bottle. "You can thank my father for this one. I purloined it from his cellar. It is an excellent drop. He is a true Frenchman; he would never allow bad wine in his home."

"I don't have any nice glasses, but if you are happy to drink out of cups, I expect we shall manage. The food is ready. I can serve while you ease the cork out of the bottle." she replied.

"If that stew tastes as good as it smells, then I don't think we shall have any problems with drinking out of mugs. Besides, warehouse living demands concessions. It's all part of the experience."

Poppy collected two plates from the cupboard and set about dishing up the beef stew. She carried one bowl to the table, then went back for the second. To her private delight, Francis not only made quick work of the wine cork, but he sliced up the loaf of bread she had baked earlier in the morning. He cut the bread exactly how Poppy liked it. Thin, so that the salty butter could be savored.

Are these the little things that change your opinion of someone? That move emotions from friendship to more?

She was still trying to come to terms with that thought as she and Francis took their seats at the table. He offered a brief prayer of grace, after which he poured them both a generous mug of wine.

"To you, Captain Basden. May you have many happy days in London, and all of your dreams come true," he said, raising his cup.

Taking a sip of her wine, Poppy nodded her appreciation. How could she respond to those words? To what her heart was asking her to risk?

She handed him the small plate of butter. "Please help yourself."

The first mouthful of the meal had them both humming their appreciation. Poppy was quietly proud of herself. A pinch of salt and pepper added an hour ago had resulted in the best beef stew Poppy had ever cooked. The tripod legs of the pot had allowed her to maintain an even spread of the hot coals and cooking temperature over the day. The meat was tender and the vegetables perfect.

Francis set the spoon down in his now empty bowl and sighed. "That was delicious. Dare I say, almost as good as our cook's, and believe me, she is outstanding. I can't begin to tell you how many people have tried to steal her away from my family over the years."

That was high praise indeed. "You say that your father has a silver tongue, but I think you can hold your own when it comes to it," replied Poppy.

She dropped her gaze to her food as a sudden bout of shyness took hold. Light banter had never been her forte, whereas the Saunders men seemed to have a natural affinity with it.

Silence sat heavy in the cavernous space, broken only by the scrape of a knife on bread. A cautious glance had her taking in the sight of Francis wiping a slice of buttered bread across the bottom of his bowl. Not a drop of his stew was going to be left to go to waste.

"How are you going with your cinnamon bales? I've seen a few loads of them being loaded onto carts. Do you have many left?" he asked.

All thoughts of food and generous gifts came to a screeching halt in Poppy's brain. Francis was her guest. Her neighbor. He was also her rival bidder for the new spice contract.

His question sounded innocent enough, but Poppy's business instincts immediately took over. Tucking a curl of hair behind her ear, she fixed her best mask of indifference to her face.

I wish he didn't want to talk about business.

The spice bid sat, a dark, heavy secret between them. Poppy had no idea how good Francis was at playing at bluff. Her reading of him so far was that he struggled to keep his inner thoughts from appearing on his countenance. If she played this moment carefully, then hopefully the wine and a sated belly would be enough to dull his wits and keep him off-guard.

Trust wasn't something Poppy had ever been able to hold close to her heart. Too many disappointments. Too many broken, false hopes.

"I'm not sure how many we have left," she replied carefully. "Only a few. Most of the cargo was already spoken for before we sailed from Ceylon. Papa negotiated the contracts. I merely hauled the cinnamon bales for him."

You know the exact count and their value. But you won't let him know that.

She could play the dutiful daughter, one who was simply doing her father's bidding. No actress could handle the role as well as Poppy did.

Smiling and playing sweet were first-rate stalling tactics that she had mastered for whenever business negotiations were getting too tight. Few men dared question a woman who had turned on the feminine charm.

Francis pushed his bowl and empty plate away. "Well, just let me know if you ever need me to find a buyer for your spices. I have connections in London who I am sure would be happy to give you a fair price."

A horrible thought crept into Poppy's mind.

Is that why you are here? To talk business. Not just for my company?

Was there anyone in the world who didn't have an ulterior motive for spending time with her?

"That is a generous offer, thank you. But I can't accept it. You have already done so much for me." *Does he like me for me? Or is this just another way for him . . . oh.*

She pushed her growing fear to the back of her mind. If she granted it more space, she may not have been able to hold back the threatening tears of disappointment.

Change the subject. Talk about anything else.

"So, your parents have gone to Scotland for Christmas. Is that an annual tradition?" This was another successful tactic which she kept in her quiver—and one which usually worked on men. If the male of the species had one common fault, it was that they loved to talk about the things which mattered to them.

His brows knitted together for a moment. Poppy picked up her cup of wine and sipped the last of it. The bottle of wine was empty. The food was gone. And the fire was slowly dying down. Francis might soon be ready to call it a night.

And if he did, what would she think? Her heart and mind were locked in a battle over deciding whether him leaving was a good thing or not. Over what Poppy truly wanted from this man.

"Yes, my family travels to Strathmore Castle every Christmas. My Uncle Ewan is the Duke of Strathmore. I'm not sure if I ever told you that," he replied.

"Your father mentioned the connection. Do you get snow in Scotland?"

Francis smiled. "Yes, we get a lot of snow. Usually just after New Year's, or Hogmanay, as it's called in Scotland. It can lay quite deep in places."

Poppy hadn't ever seen real snow. The closest she'd come was the light dusting of flakes which fell in December in Tarragona, Spain. No sooner had it settled than the sea winds blew it away.

A yawn escaped her lips. It had been a long day, and the wine was heavier than the ones she normally drank.

Francis shifted in his seat. "I suppose it is getting late, and I am keeping you from your bed." He rose to his feet and gathered up the plates and dishes. "I should wash these before I leave."

"Please, you don't have to do that. I can do them."

"I insist." He was adamant. Polite, but firm. There was no point in her arguing.

I need him to go, but then again, I want him to stay. I am so conflicted.

Why did this all have to be so difficult?

"Alright, but I shall wash, and you can dry. It won't take us take long, and the Dutch oven can soak overnight," she said.

Within minutes, the supper dishes were washed, dried, and had been put back into the cupboard next to the table. As she worked, Poppy wrestled with the problem of what she was going to do about Francis—and especially, the demands her heart was making.

She was torn. On the one hand, she ached for them to become more than just friends. On the other, the needs of her family business meant she was compelled to keep things from him. To lie.

I just wish we could be honest with one another. Then I would know the truth and how he really feels about me.

Poppy took the tea towel from Francis and hung it over a rail near the fire to dry. Everything was clean and neat once more.

"Thank you for this evening, Francis; it was lovely to share supper with you. And thank you once again for your wonderful gifts. The Dutch oven and the bath oils. I don't know what I did to deserve them."

He turned and before she had time to react, he had taken hold of her hands. The air in the room changed in an instant. It crackled with the electricity of expectation.

Francis took a step forward and closed the gap between them. They were standing in almost the exact same spot where they had been the afternoon when the delivery boy had knocked at the door with the satchel of contracts.

There was no one to disturb them tonight.

Francis leaned over her. Poppy briefly closed her eyes as his fingers brushed her cheek. Her heart was beating hard in her chest. Drumming its demands.

"Poppy?" said Francis. It was the same question and tone he had used during their earlier encounter. She understood its meaning much more clearly now. Francis was asking for her permission. For the right to touch her.

Her eyes opened to take in the two deep pools of blue. They drew her in as Francis gazed down at her. This man had more power over her than any mortal man had the right to wield.

Yes, should be the last word on her mind. *Thank you and goodni*ght were the tried and tested sensible options. They had always kept her safe.

But alone.

She broke eye contact, unsure of herself. Her aching, desperate need for this man was unmistakable. If he asked, she would let him do whatever he wished.

The problem wasn't with Francis; it lay with her. Poppy was in a constant state of flux as to what to do.

The spice contract still lay unspoken between them. She really ought to pull back. To keep him at arm's length at least until the outcome of the tender. While she knew that Francis had submitted a bid, she was almost certain he didn't know she had. That before they became lovers, they were already rivals.

If his hopes for successfully taking over Saunders Shipping rested heavily on him securing that contract, by not revealing her own role, she was being duplicitous, betraying someone who considered her a friend. Someone who was offering her more.

What if I win the contract? What will he say?

He will be angry. No, he will be livid.

He was here with her now because he didn't know the truth. Allowing his kisses would be dishonest of her. She would be taking his affections by way of deceit.

This is wrong. Why does it have to feel so right?

If things did grow deeper between them, and Francis uncovered the truth of her bid for the spice tender, he may well come to regret his actions. To see himself as being taken for little more than a cuckold.

And where would that leave her? Back to where it all started. Living next door to a man who wanted her gone. The barrels and ropes were one thing—a three-year lucrative spice contract, something entirely different. Francis would become her sworn enemy.

I should tell him. Or if not, then step back and let my head overrule my heart.

Poppy was still wrestling with her conscience when Francis lowered his head and captured her mouth. With the warm sensation of his lips on hers, her heart signaled a cry of victory. Aching need overcame all sense of reason as she welcomed his embrace.

They were kissing. Reckless desire saw all caution tossed to the wind. Poppy gripped the front of Francis's jacket lapels tight; it would have taken a Caribbean hurricane to prize her off him. She was going to take everything he offered, and consequences be damned.

This is selfish. I should stop him. But I can't.

His tongue swept past her compliant lips, seizing, claiming. Everything he demanded of her; she gave up freely. His hand settled on the back of her neck, holding her to him. The touch of his strong fingers against her skin sent a shiver down her spine.

She groaned as his other hand skimmed over her waist and hips. When he cupped her bottom, drawing her flush against him, Poppy slipped her hands from Francis's coat and wrapped them as best as she could around his middle. The only way they could get any closer would be if they were naked. If they were making love.

Oh lord, what if he wants that?

Her bed was in the corner. It wouldn't take much for him to strip her naked and claim her body completely. To make her his forever.

No. Anything else, but not that. You have to resist the sweetest temptation.

It was like the ancient sirens were beckoning for her to sail into the dangerous shoals. To allow her ship to come to grief on hidden rocks. It would be so easy to heed the call. To give in to the overwhelming urge.

And then pay the heaviest of prices.

The apex at the top of her thighs pulsed with desire. Her

body wanted that which she had withheld from it for so long. Nothing could compare to the glory of feeling the heavy weight of a man on top of her for that sweet moment when he spread her legs wide and filled her empty soul.

His fingers settled on the ties of her short jacket, and Francis drew back from the kiss. "Poppy?"

Thank heavens. He is trying to show restraint. Unlike me. At least one of us has a hold on their sanity.

Hers was hanging on by a mere thread.

"Do you want me?" she whispered.

Francis nodded. "In every way that you are free and willing to give. Though I think that tonight, we should draw the line at knowing one another in the fullest sense. I don't think either of us is ready for that. At least not yet."

He really was the gift that kept on giving. Even as she knowingly, willingly lied to him, he was seeking to protect her. Making certain that she wouldn't be left regretting that final step.

Not yet.

Love, or whatever this was, should be simple. But it wasn't. Any choice came with a cost that was either paid now or in the future.

But if I say no, I may never get this chance again with him. And I want Francis.

Her heart was determined to have its way.

"Yes. Touch me. But you have to know that I am not one of your innocent misses of the *haute ton,* Francis. I am a woman who has given and taken pleasure when it was offered. That doesn't make me a whore; it just means I have lived."

He pulled on the ties at the front of her silk jacket. One by one, they loosened.

"I would never think of you as anything other than fascinating. Exotic. A woman who has seen beyond the skies of London. You have no idea how much of my day is spent thinking about you. Of how I imagine you standing naked before me while I go down on my knees and worship your body with my tongue."

Oh.

Her lust-filled imagination had already played that particular scene over and over again in her mind. The notion that Francis was thinking the same thing had her sucking in an unsteady breath.

Poppy drew apart the openings of her jacket and slipped her arms out. The garment fell to the floor. Her light stays followed in quick time.

When Francis lifted an amused eyebrow, she smiled up at him. "The sea requires many skills of the sailor; the fast handling of clothing is but one of them. Should I keep going, or do you wish to assist?"

"Please do continue. I am enjoying this show immensely," he replied.

Gripping both sides of her blouse, Poppy lifted it over her head. All that remained between her and being naked to the night air was her light muslin shift.

Francis brushed his fingers over her right nipple, and it immediately peaked. Poppy bit gently on her bottom lip as he rolled his thumb and forefinger around the hardened bud and applied the perfect amount of exquisite pressure.

He bent his head and took her nipple into his mouth, sucking through the light fabric as he did. The fact that she wasn't bare somehow made the sensation headier. A warm hand settled on Poppy's waist, holding her in place. It wasn't necessary; she had no intention of moving away.

His fingers at the top of her skirts were not idle long. A gentle tug and the material fell with a whoosh to the floor. Francis released her nipple from his attentions and stood upright. Taking her hand, he helped Poppy to step clear of her clothing.

When their gazes locked, he gave her a hopeful smile. "Are you still comfortable with how things are proceeding?" His voice was ragged, desperate. It was good to know he was as affected by this as Poppy.

"Yes."

Francis gripped the sides of Poppy's shift and lifted it over her head. She resisted the urge to cover any part of her naked body from his view. This was not the time for her to act coy.

His eyes raked hungrily over her body, and he licked his bottom lip. "Even better than I had imagined. Poppy, you are stunning. So beautiful." The desire in Francis's voice was unmistakable.

She forced away all thoughts of the lumps on her hips and her soft rounded belly. Of her dimpled thighs. If he thought she was beautiful, that was good enough for her.

He knelt before her. "I am going to kiss you with my tongue. Stoke and tease until you cannot bear it any longer. Let me taste your sweet essence. Then you will come for me, Poppy. I will take nothing less than your complete surrender."

The first touch of his mouth on her sex had Poppy spearing her fingers into his pale hair. She shuddered as he dragged the tip of his tongue up her length, finishing with a flurry around her pleasure bud as he reached the top. And then he did it again. Over and over. Her knees were ready to buckle from under her.

He licked, sucked, and delightfully nipped at her, taking her to the point where her whole body felt ready to explode. When he slipped his thumb deep into her wet heat and stroked her hard, it was all over. Poppy shattered with a cry. "Oh, Francis. Oh, god."

His skilled ministrations continued as she slowly came down from the high of her orgasm. It was several heady minutes before her lust-hazed mind finally cleared.

She released his hair from her grip and brushed a soft kiss

over his forehead, murmuring, "Thank you. That was magnificent."

He placed a warm kiss over her curls, then got to his feet. Wrapping his arms around her, he bent and captured Poppy's lips. His embrace was warm and reassuring.

"Hearing you climax was wonderful. I hope you will offer me the opportunity to experience it again," he said.

When Poppy reached for the front of his trousers, Francis placed his hand over hers. "I thought we had agreed not to go any further tonight. I don't want you to feel any sort of obligation. It was my pleasure to pleasure you, I was honored that you finally let me touch you. Your cry when you climaxed brought me to the verge of tears."

Poppy brushed his hand away and popped open the first of the buttons on the placket of Francis's trousers. There was more than one way to bring a man to his knees. Not all roads led to full sexual intercourse. "I want to pleasure you. Let me show you the sort of education I have at my disposal."

Her hand ran along the length of him. Teasing. When Francis gave a groan of approval, Poppy offered him her mouth. Her kiss was slow and deep. When she finally drew back, she smiled up at him. "I am going to give you another type of kiss now. One I think you will enjoy."

She dropped to her knees, grinning as a strained "Poppy, you wicked girl," reached her ears.

The final button of his trousers released his erection. It was as hard and long as Poppy had imagined. Francis was a big man in every regard.

You are a beautiful, impressive beast.

Wrapping her fingers firmly around the base of his shaft, she brushed her tongue over the head of his cock. From far above her head came a strained whisper. "Oh, Poppy. You will be the death of me. Don't stop."

He shuddered as she ran her tongue along the length of

him. His fingers gripped the top of her hair as she laid a flurry of little kisses on the underside of his cock just below the head. They didn't call that spot the Cape of Good Pleasure for nothing. Rounding it always had a man sending a prayer of thanks to the heavens.

Stroke by lick by deep suck, Poppy slowly took Francis to pieces. He let out a cry when she drew back on him, and it was all over. She had reduced him to a quivering, grateful, and thoroughly sated mess.

"Thank you. Oh, that was...beyond words. Thank you."

By the time they exchanged their last kiss and said their final goodbyes, it was well after midnight. The past hour or so had seen them share the sort of sexual pleasures Poppy had almost forgotten existed. When Francis had lain her on the bed and stroked her hard and deep, bringing Poppy to a second shattering climax, she'd let the tears she had been holding at bay run freely down her cheeks.

As Poppy opened the door, Francis turned and drew her into his arms once more. "Any time you want me, I will be right next door."

Tonight, had been wonderful. Her body still thrummed with the afterglow of her release. The taste of his essence lingered on her lips.

She let him go with a promising smile, but before the door had even closed, fear and regret rushed right in. This was London. Her days of getting back on board her ship and waving at her lover as she departed were over. Those had been fleeting romances, ones without ties. Men she wouldn't have to see again.

"I will be right next door," she murmured, repeating Francis's words.

You must resist the insanity of paying him a visit late at night.

Tonight, had to be a one-time-only thing. A brief interlude between consenting adults. Leading him on was wrong.

There couldn't be any real relationship between them—not while the contract and all those lies hung between them.

But you could be so good together. If he is that skilled with his mouth, imagine what he could do . . .

No.

She had to stop thinking that way. What she had done tonight hadn't made things easier. All she had done was add another layer of complication to an already difficult situation.

The temptation had been powerful, forbidden fruit always was, and she had yielded to it.

Back in his warehouse, Francis had probably stripped off his clothes and was already laying naked on his bed, planning the next stage of his efforts to seduce her. Being who he was, he would want her next to him in that bed and for them to seal their bond— forever.

I should have said no. It was wrong to give into my desires. To create false hope.

She had no right to claim his heart. To steal a future based on a half-truth.

Tonight, they had shared a moment of beautiful intimacy. But it could only ever be that one time. Because if she did eventually win the contract, Francis would come to hate her for it. He would regret what they'd had tonight.

Their friendship would be over. In its place she would have long lonely nights of wishing 'what if.'

Poppy Basden had a lifetime's experience of those.

I have survived them before; I will do it again.

Francis was indeed thinking of how he could seduce Poppy. And how he could take matters with her further. Tonight, had been a revelation. And he wasn't just referencing the mind shattering sex.

He hadn't been surprised to discover she was experienced. This was a woman who, in her own words, had lived. While some narrow-minded men might find that a turnoff, Francis didn't see it as any sort of issue. Poppy's knowledge of sexual intimacy was a godsend in his book. Their marital bed would be a playground of heated desire.

She was a woman of the world, and if she was prepared to accept him and all his faults, he wanted to build a future with her.

This evening, they had shared precious moments, but even as they'd kissed and held one another, he'd sensed Poppy was holding something back. A part of her that she didn't feel ready to share with him.

I hope it's just her wanting time to get over her connection with Jonathan. To have a clear space in her mind. A break between the two men in her life.

She hadn't loved the blackguard, of that Francis was certain, but he could understand the need for her to maintain appearances. To avoid the sort of gossip that even the dockside workers were not immune from spreading.

He was resting, half undressed, on top of the bedclothes. His boots and shirt had been discarded. His trousers were unbuttoned, the placket laying open. His hand brushed over his hard length.

She was superb. The things she did with her lips and tongue . . . I thought I would weep and beg for mercy before the end.

His fingers wrapped around the head of his cock, and he gave a gentle tug. Closing his eyes, he settled into a rhythm of long, hard strokes.

This bed, where he currently slept alone, was big enough for two. And while the warehouse wasn't a home, for the next few weeks it could be the place where he created his future. Where Poppy slept in his arms. Where he loved, seduced, and wooed this wonderful girl.

"She is nothing like any other woman I have ever met, and that is what makes her so special. So unique."

The pace of his strokes increased and as his climax claimed him, Francis whispered into the dark, "I love you, Poppy. If you give me your heart, I will give you the world."

Chapter Thirty-Three

His parents might have been out of town, but Francis still had family members in London whom he could visit when he felt the need for company.

The morning after his night with Poppy, Francis had the need to speak to someone whom he could trust. Someone who might be able to offer him counsel. A confidant to hear his plans for the future and give him their blessing.

He should be talking to his brother Will, but the relative to whom he was closest was his cousin Gideon Kembal, the Marquis of Holwell.

The Mowbray House footman left Francis alone in the downstairs foyer while he went to fetch Gideon. As soon as the man departed, an unsettling silence descended over the empty space.

Mowbray House, in busy Berkeley Square, was never usually quiet. The Kembal family were effusive to the point of being outright rowdy. Francis had never known the place to be so still. It was as if someone had died.

Perhaps everyone is out for the day. Or maybe I am still getting used to not being around people.

The warehouse was remarkably quiet at night, with only the occasional loud singing from a group of drunken sailors on their way back to their ship to disturb the silence.

"Francis. Forgive me for having kept you waiting."

He turned, frowning as Gideon made his way down the stairs. Even the footfalls of his cousin's boots barely made a sound. The expression on Gideon's face was one of grave concern.

Sweet heavens, has someone actually died?

Gideon glanced over his shoulder at the footman who had followed him back downstairs. "Go talk to the kitchen, tell her that Mister Saunders and I shall take a light meal in the upstairs drawing room."

The footman hesitated. "Will my lord require several courses?"

Gideon waved him away with a disinterested, "I couldn't care less what we were served."

Francis, who had been hoping to share a private moment with his cousin and discuss Poppy, kept silent. Something was wrong. A terrible misfortune *had* befallen the family.

As the footman made his way down the servants' stairs to the lower kitchens, Gideon led Francis up to the next floor.

Once they were inside the drawing room, Gideon closed the door. He turned the key in the lock, then sighed. "I'm sorry; none of us have been in circulation about town of late. We are all obviously saddened to have missed cousin Maggie's wedding. But I'm afraid the Kembal family are not good company at this moment."

Francis placed a comforting hand on his cousin's shoulder. "What has happened?"

"It's Mama."

Oh, no. The Duchess of Mowbray and her daughter, Lady Augusta, were overdue to return from their long voyage to Italy. Had something terrible befallen his beloved Aunt Anne?

"She's not coming home."

His heart sank as he caught the gleam of tears in Gideon's eyes. Francis waited. Those words could mean several things.

"Papa received a letter informing him that neither Mama nor Augusta would be returning from Rome. My mother has left my father. She is going to file for a formal separation."

Francis swayed on his feet as the shock hit him. "I know this sounds unkind, but your parents are always rowing with each other. Perhaps this is just another of their arguments."

The Duke and Duchess of Mowbray had taken spousal discord to the highest level. From the day they had met, they had fought. If there had been a national competition for marital combat, they would be its reigning champions.

As a young boy, he had found their outrageous behavior frightening. It left him puzzled. His own parents didn't fight. The Kembal children, however, took it mostly in their stride. From an early age, Gideon had pressed upon him the fact that his parents' disagreements were simply a part of life. The existence of six children spoke to them having at least some moments of marital harmony.

"No, she has left him. Said he pushed her away one too many times."

"Oh, Gideon. I don't know what to say," replied Francis. What could he say? While there were socially acceptable ways to convey sympathy over a death or such loss, a marriage breakdown was something entirely different.

You didn't leave your spouse.

The *haute ton* frowned upon such things. *Till death do us part.* You may well loathe your other half, but you stayed put. For those unable to bear their spouse, it was acceptable to take a mistress or a discreet lover. You could be miserable at home while privately finding happiness in another's arms.

This wasn't, of course, how Francis viewed marriage. He wanted what his parents had. A love-match. A life partnership. It was one of the reasons he had been so set on not being pushed onto the marriage market by his eager mother. A hastily arranged union was not something he would ever consider for himself.

He had intended to raise the subject of Poppy Basden with his cousin, of his plans to woo her, but all thoughts of his own situation were quickly swept aside at hearing the news of his aunt and uncle.

If the Duchess of Mowbray had officially abandoned her marriage, then it was little wonder that Mowbray House was cloaked in a shroud of quiet despair.

Gideon sniffed back his tears and took in a deep breath. "That makes two of us who have no idea what to say. It's bad enough that it is my mother, but can you imagine the state Papa is in? This is his wife. His duchess. He hasn't left their private rooms since the letter arrived. I was the one who had to send the note to Lord and Lady Denford to explain our non-attendance at the wedding."

Francis would have liked nothing more than to offer Gideon a comforting hug, but from the stilted way his cousin spoke, he doubted it would be welcomed. This news had clearly rocked the Kembal family to its core.

"So, your father didn't know your mother wasn't coming back? I mean, not until he received the letter?" asked Francis.

Gideon shot a hard glare in his direction. "Of course not. Well . . ." He sighed once more. "Not that he told any of us children. Victoria and Coco were planning a lovely surprise party for when Mama and G returned. My sisters keep asking what went wrong and if any of it was their fault."

Francis's gaze landed on the nearby sideboard and the full whisky decanter which sat on top of it. Stepping around Gideon, he made his way over and swiftly poured them both a generous glass.

"Here. Get this down you," he said, handing Gideon a drink.

Francis shuddered as his cousin polished the whisky off in quick time. Memories of his drunken state after the wedding came flooding back, and he set his untouched glass down.

Gideon slowly shook his head. "Can you imagine the almighty scandal that this is going to create when it gets out? And it will get out. We have already been receiving cards this week from ladies expecting to be calling on Mama. The lie that she is still recovering at our country estate from the lengthy sea voyage will only hold for a short while longer. After that . . ."

He threw up his hands, then slammed the empty glass down on the sideboard. It shattered into pieces, but Gideon didn't even appear to notice, such was his distress. "She has no idea what this will do to our family. And if she does, then my mother is a wicked, uncaring woman."

Francis moved forward and pulled Gideon into his embrace. He gently patted the top of his cousin's head as Gideon finally gave up all pretense of decorum and wept openly.

This really was a disaster. What were they going to do?

Having stayed on the edge of his own family dramas during the past year, he was ill equipped to deal with the situation. The only thing he did know was that it wasn't doing Gideon any good lingering in the house, constantly worrying over the situation.

"How about you go and get changed. I will speak to the head butler and arrange some mounts. A solid morning of riding in Hyde Park will at least get some fresh air into your lungs."

Gideon drew back, wiping away his tears. "Thank you. I do need to get out of the house, if only to clear my mind for a little while."

For the first time since they had left London, Francis wished Adelaide and Charles were back home. His mother would know what had to be done in order to handle the looming scandal. The family would of course close ranks, but it was the women to whom the task of protecting reputations and future marriage prospects would fall.

"I think when we return, you and I should pen a letter to Aunt Caroline. I can send it via a fast courier to Scotland," said Francis.

As the most senior-ranking female of the family, the Duchess of Strathmore had to be informed of this unfortunate situation with all due haste. Hopefully, between her, Lady Adelaide, and Lady Mary, a plan to counter the cruel tongues of the *ton* could be formulated.

The family name and reputation had to be preserved.

Gideon nodded. "Yes, we need to address things sooner rather than later. My father is barely able to get out of bed each day, so it seems that the task of saving this family is going to fall to me. Thank you, Francis, your visit was exactly what I needed."

Chapter Thirty-Four

"An excellent choice. I am sure your friend will be delighted with such a handsome gift."

Francis gave an awkward "thank you." He wasn't one for spending time in shops, let alone going on his own to buy a tea set, but if he was going to press ahead with winning over Poppy, it was going to take more than a functional Dutch oven.

He had to convince her that his intentions were not only honorable, but that she truly had captured his heart. A delicate set of cups and saucers seemed a good way to make Poppy happy. It hadn't passed his notice that she had a soft spot for pretty items. For the things that made a place a home.

I want her to understand that I see her. That I acknowledge the hard life she has lived. She deserves all the comforts that have been denied to her for so long.

There was one particular thing that did give him pause. As he lay staring up at the brick wall of the warehouse late last night, it had occurred to Francis that his efforts to woo

Poppy could be interpreted as a sly trick on his part to secure space in her warehouse.

Having recently arrived at the docks, Poppy wouldn't of course know about the spice tender. But when he won the bid, which would be soon, he wouldn't be able to hide it from her. She would realize he needed more storage space.

That might take some explaining. She will be suspicious of my real motives.

And if they did marry, Poppy would be obliged to help her husband manage the spice contract. To possibly offer up space in her warehouse. That could well become a sore point between them.

I still need that space, but I want her more.

The issue of what he was going to do regarding Basden Line Shipping was far from settled. Before he could put a ring on Poppy Basden's finger, they were going to have to sit down and negotiate.

She needs to understand the truth of things.

After his visit to Mowbray House, Francis had ventured to Wedgwood, the china shop in York Street. He was determined to find something special for Poppy. The Dutch oven had won her favor, and he hoped to capitalize on that with this latest offering. To begin sweetening the way to the difficult conversation that would come with his marriage proposal.

While the assistant wrapped the teapot, cups, and saucers, placing them in an elegant wooden box, Francis did his best to keep his head down. The last thing he needed was for someone he knew to recognize him. A gentleman didn't venture into these sorts of places on his own. Not unless he had a special lady in mind.

His life was already problematic enough without anyone starting a rumor about him having found a potential bride. And while Adelaide might well be hundreds of miles away in

Scotland, he was under no illusion that that sort of gossip, once life was breathed into it, would find its way to Strathmore Castle and his mother with lightning speed.

If the courier bearing his and Gideon's letter could make the journey by coach in a matter of days, then so could a rumor.

Francis wanted to be in control of his life. Of his future. This wasn't just a shipping contract; this was the woman he would spend the rest of his life with. This was about the future mother of his children. He had to get this right.

If there was one thing of which he was certain, it was that his marriage would not follow the example of the warring Duke and Duchess of Mowbray. He would look to his own parents for the cues as to how to manage a lifelong partnership.

With the gift box in his hands, Francis marched straight out the front door of the shop and into the waiting Saunders town carriage. He was keen to move matters forward with Poppy.

If things went well, then he might even have a fiancée by the time the spice tender announcement was made. That would make for a red-letter day in his life.

I am sure Poppy will understand about the contract. I just need to be honest with her.

At the dock, he alighted from the coach and made a beeline for warehouse number fourteen. He rapped loudly on the front door, then waited. The sound of the key being turned in the lock had Francis taking a deep breath.

He could admit to being nervous. His plans to succeed as a businessman had been well thought through, and the numbers tallied and double checked. But when it came to the task of wooing the fairer sex, he was all at sea.

~

It had been less than a day since she had last seen him, yet it seemed like an eternity. The long, empty years Poppy had endured while constantly waiting for her father didn't measure up to the worry she had felt during the past hours.

She was prepared to admit that the sight of the white-haired Francis standing at her door was a bit of a mixed blessing. He was here. She just wasn't entirely sure if that was a good thing.

Her gaze flittered to the box in his hands, and her heart sank. More gifts. Here she was, keeping things from him while he was blindly pressing ahead with what could only be assumed as the prelude to an offer of marriage.

Francis pushed the box toward her. "For you."

Poppy shook her head. Her guilty conscious stopped her from accepting the gift. This was becoming impossible.

"Please, Francis, you don't have to buy me things. You have been more than generous already. I cannot accept your present. We are friends; and you don't have to buy friends."

He took a step forward. Poppy met his gaze. The worry on his face matched that in her heart.

What am I going to do when you discover the truth about the spice bid? How will I ever be able to look into your beautiful blue eyes knowing that they will be full of hate for me?

She couldn't ever see a way where Francis would find it in his heart to forgive her for lying to him. She had finally found the man of her dreams, but because of their business conflict, she could never have him.

He touched a warm hand to her cheek and a shiver raced down her back.

"I know we are friends, but after last night, you have to know we are much more than that. Don't let your recent experience with an uncaring male jade your opinion of my sex. I will never fail you like Jonathan did."

No, but I might fail you.

She hadn't ever cared if Jonathan was sincere, but with Francis, his sincerity meant everything. And that knowledge only served to make matters worse.

He offered her the box once more, and she reluctantly took it. Knowing Francis, he wasn't going to leave until he had handed the gift over.

With a sigh, Poppy stepped back, clearing the way for Francis to enter the warehouse. She followed as he made his way toward the private apartment on the ground floor. There was a definite familiarity about the way he moved in the space. A comfort in his easy gait. It spoke of a man determined to have his say and for her to listen.

They both came to a halt beside the fireplace. As his gaze lingered on the rug, Poppy imagined Francis recalling their encounter. Of her on her knees before him. Her memories were ones of regret mixed with a deep desire to offer to pleasure him once more with her mouth.

He took the wooden box from her hands and placed it on a nearby table, then turned to her. "I should have stayed and talked things over with you, Poppy. I didn't make love to you last night because I wanted to protect you. I told myself it was to allow you the opportunity to say no. But I was wrong. It was selfish of me to touch you and then to make you feel an obligation to do what you did. A man has no right to take the liberties I took with you—not unless he is prepared to offer more."

She ran her fingers over the ring on her right hand, avoiding his gaze. "You didn't take anything that I wasn't prepared to give. There should be no sense of obligation on your part. We were two consenting adults. We are friends, and I hope for us to remain that way."

The sigh of relief she had hoped to hear never came. Instead, a low growl of anger came from the clearly frustrated Francis. "Why won't you look at me, Poppy? Do I repulse you that much? I thought we were building a connection. The path to something more. Whatever I have done to push you away, please tell me what I can do to fix it."

~

She was holding back. And considering her luck with unreliable men, Francis could understand Poppy's position. First her father, and then Jonathan had abandoned her. But he wasn't either of them.

"I know we got off on the wrong foot. I lashed out at you because in my mind, I had already taken over this warehouse. It took a little time to accept the truth but believe me when I say I am over all that. All I want now is you."

"You don't even know me. And I barely know you. We have shared the occasional morning coffee, and you came to my home for supper. That's not exactly the sort of thing one risks their whole future over," she replied.

Francis placed a finger under Poppy's chin and gently lifted her face. "You are forgetting that I have seen you naked, and you came twice last night—once on my tongue, and the second time as I stroked you with my fingers. Let us not forget what you did to me with your mouth. I know a little more about you, Poppy Basden, than one would in a usual relationship between mere acquaintances."

She held his gaze. Quiet defiance shone in her hazel eyes. "That was just sex. And I would thank you not to raise the subject of last night again."

Ah. Now he understood. She was afraid that their connection was something sordid. A bond that had to be kept secret.

Francis wasn't having any of that. Poppy might well be thinking nothing would come of their encounter, but his mind was already made up.

"You cannot expect me to forget what happened between

us. It was magnificent, and I fully intend that we shall engage in such activities again very soon. But yes, I think we should address the issue of learning more about one another. You have met my father. Now I want you to meet the other members of my family who are still in town. Will you please come to supper with me tonight at Will and Hattie's home in Newport Street?" If he'd had a glove, he would have tossed it to the floor in front of her. The challenge had been thrown down. "And I won't take no for an answer."

Why hadn't he thought of this before? The only experience she had of him was at the London Docks. If she met some other members of his family, people he genuinely cared about, Poppy might come to view him as less of an ogre. And more husband material.

An evening spent at a private residence could be just the thing he needed in order to set their relationship, their future, on a steadier path. If things went well tonight, then he would raise the subject of the spice contract and also his wish for them to marry.

"This is not a good idea. I do not know how to behave in polite society. I have never been to a ball or a formal dinner. Francis, I haven't the foggiest notion as to how to conduct myself," she replied, throwing up her hands.

Francis caught a hold of Poppy's raised hands. Her protests gave him comfort. She wasn't saying no; she was just unsure what to do. Her life might have been spent on the high sea, but his had been lived exclusively within the *haute ton*. He would make sure she was able to navigate her way safely through society.

"Just be yourself. This will be a supper with only the four of us. Hattie works with the poor and disadvantaged at a church in the slum of St. Giles. My sister-in-law doesn't stand on ceremony—in fact, she positively hates it. Like you, Hattie is a practical woman, so I think the two of you will get along well."

When her brows knitted together tightly, a hopeful Francis reached down, rubbed his thumb over the worry line, and said, "I promise I will keep you safe. Please, come and have supper with my family. If at any time you feel uncomfortable, you just have to say you have an urgent business matter to attend to and we can leave."

Her shoulders sagged as she let out a resigned sigh. "Alright. But just as long as you understand that I don't own any fine gowns, nor do I have much capacity for small talk. If anyone starts to talk about needlework or the latest Paris fashions, I won't have a clue what to say."

He leaned in and placed a soft kiss on her lips. "I promise we will steer the conversation firmly away from delicate feminine subjects. I am sure you have plenty of interesting stories which you can share. All of them will be far more riveting than needlework. I shall come for you at eight o'clock tonight."

His heart danced a happy beat as he took in her hazel eyes, and she grinned up at him. "Are you ever going to take no from me, Mister Saunders?"

"No. Now, come. I want you to open your present."

The sooner Poppy did that, the quicker Francis could send word to Will and Hattie that they were having guests for supper this evening.

Chapter Thirty-Five

The encounter with Francis had been a mistake. A glorious one. But still an error of judgment on her part.

After a good day of chastising herself, Poppy had come to the decision that keeping her distance from the white-haired god of temptation was the wisest course of action. With only a week or so left before the winner of the spice tender was announced, that shouldn't be too difficult a task. They were both busy, and she had a ship on which she could hide.

All her plans to avoid him now lay in tatters. She was going to supper with members of his family.

What expectations will that create in their minds?

Poppy couldn't imagine that Francis regularly invited young women to dine with him, let alone meet his family.

She checked her hair in the mirror. An hour of brushing had seen the last tangle successfully defeated. It shone in the light from the lamp which hung on the wall of her sleeping quarters.

Her deft fingers and ribbons had her hair swept up into a simple bun, with whispers of blonde left free to kiss either side of her face. It was the best style—the only style—she had ever been able to successfully manage on dry land. On board the ship, she usually stuffed her hat down over a messy bun and got on with her work.

A glance at her simple charcoal wool gown revealed no specks of dust. Poppy had gone with plain and simple for her look this evening. Anything else might well stamp her as a fashion failure.

At her throat sat the black pearl necklace her father had given her on the occasion of her twentieth birthday. Poppy touched a finger to the long strand.

The pearls were meant to represent mystery, independence, and strength. She loved the necklace but had thought it odd that it had taken George Basden all those years to give her such a gift.

Papa, I was already possessed with both independence and strength long before you gave me this necklace. I had to be in order to survive.

As for the mystery? She hadn't quite figured out that part. Perhaps it was just the mystery of life, something of which few people were ever truly gained an understanding. Or it might have been simply a case of her never knowing who her father really was. George was the greatest mystery in her life.

Picking up her green cashmere shawl, she took one last deep breath and addressed her reflection. "You can do this. Get through this evening. Don't offend anyone."

As the days drew closer to the official tender announcement, so did her anxiety.

"I forgot to ask the clerk if the announcement was going to just be in the gazette or if it would be a public one, where all the bidders are expected to stand around and hear the result."

A wave of nervous nausea settled uncomfortably in her stomach. She couldn't imagine being part of such a gathering and having to deal with a shocked Francis if she was the successful bid. Not in front of all those people.

It almost made her wish she didn't win.

Don't be foolish. You want that contract just as much as he does.

"Why did I agree to this supper it was . . ."

A knock at the door interrupted her moment of self-doubt. It could only be one person at this hour. Francis.

"Come on, Poppy; you have stared down a raging Atlantic storm. You can survive an hour or so at his brother's house"

She was still sucking in deep gulps of air when she finally made it to the door.

Newport Street was a twenty-minute carriage ride from the London Docks. For Poppy, it felt more like twenty hours. She had agreed to this occasion, leaving herself with no other option than to go through with it. To endure the evening.

I want to be with Francis, but it's so hard when I know I am not being honest with him.

Whenever he was near, Poppy found it increasingly difficult to deny him anything.

From the moment she'd opened the door to him, Francis had been in full gentleman mode. Polite. Attentive. He'd even made small talk about the area of London where Will and Hattie lived.

Poppy's nerves could barely stand it. She was going to someone's home. A place where she would no doubt be judged on her social skills, or lack thereof.

I was a fool to think I could mix in polite society.

"My brother and his wife live close to Drury Lane. The theatre district has many wonderful establishments for entertainment. Opera. Drama. And of course, all the popular plays. Do you like the theatre, Poppy?"

The conversation only served to heighten her discomfort. She was a sailor. What did she know about the theatre and plays? Absolutely nothing.

Francis reached across the carriage and placed his gloved hand over hers. "Poppy?"

He is wearing gloves. The only gloves I own are thick leather ones for handling the ropes. Why did I agree to come tonight?

"I don't know. I haven't ever been to the theatre," she replied.

Poppy had been to plenty of religious festivals in Ceylon and India—colorful and noisy celebrations for various deities, which often went on for days. In her younger years, travelling through various foreign cities, she had also taken part in the days of religious observance of the Catholic church. She doubted any of those they were the same as sitting through a play.

"I've lived a different life from someone like you, Francis. London is your home, but to me it is a strange city. I have come to accept that it will take some time for me to feel comfortable here."

"I promise I shall take you to see some plays and musical performances. You strike me as someone who would enjoy them. If not, I am sure we will be able to find other things to delight you," offered Francis.

Poppy glanced down at her simple gown. All this talk of going out in society only served to reinforce her concerns over her insufficient attire. "Do you think your sister-in-law might be able to recommend me to a modiste? I would like to have some new gowns made up. Being unaccustomed to the city, I don't know any good dressmakers," said Poppy.

Francis gave her hand a gentle, reassuring squeeze. "Anything you need, you just have to ask. If I don't know where to find something in London, I can guarantee you I know someone who does."

The carriage turned off the main thoroughfare and Francis gave her an encouraging smile. "This is Newport Street; we are almost there."

To Poppy's relief, instead of Sir William and Lady Harriet Saunders's home being a grand, imposing residence, it was a simple brown townhouse hidden from the street by a high brick wall. Inside the downstairs foyer, they were greeted by Will and his heavily pregnant wife, Hattie.

"It's lovely to meet you," said Hattie.

Poppy caught the hint of an unfinished sentence. What had Francis told these people about her? Or was it more that they were shocked he was actually bringing a woman to dine with his family?

She had a sneaking suspicion that she was the first female Francis had introduced to his family. The air was thick with the scent of familial expectation.

"Will Saunders. Welcome to our home," said Will.

Poppy licked her dry lips. "How should I address you? Is it my lord, or just Sir William?"

Her experience with titles and the gentle folk of London was nonexistent, but she was keen to make a good impression. The last thing she wanted was to embarrass Francis.

Will chuckled. "I was knighted very recently, so I am still coming to terms with the whole 'Sir William' thing. To my family and friends, I am and shall always be just Will."

Francis leaned in to Poppy. "He means you can call him Will."

Poppy pretended not to catch the look which passed between the two brothers. Will's raised eyebrow echoed her same thoughts.

What does Francis, think is between us? And how soon is he planning to declare himself?

Her mouth went dry simply thinking about what she would do if Francis spoke his heart.

Will offered his wife his arm, and they headed for the main staircase. Francis did the same, and he and Poppy followed their hosts.

They were ushered into an elegant dining room on the next floor of the house. A fine table with stunning chairs had been set for supper. Poppy bit her bottom lip. The house might be of a simple construct, but the furniture spoke of expensive elegance.

"Will collects antiques," said Francis, pulling out a chair for her.

The plush cushion of the dining chair had Poppy wishing she, too, had the money to collect such comfortable pieces.

Hattie lowered herself into the chair next to hers. "Oh, it is so good to sit down. My poor feet. I am exhausted."

"I did say you should have taken a nap before our guests arrived," said Will. His words might have been a gentle rebuke, but the love which shone in Will Saunders's eyes spoke of a man deeply enamored with his wife.

While the attending footman filled glasses with wine, the men set to talking about business. Poppy was tempted to join the conversation. There was safety in familiar topics. But even with her limited social experience, she knew not to exclude the other lady present.

She turned to Hattie. "I promise we won't keep you from your bed too late this evening. I wasn't aware of your delicate condition."

Hattie sipped at her wine. "Don't worry. If I become fatigued, I shall say goodnight. In anticipation of the arrival of this baby, I have learned to protect my sleep. But enough about me—I understand you are a ship's captain. That must be interesting. And a lot of hard work."

Poppy had been anticipating this sort of question. When people asked about her life on the sea, they were always fascinated by her response. Having been in Francis's company, she had gained an appreciation as to how she could be seen as a bit of an interesting oddity by London society.

"Yes, I own several ships, and I captained the *Empress Catherine* on the voyage from Ceylon to England. It can be tough at times being the only woman on board, but it's been my life for such a long time. It's all I know," she replied.

When the first course of their supper arrived, and was placed in front of her, Poppy was relieved to see that it was a simple vegetable broth. It came accompanied by freshly baked bread and salted butter.

She had heard rumors of extravagant meals where it was expected that diners would know how to manage all manner of spoons, knifes, and specialty forks. To see soup served with only a standard spoon on the table next to her bowl took the sharp edge off her nerves.

Hattie leaned forward as best as her pregnant belly allowed. "Are you looking forward to celebrating Christmas in London? We will be attending the mass at St. Paul's on Christmas Eve; you are most welcome to join us. That is, if Francis is happy to bring you."

Poppy could of course make her own way to church, but it was becoming very clear to her that the Saunders family already viewed her and Francis as a couple.

What did you expect?

"I don't know. I haven't been to a church mass in a very long time. The last was when I lived in Spain, and that was a Catholic service."

Francis set his spoon down and turned to her. "When exactly did you live in Spain?"

The word live wasn't exactly how she would have described it. Her father had abandoned her in Spain. It had taken everything for Poppy just to survive. George had dropped her off at the front gates of a nunnery in Tarragona when she was thirteen, and it had been a long and difficult two years before she saw her father again. The nuns had been kind, but they hadn't quite known what to do with the strange English girl.

She didn't want to rehash that time with other people. And not with virtual strangers. They might well have their firm ideas as to where her relationship with Francis was likely headed, but Poppy knew better. Between now and the dream of a fancy church wedding stood the specter of the spice tender.

"I lived in Spain for two years when I was a young girl. I have lived in many places. Ceylon was only the latest. Before that I was in various cities in India, the Caribbean, and ports along the Mediterranean. I've even spent time in Africa."

Hattie's eyes lit up. "Where abouts in Africa have you been? Have you ever sailed to Freetown, in the colony of Sierra Leone?"

Poppy nodded. "I have been to many places in Africa, and yes, I've called in at the port of Freetown. Though to be honest, it's somewhere that I avoid stopping at if possible. Outside of the colony, it is still thick jungle, and the local tribes are regularly at war with one another."

Will and Hattie exchanged an odd look. Will opened his mouth, but Hattie held up her hand. "When were you last there?"

Why is she so interested in Sierra Leone?

"About six weeks ago. We stopped for fresh water and food on the journey up the west coast. But we were only in port for as long as it took to replenish our supplies, and most of the crew stayed on board ship. Freetown is not a particularly safe place. Why do you ask?"

Hattie's hands were settled on the table, but she held them together tightly. Francis's sister-in-law seemed a little too interested in the far-flung colony of Sierra Leone. Poppy was surprised she had even heard of the place.

"I ask because my parents are missionaries. They have gone to Freetown to minister to the local people," said Hattie.

Oh.

There were tears glistening in her eyes. "I was hoping perhaps you might have seen the new church they were building. Or even met my mother or father."

This is exactly the reason why I shouldn't have come. I speak too plainly for these people.

"I am sorry, Hattie; I didn't mean to upset you. I'm not used to keeping my thoughts to myself. Freetown is a fine place. I am sure your parents will do well there." Her words sounded as hollow as they felt.

Hattie pulled her hands away and rose stiffly from the table. Will got to his feet. "Are you alright?" he asked.

She gave him an unconvincing nod. "Yes, just a little tired. I might go and lay down for a moment in the sitting room. I shall join you again when the next course arrives. Excuse me."

As Hattie departed the room, an embarrassed Poppy silently stared at her hands resting in her lap. She wished she was anywhere but there.

The damage had been done. She had been too honest with her captain's review of the colony. But Freetown was a tough place, and Poppy certainly wouldn't have wanted to be a missionary in the heat of West Africa.

"I am so sorry. I had no idea," she said.

Will sighed. "Don't blame yourself. Hattie and her parents knew what Sierra Leone was like before they sailed. It was a choice. A calling they felt they had to answer."

But Hattie was here in London, and her family were a long way away. Poppy pushed back from her chair. "Let me go and talk to her."

Across the hall she found Hattie in the sitting room. She was seated on the edge of a plush sofa, wiping at her face with a lady's handkerchief. Tears were pouring down her cheeks. Poppy quietly closed the door behind her and hurried to Hattie's side.

"I am so, so sorry Hattie. I didn't mean to cause you distress."

"It's alright. I should have told you about my parents. In my silly mind, I imagined that you had met my parents and seen the new church they were building. It's probably just guilt on my part."

"Guilt?"

'I was meant to go with them, but I changed my mind and jumped ship in Gibraltar. Climbed to the end of the gang-plank and leapt into the middle of the harbor."

Poppy stared at Hattie in disbelief. This young woman had taken her life into her own hands and dropped over the side of a ship. "You are a brave woman to have attempted such a perilous endeavor. It's not something I would have ever considered doing."

Hattie patted her baby belly. "That's where I met Will. He saw me fall and swam out to save me."

"I can't believe you survived the drop. I've seen plenty of sailors go over the side, but quite a few of them got sucked under the ship and they drowned. You must have been desperate."

"I was. When you are fleeing an arranged marriage to a man you hate while headed to an unknown future, you will do things you thought impossible. I can imagine you might have had to face that sort of choice more than I have in your life," replied Hattie.

Poppy had made many life-or-death decisions during her years as a captain. But those had always been with the welfare of her crew paramount in her mind. Coming to London had been the first time she had done something purely for herself.

"I am sorry to have upset you." She couldn't think of

anything else to say. Her honesty had already caused her hostess distress.

Hattie dried the rest of her tears and offered her a sad smile. "It's not your fault. Give me a few minutes to compose myself. I shall join you back in the dining room shortly."

A reluctant Poppy left the sitting room and headed back across the hall. She was a few feet from the open door when voices halted her progress.

"What is happening with the spice tender? Have you heard anything?" asked Will.

Francis cleared his throat. "No, I haven't, which is a bit of a concern. I know they said the winning bid would find out in early January, but I expected to have heard something by now."

"Is there anyone else who is a serious contender for the contract?"

"I know three of the other four bidders, and if they keep to their usual high pricing, they won't have a chance. I'm not sure who the fifth one is, as the superintendent's office is determined to keep the names of all the bidding parties secret until the winner is announced. That's most unusual."

"Why?"

"Because it is standard practice to announce that you are putting in a bid, it keeps things above board and helps to stop price fixing. People don't trust those who aren't open about their intentions. In my opinion it's underhanded and deceitful. Trust me, when I do discover the identity of the fifth bidder, I shall make it my business to ensure that they are not allowed to enter bids for any more contracts. Not until they are prepared to play by the rules."

Poppy put a hand to her face, fighting back tears. This was the clearest indication she'd had so far as to what Francis would think of her bidding for the contract. Of how he would view her keeping it a secret from him.

By keeping her bid out of the public eye, she had innocently broken some invisible rule, one likely set by the men who ran the shipping companies around the docks. It didn't matter that she was an outsider and therefore not privy to such matters. As far as Francis was concerned, by not revealing her bid, she was guilty of dishonesty. He would see that she was punished for her transgression.

As a horrid realization gripped her, Poppy's breath grew unsteady.

Yes, but he hasn't mentioned his bid to me. Or are the rules applied differently to newcomers? And females?

"What about the warehouse? Papa said you were keen to secure the warehouse next door. Isn't that the one which Poppy owns? Have you approached her about leasing some of the space or were you waiting until after you were married?" said Will.

Poppy moved closer, shifting to one side of the door in order to stay out of sight but still be able to hear what Francis had to say. The spice tender was one thing, but she was keen to hear his private thoughts regarding her.

"I'm not sure about Poppy or what sort of future she and I may have, but I was thinking . . ."

She missed the rest of Francis's words as footsteps on the landing caught her attention. She glanced to her right and all hope fled.

The Saunders's butler was approaching, carrying a tray. On it sat the next course of their meal.

Her eavesdropping was at an untimely end.

Blast. I wanted to know what he had to say about me.

With the arrival of the food, Hattie would soon return. And Poppy, too, would have to resume her seat at the table. A seat which placed her right across from Francis. The man who would soon come to dislike her — possibly even hate her once he discovered the truth of her bid.

Hurt. Embarrassment. Anger. All these fiery emotions tangled with one another as her heart and mind fought to control her rising panic.

I need to leave, and now.

She couldn't possibly face Francis.

It took a moment for her feet to start moving, but as soon as Poppy had taken a few steps, they quickly gathered speed. She passed the butler and made for the stairs.

"Please tell Mister Saunders that I had to leave." Her hand reached for the bannister rail as she began her descent. "And could you please offer my sincere apologies to Sir William and Lady Harriet? I wish I could stay."

Poppy was down the stairs and out the front door at a fast clip. She was running by the time she made it to the end of Newport Street and into the main thoroughfare of Saint Martin's Lane. There, she flagged down a hack.

"London Docks. The main entrance please," she said.

She hadn't any money on her person, but fortunately there were enough coins at the warehouse to cover the cost of the ride. All that mattered was making her escape.

The heavens opened as the carriage pulled back into the street. Heavy rain began to lash against the window. "Thank god I managed to hail a ride. A minute or two later and I would have been drenched."

Her head rested against the leather uprights of the seat and Poppy momentarily closed her eyes. Tonight, had been a disaster. She hated herself for making sweet Hattie Saunders cry. Now the poor girl likely thought her beloved parents were living in hell on earth.

"You just had to go and embellish your old, jaded opinion of Freetown, didn't you?" she muttered.

If she ever got to speak to Hattie again, Poppy would set her right on Sierra Leone. On the progress the settlement had made over the past seventeen years since it had burned down, and how people were flocking to the colony.

Would Hattie believe me? Not after what I said.

Francis's sister-in-law would think her a liar. And so would Francis once he discovered her deception.

They will all hate me.

The carriage made slow progress across London. The rain was now a full-blown storm. The wind was accompanied with the odd bright flash of lightning. The driver up on top, who was bearing the brunt of the weather, sang a steady chorus of foul oaths.

Poppy couldn't blame the man. She had said more than her own fair share of curses while up on deck during a tempest.

When they reached the London Docks and the hack pulled up out the front of number fourteen, Poppy braced herself. "One. Two." On the count of three, she flung open the door, and dashed into the warehouse. She returned a few minutes later with a handful of coins and a handsome tip.

As she turned to head back inside, desperate to escape the maelstrom, her gaze landed on the flower pots. The pretty petunias were taking a heavy beating. One of the other pots which had only been delivered late yesterday was laying on its side, with its herbs and soil spilled out onto the roadway.

My flowers and herbs. Oh no.

The rain was coming in sideways, and the freezing-cold water soaked her woolen gown. Much as she wished to save her plants, Poppy knew better than to risk getting a chill.

She closed the door behind her. First thing tomorrow morning, she would come out to survey the damage, pick up the pieces, and decide which plants she would have to replace.

Her hand was halfway to the door, about to turn the key,

when it suddenly swung open. The door crashed against the wall as the towering form of Francis stormed inside. He paused for a moment, then with one almighty blow, he slammed the door shut.

It shouldn't be possible for an iron door to rattle on its hinges, but it did. A loud boom reverberated off the brick walls. Poppy flinched.

"You just walked out on supper! On my family. On me! Now explain yourself, Poppy," he demanded.

She was wet. Humiliated. And his accusatory demands made her blood boil. "I left because according to you, Mister High and Mighty, I am a liar and untrustworthy," Poppy bit back.

"What?"

His brows were knitted tightly together in obvious confusion. He likely thought she had gone mad. "You are not making sense. Is your sudden disappearance to do with what you said about Sierra Leone? If it is, I can assure you that Hattie is fine. She has no illusions that it is a challenging place. There was no need for you to flee like a bandit into the night. You didn't even have the good grace to say goodbye."

A tinge of red framed Poppy's gaze. Her rage now matched his. "Well, of course I didn't have the good grace to say goodnight. According to your dictates, I am a lying, deceitful person. So why would I bother with the niceties of manners?"

She turned and marched purposefully over to a nearby low bench. On it sat the beautifully boxed tea set which Francis had given to her. Poppy picked it up, hesitated for just a moment, then swiftly returned to where Francis stood.

She pressed it into his stomach, forcing him to take a hold. "Take it and leave. I shall clean the Dutch oven and have it delivered to you in the morning, along with the bath oils."

Francis attempted to hand the box back, but Poppy stepped away.

"Get out. And take your gentlemanly rules of conduct with you."

He set the box down and sighed. "I'm sorry I lost my temper. But you just disappeared, without a word. I was so embarrassed. Please, Poppy, what is going on?"

She wiped away an unwelcome tear of frustration. "The spice tender. The fifth bidder for the contract."

Francis slowly nodded, and as Poppy glared at him, a look of understanding appeared on his face. It quickly turned to one of dismay. "You are the fifth bidder? But how?"

"The tender closed the day I arrived. I saw the notice on the wall of the superintendent's office when I went to collect the keys for the warehouse. I worked all night on the proposal and made the deadline with a few minutes to spare."

His eyes narrowed on her, and Poppy was certain she could smell the tart scent of suspicion as it oozed from Francis's pores.

"You lied to me," he said.

She shook her head, annoyed but not the least surprised that he would take this tack. Blame her for his problems.

And to think that I thought you might be more than just the sum of your polished accent and fine clothes.

"Not at the outset. I hadn't even met you when I submitted my bid. If you would have a care as to recall certain facts, you would remember that our first encounter was when you decided to dump your barrels and ropes at my front door."

"But you lied to me."

"And at what point did you ever mention the spice contract to me?" Poppy stepped forward and stabbed her finger into Francis's chest. He didn't budge an inch. "You throw your so-called business rules around to suit yourself. I wasn't undermining you or lying when I pitched for the contract."

Tears rolled freely down her cheeks. A mixture of anger and hurt gripped her heart.

"And what about the warehouse? At what point, were you going to mention that you intended to marry me so you could get your hands on this warehouse? Oh, sorry. Was that too forward of me?"

Francis's lips moved, but nothing came out.

It was time to end the evening. To bring an end to this farce.

Poppy clenched her fists. "I won't apologize for the tender bid. As you are wont to say, Mister Saunders, this is purely business. Nothing more. The only thing I am sorry for, is that I crossed a line with you, one which I knew I shouldn't have done. All I can say is that I am grateful things didn't progress any further."

"Poppy," he whispered.

"I shall send a note to Will and Hattie apologizing for this evening. They don't deserve to be caught up in the middle of a business battle. Because business is all that you and I have left."

He drew closer, and despite her best efforts, Poppy couldn't look away. The hurt and disbelief in Francis's eyes tore at her soul. Whatever hope either of them had held at the start of tonight lay in ashes on the floor.

"I want you to leave, Francis. The only thing I will ask of you is that you respect the rule of English law. If you attempt to undermine my business in any way, I shall lodge legal proceedings against you personally and the Saunders Shipping Company." She bent and picked up the tea set, handing it to him once more. "Good night."

"You can't give a friend back the gift they gave you," he protested.

"Well then, you shouldn't have a problem. We are not friends; we were barely past the point of cordial acquaintances. Anything else which transpired between us I have already noted was purely an error of judgement on my part. And a misunderstanding on yours. I intend to forget about it. I suggest you do the same."

Poppy opened the door and motioned for Francis to leave. He hesitated, but to her relief, he went without a word, taking the box with him. She closed the door behind him, turned the key in the lock, and went to find some dry clothes.

She had been a fool, and the price she was going to pay was a familiar one. She was once more alone.

Chapter Thirty-Six

For the longest time, Francis simply stood in the swirling tempest staring at the closed door of warehouse number fourteen. He didn't notice the rain, only stirring when he was thoroughly soaked through and a shiver rain down his spine.

Passing the planter boxes, he stopped to set one which had fallen over to rights, scooping the dirt back into the pot and placing it safely against the wall. It was only a few yards to his own front door, but his footsteps were slow and labored. Rain dripped off the ends of his hair and into his eyes.

The only way he could be any more drenched was if he had gone and leapt into the water.

Somehow, he managed to make it inside number twelve, where he set the tea set down. He stared at it for a moment, still unsure how it had come to be back in his possession.

We are not friends.

How could Poppy say such a thing? Did she have any idea as to how he felt about her?

"No, of course she doesn't. And you didn't help things by accusing her of lying."

But she had lied to him. Kept her bid for the spice contract a closely guarded secret.

What else has she kept from me?

He went in search of a bottle of whisky, needing something to take the edge off his anger and disappointment. When he had left his brother's house, Francis had been furious. Instead of talking to him and resolving any misunderstandings, Poppy had simply fled into the night. He had never been so embarrassed in all his life.

But storming into her home hadn't been the wisest course of action. It had only served to further inflame the situation.

You came to her door full of sound and fury. Of course, she fought back.

He was tempted to go back next door and confront Poppy once more. But she had demanded that he leave. And if he had learned anything from his short time with her, it was that when Poppy wanted to be left alone, you didn't fight her.

It had all gone so horribly wrong.

The first glass of whisky took the chill off his bones, but as Francis reached for a second, he stopped himself. He wasn't going to add to his troubles by drinking himself into a stupor. When he spoke to Poppy again, and he was determined that he would, it would be with a clear head.

Dropping his sodden jacket onto a chair, he reached for his cravat.

"Bloody hell," he muttered. Damp linen was nigh on impossible to handle. It took a good five minutes for him to finally work the knots of his neck cloth free. Shirt, boots, and trousers soon followed.

He would kill for a hot bath.

The familiar vision of a naked Poppy in her tub dropped into his mind, and Francis quietly swore. He had imagined it so many times, he had convinced himself it was real. After tonight, he feared he may well have lost any chance that he may have ever had of sharing her bath. Of sharing her life.

Francis rubbed himself dry with a towel, then put on fresh clothes. Outside, the storm continued unabated. Poppy was just a few short yards away, but in the dark and the rain, it seemed like she was on the other side of the ocean.

He stoked the fire, bringing the embers back to life. His big, comfortable bed beckoned, but the chance of getting sleep appeared all too remote. Emotions swirled in his brain.

Seated in a chair, Francis stared into the flames. He wished that his father was still in London. For the first time in a long time, he was in grave need of Charles's counsel.

Like a schoolboy destined to keep repeating the same mistake, he had once more erred. Assumed that things were set in stone when in truth they were not.

He had accused Poppy of lying to him when he had been guilty of the same crime. The warehouse wasn't his, and neither was she.

His hands scrubbed over his face, and he let out a tired sigh. "What will I do if she does win the contract? No. You fool. That is not what is important. Sod the contract. It doesn't matter which of us wins it."

Not even business was worth him losing Poppy over. Nothing was.

I'll talk to her in the morning. A night apart will give us both a chance to calm down.

First thing tomorrow he would go, cap in hand, and apologize. Then, when she was ready to talk, Poppy and he would have an adult conversation about the tender and their future.

His eyelids grew heavy, and they fluttered closed. Francis woke a few minutes later with a start. "I must be more tired than I realized."

There was no point in fighting sleep, and if his mind was

well rested, then hopefully tomorrow he might be able to think more clearly. Settled thoughts would help to stop emotions from taking over. A rational conversation and considered outcomes were the best thing for them both.

"What was it that Jane Austen wrote? Ah, yes. Angry people are not always wise," he muttered.

It was a hard lesson he was still finding hard to digest; his temper was often his own worst enemy. But if he was going to make headway with Poppy, it was something he had to get under control.

He climbed into bed and settled beneath the thick blankets. The mattress was soft and comfortable—the best that money could buy. Until tonight, Francis had always appreciated the generously sized cushion. Now it just seemed empty.

His bed lacked the soft, warm body of a woman. But not just any woman—the bright and chirpy Poppy was the only female he wanted sleeping beside him.

She was angry tonight, her behavior so unlike her normal ray-of-sunshine self. And it was all his fault. He had hurt her, and in doing so, had wiped the smile from her face.

Little wonder she has such trust issues when it comes to men. Males are constantly failing her. I might think I am better than him, but the truth is when it comes to Poppy, I am just as bad as Jonathan.

As his eyes closed once again, Francis made a vow. Whatever it took tomorrow to make Poppy happy, he would do it.

I need to see her smile again.

When the dawn came, Francis dressed and made his way out the front door of number twelve. He stopped by the planter boxes and checked on the flowers and herbs. They appeared to have survived the night and were mostly intact. The pansies looked a little worse for wear, but he knew from his mother's gardening efforts that they were a particularly hardy flower. A little sunshine and some calm wind would see them return to full bloom.

He knocked on the door of number fourteen, then took a considered step back. He wouldn't be making the same mistake of barging in the door as he had done last night. Today was a day for laying down arms and offering to conduct peace talks.

The door of the warehouse remained shut fast. He knocked again, then crossed to the window and peered inside. There was no light to be seen, and from what he could make out, the fire had been extinguished.

A horrid sense of foreboding crept over him. Surely Poppy hadn't gone back out into the storm last night. It had been raining cats and dogs until the early hours of the morning.

He knocked one last time. "I will come back later. We need to talk," he called through the keyhole.

Francis turned, making ready to head next door. He would write a short note, then come back and slip it under the door. *She must have gone to the early market at Spitalfields.*

His gaze flitted over the water, and the first rays of sunlight as they danced across its surface. The light ran all the way from the edge of the wharf out into the middle of the docks.

"Oh, no," he muttered, as the chill of understanding sunk into his bones.

The *Empress Catherine* was gone.

Chapter Thirty-Seven

It hadn't taken much effort for Poppy to hastily put together a crew to sail the *Empress Catherine* back down the Thames and into the North Sea. Within half an hour of her setting foot inside the nearest dockside tavern, she had all the sailors she needed. There were always plenty of crew members looking for a couple of days' cash work while in port.

With no cargo to haul and an empty berth at the dockside ready and waiting for their return, it was an easy choice for men looking for drinking money.

The wind bit through Poppy's coat with wicked ease. It added just another layer to her already miserable mood. In her muddled state, she had only put on her land coat when she'd left the warehouse the previous morning. As the *Empress Catherine* made its way north, hugging the Suffolk coastline, she silently chastised herself.

How long have you been a sailor? And what sort of captain takes her heavy weather coat off the boat? And you forgot your sailing skirt and trousers. This full-length gown is a bloody nightmare.

A matter of weeks and she was already becoming a landlubber. Set in her ways of living on land. Just as she had always wanted.

But that particular dream had always been a fancy one, one she had imagined when she was well rugged up against the elements. It was not so endearing now as the mocking wind dug its icy fingers into her chilled skin.

And to top it off, there had been that horrid confrontation with Francis. She had said things she bitterly regretted. The hurt on his face haunted her. In the days since then, Poppy had barely slept.

Her lies had carved a deep ugly chasm between them—one she feared she may never be able to find a way across.

Yes, he was a stubborn, pig-headed male. Weren't they all? But she had been the one who had allowed matters to develop between them to a point where Francis had obviously concluded that she held no secrets.

He had made assumptions about her, dangerous ones, while she had kept to the safe course of not telling him anything which might eventually cause her pain.

It had always been this way when it came to men.

Her father had kept her at a distance, and it was only as she grew that Poppy came to realize why. He blamed her for his wife having died in childbirth. His daughter only served as a constant reminder of what he had lost.

And Jonathan. He was simply a means for George Basden to finally wash his hands of her. If she was someone's wife, she was no longer his problem.

Standing at the helm, Poppy adjusted her stance and gave the wheel of the *Empress Catherine* a small turn starboard.

Concentrate. Captain Basden. Stop allowing yourself to stay lost in your thoughts.

The deck of the ship was wet and slippery. And while the North Sea didn't have large waves this close in, they could still be quite choppy. The boat did a never-ending dance up and down, which forced Poppy to constantly check her steps.

Much as she tried to maintain her concentration, her mind kept flitting back to Francis.

He was a different story. Much as he frustrated her, Francis seemed to genuinely care. If she had treated Jonathan or her father as she had done the other night, neither of them would have given a damn.

They most certainly wouldn't have come crashing into the warehouse full of wrath.

She sighed. Francis cared about her. When he wasn't angry with her, he respected Poppy. If he didn't, he wouldn't have held back on their physical connection. And he most certainly wouldn't have invited her to supper with his family.

I don't know how to deal with someone who cares. A man who wants to protect me.

She didn't know much, but she knew that you didn't push those sorts of people away. That you didn't keep secrets from them.

And you most certainly didn't turn tail as soon as they had left your home, then race back out into a storm and offer a ship's crew an extra coin if they came right then and made your ship ready to leave port at first light. Only a coward did that.

I am Poppy Basden, and I am a coward. A ship-owning, North Sea-sailing coward.

A shudder ran through the *Empress Catherine,* and Poppy snapped out of her thoughts. She had been too busy thinking of Francis and had missed the obvious signs of shallow water. Only a raw, barely blooded captain would have made such a fundamental error.

"Bloody hell, we will be smelling the ground if we don't pull away. Another hand on the wheel," she bellowed.

One of the crewmen raced to stand alongside her at the

wheel. Her long, sodden skirts made it almost impossible to stand. The sailor grabbed hold and turned the wheel as Poppy helped to feed it up. The ship lurched to the right, and a second shudder rippled through the deck.

"She's coming 'round," he cried.

A wave crashed over the side of the ship, and Poppy's already unsteady feet were swept out from under her. She went down, her face repeatedly smashed by the bottom spokes as the wheel kept spinning.

Pain tore through her head, blinding her vision. Her sailor's vocabulary got a full workout as she struggled to her knees. Saltwater swirled around her skirts. She was drenched.

Wincing thought the agony, Poppy made herself a promise. This really was the last time she would captain a ship. Her heart and soul were no longer that of a sailor, and her body couldn't handle any more punishment. She would be a damned fool not to walk away.

Next time, she might not be so fortunate.

"Turn her around. Let's head back to London."

Chapter Thirty-Eight

L*ate Christmas Eve.*

Francis sent the staff of Saunders Shipping home early, wishing them all a merry Christmas and handing each man their five-pound annual bonus. Good clerical staff were hard to come by, and Charles had always stressed the need to show an appreciation for their efforts. Nothing said it better than a generous bonus at the end of the year.

With the office now empty, Francis packed away the ledgers and tidied the desks. It wasn't something he normally did, but anything that kept him busy was welcome. He had politely declined Will and Hattie's offer to join them for the midnight mass at St. Paul's Cathedral. He wasn't good company for anyone at the moment.

It had been almost three days since he had last seen Poppy—since their fight. Worry as to where she had gone sat constantly in the forefront of his mind. If he could just see her again, apologize for the way he had spoken to her and throw himself on her mercy.

I have to find a way forward with you. Where are you?

He continued to check the dockside on an almost hourly basis, searching for any sign of the *Empress Catherine,* but the ship was nowhere to be seen.

"This is her home; she wouldn't have left London just because we had an argument."

Poppy had made it clear that she was putting down roots, making plans to stay. She had to return.

Please come back.

After finishing up, Francis took a stroll outside. The early evening air helped to clear some of the fog in his brain.

This was a year where he had seen all of his siblings meet their respective soul mates. Will, Eve, and Caroline were all happily wed to good people.

But Francis had somehow managed to convince himself that he was immune to such a thing. That love simply wouldn't happen to him.

And yet love had found him. He was bound tight with its bonds of longing. Of wishful regret.

Passing the front of warehouse number fourteen, he glanced toward Poppy's flowers and herbs. He had made sure to check on them each day, even slipping out earlier to water the parsley.

His gaze went from the planter boxes to the light which shone through the ground-floor window. His heart skipped a beat. Someone was inside the warehouse.

He checked back to the water. The berth which the *Empress Catherine* normally occupied was still empty.

He turned back to the warehouse and checked the lights. Yes, someone was definitely inside.

Doing his best to calm his racing heart, Francis knocked on the door. Poppy might not have been home, but the person within might at least be able to give him an indication as to where she had gone. And, more importantly, when she might return.

The sound of shuffling feet reached his ears followed by the click of the key turning in the lock. As the door slowly opened, Francis had an unsettling thought. What was he going to say?

Good evening. I was wondering if you could tell me when Miss Basden is due back? Who am I? Oh, just the nosey neighbor from next door.

His mind was still scrambling to come up with something plausible to say when the person on the other side of the door stepped forward and into the early evening light.

It was Poppy. A badly injured Poppy.

His gaze took in her half-closed eye. The right side of her face was a sickening patchwork of black and blue bruises. And the huddled way that she held herself was the posture of someone who had just crawled up from the floor after a vicious beating.

A heavy stone settled in the pit of Francis's stomach. The sight which met his eyes was too unreal to be true. He took a tentative step forward, almost too afraid to speak, and whispered, "Poppy?"

"Hello."

"Wha . . . what happened to you?"

He stopped on the threshold, suddenly recalling their last encounter. Of her demand that he never darken her doorstep ever again. "Please, Poppy, let me help you. Let me come in." His voice was a concerned plea.

She beckoned him inside. "If you must, but hurry. I would rather not stand with the door open. The air is a little fresh, and I am embarrassed for people to see me like this."

Francis closed the door behind him, then reached for Poppy. To his bone-deep relief, she didn't push him away. He gently wrapped his arms around her, wrapping her up in his comforting embrace.

"What happened? Who is the blackguard that hurt you? I shall bring the authorities and the full force of the law down upon his head. He will rue the day he decided to attack you and take your boat."

Poppy's good eye met his, and she gave the barest shake of her head.

"No one took my boat. And as for this mess, it was an accident. You don't have to be my hero, Francis. I don't need one."

He brushed his hand gently over her bruised and battered face. "I would beg to differ." He offered her a soft smile and she sighed. Her small hands came to his chest, and she leaned into him. The relief that flooded him was overwhelming.

She is back with me. She is home.

Their lips met in a soft, tender kiss.

Chapter Thirty-Nine

When Poppy woke later than night, it was with a start. Her immediate attempt to sit upright was foiled by the large arm and leg which pinned her to the bed. The best she could manage was a gushing, "What?"

"It's alright. I am here," said a voice.

It was a familiar one. Comforting. Friendly. And thoroughly male.

Francis.

Of course. Now I remember.

Francis Saunders. Or rather, Saint Francis, if the way he had fussed over her was any indication.

Her explanation about the accident on board the *Empress Catherine* had been met with a good deal of clucking and a great amount of mothering. Heaven help her if she had actually been seriously injured.

He had been all for summoning a physician, finally relenting when she threatened to throw him out of her warehouse.

But I am not in my warehouse.

"How did we end up here?" she asked.

"My place had the fire going, and you didn't have any food. I thought you promised to give up complaining about me bringing you here." Francis shifted in the bed and released Poppy from his limb prison. She rolled over to face him.

Her snow-haired nurse was dressed in a white linen shirt, no cravat. He sported loose trousers, and no shoes or socks.

Fully dressed, he was a devilishly handsome man, but in this state of partial undress, Francis was breathtaking. Her fingers itched to touch his ruffled, sleep-mussed hair.

"What time is it?" she asked.

He nodded toward the clock on the wall. "A little after three in the morning. Merry Christmas, Poppy."

Christmas Day. When had that suddenly rushed up? The last day she could recall with any clear certainty was the twenty-second, the evening they had gone to supper with Hattie and Will.

Poppy flopped onto her back. She had made such a mess of things that night. And then she'd had the argument with Francis, when she had told him that they were not friends and that she hadn't ever wanted to see him again.

"Merry Christmas, Francis." She sucked in a deep breath. "And I am sorry."

Francis closed his eyes for a brief moment. "So am I."

Neither spoke again for a time. She was grateful that he didn't feel the need for them to rehash it all. They were both sorry for everything. And that was enough.

And her face still ached.

She reached across the bed, and finding his hand, threaded her fingers with his. Francis gave a gentle reassuring squeeze.

"What do you do for Christmas? I mean, here in London. I know you normally go to Scotland, but what will you do this year?" she asked.

"I would take you to a service at St Paul's cathedral later

this morning, but I don't think you should be out in public. You need to rest and recuperate. Your bruises are only going to get worse as the swelling goes down."

"You are right, though it is a pity. I haven't ever been to a Christmas Day church service. Maybe next year." Having lived much of her life in countries where Christianity was not practiced and also sailing on the high seas, the opportunity had simply never presented itself until now.

"Let's see how you are healed in a few days. I can always take you to a service on New Year's Eve. Will and Hattie will be going for sure."

Poppy let go of Francis's hand and rose to sit up in the bed. They had apologized to one another, and that was a good start. The kiss had been a tender act of atonement. But there were things which still remained broken between them. The issue of the spice contract was one. The other, his family.

She wasn't sure where to begin or even how to try to mend things.

"I didn't mean to lie to you about the tender. Or rather, I regret choosing not to tell you," she began.

The bed shifted on its frame as the hulk that was Francis moved and sat upright. "You had your reasons. And considering how I reacted when I found out, I would say that your concerns were well founded."

She lifted her head, and their gazes met. Poppy closed her good eye as Francis brushed his fingertips gently, almost reverently, over her bruised cheek.

"I thought the spice contract was the be all and end all of everything. The past few days have pulled my ill-conceived priorities into sharp relief. And I am willing to admit that I was single-minded in my desperate pursuit of beating everyone else. Of winning," said Francis.

His honesty humbled her. Poppy swallowed back the tears which threatened. She didn't want to cry; she wanted to talk.

To clear the air between them. "I didn't trust you. I let my initial impression of who you were, continue to guide me. Even after we became friends, I kept my distance."

"Are we friends? It was hard to hear you say that we weren't," he replied. The tremble in his voice tore at her soul.

"Yes, of course we are friends. I was angry with you that night. And I was embarrassed. Humiliated. I hurt Hattie, and then I overheard you and Will talking about things. How you thought that the secret bidder lacked honor."

She wiped at her tears, unable to hold them back as the emotion of that night came flooding back in. "And then you told him you didn't know what sort of future we might have. As soon as I heard that, I had to leave."

"I'm sorry you did. Because if you had stayed, you would have heard the rest."

She wasn't sure if she wanted to hear what else Francis had said that night. What other pain his words could inflict.

"I told Will I wanted to marry you. But that I wasn't sure how to go about it. I mean...how we would make things work between us. You are an independent woman, Poppy. Someone who has had to rely on herself for much of her life. But marriage is a partnership. I'm just not sure if that is what you want."

His words stung. They were honest, but the truth they held bit deep. Marriage was a union, two people working together and forging a future. United in purpose. Poppy had never had that sort of connection with anyone. She had no real experience of what a true partnership or marriage even looked like.

"Do you know what you want?" he asked.

She shrugged. The kind of union she had imagined she would have had with Jonathan had never been a partnership. They would have been two people at constant cross purposes. Both fighting for something they didn't understand.

"I don't know what I want. Can you accept that it is difficult for me to crave something which I have never known? I didn't have a family growing up. Your understanding of marriage has likely been formed by the couples you have had in your life. I've had no such thing. No guidance which I could draw upon."

A strong but gentle hand settled around her waist. Francis drew her closer. Poppy rested her good cheek on his chest, closing her eyes as he bent and placed a kiss on her forehead. "I know you probably think you don't have much of an idea, but would you be open to letting me share my knowledge of family life with you? To showing you what we could be if we decided to make a future together?"

He still wanted her. Poppy hadn't been expecting that. She had thought he was simply being kind. "What about the spice tender? You speak of us possibly sharing a future, but what will you do if I win the bid?" she asked.

He hummed softly to himself for a moment. A wry grin crept to Poppy's lips. She could just imagine Francis still thinking himself the odds-on favorite to win.

She pulled out of his embrace. "I know you think it impossible, but if I did win, it wouldn't be the first time I have beaten a man in a man's game. You have to take things seriously. We have no future if you cannot deal with me in business."

It was hard enough to negotiate contract terms at the best of times, but this was no ordinary haggling over conditions and profits. Any decision that they made would have lifelong repercussions. Marriage would take much of Poppy's power out of her direct control and place it in the hands of her husband.

"When is your father arriving? I mean, when is he really planning to come to England? Because if you win the bid, then we cannot marry until he is here. My wife can't be my main competitor."

Hard and clear facts followed by a question she had long been avoiding. The only positive was that Francis was thinking along the same lines as Poppy. Of the nuts and bolts—the practicalities of them being man and wife.

When it came to the subject of Francis, Poppy's private emotions toward him were a sticky hot mess of want and need. A lifetime of hoping that someone might come to care for her lay unfulfilled.

Don't get your hopes up. He cares for you—that is obvious. It's more than you thought you would ever have.

If he respected her, listened to what she had to say, she should be grateful. Respect began with telling one another the truth.

"I don't know when my father is coming. He said he would be sailing in June, which means he could be here next December. But when it comes to George Basden and his arrivals, he tends to disappoint," she said.

Departures were even more heartbreaking. How many mornings had she woken in a strange city only to find a note from her father informing her that he had sailed with the morning tide, and that he would be back soon? *Soon* could be weeks, months, and in the case of Spain, two years.

With that thought burning in her mind, Poppy climbed out of Francis's bed. Her right foot hit the floor, sending a protest of pain up her leg. "Ow," she cried.

Francis was at her side in an instant. "Where does it hurt? How about you get back to bed and rest?"

She waved him away. All this attention and fussing was so utterly foreign to Poppy. Sailing was a dangerous endeavor; bruises and aches were just a part of the sailor's life.

"Please, Francis, you are smothering me. I am fine. The

bruises will heal. You haven't seen half the scars I have on my lower torso as a result of trips and falls."

He let out a snort, and for a second, Poppy wasn't sure if it was in frustration or if it was in response to the mention of her body. Of the fact that he planned to see all of her naked at some point.

She didn't want to go back to bed. What she needed more than anything was a hot bath and to soak her tired muscles. "I'm going to go home and build up the fire. After I have warmed up some water, I am going to pour it into the copper tub and have a wash. I might even splash a drop or two of the bath oils you bought me."

Everything else—her father, the spice tender, and most especially, the subject of marriage—could wait. Poppy wanted hot water and then sleep.

Francis grabbed his coat and slipped his feet into a pair of gentleman's slippers. After that, he headed to the fire.

He retrieved the large fireside kettle and carried it over to her. As he set it down, Poppy frowned. "It's a bit late to be making tea, don't you think?"

"I am not making tea; I am bringing this kettle with us. It's full of hot water—perfect for your bath. And don't bother trying to say anything about my not coming to help. Until either your father arrives, or you and I are wed, you should consider yourself under my self-appointed personal protection."

She reached for his coat sleeve. "You seem a tad eager over my taking a bath, Mister Saunders. Have you been giving the prospect of seeing me naked while I soak in those special bath oils much considered thought?"

A bemused smile sat on his face. "More than I am prepared to admit." He nodded toward her coat and boots. "Now get dressed, young lady; it's raining outside. It might be a short walk to your front door, but I am not having you catch a cold. Come on."

She was three years older than him. Had captained her own ship and crew. But nothing was going to make Poppy Basden protest his command.

Especially not with the way Francis's stern words sent heat racing to her core.

"Yes, Mister Saunders," she replied.

He raised an eyebrow in her direction, but she caught the hint of a grin on his face. The idea of taking a bath suddenly took on a whole new meaning.

Chapter Forty

"There. That should be enough to let you have a bit of a soak," said Francis, emptying another pot of hot water into the tub.

As soon they had arrived at Poppy's warehouse, Francis had set to work. While Poppy undressed and slipped into her nightgown, her knight in shining armor made trips back and forth to the water pump in the laneway outside. Every pot and kettle he could muster was pressed into service. The fire was stoked and brought to life.

Within half an hour, the copper tub was half filled with warm water. When Francis gave the word, the fussed-over Poppy was allowed to pour some drops of bath oil in.

"You will need to take that off," he said, eyeing her nightgown. The hunger in his voice was unmistakable.

Please let it be for me.

She glanced at her attire, unsure of how to proceed. Did he want her to strip off while he retired to the front of the warehouse and allowed her some privacy? Or did he have other plans?

Please don't be a gentleman. I want you.

Francis came to stand before her, and a now familiar game began.

"Poppy?" he murmured.

"Yes," she replied without hesitation.

When he reached for her gown, she placed a hand on his chest. This was something she wanted to do. Had to do for herself.

"Don't be shocked when you see my scars. I have quite a collection." Arms crossed, she lifted the nightgown over her head and let it drop to the floor.

Francis took a step back, his gaze roaming over her body. He touched the long, red angry scar which ran from the top of her hip most of the way down her right thigh. "What happened here?"

Trust him to go for the biggest, nastiest mark on her body. "I slipped coming down from the crow's nest onboard one of our ships. Hit a sharp piece of the rigging as I fell. Fortunately, I managed to grab hold of one of the ropes, so I didn't smash into the deck. Nasty accident, which resulted in two weeks in bed and forty-six stitches."

"Oh, Poppy. They must have had to give you a gallon of rum to get those stitches into you."

She lay her hand over his where it rested on her old wound. "I was still in charge of the ship. I had to stay lucid. That was the neatest stitching I have ever done."

He let out a gasp. "You sewed your own wound?"

"Yes. Swore like a naval midshipman the whole time, but yes, I did. I wasn't prepared to trust anyone else to do the job. This was my life. And I was determined not to have the stitches come undone, or worse, become infected," she replied.

Poppy was proud of her scars. There were other ones and dark marks on her body; in time, she would tell Francis the story of them all. But the water would have long gone cold if she did that now.

He offered her his hand. "Come. Let's get you into the bath."

The moment the tips of her toes tapped the warm water, Poppy hummed with happiness. She had dreamed of this moment, relaxing in her own tub, in her own home, in front of a fireplace. The weight of the moment settled around her as the warm water caressed her skin. This was heavenly bliss. She could do this every day.

Hands gripping either side of the tub, she lowered herself in. Her sore and tired muscles protested as she touched the bottom and let go.

Francis knelt beside the bath, washcloth in hand. "Let me be your servant."

"How does that work? I mean, I have never had a servant. And I didn't think you employed them to wash you."

He leaned in and whispered in her ear, "How about I show you."

Poppy licked her lips as Francis's gaze settled on her breasts. Hunger blazed in his bright blue eyes. Desire for her. With the way he looked at her, she truly believed she was beautiful. That this man could love her. She nodded, swallowing deep as Francis sat back and stripped off his shirt.

Oh, yes.

"One of the things about being tall is that I have extremely long arms. Lay back, Poppy, and let me show you how much of a godsend that can be."

Resting her head on the end of the tub, Poppy closed her eyes. A shiver rippled down her spine at his first touch. His fingers brushed her already peaked nipple. When his thumb and forefinger gently squeezed the tight bud, the core of her sex tightened.

"Francis," she whispered.

Warm, tender lips captured her mouth. Poppy gave herself up to the kiss—to the gentle lure of the man who had captured her heart.

His fingers traced lightly over her breast, then continued on down over her stomach. Anticipation flared bright within her body. Burning need flamed a hunger only he could sate.

When his roaming hands reached the soft hair of her sex, he stopped. Poppy shifted her position, opening her legs wider. "Yes. Don't ask. Just take."

From beside her came the deep, wicked words. "I plan to give first, after which you can decide if I get to take."

Her back arched as he slipped his finger deep into her heat. His clever thumb circled around her pleasure nib. Every stroke had her whimpering with aching need.

Poppy had imagined this moment, pictured it in glorious detail. Nothing could compare to the reality of having a semi-naked Francis beside her, his hands creating wonderful mischief with her sex.

As heat built inside her, she stayed his hand. "I want to come, but not this way," she whispered.

"How?"

"I want you inside me."

When he didn't respond, she cracked open an eye. Deep blue pools of desire stared back at her. There was no sense of hesitation in them. The only words she could possibly use to describe what she was feeling were *humble gratitude.*

She was trusting him.

Francis knelt over her, capturing Poppy's mouth in a toe-curling kiss. His tongue delved deep, and she answered his siren's call.

Yes. Yes. Yes.

He drew back. "You need to know that if we become one tonight, it is forever. If we fight or disagree, there can be no getting on board a ship and leaving. My bed—our bed—is where we both sleep from now on."

Sex had never been this way before. There hadn't been the expectation of more. But Francis was being honest and clear with her, leaving no doubt as to what tonight meant for them and their future.

This moment should have been an easy one. And for many other women, that was what it would have been. He was offering her a life by his side.

Poppy wanted more. She was determined to have it. And if Francis couldn't or wouldn't then . . .

A line of worry appeared on his brow. "Don't you want me? Or is it that you don't think you could ever love me?"

Love.

A simple little word, yet so powerful.

She climbed to her feet. Sitting naked in the water had her feeling vulnerable. Francis wrapped his arm around her waist and lifted Poppy out of the tub, setting her onto the fireside rug.

Her lifelong problem had always been trusting men. Having them make promises with no intention of ever keeping them. Francis was asking for forever. What sort of promise was that?

He didn't let go. Instead, he pulled her hard against him. "I want your love. And I shall do whatever it takes to claim it. Poppy, there will never be another woman for me. You are it. The love of my life."

Her knees almost went from under her. He loved her. "Say it again. Please."

He nodded. "I love you, Poppy Basden. I shall have no other but you."

Francis. You are all I have ever dreamed that love could be.

"I love you, Francis. When I said I didn't need you to be

my hero, I lied. I've waited my entire life for you. Swear to me that you will never leave me alone."

"I swear. From this day forth, you and I are one."

Her heart swelled at his vow. For the first time in her life, she trusted a man to be there for her. That he would always be by her side.

I will never be alone again.

"Take me, Francis. Here. Now. Our forever begins tonight."

Poppy worked open the front of Francis's trousers, freeing his hardened erection. When it slapped against his stomach, he let out a groan of need. Taking him in hand, she stroked her fingers along his length. "This belongs to me now," she purred.

Yes. Use me, for your pleasure.

As Francis lifted her, Poppy wrapped her legs about his waist. Then slowly, carefully, he lowered her onto his cock. The sweet heat of her body welcomed him as he thrust up. For a moment they stood both breathing heavy.

"Bed?" he asked.

"Table. I want this raw and heated. We can sleep later."

It was a shuffling struggle to make it over to the table. Francis stopped every few steps to pump his cock inside Poppy as if they couldn't wait for even the short moment it would take to get there. She was a greedy girl. "More. Harder," were her words of encouragement.

When he finally got her to the table, he tumbled her onto her back. Poppy didn't let go. She might well have been bruised and sore, but she clearly knew what she wanted. He exulted in her heated desire.

"Now claim me. I want it hard and deep. I want you to

mark me with your kisses and bruise my hips with your thumbs."

Francis leaned over her. It took an almighty effort on his part to slow his long strokes. To make this first time last. "You are not the shy virginal wife I'd once thought I would be bedding."

She clutched at his arms. "I can play sweet if that's what you want." The wicked grin on her lips held a lifetime of promise.

He nipped at her earlobe.. "No. I want you wild. Windswept and carried on the storm. You, Poppy, will never be a placid wife in public. Why the devil should I want you to be anything but your fiery best when you are naked in my arms?"

He was done with talking. It was time to let his body speak for him. To show her how she set his blood aflame.

With hands either side of her hips, gripping tight, just as she wanted, Francis took Poppy in a frenzy of hard, deep thrusts. Pumping in and out. His soul burned bright as she urged him on. Demanding. "Yes. Oh god, Francis."

Her scream of completion had his heart almost fit to burst. The last of his control was torn away as he lay over her and ravished her body.

When he reached his own climax a few thrusts later, Francis's world stopped. He gazed down at Poppy utterly in awe of her. Being with this woman meant more than he could ever have imagined.

He collapsed on top of her, heart racing, chest heaving.

In the silence came Poppy's voice. She spoke the one word which touched his soul. "Forever."

Chapter Forty-One

Christmas might have closed the shops and seen servants given a day or two of leave, but the busy London Docks never ceased. A visitor at his warehouse on Boxing Day afternoon roused a sleepy Francis from his bed. "My empty bed," he quietly mumbled as he went to answer the door.

Poppy had sent him home a few hours earlier, citing her need to get some urgent paperwork completed. He had protested, but as soon as he'd stepped inside number twelve, he'd headed for his bed. Men might talk about wanting an insatiable woman, but the reality of it was exhausting.

I need a nice long nap.

Once he had his energy levels back, he would return to Poppy, heat up more water, and then join her in the tub. He was still mulling over the details of how he was going to get running water installed inside her warehouse as he unlocked the door and opened it.

Standing outside was one of the superintendent's clerks. He recognized the man from his regular trips to the nearby offices.

"Good afternoon, Mister Saunders. And a merry Christmas."

"Good afternoon, and a merry Christmas to you too. I'd thought the offices would be closed for at least a couple of days," replied Francis, blinking in the bright sun.

The clerk shook his head. "A very pleasant half-day holiday yesterday, but with another ten ships arriving today, it would be impossible to close the office up for any longer. But I am not here just to offer you my felicitations of the season. The superintendent is requesting your presence in his office at your earliest convenience. He will give you an update on the current state of the spice tender."

Francis's sleep-hazed mind cleared in an instant. This could be just the news he was hoping for—the initial chat where he would be promised the contract.

"Excellent. Tell the superintendent I shall see him shortly."

He closed the door, then with fisted hands, he punched the air with delight. All his hard work was about to come to fruition. "The spice contract will be mine. Yes! Wait until I tell Poppy . . ."

His arms dropped to his sides. If he won the tender, then that meant she had lost. Victory would come at the cost of seeing the woman he loved suffer defeat.

They had made a private commitment to one another last night. How they would manage publicly and in business was going to take some careful planning. Poppy deserved to share in his victory.

And she has the right to hear about the contract from me, in private.

Things really had changed for him. Only a short while ago, seeing his rival vanquished would have brought him nothing but joy. Falling in love with Poppy had shown him the truth of his failings.

He had come to realize that he could be a success in business, and it didn't have to come at the cost of losing his soul.

This was why she was a better person than him in so many ways. While he was only starting out on the voyage of self-discovery, she had learned to accept all sides of her personality. To understand her insecurities. With her love and support, he hoped in time to experience the same growth.

"I have to talk to her. She will be crushed by this news."

It had never occurred to Francis that victory could feel so hollow. The spice contract had at one time been the only thing he cared about. Poppy had reset his priorities. Put things back to the way they used to be, the way they should be.

She now came first in his life. The woman he loved always would.

Chapter Forty-Two

Poppy was headed out the door when Francis appeared in front of number twelve. She gave him a wave. "You look like you took a nap,"

As he drew closer, she caught the worried, apprehensive look on his face. Something wasn't right.

They met halfway between their respective warehouses. Francis nodded at Poppy's buttoned up coat. "Where are you off to, young lady? I thought you were going to stay out of sight until your bruises had healed."

He was so damn sexy when he tried to be strict with her.

I wonder how he is going to take the news about me being summoned to the superintendent's office.

"Sailors don't have the luxury of staying in their hammocks if they get hurt. I had fifteen stitches in my face when I helmed the *Empress Catherine* around the Cape of Good Hope two years ago."

Lifting her hair, she turned and revealed the thin line of a scar which sat behind her right ear—three inches of blood and pain caused by a loose flying jib. She hadn't shown Francis that scar before.

"Were you on your way back to me?" she asked, attempting to sidestep his question.

Francis reached down and took a hold of her hand. Poppy steeled herself. He must have heard that he didn't win the contract.

Managing his disappointment while stuffing down my own glee is going to be tough.

"I received a summons to attend the superintendent's office as soon as possible," he said.

He did what?

"So did I."

"What?"

"One of the clerks came to see me a few minutes ago. I was going to come and see you as soon as I returned." She hadn't wanted to speak to Francis before the meeting but had fully intended on heading straight to number twelve on her way home. They were committed to one another and there was not going to be any more lies or secrets between them. If she had won the contract, she wanted him to be the first to know.

Whichever of us wins, we are both victorious. And for that, I am glad.

"The man from the superintendent's office didn't mention you would also be attending, but then again, I don't expect that they know of our connection. I was on my way to see you now— before the meeting," said Francis.

Poppy silently accepted his gentle rebuke. The fact that Francis wasn't raising his voice or outright accusing her of lying to him was hopefully a sign of his emotional growth. Of acknowledging his role in keeping the peace in their relationship.

"Why don't we go together? If they have granted the tender to another bidder, then at least we can drown our sorrows as comrades in arms," replied Poppy.

He firmed his grip on her hand. "Let's do that. I will be surprised if they have given it to someone else. From what I understood, the other shipping agents were pricing their bids much higher."

Poppy knew these things were never set in stone. Until both parties had inked and sealed a contract, there was always room for change.

They began to walk the short distance from building number two toward the front entrance of London Docks and the main office. As they reached the front door, Poppy let go of Francis's hand and turned to him. "Whatever happens in the next few minutes, can we agree that we won't let it come between us? If one of us has been awarded the contract, the other has to accept the decision with good grace."

He paused for a time, nervously biting his bottom lip. She could imagine that for a man like Francis, failure wasn't something he was used to accepting or even experiencing. In his world, men took what they wanted and were treated like gods.

Discovering that he was in fact a mortal could be a painful lesson.

"Agreed. But we are going to have to have a frank and honest conversation about how to handle the spice deal going forward," he replied.

"Yes, we will. Neither of us wants to feel that they are sleeping with the enemy."

He stole a kiss. "Our love is more important."

Francis held the door open for Poppy, then followed her inside. His breathing was shallow and his head a little light by the time they were shown into the superintendent's office.

Memories of his previous humiliating visit to this place still burned in the back of his mind.

The superintendent rose from his chair, and looked from Francis, to Poppy, then back again.

"Ah, Captain Basden. Mister Saunders. How good of you to come. I wasn't expecting the two of you at the same time. I apologize if my office made a mistake with your appointment times. I can see you both separately," he said.

Francis and Poppy glanced at one another. Poppy gave him a gentle smile. "Mister Saunders and I are more than happy to have this meeting together. The outcome effects both of us."

The superintendent's brows knitted together, his lips forming into a small *O* as a look of realization appeared on his face. "Right, well, then shall we begin?"

Poppy took the seat to the right of Francis, and they waited patiently while the superintendent shuffled a few papers around on his desk. It was tempting to reach out to her once more, to hold her hand as they received the news of the tender, but when he glanced at her out of the corner of his eye, her gaze was fixed forward.

Captain Poppy Basden was sitting up straight in her chair, her business mask firmly in place. Francis's heart did a little dance at the sight. This was the woman who had rounded both the tips of Africa and South America in the teeth of a howling gale.

More importantly, she was the woman who had torn his indulgent self to pieces and remade him as a better man last night. As she lay naked beneath him on the table, all he could think was how bloody magnificent she was, and that she was his forever.

I am so proud of you.

The superintendent ceased his fidgeting and rested his hands on the desk.

"Now, this is not the usual way these things are done. The winner of the tender is normally notified before all the other bidders. But in this case, the other three bidders priced themselves out of the running from the outset, which left only two financially viable bids—the one from Saunders Shipping and the other from the Basden Line."

Francis resisted the temptation to shift in his seat. This was good news. So far, only he and Poppy were in the running.

The superintendent opened his desk drawer and took out a hip flask. He unscrewed the lid and helped himself to a generous swig. *He is steadying his nerves. This does not augur well.*

"So, to continue, I have spoken to the contracting party, and they reviewed both submissions with the result that neither of your companies have been awarded the contract."

"But . . ."

The superintendent held up a finger at Francis's protest. "The problem isn't with the bids, per se, but rather with the two of you."

What?

Poppy and Francis exchanged puzzled scowls.

"Captain Basden, I must say that your bid was excellent. Detailed and well costed. You have a suitable warehouse and a ship which can easily handle the size of the contract cargos. Where you fail is that you are new to London and lack suitable connections. There is also the issue of you . . ." He cleared his throat.

"Of me being female," said Poppy.

The superintendent nodded. "Some traders will not wish to deal with you. If your father were here, it might be a different story. But I cannot recommend your bid."

Fury simmered within Francis. Poppy's bid was being rejected simply because she was an outsider and a woman.

The two things I judged her over when she first arrived.

Francis barely had time to force his growing anger down before the superintendent turned his gaze toward him.

"As for you, Mister Saunders, again, a well thought out and costed bid. Though it lacks several pertinent things. The situation with regard to the warehouse storage is not ideal. You lack a suitable ship. And I have reservations about your ability to work with other traders. Again, if your father was still involved in the company, it might be a different proposition."

Does not play well with others.

The past few weeks without Charles had taught Francis a few hard lessons. Poppy had also been the most excellent of teachers when it came to the subject of Francis learning to accept others. To seek and find common ground.

It would appear, however, that those lessons had come a little too late to save the spice contract. In future, he would put them to good use.

"Thank you for your consideration," said Poppy.

She went to stand, but the superintendent waved his fingers down. "Don't be in such haste to go and lick your wounds, Captain Basden. I might have a solution to the problem if you are willing to listen."

Poppy resumed her seat.

"I was pleased to see that the two of you arrived together this afternoon. From what I hear, you have buried the hatchet and become good neighbors."

You could put it that way.

If they were not going to win the contract, the consolation prize had to be another afternoon naked in one another's arms followed by a splash in the copper tub. Francis was fast gaining an appreciation for a shared bath.

"The thing is, between the two of you, you actually have all the ingredients to manage this spice contract. You just need to find a way to work together."

Poppy shifted in her seat. "So, what are you proposing?"

"A joint bid—one which your companies can adhere to in both letter and spirit. I am going to give you two days to come up with either a new submission or a letter declining my offer."

The superintendent rose from his desk and began collecting his papers. "I shall bid you both a good day. Captain Basden. Mister Saunders."

Poppy was out of the office in quick time. Francis could barely keep up with her. She was taking three steps for every one of his long strides, but it was still a good thirty yards from the front of the superintendent's office before he finally caught up with her.

She brushed his hand away as he attempted to take a hold of it.

"Poppy, wait. I know you are disappointed. And what he said about you being unsuitable because you are a female wasn't fair, but we need to talk," he said.

"No. I won't wait. And if you think he is the first man to treat me that way because he thinks women are the weaker sex, you are more stubborn and naïve than I'd thought."

Naïve?

Francis stopped dead in his tracks. Poppy thought he was naïve. He knew he was stubborn, but she thought him a green boy.

Poppy kept walking. She was close to the front of her warehouse before a stunned Francis caught up with her once more.

"I had no idea you thought me a fool," he said.

She pulled her key out of her coat pocket and slipped it into the lock. The door swung open. Poppy stepped inside while a hurt Francis lingered on the doorstep.

"I did not say you were a fool, nor do I think that you cannot work with others. I said you were inexperienced. And you are. If you knew how to play the game, you would have got that contract, and they wouldn't have even opened my bid," said Poppy.

"And if you had been a man, I wouldn't have stood a chance."

She met his gaze, her expression one of steely determination. "Exactly."

He turned to head home, unsure of his next steps. A hand grabbed a hold of his coat sleeve. "Don't tell me you are giving up, Francis Saunders. What happened to the man who was going to rule all of London?"

"I think he might have just been shown that he is not the heir apparent. And according to the woman he loves, he is nothing more than a schoolboy."

Pulling firmly on his coat, Poppy towed Francis back toward her front door. Once they were inside, she kicked it closed.

"Now what are you going to do?" he asked.

"Not me—*we*. Remember, forever together? We are going to submit a joint bid and bloody well win. So, stop with the long face."

At her words, his mood lifted immediately. Francis wrapped his arm around Poppy, pulling her to him. "I'm sorry. My two-minute sulk is done and dusted; I promise. Thank you for indulging me."

Her fingers teased at the knot of his hastily tied cravat. "See? You are making progress. No more barrels or ropes being tossed about. And you are becoming aware of when you are pouting. Perhaps you might want to put your lips to better use, Mister Saunders, and kiss me."

They both might have been thrown by the loss of the tender bid, but as he claimed her mouth with his, Poppy sent a silent thank you to the heavens. Her anger and disappointment went into the kiss, into the fevered meeting of tongues and lips. When Francis grabbed a hold of her ass and drew her hard against him, she didn't resist.

They could try to take away her hopes of winning the spice contract, but nothing would stand in the way of her stamping her ownership on this man.

The kiss slowed, moving from a frenzy to a gentler embrace. Francis drew back, then proceeded to drop a thousand butterfly kisses over Poppy's face. Every one of them sent a spark to her heart. This wasn't a prelude to sex; it was the sweet entrée to love-making.

"Am I really that much of an ogre?" he asked.

Resting her hand over his heart, Poppy smiled up at Francis. "No. Though at times you can be a bit like a hungry Bengal tiger chasing after a herd of spotted deer. You send everyone scattering in all directions."

He wasn't an evil man; he just had to learn to curb his temper and try to see things through the eyes of others. She trusted that in time, that growth in his character would come.

Francis sighed and kissed Poppy once more. "I am surprised that you are not fuming over the outrage of having your contract bid rejected. You are possessed with an infinite amount of patience."

"No, I am not. There have been times when my lack of a penis has caused me to lose out on contracts and even the prime berth at a dock. And I can tell you, I didn't always swallow down my disappointment. There were times when I made my views loudly heard. Don't forget, I did fire a pistol at you."

But if she was honest about it, Poppy did hold her tongue

better than Francis did. Her upbringing had meant a life of constantly weighing up the possible outcomes of her words and actions. She had always stood to lose more than anyone.

She had long ago come to terms with only dealing with the things in life she could influence or change.

"We need to get moving on putting the bid together. If you go and get your papers and then bring them back here, we should be able to have most of the work completed today," said Poppy.

She rolled her eyes at the sight of the scowl which appeared on Francis's face.

"What's wrong with my offices?" he replied.

"Nothing. But I have a stew cooking in the Dutch oven. The fire has been lit and this space is warm." Poppy turned her hands over, flat palms up. Answer presented.

Francis growled. "I have an even better idea."

He marched over to the fireplace, grabbed hold of two dishcloths, and placing them either side of the Dutch oven, proceeding to lift it out of the embers. "I have a fireplace. And now I have the pot. We will work on the bid in my warehouse. Then we shall eat."

"But—"

He headed for the door, and Poppy had no choice but to follow. As he stepped back, allowing her to open it, Francis fixed her with his stern gaze. "You made a promise to me, and I intend that you shall keep it."

"And what is that?"

"Tonight, and every night from now on, you sleep in my bed. I told you that you are under my protection, and I meant it."

She should have been angry at his overbearing behavior. Love, however, made her think otherwise. It made her feel a touch giddy with happiness. Poppy nodded. "I like being under your protection."

He bent his head and nipped at her bottom lip with his teeth. It sent a shiver of hot need through her body. “You are mine, and I shall always keep you safe.”

Chapter Forty-Three

"Are these figures correct? I mean, I hadn't really looked at the whole bid this way," Francis said.

He and Poppy were seated side by side at the table in his warehouse, papers piled up in front of them. They had worked through the numbers several times, and while they seemed to add up, he couldn't quite make sense of them.

His finger tapped at the top of the page, where the shipping calculations for the boat had been calculated. "Here."

I think she might have made a mistake.

He had been accused of not being able to work with others, something he knew he would have to remedy, but that didn't mean he couldn't question when things didn't seem right. Poppy leaned forward and stared at the number Francis was pointing to, then nodded.

"That's correct. She's carried those cargo levels, and a good deal more, before," she said.

He hadn't been into the lower parts of the *Empress Catherine*, but the length of her hull had never impressed on Francis that she was capable of supporting hundreds of bales of spices.

I would like to see for myself before we submit this bid.

"Speaking of ships, when is your boat coming back to the dock?"

Poppy had returned on Christmas Eve, but the *Empress Catherine* was nowhere to be seen.

She shuffled some papers around, all the while muttering under her breath. Francis caught a few of the words. It seemed like she was counting. He hoped that was what she was doing, not mumbling curses about his mathematical abilities.

"She is berthed further down river. There was no point having her here and incurring dock fees. And especially not until the spice contract is settled. The London Docks charges a pretty penny for tying up here." Poppy pushed back from the table. "I think that should do for the day. My brain can't handle anymore, and I am hungry. How about we eat, then you can show me where you keep your ink pot?"

"Is that a euphemism?" *I hope it is, because the last thing I want to do is to go through more books of account.*

Bookwork hadn't even made the list of activities Francis planned on doing once he succeeded in getting Poppy over to number twelve. Having her naked and beneath him was at the top of his priorities. Hearing her cries of completion came a close second.

His hopes lifted as she rose from her chair. Poppy bent and placed an inviting kiss on Francis's lips. "There is a rule of thumb that all good sailors live by. Food, fornicating, and a full night's sleep. I want to see your ink pot, so I know which is your desk. We need to test if it is sturdy enough for sex."

If his blood hadn't already been rushing to his manhood, Francis would have blushed at Poppy's words. "You are incorrigible. Scandalous. And my family is going to think you fabulous."

The smile died on Poppy's lips. "I don't expect I will be

able to use such language in front of your mother. Are you sure she will think me wonderful? I've already offended the two members of your family whom I have met. Who is to say I won't upset the rest?"

As he rose from his chair, Francis bent and placed a kiss on Poppy's forehead. "Don't forget you have met my father, and he thinks you are the bee's knees. If you keep feeding him plenty of freshly made French toast, he will defend you against the entire Radley clan. As will I."

Poppy didn't speak the same way as the rest of the women of Francis's acquaintance, and to him, that was perfect. The fact that she could sail a ship and cost a business proposal far outweighed any shortcomings she might have with social graces.

She was bright and intelligent, and made his heart go pitter-patter. He was hopelessly in love with her.

"And if you are still unsure of yourself in polite society, take heart. My mother will make certain that you shine. She knows all the best people." He glanced at the tender document. By combining their resources and skills, they had put together a solid proposal. A little more spit and polish in the morning, and it would be ready for submission.

This will hopefully be the first of many successful tender bids that we create.

While Poppy dished up their supper, Francis carefully cleared the papers to the other end of the table, making room for them to eat.

There was an easy, comfortable way between the two of them. Without having to talk, as one worked, the other went about doing what was needed. It was a sweet dance of domesticity. By the time Poppy brought the plates of food over to the table, Francis had laid out the spoons and napkins. Everything was ready.

If I could have this simple perfection every evening, I would happily live out the rest of my days and not yearn to attend another fancy ball or elegant soiree.

But only if that was what made Poppy happy. If she wanted to enter London society and experience the gaiety and light, he would be with her every step of the way.

As her husband.

When supper was over, they cleaned the dishes. Poppy washed, and Francis dried. If the staff of the shipping company could only see him now.

I should give them a few more days off. The ledgers can wait.

He caught himself smirking over that thought. When had he reached the point of not worrying over the books of account? The mighty were truly fallen.

"Oh, that reminds me," said Francis.

After hanging the tea towel up over the rack near the fire, he made an excited dash over to the cupboard near his bed. When he returned to Poppy's side, he was holding something very special behind his back.

"Close your eyes, and hold out your hands," he said.

She gave him a quizzical look but did as she was instructed.

Francis placed the heavy set of books in her hands. "Now you can look."

Poppy opened her eyes and glanced down. "What are these?"

Francis took the topmost book and held it up. "The latest and probably last books from Jane Austen. Two full novels published over four volumes. This first one is called *Persuasion*, and the second story, *Northanger Abbey*. They were released only this week."

He couldn't hide his excitement. He had been waiting months for these books to arrive. His plans had been to sit up late at night and devour them but matters with Poppy had concentrated his mind.

"You bought me romance novels? Oh, Francis, I don't know what to say."

Much as he wanted to pretend otherwise, it was only fair that he told Poppy the truth of his private passion. "Actually, I had ordered them for myself. Some time ago, I found Eve's copy of *Pride and Prejudice* and decided to read it. Just for a lark. But I must confess that I found it a fabulous read. I've read all of Austen's books."

Poppy held the rest of the books out to him, offering them back. Francis shook his head. "Please. I want you to have them, Poppy. Though the gift does come with one condition. You have to let me read them when you are finished."

A laugh left her lips. "Big bad Francis Saunders is a romantic at heart. That's wonderful. But if the stories are set over different books, we can take turns reading them. I can read *Persuasion* while you read *Northanger Abbey*."

He considered her offer. Typical of Poppy—she had a ready-made solution to a problem. But Francis had a better idea. "Or we could snuggle up in bed together each day and read to one another."

She trained her hazel eyes on him, clearly not buying his story. "You know as well as I do, my love, that if we tried reading in bed, we would never get any of the books finished."

Poppy handed Francis the bottom two volumes. "*Northanger Abbey*. And don't you dare give away any of the plot."

Chapter Forty-Four

"I love you." Poppy hadn't meant to say the words as Francis filled her with his morning erection, but her heart demanded it. Having confessed her love to him, the sentiment now slipped easily from her lips. If he was going to claim her body, it was only right that she yielded her soul.

"I love you too. And I shall till the day I die," he whispered in her ear.

His thrusts were long and masterful. Francis was an expert at building the tension slowly. He might well have been a green boy in some aspects of business, but he knew his way around a woman's body like a skilled craftsman, kissing and touching her in all the right ways, in all the best places.

She wrapped her legs around him, hooking her ankles together. This position allowed her to take him more deeply while Francis was then able to angle his thrusts hard against her sensitive bud. Every stroke sent pleasure through her body as he hit the perfect spot.

In comparison to their wild coupling of the previous night where they had let loose on top of Francis's desk, this morning's sex was sleepy and gentle.

Poppy lay back in the bed and let her man have his unhurried, delicious way. His hips rocked back and forth as he brought her to climax. He stilled above her a moment or two later, then rolled off to one side.

She scuttled over and lay her head on his chest, listening to his heart as it slowly returned to a steady, slower rhythm.

"I think we should do one last check of the proposal this morning, then walk up to the office and submit it," she said.

"If you think your bruises have started to fade enough, then I am going to take you somewhere nice, and we can have a long breakfast. You make me a hungry man in more ways than one," replied Francis.

She gifted him a tender kiss, then climbed out of bed. "I will stoke the fire and get us some hot water. I can't function very well until I have had at least two cups of coffee."

Poppy stopped and came back to Francis's side of the bed. "Your mother won't expect me to drink tea when I visit with her, will she? I know it's become a bit of a thing here, but I am a coffee drinker to my bones."

He leaned up on his elbow. "We drink both in our household, though Papa is dead set against drinking tea."

"Good. I knew I liked him for a reason."

She went back to the fireplace and picked up the kettle, sloshing it about to check for water. "Hmm, there isn't enough in here for the two of us. I shall get dressed and go and get some water."

Francis swung his long legs over the side of the bed. "If you do that, I will get the fire going properly again."

A little extra kindling and a small log soon had the fire crackling back to life. While Francis waited for Poppy to return, he dressed and raked a brush through his hair.

Poppy still hadn't made her way back to the warehouse by the time he was fully clothed, and the breakfast cups ready.

She must have dropped in next door to pick up something, I am sure of it.

When another five minutes had elapsed and she was still nowhere to be seen, Francis put on his coat and headed outside.

The first thing he saw was a sailing ship—a huge three-masted clipper, fleet and slick—berthed at the dock where Poppy's ship belonged.

"She is going to be livid," he muttered.

A steady procession of boxes, crates, and barrels were being lifted off the ship and placed on the Basden Line side of the wharf-side pavilion. Francis turned, in a hurry to alert Poppy.

"Francis!"

He stopped mid-stride and spun on his heel. At the top of the gangplank of this newly arrived, enormous ship stood Poppy, waving to him.

She strolled down the walkway, and Francis rushed to meet her at the edge of the road.

"I shall go to the superintendent's office immediately and demand that this vessel be moved," he said.

The grin on her face had him confused. Why wasn't she angry?

"Not until Captain Lewis says it is ready to sail," she said. Poppy pointed back to the ship. A thin, grey-haired man was making his way toward them. When he arrived at her side, he bowed to Francis. "Good morning. Captain Jeremy Lewis at your service."

A still confused Francis offered him his hand. "Francis Saunders. Whose ship is this?"

"The *Tarragona* is mine. I own it and the *Empress Catherine*," replied Poppy.

Captain Lewis looked from Poppy to Francis, then back again. "Is there a problem, Captain Basden?"

"No. Mister Saunders wasn't aware of the existence of this ship. Not until the last few minutes."

He caught Francis's eye and a definite sizing up moment quickly followed. Whoever Captain Lewis was, he was trying to figure out where Francis stood in all of this.

"Where is Jonathan?" Captain Lewis asked.

"Somewhere off the coast of Portugal I expect. Jonathan and I agreed to end our business partnership. He signed articles for a ship sailing to Cape Town."

Francis held the other man's gaze confidently, but without threat. He was doing his best to take his cue from Poppy's signals.

Poppy brushed her hand against Francis's arm and smiled up at him. "Mister Saunders and I are forming our own partnership."

I think her message is clear, Captain Lewis.

The captain's face softened. "Good. I am glad that Jonathan has gone. He is not a bad chap—just not good enough for you. George made a mistake in choosing him—not that he would admit it."

Whoever this man was, Francis liked him. And Captain Lewis seemed to have a close personal connection with Poppy.

"Speaking of George. Could I have a private word with you, Poppy?" Captain Lewis asked.

The happy expression on Poppy's face evaporated in an instant. Her hand slipped down, and she touched Francis's palm. Their fingers softly entwined. "Francis and I have no secrets. Whatever you have to say to me, you can say in front of him." She drew in an audible breath. "Papa isn't coming, is he?"

Her voice broke on that last word, as did Francis's heart. Hadn't her selfish father made Poppy suffer enough?

"No, he is not. He is chasing a new contract in Singapore, after which I understand he will be remaining in Ceylon. He sailed just before we left. I asked him to at least write a letter for you, one I could personally deliver, but he said no. I must confess, I do not understand the man," replied the captain.

Francis gave Poppy's fingers a reassuring squeeze. *Neither do I. But I am here for you.*

She released her hand. "No, but I for one do understand my father—only too well. Thank you, Captain Lewis. Please excuse me; I have to finalize an urgent contract proposal. It was good to see you safely arrived. You should come to supper with us tomorrow night."

A confused Francis followed Poppy back to number twelve. Once inside, he braced himself, unsure of what was to come next. Tears. Rage. Or the silence of desperation. Poppy had seemed so utterly resigned to yet again being failed by her father.

Whatever she needed, he was determined to be there for her.

"We should get this proposal delivered to the superintendent's office." She picked up the papers and gathered them into a pile.

"Poppy?"

Her hands stilled. "I should have told you about the *Tarragona*. I didn't because I had to be absolutely sure about you before I did. It's not good business to go telling your competition that you own a large ship."

She had retreated to the safety of another subject. Anything to avoid talking about her father.

Francis went along with it. "Can I assume that the *Tarragona* is the ship we are putting up for the spice contract? It makes more sense if it is. I couldn't work out your numbers, but that's because I thought you were talking about the other boat. The *Empress Catherine*."

"The *Empress* is a pretty boat, but no, she was never going to be used for the bid. I won't have her for much longer. She is moored downriver while a potential new owner takes a good look at her."

Poppy was selling the lion ship.

"You would really sell her? I can't believe it."

"She will always be the boat of my heart, and I shall miss her. But she will fetch a good price. One which will give me the capital to set up properly in London."

The proposal papers dropped to the desk and Poppy screwed her eyes shut. How many times had this happened in her life? She had made plans based on her father's promises, and he had let her down.

"Though if we are to marry, the money, along with everything else, won't be mine. It will be yours."

With slow, measured steps Francis came to Poppy. He bent and kissed her softly on the lips. "My love. I know you are hurting. Your father has betrayed you yet again."

Her glassy eyes met his. "George Basden has failed me for the last time, but oddly, I feel relieved. He can't disappoint me anymore. Why? Because this time, it's different. I have you. I am not alone. And I never will be again. Oh, Francis, promise me that you won't ever leave."

"I swear I will be by your side until the day I draw my last breath. I love you. My word is my bond."

She was pinning her whole future on the promises of a man. Not her father, but still, another male who could fail her. Francis was determined that with him it would be different.

"Francis, would you be open to a proposal?"

His brows lifted. He was the man; men were the ones who proposed. Poppy sniffed back her tears. "Not that sort of proposal. Though I am open to such an offer, if you are inclined to make one. I mean a business proposal."

Francis was more than ready to make her an offer of marriage, but from the expression on Poppy's face, this proposal of hers meant a great deal. His could wait for a little while longer.

We have the rest of our lives.

"Go on," he replied.

"The money from the sale of our house in Ceylon was meant to go toward buying a house here in London. He swore on my mother's memory that he would finally give me a proper home. Well, I am going to hold him to that promise. As an unmarried woman, and a director of the company, I still have full legal power over the ownership of the warehouse. I can sell it if I wish."

"Right."

"This is what I want to do. Step one: I go through with the sale of the *Empress Catherine*. I then lend you the money I receive. Step two: You use it to buy the warehouse from me."

I end up owning the warehouse while owing Poppy money.

"Is there a step three?" he replied, trying to get his head around her line of thinking.

"Yes. You make me a full partner in a new venture called F. and P. Saunders Shipping. This will be the company which bids for the spice contract. In time, you buy your father out of his share of Saunders Shipping and you fold the two companies in together."

This all made sense, but marriage would invalidate some of the transactions. Once Poppy was his wife, she would no longer have her own legal identity.

"You do realize that if we marry, the loan to you won't exist anymore. You and I will be one legal person. I can't owe myself money."

All loans would be extinguished, and Francis would be the

owner of the warehouse, and he would have the money from the sale of the *Empress Catherine* at his disposal.

"Yes, and that is where step four comes in. After you give me the money to buy the warehouse, I give it back to you as my dowry, along with the *Tarragona*. But there is one condition that will come with my marriage settlement; my solicitor will put it in writing. And it will not be negotiable."

Of course, there was a condition. This was Poppy—she was always one step ahead, trying to find a way to win. This time, Francis sensed he knew what she was going to say. "When everything is finalized and we are married, you want the money from the sale of the *Empress Catherine* to go toward a house. That's it, isn't it?"

Her first real home. A place where Poppy could have a garden. Where she could bake. And where they could raise a family. "Yes. Am I asking too much?"

"No, you are not. I love you. You deserve to have somewhere that you can call home, I couldn't think of a better use of the money from the sale of the ship. I would be honored to be able to share that home with you . . . as your husband."

Francis dropped to one knee. It didn't matter if he didn't become the most successful businessman in London, although with this woman as his partner he stood a good chance of succeeding.

The things which Francis saw as being important had changed. It wasn't business, nor was it his misguided need to compete with his relatives. It was the woman standing right here in front of him.

"Poppy Basden, will you marry me?"

Chapter Forty-Five

"What do you think your mother is going to say when she discovers that in the short time since she left town, you have not only gotten yourself a fiancée, but that you have gone ahead and booked the cathedral for the wedding? Won't she be a little ticked off?" Poppy asked, shifting her pillow.

It was early, and the morning sun had barely touched the window above their bed. Poppy's usual habit of taking her coffee outside and watching the sun rise had recently changed. The dawn couldn't compete with the lure of staying in bed with a naked, warm male.

Francis had moved with such uncommon haste to set the wedding date that Poppy's head was still in a spin.

"Don't worry. There is another family matter which will have my parents back in London very soon. But you should prepare yourself for a long list of modiste appointments and house inspections as soon as my mother gets home," replied Francis.

He thinks shopping is a chore. I can't wait.

They had agreed to divide and conquer over the next

month. Francis would work with Captain Lewis to get the warehouses and the *Tarragona* ready for the newly secured spice contract. Poppy would deal with wedding preparations and finding them a house, as well as handling some of the paperwork in the business.

The future Mrs. Saunders had extracted the price of two new gowns from her fiancé as part of the naked negotiations that they'd conducted over that piece of work.

Once they were married, they would jointly manage F. and P. Saunders Shipping. Francis would concentrate his efforts on securing new contracts while Poppy would run the day-to-day side of the business. All major decisions were to be made between them by agreement.

A still half-awake Poppy rolled over and rested her hand on Francis's chest. Her fingers toyed idly with the dusting of fine white hair before settling to draw light circles around his left nipple. The bud went pleasingly hard.

"If you keep that up, future Mrs. Saunders, I shall have to take matters firmly in hand."

She grinned. Poppy liked nothing better than when Francis took matters in hand. Her own hand dipped below the light bed coverings, searching. She found her prize and gave it a gentle squeeze. "You are definitely getting firm, Mister Saunders. Though I suggest you might want to move if you plan on doing something about it."

"Hmm?"

"We have a long day ahead of us."

This morning, they were due to sign the agreement for the new spice contract, followed by a trip into central London to finalize the sale of both the warehouse and the *Empress Catherine*. And then later in the evening, they were hosting Will and Hattie for supper. Poppy had found a new recipe for lamb shanks she was going to try.

"In fact, we really don't have time for this," said Poppy, releasing her grip and sitting up.

As she went to swing a leg over the side of the bed, her world suddenly shifted, and she found herself pinned under a large, naked Viking.

"Minx. We will always have time for this. For us."

Poppy sighed with happiness as Francis brushed his lips over hers. "I can't believe this all began with a battle over some silly barrels and rope. And look where it ended."

Francis grinned down at her. The early morning light shone in his dazzling blue eyes. "I might have lost the war over the barrels, and rightly so, but *we* won at everything else. And this is not an end; it is only the beginning."

Epilogue

L*ate January, 1818*
The Empress Catherine, somewhere off the coast of Kent.

Gideon Kembal, Marquis of Holwell, wanted to die. Death had to be better than how he was feeling right in that moment. His eyes were already closed, so the undertaker would be saved the task.

"That is probably the safest place for you right now. I wouldn't attempt moving about the boat anymore; you will only find yourself throwing what's left in your stomach over the side," said a familiar voice.

He cracked open his eyes. A pale-haired beauty stared down at him. He was still trying to bring her into sharper focus when a ball of white appeared next to her.

"Yes, you don't look at all well. Poppy, what color would you say Gideon's face is right now? Putrid green?"

"One does not mock the seasick, Francis. I would have thought you might have at least a little sympathy for your poor cousin."

The boat reached the top of a wave and gave a little dip as it came down the other side. Gideon gripped the floor of the deck with his fingernails. Flat on his back at the stern of the ship, he was living a nightmare.

He had taken up the offer to join the newlyweds while they enjoyed a short jaunt up the coast to say a final farewell to Poppy's lion ship. Upon their return to London, the *Empress Catherine* was going to be handed over to her new owners.

"I thought this would be a nice, easy sail. But I just want to die," he muttered.

Francis took a seat on the deck next to him. "They say that there are two phases of being seasick. The first is when you fear you are going to die. And the second is when you fear you might live."

"Francis!" scolded Poppy.

Gideon mustered a laugh for his cousin. When they got back to dry land, he fully intended to kill him, but still, it was a good jest. "It's a pity I have nothing left in my stomach. Otherwise, I might soil your highly polished boots."

"Take heart, Gideon. I have ordered the crew to turn for home. You have suffered enough for one day," said Poppy.

When the ship finally berthed at London Docks late that evening, Francis helped the lightheaded Gideon down the gangplank. The stricken marquis was still swaying as he stepped through the door of the F. and P. Saunders Shipping offices.

Poppy raced and grabbed a chair, holding it steady while her husband lowered Gideon gently down into it.

Once seated, Gideon gripped the arms tightly. "Thank you. I might just stay here until the room stops moving."

"I shall make you a cup of tea. I know your stomach is churning, but you need to hydrate your body. It will help you to recover faster," said Poppy.

There was a lot to be said for having a cousin-in-law who understood seasickness as well as Poppy Saunders did.

Gideon gingerly lifted his head. The worst of the giddiness was beginning to subside. *Thank the Lord for small mercies.* Francis pulled up a chair next to him.

Don't say it. Please.

"Are you having second thoughts? I mean, after today, no one could blame you if you didn't undertake the trip," said Francis.

One short excursion in the English Channel had thrown all of Gideon's plans into disarray. If this was what a day's sailing was going to do to him, how would he manage six weeks?

"You've heard the rumors. I can't sit by and do nothing."

When the Duchess of Mowbray hadn't returned from her trip to Rome in time for Christmas, the rumor mill had started to whisper.

Did you hear she has left her husband?

All the Kembal girls will be ruined. No decent chap will want to marry them.

I heard she has taken on an Italian lover. Scandalous.

Vicious, spiteful rumors.

Gideon knew the first one to be true. He had seen the letter. Knowing the *haute ton*, the second was also likely.

As for the third? He would have pistols at dawn with any man who said such a thing about his mother.

A cup of tea appeared under his nose, and he gratefully accepted it. He waved away the sweet biscuit that Poppy offered, hoping she wouldn't take offence. Francis's new wife was an excellent baker as well as a top-notch sailor—a strange but winning combination of skills.

"I shall pack you some to take home to the others," she said.

"Thank you."

Poppy placed her hand over his and softly sighed. "I'm sorry about what has happened with your parents. I didn't grow up with much of a family, but I know that when things go wrong, it hurts."

"I have to go to Rome. My father has aged ten years over the past month or so. My sisters and younger brothers dare not show their faces in society. Our family is falling apart."

If it meant him having to spend weeks at sea lying prone on the deck of a ship, he would do it.

I just don't know if I will survive the voyage.

If he died at sea, it would mean the loss of the immediate heir to the Duchy of Mowbray. His brother Richard would have to step into his shoes. Richard, who had no head for numbers, too much of an appetite for foolish wagers, and who was determined to never marry would make a terrible duke. The line of the Dukes of Mowbray would fail with him.

"I need a ship that will take me to Italy, under the command of a captain who will keep my identity secret. If anyone finds out that I have left England to bring Mama and Augusta home, all hell will break lose."

The rest of the Radley family had done what it could to keep the scandal at bay, but unless the Duchess of Mowbray returned, nothing would silence the gossip.

"I think I know someone who can help you. Count Nico de Luca runs ships between London and Civitavecchia, which is the main port just up the coast from Rome. I can go and have a quiet word with his local representative if you like," said Poppy.

"We will do everything we can to help you," added Francis.

Gideon stirred from the mire of seasickness. "Just a moment. I know the de Luca family. They are who Mama and G are staying with in Rome. They should be able to help me with securing private passage to Italy."

How could I have forgotten that they are involved in shipping?

This was the first real piece of luck he'd had in some time. His mind began to formulate a plan.

He could pretend he had departed for the family estate just outside of Leicester while in truth he had sailed out of England. No matter the personal cost, he was determined to answer the call of duty.

And if it meant being able to confront his mother, getting her to see reason, and finding a way to get her to come back to England, it would be worth it.

Six weeks of hell at sea followed by lord knew what was waiting for him in Rome, and then six weeks back again. A trying journey lay ahead.

He was the Marquis of Holwell. The future Duke of Mowbray. But none of it meant anything if he couldn't get his parents back together.

I have to save my family.

Turn the page to read the first chapter of Gideon and Serafina's story in...

Tempted by the English Marquis
The Kembal Family
When love conquers duty

Sign up for my newsletter and receive your FREE BOOK.
A Wild English Rose

Regency London's wild child is about to meet her match...

Award-Winning Series
The Duke of
Strathmore
He will tame her
wild heart...
Sasha
Cottman
A Wild English Rose

Tempted by the English Marquis

September, 1816
Mowbray House, Berkeley Square, London

Gideon Kembal, Marquis of Holwell, took his coat from the downstairs footman and tucked it neatly under his arm. He was in much too much of a hurry to make his escape to bother with stopping and putting it on.

I need to get out of here before Mama corners me.

His parents were upstairs in the drawing room hosting some guests. Gideon couldn't recall who their visitors were or where they were from. In truth, he hadn't actually been paying that much attention when the Duchess of Mowbray made the announcement at breakfast earlier in the week. People were always coming and going from the Kembal family home.

Gideon's brain had registered but a few of Lady Anne's words. Some gentlemen and a young lady. The woman was beautiful and apparently accomplished. That was more than enough to set his nerves on edge.

In the eyes of the *haut ton*, and by default also his mother, at five and twenty he was more than ripe for marriage. Any suitable female who happened to breathe the same air as him was therefore considered a likely candidate for the role of his future bride.

Not bloody likely. I will choose who I marry, thank you very much.

Once he was safely outside, Gideon paused at the top of the stoop. A sly grin sat on his lips. He had successfully eluded his mother.

His gaze took in the evening bustle of busy Berkeley Square. Carriages and people were a constant in this part of central London. Gideon loved it. He wouldn't live anywhere else.

Slipping his coat on, he quickly checked the pockets. Both hands came up empty.

Deuce. Where is that card?

There should have been an invitation to a private party within one of the pockets. Panic crept into his blood as he checked the inner pockets, swearing under his breath when his searching fingers touched the lining.

A horrid realization dawned on him. "Oh, no. I took the card out to check what time the soiree kicked off. I must have left it upstairs!" he muttered.

He turned his gaze back toward the front door of Mowbray House. Just how fast could he dash inside, make it up to his bedroom, and retrieve the invitation? All without being caught by his mother.

Speed was not, however, his main problem. The duchess's acute hearing was. The slightest hint of a footfall would have her stepping from the main drawing room and seeking out her eldest son.

But with no clue as to the exact address of the party, Gideon resigned himself to the perilous task. He would have to risk it and hope that his parents were too busy with their recent arrivals to bother with him.

Come on, lady luck. Smile upon me this evening.

He put a finger to his lips as the perplexed footman opened the front door once more and Gideon slipped inside. One step followed by another, he raced up the stairs. Upon reaching his bedroom, he slowly opened the door, doing his utmost not to make a sound. He scurried over to his dressing table and snatched up the card.

"Now to make a fast but stealthy escape."

Once more out in the hallway, he quickly headed for the staircase. Freedom and a night of drunken frivolity beckoned. He had just put his front foot on the top step when the door of the drawing room at the end of the hall opened.

"Ah, Gideon, just who I was looking for. What a spot of luck. I thought I might have missed you."

Damn. Damn. Damn.

Silently cursing his own stupidity, Gideon turned to face his mother, Lady Anne Kembal. If he had departed but a minute earlier, he would have gotten clean away. Now, there was nowhere for him to hide.

"Mama. I was just heading out; I'm late for a party. I shall see you at breakfast," he said, making to head down the stairs.

"Oh. You can spare your mother a few minutes, can't you? I mean, it would be terribly rude of you not to come and greet our guests. And I didn't raise you to have poor manners, now, did I?" replied the duchess.

The expression on his mother's face held more power than her words ever could. Only a foolish young man would try to flee from Lady Anne and her parental expectations.

"I am running a tad late, so would a quick hello suffice?" he offered. Gideon wasn't above haggling. Or begging.

"Five minutes—ten at tops. Stay for one glass of wine and make our guests feel welcome. Augusta is already playing hostess with the young lady, so I promise it won't be too taxing on you."

A reluctant Gideon followed his mother into the formal drawing room. He could manage five minutes. Years of social gatherings had equipped him with the ability to down a glass of wine swiftly while maintaining his manners.

His mind drifted elsewhere, but his gaze was focused on the back of the silver evening gown worn by the duchess. When she came to a halt, Gideon stirred, lifting his head.

He caught sight of two dark-haired gentlemen standing, talking to his father. From the look of them, and their manner of dress, they were not English. Gideon had just ventured a guess that they might be French when one of the men spoke.

"Is this your son, Your Grace? He looks like you." The Italian accent was unmistakable. It wasn't just the elegant way the gentleman rounded the curves of his words; it was the speed with which he spoke.

The Duke of Mowbray, Clifford Kembal, beckoned his son over. "Gideon, come meet Count Nico de Luca and his cousin Matteo."

What followed was a quick dance of bowing and handshaking, and a sharing of smiles. He might well wish to be out of the house and on his way to the party, but Gideon would never be so crass as to disappoint his father when greeting guests.

"So, what brings you two gentlemen to London?" he asked.

Count de Luca, who was the shorter of the two—though both men were well over six feet—nodded to the duke. "We were just telling your father about our shipping business. The de Luca family has been involved in the Mediterranean sea trade for several hundred years. Our company has offices near the new London Docks at Wapping."

"And I was telling the count and Signore de Luca about your Uncle Charles and the Saunders Shipping Company being based at the North Quay warehouses," added Clifford.

Gideon's uncle on his mother's side was a French émigré and had established a successful import and export business in London. Gideon's cousin Francis worked with his father in the company, and they had plans for Francis to take it over when Charles eventually retired.

"I went to school here in England when I was young, my mother was born here. Our family knows the Duke and Duchess of Strathmore. And my wife was English," said the count.

That would explain his near flawless grasp of the language.

"I'm sorry for the loss of your wife," said Gideon.

Nico and Matteo looked at one another, then Nico softly laughed. "My wife, Isabelle, is very much alive and well. When I said she had been English, I meant she became Italian when we married. If she wasn't heavy with our first child, she would have made the journey with me."

Gideon caught his father's eye and the look of expectation which sat on the duke's face. He silently cursed his bad fortune in not having earlier made it successfully out the house. Having assumed he wouldn't be meeting them, he hadn't bothered to find out anything about these gentlemen. Guests having to explain who they were and their connections to the family only served to highlight Gideon's apparent lack of social graces.

I should have greeted them by name, not stood like a statue while Papa had to make the introductions. What a clod.

"When Nico decided to come to England, he invited one of my younger sisters and myself to join him. Who would be foolish enough to pass up the chance to come to see the great city of London?" Matteo asked.

Matteo de Luca gestured to the other side of the room.

Gideon glanced over his shoulder. His mother, sisters Augusta, Coco, and Victoria, and another young woman he didn't recognize were chatting amongst themselves near the window. The duchess was pointing to something in the garden and the group appeared genuinely interested.

Mama has always been able to hold a room.

"That is my sister Serafina. She has been most eager to learn and practice her English. On the boat from Rome, she spent hours studying the phrase book and getting Nico to engage in . . . how do you say? Polite conversation," said Matteo.

"Serafina is going to be staying with us while her cousin and brother are busy with business meetings. She might be closer in age to Victoria, but it would appear that she and Augusta have hit it off right away," said the duke.

Gideon studied the back of the young Italian woman, taking in her long glossy black hair. She was dressed in a dusky pink gown, which flowed elegantly from her slim shoulders all the way to the top of the cream shawl she had draped over both arms.

If she was around his sister Victoria's age, that would make Signorina de Luca likely about eighteen or nineteen years old. A touch too young for Gideon's taste. He found most girls at that age either acted giggly and silly around men or worse—they had been trained as husband hunters by their fortune-seeking mamas. The *haut ton* hadn't dubbed them simpering misses without good reason.

In his opinion, it was only as they got closer to the time when marriage became a part of their future plans, that young women discovered a sense of self-regard. A certain steadiness of mind, which a wife needed to possess.

Not that Gideon had the slightest intention of marrying anytime soon. The Marquis of Holwell was far too busy living the riotous life of a young, wealthy nobleman. When it came to wild oats, he had plenty of them left to sew.

He had a role to play in ensuring the line of ducal succession would be fulfilled, but with a still healthy father, and two strapping younger brothers to help secure the bloodline, Gideon was in no particular hurry to wed.

And as much as it vexed his mother, he also didn't consider any of the current crop of eligible misses to be worthy of his attention. He would find a wife when he was good and ready.

"Excuse me for a moment," said Clifford. The duke crossed the floor to where the women were gathered and spoke briefly to his wife. Lady Anne's gaze settled on Gideon, and she nodded.

They are going to make the final introductions. Excellent. I shall give it a few minutes and then I can take my leave. I have a drunken soiree to attend.

He was still considering which of his lady acquaintances might be up for a midnight rendezvous in a carriage in Hyde Park when his mother approached. Behind her trailed her three daughters. His view of the young Italian woman was obscured by his sisters Victoria and Coco, who preceded Serafina and Augusta.

"Serafina. Serafina," Gideon muttered to himself. He was terrible with names but after his earlier faux pas, he was keen to make amends.

When Lady Anne reached him, she held out a hand. "Serafina, would you please join me?"

"Gideon, Lord Holwell, may I introduce Signorina Serafina de Luca, recently arrived from Rome," announced the duchess.

His gaze shifted from his mother to the young lady who stepped forward, bowing her head as she dipped into a deep curtsy.

Time and the world stopped for Gideon.

Stunningly beautiful. There wasn't any other way to describe Serafina. Gideon took in her sable tresses. The way her hair gleamed in the light from the chandelier was like seeing the moon reflected on the midnight waters of the sea.

As she rose, Serafina gifted him with a smile that set his heart racing. Full, red lips drew him in. When she fluttered her long, dark eyelashes at him, Gideon feared he might faint. Her deep brown eyes had him swaying on his feet. This girl. This woman. Incredible.

His mother's voice came to him from somewhere distant. "Gideon, are you alright?"

He nodded. "I am magnificent. The picture of utter perfection."

A loud indignant huff reached his ears, and he turned to find his sister Augusta, or G, as she was affectionately known, glaring at him. "Oof, you are far from perfection. But you are being perfectly rude to Serafina."

"Serafina," whispered Gideon, still in a half daze.

"It is a pleasure to meet you, Lord Holwell."

I can assure you that the pleasure is all mine.

"Serafina will be our guest at Mowbray House for the next two weeks. While Count Nico and Signore de Luca are busy with their business, we thought it might be nice for her to come and stay with us. She can spend time with the girls and also see some of the city," said the duchess.

"And where are you from, Serafina?" asked Gideon. He wasn't about to leave his daze anytime soon.

A cool hand was pressed to his forehead. *What the devil?*

Gideon shied away from his mother's touch. He wasn't a young boy. "Mama. Please," he protested.

"I was just checking to make sure you were not unwell or coming down with something. You are behaving most peculiarly, Gideon," said the duchess.

He wasn't ill, but he could confess to feeling a touch odd. "Perhaps I need a drink."

Yes, that would solve his problems. A stiff drink, preferably a large one.

A warm hand brushed against his fingers, and Gideon glanced down. As Serafina slipped her hand gently into his, he swore he heard a choir of heavenly angels. Unlike his mother, this touch was most welcome.

"Lord Holwell, I am from Rome. The Eternal City," she said. Her heavily accented words slipped beneath the buttons of his linen shirt and settled on the naked skin of his chest. There they rested, softly stroking over his erratically beating heart. "Have you ever been to Italy?"

Stirring as best he could from his trance, Gideon slowly shook his head. "No, though I have always wanted to visit. It would be wonderful to see the Colosseum, the Pantheon, and of course Saint Peter's Basilica."

Get your head together. Stop making an ass of yourself.

A footman handed him the long-awaited glass of wine. Gideon took it with his left hand. The fingers of his right were still entwined with Serafina's, and as far as he was concerned, it would take a horde of gladiators to prize them apart.

He had heard that Italians were an expressive people and less reserved than the English. Gideon was enjoying his first experience of this cultural difference. His gaze remained settled on their joined hands.

Her skin is so warm and soft.

When Matteo de Luca cleared his throat, Gideon snapped out of his daze. He immediately released Serafina's hand.

"Palazzo Lazio, our family home, is situated not far from the Colosseum. And we have relatives who work within the Holy See," said Matteo.

Gideon nodded. "That sounds wonderful."

He really ought to be engaging Matteo in conversation, but his attention was held captive by the young woman who stood before him. Gideon's heart did a little dance of joy at the thought of her living in his family home for the next two weeks. Of the many opportunities that might present themselves for him and Serafina to spend time together. Opportunities which he found himself suddenly intending to create.

"Do you wish to see London, Serafina? Because if you do, I might be able to find the odd day or two in which I can play tour guide. You are a guest in my family home, so it is only right and proper that I offer you my services," he said.

I will be free every day for the next two weeks, because I intend to cancel everything in my diary.

By the time he had finished showing the enchanting Serafina around London, she would be able to write the definitive tourist book.

"I have toured some parts of the city already. Of course, it's different from Rome. London is a modern city, with a large population. Rome is much smaller; we have everything all . . . how do you say it?" She pushed her hands together.

"Squashed?" offered Lady Victoria.

Gideon was fond of his younger sister, but he would much rather she was somewhere else right this very minute. The remote northern islands of Scotland would do nicely.

He smiled at Serafina. "Compact. Neat. But still beautiful and precious. While you are here, Serafina, I would love to be able to show you some of the special places in London." Gideon nodded toward Matteo and the count. "With suitable family members acting as chaperones, of course. If that is acceptable."

He ignored Augusta's "What about me?"

Count Nico and Matteo both nodded their agreement.

Gideon's heart swelled with pride knowing that the Kembal family was being trusted with such a loved young woman.

I can be a gentleman and play host.

If he spent time with their guest and his younger siblings, Gideon could score valuable points with his parents. It would also give him the chance to get to know the lovely Serafina a little better - even if only friendship came from their connection.

A blushing Serafina returned his smile. "That would be lovely, Lord Holwell. Thank you. And perhaps someday if you come to Rome, I could repay the favor."

"I would like nothing more than to see your wonderful city through your eyes," he replied.

The party invitation lay forgotten in his jacket pocket. There was nowhere else in all of London that the Marquis of Holwell would rather be than right there with the bewitching young lady whose looks rivaled those of the Mona Lisa.

Gideon made himself a secret promise. One day, someday, he would go to Rome. And Serafina would be the beautiful young woman who shared the secrets of the ancient city with him.

Someday.

READ
Tempted by the English Marquis

When Love Conquers Duty.

Gideon Kembal, Marquis of Holwell, vows to save those he loves from the shocking scandal which threatens to tear his family apart. Duty bound, he sails to Italy, determined to bring his wayward mother and sister back to England.

Serafina de Luca is the obedient daughter of one of Rome's most wealthy and powerful families. Despite her heart's secret desire, she knows her future lies in a loveless, political marriage.

Arriving in Rome, Gideon finds himself at war with his mother. His only respite is found in the company of the enchanting Serafina who offers to show him around the ancient city.

The attraction which sparks between them soon becomes a blaze of passionate temptation. Serafina accepts Gideon's offer of a life with him in England.

When their secret romance is exposed, her family is outraged. Serafina faces the heartbreak of being forced to marry a man she barely knows, while Gideon finds himself fighting an honor duel, to the death.

As hope stands on the edge of bitter despair, can the eternal city deliver them a miracle?

Tempted by the English Marquis
is a standalone story in the
Kembal Family Regency Historical Romance.

Also by Sasha Cottman

SERIES

The Kembal Family

The Duke of Strathmore

The Noble Lords

Rogues of the Road

London Lords

The Kembal Family

Tempted by the English Marquis

The Vagabond Viscount

The Duke of Spice

The Duke of Strathmore

Letter from a Rake

An Unsuitable Match

The Duke's Daughter

A Scottish Duke for Christmas

My Gentleman Spy

Lord of Mischief

The Ice Queen

Two of a Kind

A Lady's Heart Deceived

All is Fair in Love

Duke of Strathmore Novellas

Mistletoe and Kisses

Christmas with the Duke

A Wild English Rose

The Noble Lords

Love Lessons for the Viscount

A Lord with Wicked Intentions

A Scandalous Rogue for Lady Eliza

Unexpected Duke

The Noble Lords Boxed Set

Rogues of the Road

Rogue for Hire

Stolen by the Rogue

When a Rogue Falls

The Rogue and the Jewel

King of Rogues

The Rogues of the Road Boxed Set

London Lords

Devoted to the Spanish Duke

Promised to the Swedish Prince

Seduced by the Italian Count

Wedded to the Welsh Baron

Bound to the Belgian Count

Available in audio

My historical romance novels are set around the Regency period in England, Scotland, and Europe.

Join my VIP readers and claim your
FREE BOOK

www.ingramcontent.com/pod-product-compliance
Lightning Source LLC
LaVergne TN
LVHW050927080826
845145LV00001B/240

9781922366368